MW01601955

A MILE OF DREAMS

A MILE OF DREAMS

A Novel by

Jim Trevis

Copyright © 2010 by Jim Trevis.

Library of Congress Control Number:		2010908802
ISBN:	Hardcover	978-1-4535-2303-2
	Softcover	978-1-4535-2302-5
	Ebook	978-1-4535-2304-9

All rights reserved. No part of this book may be reproduced or transmitted
in any form or by any means, electronic or mechanical, including photocopying,
recording, or by any information storage and retrieval system,
without permission in writing from the copyright owner.

This is a work of fiction. Names, characters, places and incidents either are the
product of the author's imagination or are used fictitiously, and any resemblance
to any actual persons, living or dead, events, or locales is entirely coincidental.

This book was printed in the United States of America.

To order additional copies of this book, contact:
Xlibris Corporation
1-888-795-4274
www.Xlibris.com
Orders@Xlibris.com
78773

A MILE OF DREAMS REVIEWS

A Mile of Dreams is a fine, multi-textured first novel by Jim Trevis. On the surface, it is a classic, coming-of-age story of a rural Minnesota teenager. Young Joe Mitchell struggles to achieve athletic glory, churns with the emotions of first love and grapples with adult-like family responsibilities. On deeper reading, however, the novel is more about strained family relationships as rural culture transitions from isolated, one-family farms to modern, commercial agriculture.

A Miles of Dreams is an extremely accurate portrayal of the sheer volume of work a 50-cow dairy farm requires, consuming nearly every waking hour of the family. Over the years, this 5 a.m. to 9 p.m. grind wears down the family, gnawing away at them physically and emotionally, jeopardizing the very relationships that family farms are supposed to embody.

Because of the workload, Joe has never been allowed to participate in school sports. Now in his senior year, Joe yearns to be an athlete and finally convinces his father to allow him to run track. That decision drives the novel into unexpected twists and turns. Having to reach their own grand pledge to help Joe achieve his dreams, his parents also come of age—once again finding that relationships—parents to son, husband to wife—are far more important than farm mortgages.

And therein lies the novel's true message. Urban readers, now three and four generations removed from agriculture, need this novel. Visions of life on red-barned dairy farms is and never was the idyllic situation all of us think we see as we speed by at 60 miles per hour. Farmers are real people with real relationships that can become as challenged as any two-earner family in the largest city. But farmers must also cope with the vagaries of livestock, weather, machinery breakdowns, fatigue, physical injuries and global markets while also trying to keep their relationships whole. Few of us could survive this maelstrom. I wish I had written this novel.

Jim Dickrell, Editor, Dairy Today magazine

This is an engaging novel about a young man's journey to adulthood. Joe Mitchell, the only child of a Minnesota dairy farm family, doggedly pursues his dream of becoming a star on his high school's track team during his senior year. Joe's goal is hampered by troubles and turmoil on the farm. While chasing his dream, Joe learns valuable life lessons. Perseverance, a strong work ethic and unwavering commitment to family are what matter most.

Anyone who has grown up on a farm will relate to Joe's yearning for independence and opportunity, and his awareness of the powerful pull of the land and all that it represents. Rural and urban readers alike will enjoy and appreciate this book. It offers a much-needed perspective on farm life. A wonderful story, well told! I really enjoyed this book.

Linda Tank, VP Communications, CHS Inc.,
Fortune 100 diversified energy, grains and foods company

A Mile of Dreams is a wonderful story that I thoroughly enjoyed. In fact, I devoured it this weekend, and now I'm sad tonight because I wish I could spend more time with those characters because I absolutely loved them. It was over too soon. I laughed aloud, cried, re-read small sections just to savor the wonderful descriptions and rich images. It's great story-telling and very inspiring. I'm amazed. The book really deserves to be read.

Lonnie Howard, Sante Fe poet

To my parents, Walter and Marie,
who long ago put away their own dreams
so that I could fulfill mine.

ICED IN

In his daydreams—the ones he folded into his filthy pillow every night and the ones he resurrected in the predawn darkness—he was always a different Joe Mitchell. In the spring, Joe's daydreams found his curve ball dropping like a guillotined head across home plate. Winter found his winning 20-footer hitting nothing but net. He lugged a hulking linebacker into the end zone to win the homecoming game in his favorite fantasy. The pug-nosed behemoth slammed Joe to the frozen turf in defeated anger. Joe was, of course, hurt. All the better. A hero, and bruised in sealing the victory. His injury drew an audible murmur from the imaginary crowd. Concern turned to cheers as he stood, aroused by the smelling salts, his sweaty hair wild and steamy in the late October chill.

If his father or chores didn't distract him, Joe clutched that particular dream to its sweet end. His teammates lofted his aching body onto their shoulders, and it was all he could do to reach down and touch the warm fingers of one of the cheerleaders—Helen or Nancy or Michelle—whichever one he had chosen as that dream's lover.

No matter the daydream, in them he was Joe Mitchell—confident, talented, and astounding. The someone he was not.

The someone he was rose to the burr of the alarm. It was his 18th birthday. A day to relish, and a day of remembrance. His thoughts fell backwards first. "You're 13 now, old enough to help," George had simply said. Today marked his fifth straight year of rising daily to 5 a.m. darkness. No sleeping in for Joe. Not on Christmas, or Easter, or his birthday. But that would all end soon.

Joe pocketed these thoughts and rolled out of bed and onto the frigid floor. The room's only warmth climbed roundabout up the stairway from the two oil-burning stoves below. He tugged on the light string and shivered as he donned shirt, jeans and socks in the bare bulb's glare. Grabbing his heavy work shoes, he tiptoed down the scalloped wooden stairs to the kitchen. Joe sidled up to the stove and laced up his boots. Then he lifted the lid of the Amana freezer and copped two frozen brownies from a plastic ice cream pail. One he shoved into his pocket; the other he sucked on while donning coat, cap and gloves. His work clothes reeked of the barn. The rancid odor assaulted him anew each day. He could always detect it as he slipped on his coat, and feared that his body soaked up the stench like a sponge, only to release it, despite his raw scrubbing, once at school.

Joe gnawed the first brownie into submission on his way to the barn. The round-topped building looked like a Conestoga wagon against the blue-black dawn. Lights shown dimly through dirty windows the length of the structure, their pattern broken only by the huge, square window of the attached milk house. The 50-foot tall silo stood like a sentinel at the south end of the barn.

Joe entered the barn through its massive wooden door. The hum of the generator and incessant click-click, click-click of the milking machines floated above the cows and collected with the condensation dripping from the barn's low ceiling. The stanchions held 50 Holsteins. Gutters and a 10-foot wide floor behind them split the barn length-wise. Mangers and a walkway ran in front of the cows on both sides of the barn. Whitewash covered the cement block walls. Some of the windows hadn't been spared from the recent spraying. Joe knew. He had spent his recent Saturdays scraping them clean with a razor blade.

Joe father's head appeared over a cow's back at the far end of the barn.

"These cows won't feed themselves so get some silage down," George hollered above the machines. He disappeared for a second and then popped back up. "Put some speed behind it today, Joe. I've got two cows with mastitis and a fresh heifer to deal with before you run off to school."

Joe turned toward the feed room, cursing mastitis and edgy heifers. He wanted time to soak in the tub, for it was a rare day—Troy in the regional basketball finals and he getting to go because of his birthday. No afternoon chores or evening milking.

He tugged his cap down over his ears, pushed the steel cart beneath the silo's chute, and started his twice-daily climb. The chute was tomb-like but its darkness didn't matter. He knew the exact space between the rungs. Half way up the chute, a sliver of light revealed the door he sought. Grabbing hold of its rungs and pushing inward, he followed on his hands and knees onto the half-frozen silage. On the far side of the silo, a mechanic's lamp dangled from a 12-pronged fork. He placed the lamp on the silage and watched its arc of light illuminate his breath. Hefting the fork, its steel handle cold through his gloves, he started heaving the chopped corn through the open door.

Joe worked methodically, always working counter-clockwise. Sometimes close to the chute door, working in rapid spurts like a boxer. Then straining to heave forkfuls from 16 feet away. So much repetition. After 60 forkfuls, Joe rehung the light on the upturned fork, and eased himself backward into the chute, pulling the door shut behind him. An updraft of air sent bits of silage fluttering down his shirt and into his eyes and nose so that he finished his descent blindly.

Joe wheeled the full cart into the barn. The hungry cows strained their thick necks and exposed eggplant tongues. Joe reached Abigail, the fresh heifer. New to her stanchion, she swung her massive head right into Joe's toss. A fork tine pierced her nose, and she recoiled wide-eyed. The silage scattered over the manger and into the straw bedding at her feet.

"What the hell are you doing up there?" George yelled.

"Abigail butted my fork," Joe said defensively.

George moved down behind the row of cows toward the commotion to see Abigail extending her long tongue to stem her bleeding nostril.

"Goll darn it, Joe, how many times I have to tell you to slow down."

"You told me to hurry up just a while ago."

"Well, not so fast that you're maiming cows," George scolded. "Now she'll probably kick like a mule when I hang that milker."

Joe proceeded to the next cow, cursing Abigail under his breath. He didn't dare curse George. There was the night's game to consider.

Joe repeated the circuit with a ground mixture of corn, oats and molasses. Five scoops for Jean, a just-fresh Holstein the size of an Indian elephant. Two scoops for Marcie, a feisty kicker with a bone-white face and devilish black patch around one eye. Joe knew everything about them—from how much feed each received and milk they produced, to which ones laid for him with a urine-soaked tail.

Joe hustled next to feed the outside stock. He shoveled silage into a rusty bushel basket and swung it onto his right shoulder. Threading between icy spots, he traversed the 70 yards to the steer shed. By now the morning gleamed silver. Joe passed the squat steel grain bins, the dilapidated tool shed with its faint odor of oil, and, finally, the pump-house beneath the windmill. The young steers awaited him, their frothy breath steaming above their heads. Joe dumped the silage amongst the bobbing heads and watched the dominant steers butt the younger stock aside. By the fourth of his seven trips, though, even the meekest feasted eyeball deep in the feedstuffs.

His final chore, watering the steers, required hauling five-gallon pails from the pump-house, as the hoses lay frozen. Joe had dreaded this chore all week, especially since Easter fell in March. Sure enough, when he entered the shed and pinned the door open, the peeping began. The door's rectangle of light revealed two ducklings in the water tank, their legs frozen solid in the ice.

The sight was all the more hideous because one of the ducklings was green and the other red. Part of Henson's Easter promotion. Buy so much feed and get duck eggs injected with dye. Kids can pull the eggs right out from under the incubator lamp, the ads said. They'll love guessing what color the ducklings will be when they hatch. And hatch they did. Folks found downy purple, blue, green or red ducklings. Ruth bought into the gimmick despite Joe's protests. Ducklings should be born when the grass and not they are green, he chastised. But one year the ducklings lived, and Ruth reminded Joe they provided several free meals in the fall.

Now the ducklings chirped incessantly, swaying back and forth like cotton candy. Joe didn't hesitate. He picked up one in each hand. Their legs broke off easily, leaving their webbed feet encased in the ice. With all of his might, Joe heaved one duckling, then the other, against the wall. Joe hated killing them, but they were doomed the minute they dove into the tank from the shed's hay bales. When the cattle drank, the water level dropped. The ducklings couldn't scale the tank's smooth metal sides. During the frigid night, the water froze around the tired ducklings.

The first year he had been unable to kill them. He retrieved boiling water from the house and thawed them out. But their legs were long dead, and the crippled birds had rolled and twisted spastically on the shed's floor when he left for school. He found them half eaten by the cats during his evening chores. Dumping their remains in the garage only brought Ruth's wrath. So he used the wall quickly and mercifully now. Still, the doing upset him terribly. The birds chirped in the brief arc from hand to wall, then hit with thumps and fell silent.

Their death reminded Joe again how much he wanted to leave the farm. Farming was a way of life for George. "Nothing a man can do is nobler," his father would say. Five years had tattooed a different impression on Joe. For everything planted and nurtured, Joe saw something else kicked, cursed or tossed against a wall.

Joe stooped for the dead birds and flipped them into one of the pails. With a rusty axe nestled by the door for this purpose, he smashed through the tank's inch-thick ice and watched the water gurgle up through the hole. He swung again and again until all was dirty diamonds of floating ice. Picking up his pails he hurried to dispose of the ducks because George needed him. He would have to skip either breakfast or bathing. With the night's game, he reached in his pocket for the second brownie. Bathing was more important.

SILHOUETTES

Like twin comets, the lights from the stream of oncoming cars tossed the occupants on the bus in and out of darkness. They made silhouettes of the heads of those sitting in front of Joe and he knew his mane created a silhouette to those behind him. That silly distraction stuck. Anything was better than thinking about the game.

Harrison Central 59, Troy 57. A half-hour earlier the world seemed to end with the soft swish of a basketball. The loss plunged Joe into a foul mood, so he sat alone behind the sniffling cheerleaders.

Conference champs and going to state. That's what everyone predicted. One couldn't buy a loaf of bread, get a buzz cut or pump gas in Troy without someone chattering about the Trojans. They had become a big deal in the small town. First the district finals, then a convincing win in the regionals, and on to state. The path was certain—destined—regardless of what the city papers said. All the pre-game ballyhoo focused on Central's tougher city conference and 6'9" center. Still, the Trojans and their fanatic following of farmers and merchants believed Troy would win. Now the season was over. The townspeople would cheer the returning players and tell them they were still champions, that they could be proud because they put Troy on the map. Coach Sauer was likely telling the team the same thing on the trailing team bus—that there was no shame in the loss, and that the players would grow from the experience and what a fine season it had been, and—oh, it was all such a bunch of crap!

Joe stewed, suffering a fan's eternal curse. He had mentally run up and down the court. But he poured only his nerves into the effort. Harrington could float a baseline jumper, or Perkins could snare a rebound. They could make things happen. Feeling more depressed with these thoughts, he watched more comets speed his way.

"Mind if I join you?"

Startled, Joe looked up to see Annie Jensen, one of the wrestling team's cheerleaders.

"Of course, Annie."

Annie plopped beside him. Joe caught her scent, a mixture of chewing gum and light perfume.

"Too bad about the game, huh?" Annie offered immediately.

"Yeah, I don't know what happened. Greg couldn't buy a basket."

"My hopes had been so high. I thought for sure we'd win," Annie continued, her anguish evident, too. "But those refs. They called so many fouls against us."

"That's for sure. I kept looking for their seeing-eye dogs."

Annie giggled half-heartedly. She played with her gloves for several quiet moments. Then she sighed. "It doesn't matter any more. Season's over."

"Yes it is," Joe said. "I bet Mark won't be fun to be with tonight."

"I imagine not, but that doesn't matter, either. We're not together anymore."

"You're not? When did this happen?"

"Right after Snow Days."

"My gosh, you two have been dating all year. What did he do to ruin it?"

Annie smiled. "What makes you so sure it wasn't me who ruined it?"

Joe regretted his outburst immediately, yet it was based on long observation.

"I just assumed. He's the type who wouldn't appreciate what he's got."

Annie leaned closer. "What makes you say that?"

"Never mind, I shouldn't have said anything."

"No, please Joe, I need someone to say what I've been thinking." Annie rested her hand on Joe's arm. "It's been pretty rough since the break."

A comet lit Annie's face for a brief moment. Her auburn hair cascaded over her coat collar, her bangs sweeping across her forehead in a half moon. The perfect teeth seemed carved from the same lunar white. Only a slightly dimpled chin marred her perfection. The comet passed, casting them again in semi-darkness. What a beautiful face, Joe thought. He wished for more comets so he could again see her eyes, and soak up the warmth and goodness that he often imagined behind them.

"Well," Joe began, "it's that he's got just about everything. Homecoming king, captain of the basketball team, that Impala, and the best catch in school."

"You think I'm the best catch?" Annie asked, bemused.

"Hands down." He blushed at the quickness of his response. Taking more time, he added, "People who have so much usually think they deserve it. They stop earning it. That's what I think."

Annie pulled away and slumped back into her seat. The bus driver downshifted to climb a hill, and the grinding of the gears filled the silence between them.

"Are you sticking around for the team bus?" Annie asked.

"Yeah, I guess so."

"Could I hitch a ride home with you? Betty planned on giving me a ride after getting a pizza. But she says Dave'll be too bummed. Says he'll want to go neck straight away. I don't think it's too far out of your way. You're south of town, aren't you?"

"Yeah, past the trestle on Highway 17. It's no problem to run you home." Joe's thoughts turned instantly to the muddy Dodge pickup.

"Great," Annie said. Then she added, "I could still go for that pizza. Can you stay for that, too?"

"Pizza sounds great. I get hungry when I get worked up. Right now I could eat a Buick."

"Why didn't you go out for the team?"

Joe chortled. "At 5'7" I wouldn't have been what you would call a dominating player. Besides, I have to help my dad on our farm."

"All the time? Isn't that mostly a summer thing?"

Joe began to fidget. *Yes, All the Time, as long as he could remember.* "It's a dairy farm. There's always work."

"Well, how about baseball? Or track?"

"Spring's the worse time of all because of planting," Joe replied tersely. He didn't want to elaborate with Annie because the farm embarrassed him. He changed the subject. "What about you? What are your plans to make your last months at Troy memorable?"

"Wrap up the yearbook. I've got to hit the books, lock in a college. Not much time for fun. There's just too much going on."

Turning to other things they had in common, Joe and Annie soon were laughing about Mr. Carter, the social studies teacher being audited by the IRS the very quarter he was teaching the seniors about taxes. And Mrs. Sandowski, the cheerleading coach, who had broken her toe doing a handspring. Eventually their conversation waned. Joe wanted desperately to keep it flowing freely, but he couldn't think of anything to say.

Joe returned to gazing out the window as the bus churned away from the suburbs and through a stretch of rolling hills. Soon the first farms appeared bleak and shadowy amidst the snowy fields. Occasionally a yard light beamed brightly. One illuminated a farmer trudging up to the house from his barn, his dog, anxious to play, bounding around him. Finally, small houses that marked the outskirts of Troy appeared. The bus hummed with conversation now. The driver switched on the interior lights as he turned down the school's drive. On cue, the cheerleaders broke into the school rouser and were joined by a smattering of students.

The buses degorged the students into a sea of lights and eerie exhaust from the waiting cars. Parents honked from behind dark glass when they spied their son or daughter. Students with cars revved the cold engines to chase away the March chill—a lost cause since most of them hollered out of open windows to friends. They honked their hellos, good-byes and follow-mes across the parking lot.

About 60 students and parents awaited the team bus. Annie and Joe huddled out of the wind in the school's entryway. Annie shivered next to Joe, her coat collar raised to cover her ears. Forgetting his own vanity, Joe donned his stocking cap when the top of his ears began to sting. Instinctively, he rubbed Annie's arms to keep her warm.

"Thanks, Joe. Brrrr. We could go in, but I want to find Betty first to tell her about the change in plans," Annie said through her muffler. She stood on tiptoes in search of her friend. "There she is. Betty!" She waved across the milling crowd.

"Hi guys," Betty Carlson yelled back. She approached them from the last student bus. Wrapped in a hooded jacket, she resembled an Inuit except that she stood 5'10", which was one reason she was Dave Wilson's steady. The Troy strong forward was among the few who towered over her.

"Isn't it awful that we lost?" Betty said when she reached them.

"It's worse than awful," Joe said, truthfully for him.

"Oh well, they did their best. And we're the first senior class ever to go to the regional finals."

"You still think Dave will want to just take off?" Annie asked.

"Probably. When we lost the Franksburg football game, he didn't even want to talk to me. And this is worse. This game meant something."

Annie turned her face inside her raised collar again. Her words came out as vapor. "I figured that, so either way, I've asked Joe to give me a ride."

"Could you, Joe? That would be great. Just in case."

"Hey, it's no problem."

Ten minutes later, the team bus rolled down the hill toward the school's entrance. The cheerleaders began the Troy rouser as the fans formed a corridor. The players hurried off the bus, freshly showered and sullen. Clapping and cheers, mostly from girlfriends, solicited half smiles in return. Even more now in their defeat, because people felt sorry for them, Joe wished he were one of them. They filed under an arbor of adulation, soaking up the season's final recognition, as close to conquering Caesars as teenagers could ever hope to be.

Dave Wilson slipped out of the stream to join them. "Hello Betty," he said, slipping an arm around her. "What's up?"

"Well, you're in a good mood for losing," Betty said, surprised.

"I left the loss back in the shower. Coach gave us a good talk. For once he was human."

"Well, then, do you still want to go get a pizza like we had planned?" Betty asked.

"Sure, I could use some of Mel's grease for these aching joints. I'm whipped," Dave said. He stretched backwards, groaning for emphasis. "Who's all coming?"

"The usual gang," Annie said. "Joe, too."

"Is that right, Little Joe?"

"Sure, sounds like a good idea."

"Your stomach will have to be the judge of that," Dave said. "Mel uses salmonella for seasoning." Dave laughed at his joke. "I'm going to hurl that one at him tonight."

"You better get inside," Betty said, mussing his hair. "Ice is forming on your head."

Dave felt his still wet scalp. "Jeez, I hope this winter ends soon. Be back in a sec, guys. I've got to unload this crap one more time," he said, hefting his gym bag.

The three of them waited inside until Dave returned. Then, as pairs, they ran out into the last of the winter's cold. Joe opened the door to the Dodge and started to brush off the seat. "It's okay," Annie said, and scooted into the cab. He slammed her door, ran around the front of the pickup and hopped in on the driver's side. He shifted the pickup noisily through its gears and up the school drive, turned right down Main Street to the one stoplight that marked the right turn to Troy's only pizza joint. Parking, Joe ran around to Annie's door before she had a chance to open it. She released a small laugh.

"What?"

"Nothing," Annie said, still smiling.

Mel did his best to create an Italian experience. With the last name Vansek, he failed miserably. Dusty plastic green vines and purple grapes hung from a wire mesh along the low ceiling. A poorly painted mural of a gondolier poling down a canal covered one wall. Students already filled most of the high-backed booths on the far side of the room. The foursome managed to get the last booth next to the jukebox, which belted out "Lady Madonna."

Mel worked behind the counter, a green sweater revealing his too-frequent consumption of his own pizza. When he wasn't shuffle-boarding pizza into the ovens, or taking orders from a waitress, he kept a sharp lookout for beer or schnapps. He loved the kids, but he cherished his dining license more.

"Hey Mel, got a winner yet?" Dave yelled above the clamor.

"Not yet," Mel hollered back. "Bunch of lightweights so far. Must be the loss."

"Well, then, light on the salmonella seasoning tonight, okay?"

Mel grinned, rubbed some tomato sauce on his shirt, and shook his head. "Heard it before."

"What are you trying to win?" Joe asked, amused at Dave's insult.

"Haven't you been here on game nights?" Dave asked.

"No, this is my first game of the season."

"We've got to get you out more, Little Joe," Dave said. He gave Joe's shoulders a jovial hug. "Here's the deal. On game nights, Mel awards the table with the best slam against his pizza a free one. Why don't you give it a shot?"

Joe's mind raced while Dave and the girls waited on him. He burned under their stare. After what were mere seconds but seemed an eternity, Joe yelled: "Mel uses sliced big toes for pepperoni."

Mel's laughed and clanged his bell, signifying the night's winner. "One big toe pizza coming up for the jukebox table," he yelled, as Dave and the girls cheered.

While they ate their pizza, some of the basketball players straggled into the room. They slipped easily into seats reserved for them. Two starters, Greg Harrington, a lanky lefty whose career as a hustling point guard had just ended, and Mark Perkins, the team's leading scorer and Dave's counterpart at forward, came over and squeezed into the booth next to Joe and Dave. Greg removed his letterman's jacket and rolled his sweater sleeves up his skinny arms. He sported a crewcut from which an elbow-induced lump rose like an acorn. Greg sat sullen and withdrawn. He ordered a Coke and downed it quickly, and then seemed content to suck on his ice cubes. Mark, his dark eyes passionless, shrugged away questions about the game as deftly as he dribbled between his legs. Only the pizza interested him, and he grabbed a lukewarm gooey piece.

"It's too bad you guys lost," Betty said.

"The refs cost us the game," Greg said.

"Refs, hell," Mark said between chews. "What were you, two for 20 from outside?"

"Screw you, Mark," Greg retorted. "I took about 10 shots, and I was getting hacked on half of 'em, but those city refs had it in for us."

Mark glared back at Greg for a moment, and then licked a streak of orange grease off his finger. "Whatever," he said.

"Well, there's still baseball," Betty said effervescently.

"Do you think the baseball team will go as far?" Annie joined in from the corner.

"We should win conference . . ." Greg began.

"And lose in districts," Mark finished the sentence.

"Well, we'll do better than you turkeys in track," Greg said, irked. He crunched down hard on an ice cube for emphasis.

"Don't be so hasty to pass judgment, we've got a chance at the title this year," Mark said.

"Get real," Greg grunted, tapping the last cubes from the bottom of his cup.

"You running the half mile again this year Mark?" Betty asked, ever the appeaser. "It would be exciting if you went to regions again."

"Nope, I'm moving up to the mile. O'Reilly's orders. He figures I can win it unless Langley from Webster has had a sex change. Crazy will be our half miler."

Mark seemed suddenly bored. He scanned the room to weigh its potential. The crowd was subdued and thinning. He turned back to the booth.

"Got a ride home, Annie?"

"Joe's taking me."

Mark's thick black eyebrows arched. He turned to Joe. "As I recall, that would be out of Joe's way. I'm leaving soon. I could just drop you off on my way home."

"No, I'm going with Joe," Annie said emphatically.

This time Mark leveled his piercing stare at Annie. She glared back at him defiantly. An uncomfortable silence fell across the booth. Betty caught Joe's gaze and rolled her eyes as if to say "here we go." Joe became conscious of the jukebox. Someone had pushed "Lady Madonna" again. *Lady Madonna, baby at your breast, wonders how you manage to feed the rest.*

"Suit yourself," Mark finally said. He tossed his napkin onto the remnants of pizza and rose from the table. "Catch you guys, later, and thanks for the pizza," he said, reaching for his billfold.

"No need to pay," Dave said. "Joe won the pizza tonight. Sliced big toes for pepperoni."

"He did? Well, it seems to be Joe's lucky night all the way around," Mark smirked. He wandered away to join some other teammates with Greg at his heels.

"We've got to get going, too," Betty said, rising. "Or are you too tired to play anymore one-on-one tonight?"

"Depends on the opposition," Dave said, circling his arms around Betty from behind, "and if the objective is to score."

Betty groaned. "I can't take this on top of Mel's pizza. Thanks for sharing, Joe."

"No problem. It was fun."

"See you two Monday," Dave said, guiding Betty toward the door.

Joe left a 50-cent tip and escorted Annie out the door. They slid across the frozen parking lot, the wind whipping at their backs. Joe again opened Annie's door. They sat and shivered while the old pickup warmed.

"I should have let you wait inside while this baby heated up," Joe said. "But it never really ever warms up."

"That's okay. I'm fine. Really," Annie said, well bundled.

They said nothing as he turned the pickup west on Elm Street past Troy's small businesses—Sally's Beauty Shop and Glen's Electric, then the Red Owl grocery store and Nedeen's Drug Store. The street's few other small businesses fell away in the next block, and the town's oldest houses appeared stately in the moonlight.

"Sorry you had to witness our . . . differences back there," Annie said. "I didn't mean to get Mark pissed at you. He can be a great guy one minute and a jerk the next. Towards the end, I never knew which one would show up," she said tiredly. "He can be abusive."

"Physically?"

"No, he's never laid a hand on me. I mean verbally."

"I'm glad you turned Mark down."

They approached Maple Crest, the new housing development west of Troy. Here the huge houses loomed like castles behind their moats of snow-covered lawns. Annie navigated, pointing with her gloved hand where to turn as they weaved down curving avenues framed by look-alike houses.

"I've been thinking about what you said on the bus, about Mark taking things for granted," Annie said as they crossed Jade Street. "I think you're right."

"I know I am."

"Why's that?"

Joe fiddled with the heater. Enough time had passed so that the fan at last kicked out some warm air. *Because he's the opposite of me,* Joe wanted to say. Instead, he said plainly: "Just look how he treated Greg back at Mel's. Greg's his best friend, wheeling from the loss, yet Mark slammed him. You don't do that if you care about other people's feelings."

"You don't think highly of Mark, do you? Is it because he's a jock?"

"Hell no. I wish I were. I'd cut off my right arm, wrap it in a bow and give it to Coach O'Reilly if I could get on the track team."

"Why don't you go out then?"

Why don't I?, thought Joe. *Why doesn't a black man spit in a Klansman's face? Ramifications.*

"Can't. Like I said, spring's the busiest time on the farm."

"Are you really that dedicated?"

"No," Joe laughed. "The truth is my dad would probably cut off my arm himself if I even approached him with the idea." He tried to imagine what George would actually do if he asked. *Ramifications.*

Annie told Joe to slow down, and moments later they eased up the Jensen driveway.

"It would be nice if you went out for the team," Annie said. "You could whip Mark's butt."

Joe snorted. "Are you kidding? Even if I went out, he made the regions last year."

Annie scooted over the seat and pecked Joe on the cheek. "Thanks again for the ride." She slid back across the seat. "This time I'll get the door."

As she opened it, she turned back to Joe. "If you went out for track I could see you after school sometimes. The yearbook's due soon, so I stay after most days."

The light over the Jenson's front door blinked on. Annie waved and scurried up the walk as her mother waited.

"Who was that who brought you home," Donna Jensen asked Annie as she shut the front door behind her youngest daughter.

"Joe Mitchell, he offered to give me a ride after the game."

"I don't remember you mentioning a Mitchell before. Should I know him?"

"Do you need to?"

Mrs. Jensen huffed. "Why do you have to be that way? Elizabeth never was. Is it a crime that I worry about you?" She turned her stout body away in an expression of hurt, and sighed as she settled back on the sofa.

"He's just a friend. We have some classes together." Seeing her mother eyeing her quizzically, Annie added, "We're not getting married yet, we thought we'd wait for the baby to be born."

"Don't sass. I know you think I'm prying again," Mrs. Jensen said, wagging a finger at Annie. "Well, I need to pry, especially with Mark calling twice in the last 10 minutes."

"What does Mark want?"

"I thought you could tell me. I thought you two were through but he sounded pretty upset and I don't think it was about the game."

"Well, we are through, and I can ride home with whomever I want," Annie pouted. Just then, the phone rang again.

"Why don't you repeat that to Romeo, then," Mrs. Jensen said with irritation. "And remind Mark not to call this late."

Annie answered the phone in the hallway.

"Hello, Annie. This is Mark. Remember. The guy you love."

Annie twisted the phone cord nervously around her fingers. "Not anymore." She spoke softly so her mother couldn't overhear.

"Look, if you want me to say I'm sorry, I'm sorry. Only thing is I don't know what I've done." His voice floated plaintively over the line.

"That's the problem, Mark, you're not even aware of how you treat me. You denigrate me when you're around the guys. You tease me mercilessly."

"That's just being one of the guys . . ."

"And I don't like it when you drink," Annie continued. "It makes you rude and mean."

"If you're still mad about Snow Days, blame Harrington. He brought the schnapps. Anyway, if your goal is to get even, you've succeeded. It's been bad enough you've ignored me these past few weeks. But to replace me with Mitchell is downright cruel."

"I haven't replaced you. Like I told you earlier, I've dumped you."

"He's a farm boy."

"So?"

"And a loser."

"That's not true."

"It is. You'll see. And here's something else that's true. You're still in love with me. People don't lie about things when they're in each other's arms. I haven't forgotten the things you've said." He softened his tone. "Have you, Annie?" He waited for an answer and when none came, he added, "What do I need to do to win you back?"

Annie remained silent. Breaking up had been traumatic. She still at times struggled with her decision. Looking through the doorway, she saw her mother eyeing her and then feigning interest back to her book.

"Mother says not to call this late," she said, and hung up.

RAMIFICATIONS

Joe spent all of the next week trying to work up the nerve to ask his father's permission to try out for the track team. He feared the encounter, but Annie weighed constantly on his mind. He read much into her goodbye kiss and comments about seeing him after school. Finally, on Sunday, Joe could stand his indecision no longer. During the evening milking, George flowed from cow to cow, his crumpled hat pressed against one flank after another. The milking machines, all stainless steel and black rubber, emitted their sucking sounds. George sometimes folded himself into their rhythm. Humming old tunes, he patted the cows, stroked and scratched them, as if only something so docile and obedient could capture his affection.

Joe waited for the lullabies while quietly and efficiently performing his tasks. His stomach twitched, knowing the dream stayed alive as long as he didn't pop the question.

Above the milkers' chink-chink, chink-chink, George's faint humming began. He squatted next to Penny, head bent so he looked down into the straw. Joe approached quickly, and let the words tumble out.

"Dad, I was wondering. Can I go out for track this spring?"

There, it was out, his anxiety pricked.

George swiveled his head, as if it were affixed to Penny's flank. He seemed confused by the question. "What?"

"Running for school. You know. Hundred yard dashes or the mile."

"When would this be?"

"Right after school."

"What about your work around here?"

"I can do the chores and milking when I get home about six."

"Six!" George's head snapped away from Penny, acknowledging for the first time Joe's request. "These cows have to be fed by six so we can milk right after supper. And who's going to do that when I'm in the fields?"

Argument No.1, the threat to the all-important crops. Joe's request might as well have been August locusts. Counting on this question Joe parried with a prepared solution.

"I can catch a ride home with Larry Pressler instead of taking the players' bus. He comes home from the vo-tech about 5:15 and could pick me up. I'd be home by 5:30. I'd skip supper till late. I'll work hard to make up the time."

George turned back to his machine, methodically squeezing each of the four tubes to check Penny's milk flow. Into Penny's side he said, "No."

"Please Dad . . ."

"I said no. You'd come home and rush through your chores. You'd feed the cows too much or too little. Stick a fork in their noses like the other day. Mess up their production. I'm running a business here, and I can't screw it up so you can go run in circles."

Penny kicked at the milker, catching George's arm instead. "Dang it, hold still, you cockeyed buffalo," he roared, leaning harder into Penny's side. Penny quieted, and George fell into a fuming silence.

Joe scratched a pattern in the lime on the floor with his shoe. He felt selfish for asking and angry for feeling selfish. Other guys in school did as they pleased; yet he was tied to the farm, no better off than a slave. Track had suddenly become the most important thing in his life—a taste of the chains coming off. How could he explain that? Even in his own mind, his needs paled against their livelihood.

"Please, Dad, it's my senior year. Other guys go out for sports year-round all through high school, and I've never competed in anything."

George mulled over this fact for several long seconds. He leaned back into Penny's side and stared blankly into the straw. Then he looked Joe square in the eyes.

"Other guys don't make a living farming." He didn't say it harsh or mean. The rejection came out honest and true, under control. "I'm competing against a banker's note and Mother Nature to boot. I'm sorry, but I can't afford watching my corn crop ruined by a killing frost because it was planted too late because you were off running."

Joe was crushed. His hanging arms ended in clenching fists. "It's not fair, and you know it."

"No, it's not fair. But it's our life. Now let's drop this crazy talk."

The milking machine cups gasped noisily at Penny's udder. George stood up, pulled off the machine, shut off the air valve and tugged the hose from the vacuum line. Removing the milker's lid, he poured their liquid income into a tall steel pail, and moved onto the next cow, all in silence. Angry, Joe removed the milker strap from Penny, kicking her in the leg when she innocently pressed against him. He strapped up the next cow, washed her udder with an iodine and water solution and, seething, hoisted two full pails of milk.

What does he expect of me? George thought as Joe walked toward the milk house. I work from 5 in the morning till 9 at night as it is. He nestled against the next cow, Linda, seeking relief, but the guilt started pulsating through him. The milker's vacuum line seemed to suck at his resistance.

Joe can't see the importance of all this, of his help, George thought. He doesn't connect this with the clothes on his back or the food in his belly. Joe wants to play when I've got Casey's Implement waving a $2,000 overdue bill in my face. But hell, he's right. Works like a son-of-a-bitch. He's like a whirlwind the way he whips through his chores. I push him, and he doesn't complain or ask for things because he knows there's no money.

Linda whipped a stinging tail across the back of his head. George grabbed it, gave it a twist that drove Linda against the stanchion bar. The slap fortified his resolve.

"Hell, I never got to be so carefree at his age," he mumbled out loud. He continued his dialog internally. Had to quit school in the eighth grade to help Dad—had to, there was no choice. No milkers then, either. It took all three of us boys to milk the cows. And if we complained, it was the rough side of the razor strap. There was work, pure and simple. You didn't have to like it. It's how things were.

The rock music exploded down the middle of the barn, jolting Holsteins and George alike. George jumped across the gutter. The radio rested on a plywood platform he had built above the walkway to the milk house. Joe stood beneath it, looking back defiantly. Joe hoisted the pails again, and made his way up the walkway. After turning the radio down, it took George several minutes and no returned pails to realize he was alone with his cows for the rest of the milking.

Ruth knew from the way Joe kicked off his boots against the mudroom door that something was amiss. Entering the kitchen, Joe peeled off his coat and hat and hung them on his hook in silence.

"What's the matter?" Ruth asked.

Joe walked past and started bounding up the stairs to his bedroom.

"Joe, you come back down here and answer my question," Ruth hollered. Joe audibly halted on the steps, and in a few seconds he stood before Ruth, his face closed.

"I won't have you running away from me when I'm talking to you, Joe," Ruth scolded. "It's disrespectful."

"Sorry," Joe said curtly.

"You going to tell me what happened?"

"Nothing."

"Nothing? Then I guess you better go back to the barn and finish milking."

"That's not going to happen."

Ruth walked to the kitchen table and sat down.

"Sit and tell me what's wrong."

Joe bent into the adjacent chair morosely. "It's everything. This place, the work. Dad always bossing me. I have no fun. No life." Joe suddenly seemed to run out of steam. He dipped his forehead to the cold Formica and covered his head with his arms. His fingers moved slowly back and forth through his blond hair.

"Can't even go out for track my senior year," he mumbled into the table.

So that's it, Ruth thought. She rubbed the side of her face with her hand. Joe might as well have gone for George's jugular. Still, she knew her Joe. He wouldn't have asked unless he truly desired it.

"You know spring's the worst time for sports."

"Every season's a worst time. Has been for all of high school. It's just that this is my last chance," Joe said, raising his head, a forlorn look on his face. "You see it, don't you? Why I'm asking?"

"Of course I do," Ruth replied sympathetically. Spring brought Joe's graduation ever nearer, and with it the prospect of no Joe at all. That fact hung perilously over the family, like the threat of June frost. George desired Joe to stay on to become a partner some day. Joe planned on attending Belton Junior College. Ruth alone knew this. Joe talked to her.

"Will you talk to Dad? Make him understand?" Joe implored.

"I will Joe. But I make no promises on the outcome."

That mollified Joe. He sat up straight and exhaled deeply.

"Hungry?" Ruth asked. "There's some chocolate cake left."

Joe nodded. He watched Ruth cross the huge kitchen to retrieve the cake pan. He had always thought his mother was attractive. Her blond hair had begun to streak with gray the color of pipe smoke, and her crow's feet marked her hours outdoors, but her high cheek bones gave her the radiance of a younger woman. Watching her work, Joe noticed the black night through the window behind her. He suddenly wondered how she survived being alone all day during the merciless winter months. Joe at least had his classmates. George spent most of his days in the barn or the fields. Neighbors were distant.

When Ruth placed a piece of cake the size of a brick before him, Joe asked, "Are you happy, Mom?"

The question startled her. Joe seldom probed. She mulled over her answer as she fetched the half-gallon jar of milk from the fridge and poured Joe a glass. It was milk from the bulk tank, thick and creamy.

"I'm as happy as can be expected," she answered as she set the glass down.

"What does that mean?"

"I've got you," Ruth said, reaching out and touching his cheek before he could move away.

"Stop it, Mom," Joe said through a mouth chockfull of devil's food. He gulped some milk to wash the cake down, and looked back at Ruth, milk-mustached and inquisitive. Defying George for the first time suddenly seemed like a rite of passage that now entitled him to this line of questioning. "Don't you get lonely here?"

"Yes. I hate the silence. Hate it more than you can imagine. What can I say? I married a dairy farmer," Ruth said. Lordy, why am I telling Joe this, she thought. She had never spoken of it before.

"My mother warned me against it, having married one herself. But George is a good husband. He takes good care of me. Sure, I'd like to dally over coffee and dessert instead of talking about the baler breaking down, but this is our life."

"That's what Dad said. That this is our life." Joe sighed again, and placed his fork on his plate. He shut his eyes, overwhelmed again by the futility of his dreams.

"Joe," Ruth said. "This is *our* life, Dad's and mine. Not your life, unless you choose it. I know you want to leave. Dad is fighting to keep you here."

Joe looked at Ruth as if he were about to cry. "I don't want to fight, Mom. I just want to be happy," he said with finality. The hard look returned to his face. "Can I be excused? I'm really tired."

"Sure. I'll talk to George."

Ruth sat quietly in the kitchen, the overhead light suddenly too bright, the room too barren, with Joe upstairs. George would be up soon and, as he had skipped supper to talk with Charlie Wharton, the Pioneer seed dealer, Ruth busied herself heating up beef roast and refrying mashed potatoes. Ruth hadn't really minded the dairy in the beginning. She loved George madly and pitched in at his side in the early years of their marriage. She thought then of having a large family—half a dozen sons who would raise prize-winning stock and crops while she and George rocked on the porch and admired their work. But after Joe, she had two miscarriages. The second came at seven months. Ruth blamed the blue baby on overexertion from helping George with the stock. She hadn't entered the barn since, not in 14 years.

George didn't escape the agony of a lost child, either, she knew. He yearned to recreate the life of his father, who reveled in the goodness and honesty of hard-working sons.

A second thud of boots heralded George's arrival. He, too, entered in silence, laying yellow work gloves upon the freezer. Flipping the potatoes in sizzling butter on the stove, Ruth waited for him to speak, but George was more reticent than Joe. He took off his coat and hat, unsnapped and climbed out of his blue bib overalls, and walked past her to the washroom. Ruth waited while he scrubbed off the day's labor, and noted that it took him longer than usual. When the water stopped running, she dished up his food from the blackened frying pan, sliced the rye bread he loved and filled his milk glass.

George said grace to himself, and then set upon his meal. He ate hungrily. His jaw clicked as he chewed—one of his annoying idiosyncrasies. But he was still a handsome man, this George she had married. Ruddy complexion and wrinkled by the years in the field, his face possessed steel blue eyes and thick brows that detracted you from his receding brown hairline. His smile showcased strong straight teeth ("My pearls," he called them when his vanity surfaced). With the tubular bibs off, he still displayed the tapered, muscular build that first attracted her.

"I suppose Joe came through here bellyaching," he said between chews.

"What did you two fight about?"

George fiddled with his fork, plowing furrows into his potatoes. "He wants to go out for track, for Christ's sake."

"Yes, he told me. And you said no."

George attacked his meat, slicing it with vigor. "Of course. He'd be missing chores every night. Not getting home till six."

"We've never let him go out for any sport. Isn't there a way?" Ruth ventured.

"Now, don't you start in on me," George snapped. Leveling his fork at her, he tapped it in midair as if playing a drum roll. "You know I can't get the work done without him. Maybe in the winter, yes, but in the spring I've got the field work."

"Shhh, not so loud, he'll hear you."

"I don't care," George said. Then, putting both fists on the table, knife and fork upraised for effect, he bellowed through the walls and up the stairs, "I don't give a damn if he hears me!"

"Stop shouting, George."

"You coddle him too much," George said, returning to his meal. "He's not a baby anymore."

Despite her intention, Ruth's temper rose. "You're right," she whispered harshly. "He's not a baby. He's 18. He can be drafted and get killed, but he can't go out for track."

"All I told him was he couldn't because of the field work. He blasted the radio on me. Probably cost us a hundred bucks in production by spooking the cows."

Ruth maneuvered her chair closer to George in a conciliatory gesture. She placed her hand on his forearm. "George, this is Joe's senior year, and he works so hard . . ."

"And I don't?" George interrupted. "Do you want me to get up at 3 o'clock instead of 5? Come in at 10:30 instead of 9? Why don't I just give up sleep completely? Our heads aren't that high above water. You do the books. No, Joe's turning sassy, and I won't stand for that as long as he's living under my roof. I give in here and he'll just want something more."

George's face turned a dark red. He picked at his food, rapidly losing his appetite. He dropped his fork to the plate with a clatter. "You just don't see what's happening here because you can't see Joe as anything but your baby. If we would have had other sons, this wouldn't be an issue."

"Oh, George," Ruth said. She turned away, visibly upset over the reopened wound.

Already damned, George continued. "You don't like the way I run this farm, you find someone who you'll do better by. Let Joe go out for track. Spend your days carefree, your head in the clouds like his. And don't worry about me. I'll just be here mucking around knee deep in shit as usual."

Ruth stood up from the table and walked around George into the livingroom. George pushed his chair back with an audible scraped along the linoleum floor, grabbed his gloves and coat, and retreated out the door. He headed for the barn where the Holsteins never questioned his judgment.

Later, when George crawled into bed, Ruth lay square-shouldered away from him. He shivered while the cold sheets warmed around him. He lay there for several minutes, knowing Ruth was awake. Together they shared the sound of ice cracking on the roof. At last he moved toward her warmth.

"I'm sorry, honey. I lost my temper."

Ruth didn't respond. George hated it when she didn't forgive him instantly. It was only here, in bed, that Ruth controlled him. He rubbed her shoulder through her flannel pajamas and continued. "It's just that I'm so frustrated. I want the best for Joe too, but I work all day, every day, and still can't get ahead. Can't buy you new clothes at Twain's or take you on trips. I can't seem to do anything right. On days like these I feel so worthless."

"No, you're doing your best," Ruth said dispassionately, keeping her back to him.

George had hoped she would turn into his arms. He didn't want to beg, as he was too proud and still too angry to admit he might be wrong. Ending his overtures, he rolled away, hating the widening distance between them.

Above them, a chunk of ice broke free, scuttled along the pitched roof, and slipped into silence over the eave.

"I'll figure out something," he said. "Maybe he could miss some practices. On days it rains it won't matter. Or maybe this early thaw will last, and I can still get the corn in by early May with him gone."

"You do what you think is right, George."

BLOODLINES

Nary had a word passed between George and Joe over the next two days. Joe went to school knowing only that his parents had discussed the matter, and that George was "thinking about it." In the meantime, Annie asked Joe why he hadn't signed up for track. The friendliness in her voice tossed him deeper in gloom. The deadline for signing up came and went, and Joe had no answers.

Joe approached the weekend with trepidation. Winter hung on as annoying as a wood tick. The slush meant George would find a task requiring both of them to work indoors. Joe feared his pent-up anxiety would erupt between them, and forever doom his chances.

After the morning milking, they trudged up to the house together. On weekends, Ruth cooked huge breakfasts. The kitchen table held a platter of sausage and eggs over easy, a plate of toast, coffee for George and the home-grown honey that Joe slathered in an amber sheet across his bread. Ruth didn't join them, having eaten earlier. Instead, she stood next to the stove, boiling something in the two enormous pots she used for making strawberry jam.

Joe thought nothing of it, his mind on track. While they ate, the silence between George and Joe hung thicker than the smell of the sausage, yet when Joe caught Ruth's eye she winked at him.

George swiped up a yellow streak of yolk with the last of his toast, swallowed the morsel, and drained his coffee cup. Wiping his mouth on the back of his hand, he said, "I'll be killing some chickens this morning. When you're done, Joe, come out to the machine shed."

Joe bit his tongue. One of the worst jobs on the farm. Only one worse was mucking out the steer shed in April, and dealing with the rats that sprung from their winter nests in the matted straw and manure. He waited till George left before speaking.

"Unless he's going to say yes to track today, I'm not helping slaughter chickens."

Ruth smiled. "Wear something you don't mind tossing when you're done."

"He's going to let me?"

Ruth began clearing plates. "Go fetch some five gallon pails to hold this boiling water. Be quick or George will be waiting on you."

Joe didn't bother changing. Any of his work clothes were expendable in his opinion. His jacket and jeans were in tatters, stained by manure and mud, and quite appropriate for the grim task. With gloved hands, Joe helped Ruth pour the scalding water into the pails. Bent under their weight, he left the house and walked in jerks toward the machine shed. The water sloshed and steamed into the frigid air. Ahead of him, a chicken dangling from each hand, George emerged from the chicken coop. They bought 50 chicks twice a year. The spring batch scratched its way through summer weeds until plump enough to feel George's knife. The fall batch enjoyed shelled corn and lamp heat, but met the same fate.

Joe reached the machine shed in short order. One side of the A-frame building held farm equipment, the other bales of bedding straw for the steer shed. The straw was now almost gone, and in the empty space, suspended from the rafters, five twine nooses hung. Two already contained George's just-captured chickens. Tied upside down by their yellow feet, they fluttered and swung like tethered balls. Their beating wings released small white feathers that drifted slowly to the straw floor like snowflakes.

"Set the pails over by the door where there's better light and help me get three more," George ordered. "We need to work fast before that water cools or you won't be getting those pin feathers out."

As a pair, they entered the coop. The chickens squawked and scurried away from the door. The dust they kicked up commingled with the smell of their droppings and almost overpowered Joe. He was accustomed to the smell of all kinds of animal waste. Pig manure was by far the foulest, but in a confined, heated space, chicken shit smelled acrid and awful.

"Grab their feet. First one to get two birds wins," George said, enjoying himself.

They moved stealthily towards the chickens, which piled together in a white mound against the far wall. Only their red cones revealed individual birds. George feigned to the left, and the clucking drift swung in an arc towards Joe. The first few frightened birds tried to run by him. Joe made a mad grab and missed. Then the whole flock surged toward him. The fat hens could barely get airborne, but the ones that did flew right into him. Joe felt their sharp nails against his leg, and their frantic wings brush by.

"Grab 'em, Joe!" George yelled.

Joe blindly obeyed, sweeping and closing his open hands into the fluttering storm. At last he caught a single leg. The chicken struggled and pummeled his arm with both wings as he lifted it above the others.

"Get her other leg and keep her head down. Then she'll quiet."

It sounded like a simple task, with one leg already in hand. The chicken had other ideas. It came straight for Joe's face. Joe saw three long toes, the color of mustard, inches from his eye. In a flash he whacked the bird against the wall, which stirred up the entire flock again. When the flurry subsided, Joe's chicken looked up at him through dazed eyes.

"That works, too," George said, two birds in hand. "Let's go. Three's all we need."

Back in the shed, George fashioned the slipknots over the birds' feet. Their two groggy predecessors watched passively as the new birds went through their own gyrations.

"Stand back, Joe," George said. He grabbed the first chicken by the head, shrouding its eyes with a gloved hand so it didn't see the bone-handled knife in his right. George stretched the neck and slowly stuck the blade through it. The chicken let out a muffled, mournful squawk as George retracted the blade. The blood flowed from the severed jugular and wrote the bird's epitaph in circular red lines on the straw below. The dying bird began to flail, and the blood spurted in an ever-widening circle. It didn't deter George. He moved to the opposite end of the gallows and executed another hen as the life drained from the first. After several minutes, the first bird hung dead above a pool of blood. Joe's part in the slaughter began. Loosing the bird, he carried it to one of the pails and submerged it. The feathers' contact with the scalding water unleashed yet another offensive odor. Joe swirled the bird around for a minute, then withdrew it dripping wet. Sitting down on the front end of the corn picker, he worked with a practiced hand, pulling great gobs of feathers off the carcass. The warm feathers felt good against his cold hands, and he moved with precision to pull out any stubborn pin feathers. Shortly, the bird was completely plucked. Joe noticed the vertical knife slit in its throat, and the scaly lids shut forever over the dead bird's eyes. Next Sunday's dinner, Joe thought as he placed the carcass in a bushel basket.

Joe plucked one more bird while George's more practiced hands cleaned three. Then Joe went to retrieve more boiling water while George fetched additional birds. Soon they were in sync again, a regular assembly line of noose, knife, blood and feathers, wet and bloody from their task, and both reeking terribly.

George pulled the last two birds down from the gallows and handed one to Joe. They plucked in silence, the feathers now mounded in twin piles at their feet.

"I've come to a decision on this track thing," George said, never slowing, never raising his head. Joe slowed, however, squeezing hard on his fistful of feathers. "You can go out for the team but only under several conditions." George let the bird dangle and looked up. "First I want you to know I don't like this, Joe, not one bit. You and Ruth ganging up on me when you know full well the workload around here come spring."

Joe dropped his eyes. He hadn't expected a lecture.

"But I've got to keep the peace, so I've come up with this here compromise. Are you listening to me?" George asked brusquely.

"Yes, Dad," Joe said meekly.

"Condition number one. You can't stay the whole darn practice. Cows got to be milked regular, same time morning and night. You've got to have the cows fed by 6 p.m. Next condition. I'll be working harder because of this. I expect you to work harder when you're at home. That means weekends will be a son of a bitch for you."

Big whoop on that one, Joe thought. He'd sacrifice his Sunday afternoon—the only free weekend time he had anyway—if it sprung him for track during the week.

George returned half-heartedly to his bird. He picked at dripping feathers beneath a wing. "Last condition, and it's harsh, but I'm serious about not threatening our livelihood. Some days I might just have to say 'no track'. Might be I got to push because of the weather to finish planting. Might be something worse. Could be lots of things. If I see this isn't working, I might just change my mind."

Joe fiddled with some stubborn wing feathers on his own bird. He eyed the work of the executioner, his father, and didn't doubt the truth behind George's words. A goof up, three straight days of May rain, or a busted plow blade could jeopardize all.

"Those are my conditions, Joe. Do you accept them?"

"Yes."

"Well, then, finish plucking that bird. Then go tell Ruth to spread newspaper on the kitchen table. I'll be up to gut these birds shortly."

ON PAPER

The smell of the locker room in the morning always caught Coach O'Reilly off guard. The mixture of sweat, liniment and ammonia permeated his office between phy-ed classes and after school when he coached. But then the showers moistened and softened the odors. Early like today, they hung dry and rancid in the air, a layer of sweaty shellac brushed over the tiles and metal lockers. They grabbed him by the nose and shook him awake.

He was a large, tall man, and the worn office chair squeaked in defiance as he eased himself into its cracked folds. His red hair flowed in disarray over his scalp, untamed by comb. While his once muscular build was settling, his barrel chest and thick neck still commanded attention.

Coach O'Reilly was not a man prone to rising early. Even now, he wondered if he wasted good sleep over a pipe dream. On paper, the track team looked promising. Ten returning seniors, an unusually high number considering most seniors traded glory to pump gas or bag groceries in order to afford a jacked-up Chevy. About a dozen good juniors, too, eight of them returning lettermen. The rest of the juniors could contribute if they improved on their previous year's performances. The sophomores remained a question mark, except for Crazy Nolan. No, on paper they looked good, very good. He made champions of them with his pencil, jotting down potential times in the dashes, and trying out possible combinations for the relays.

Coach O'Reilly belched loudly into the cramped room. He recoiled inwardly from the acrid taste. Nervous stomach and the first starting gun still three weeks away, he thought. Boy, it's going to be a long season.

Webster represented the stiffest competition. Conference champs last year, and good sprinters and relay teams. And Langley. Franksburg could be a dark horse. No, not Franksburg. No lung men.

Coach O'Reilly snatched the Camels out of his shirt pocket and tapped one out of the pack. He inhaled deeply on the filtered cigarette, leaned back and put his feet up among the schedules and flyers that cluttered his desk. Watching the smoke curl upward, listening to more rumblings in his stomach, he gloated silently over his prospects. The Troy School Board considered track a second-class athletic endeavor. So the football team received new helmets and travelling uniforms, while Coach O'Reilly made do with old spikes and faded jerseys. Runners were either retards, uncoordinated wimps, or farm boys, Coach Simpson reminded him with each new track season. Coach O'Reilly had long ago tired of such barbs from his baseball counterpart. Usually, the other coaches were right. He was stuck with the less agile, the long-legged, gawky kids who could run and little else athletically. But this year he gained Jerry Porter, a transfer student, as a legitimate pole-vaulter, and Henry Thompson for the high jump. The school's first black, Thompson, and he could jump over a station wagon. Porter and Thompson, along with Dave Wilson in the shot put, gave him a solid nucleus for the field events. With Perkins switched to the mile, and Crazy Nolan coming on like the next Jim Ryan in the 880, he just might pull it off and make Coach Simpson eat his words.

The cigarette suddenly burned his throat. Coach O'Reilly dropped his feet and crushed the butt out against the stained insides of the metal trash can. He returned to his charts, and was deep in strategy, matching sprinters in the mile relay, when a knock against the glass startled him.

"Excuse me, Coach, could I see you for a minute?" Joe asked from the doorway.

Coach O'Reilly sat upright. He waved away the lingering wisps of smoke. "Little early to be sneaking up on someone, isn't it?"

"Sorry, Coach. I got to school early and the janitor told me you were down here."

"Well, come on in," Coach O'Reilly said, motioning to another chair. "Mitchell, isn't it?"

"Yes sir. Joe," he said. He sat stiffly along side Coach O'Reilly's desk.

"Ever finish that gun case?"

"No sir, I keep meaning to, but there's no time."

"Well, you should finish it. You had a nice design going. And you knew your way around wood. When was that? Two years ago?" Coach O'Reilly asked.

"Yes, sir, I was a sophomore in your Industrial Arts class."

Coach O'Reilly grunted, pleased with his memory. "What do you want this early? I'm not serving breakfast you know."

Joe fidgeted. "I was wondering if I could still sign up for the track team."

Coach O'Reilly rolled back in his chair. "Where have you been, Mitchell? Everybody else signed up more than a week ago. Had their physicals already.

Hell," Coach O'Reilly said, scratching his belly, "uniforms and spikes have been distributed and practice starts tomorrow."

"I know, Coach, I'm sorry. It's just that I only got permission Saturday."

"Permission? Who gave you permission? You on parole or something? Do I have something to worry about?" Coach O'Reilly chuckled. He didn't mean to pick on Joe, but he looked so sheepish, eyes downcast, afraid to meet his own. And his latest pairings in the mile relay left him feeling jolly.

"No sir. My dad's got a farm about three miles south on Highway 17 and he needs my help in the spring, so I had to clear it with him first."

"Doesn't he need your help this year? Corn and beans growing themselves these days?" he snorted out loud this time, doubly pleased with his wry wit.

Joe lapsed into silence and pursed his lips in growing anger.

"Something wrong Mitchell?" Coach O'Reilly asked.

"I'm still wondering what your answer is," Joe said.

"Well, I'm inclined to say no," Coach O'Reilly said.

"No?"

"Yes, no. Waiting this long to come forward says you're not serious in my book. Most of the guys on the team have already been running for a month on their own. They know we've got a chance at the title this year. So yes, my answer is no."

Joe's whole body tensed. This continuous progression through defended doors was wearing him down. Dejected, he turned to leave.

"Hey, wait a whore's minute. If you don't want to be on the track team, you just keep walking."

Joe about-faced. "You just said your answer was no."

"Maybe I was just testing your mettle."

"Seems like everybody is," Joe mumbled to himself.

"What's that? Speak up if you've got something to say."

"What's . . . the . . . USE," Joe said slowly and with sudden insolence. "You don't want me. And even if you did, I have to skip out of practice early for chores."

"Skip practice?" Coach O'Reilly bolted forward in his chair. "If I allowed that I'd have every runner hustling for a job instead of for me."

"It's not a profit I'm making feeding cows," Joe said angrily. He seemed ready to literally pounce on Coach O'Reilly, and the coach held out his hands in appeasement.

"I know that Mitchell. I've lived in this hayseed hamlet long enough to know. But I'm not running a democracy here. You do things my way or not at all. No exceptions."

Joe stood leaning against the doorway. He told himself he should have known by now that he never got what he wanted. "Like I said," he repeated smugly, "What's the use?"

Coach O'Reilly watched Joe suffering, and eyed him seriously for the first time. Despite Joe's size, he had the look of a runner. Jack Sprat's leanness. A farm kid's muscles. And something smoldering inside him. A flame that could be fanned?

"You any good? Have you ever raced?"

"I really don't know," Joe said, tensing. "I'm pretty fast, I guess. That is, I can keep up with our Super M in second gear for a ways. Are you going to let me join?"

"Hold your horses," Coach O'Reilly said. His stomach churned again, reminding him of his nervousness and, now, hunger. "You're short for a sprinter, too short for the distances probably as well." What's the harm, though, he thought. Maybe he could contribute if someone else drops out. If not, he could butt Mitchell off the team for missing practice.

"How late can you practice?"

"I could practice until 4 and then run home. That would give me plenty of running time. Oh please," Joe begged. "I'll run whatever races you want. I'll do anything."

"Well if you're running out past the trestle, you'll be a distance man," Coach O'Reilly said, mollified. "Had a physical yet?"

"No sir!" Joe half shouted.

"Better see Doc Crow tomorrow. He won't know if you're healthy or not, but he signs the paper," Coach O'Reilly instructed. "If you pass, see Bobby Thorton, the student manager, tomorrow about a uniform. Practice starts at 3 sharp."

HALLWAYS

Joe arrived late for the first practice, having gone first to turn and cough for Doc Crow. As he entered the locker room, his new teammates streamed by him. Bobby Thorton, the diminutive equipment manager, awaited him. Bobby found Joe a blue sweat suit, with "Trojans" blazed across front and back in flowing gold cursive. Between pushing his glasses up his nose, Bobby next supplied Joe with spikes and, finally, a sleeveless white top and silky navy blue shorts.

"31. That'll be an easy number to remember," Bobby said, displaying the back of the jersey. "July's got 31 days, and I was born in July." Bobby grinned. "I've got to find ways to remember numbers. There's so many, and the guys get pissed if I screw up."

The thought of belligerent runners waving jerseys in his face turned Bobby's grin upside down.

"July's a good month for a birthday," Joe said. "Mine's March 15th, the ides of March. That's the day they killed Julius Caesar. He's the guy they named the month of July after."

Bobby looked perplexed, but Joe continued. "March is a lousy birthday month. You get a bike or ball glove for your birthday and it can be snowing outside. Summer birthdays are better."

Bobby nodded over these nuggets of wisdom. He had never thought of his birthday in quite this special way. Nor that Joe's birthday, in March, was magically linked to his in July.

"You think kinda different, don't you?"

Joe leaned in over the half door of the equipment room and motioned Bobby close, so close Joe smelled tomato soup on Bobby's breath. "Here's a secret I want you to keep." He rotated around to emphasize the need for secrecy, even though the locker room was cleared. "I am kinda different."

Bobby's face slowly lit up. "Guess what, Joe?"

"What?" Joe whispered.

"So am I."

"Well, then, the two of us better stick together."

They shook hands, and while Joe dressed, Bobby affixed a label with Joe's name on it to one of the middle row lockers. Joe traced the embossed letters as if they were magical. His name hung among those of the other athletes—names known throughout the school, names with the most footnotes in the yearbook, names that carried weight. For the first time in a long time, he was glad to be Joe Mitchell.

Joe joined his teammates minutes later. They had finished their warm-ups and stood in a quadrant of the school gym, the rolled-up bleachers behind them. Kitty-corner from them, the baseball team gathered. The players there played catch, the smack of the balls in leather echoing off the cement walls. To protect the track team from errant throws a floor-to-ceiling netting split the gym.

Coach O'Reilly had lined the tracksters up in six rows. As Joe slipped into one, Coach O'Reilly began strolling among them while his assistant, John DeAngelo, leaned against the wall with folded arms. With each pass between the track and fieldmen, Coach O'Reilly said nothing. He finally completed his meandering loops, faced the team and placed his huge hands on his hips.

"I know you're all dying to know why I just took a stroll here," he began, his voice booming. "It's because I've sized up your potential on paper and I wanted to see if that potential pales up close and personal." He paused for effect. "It doesn't. And that's good. Because this year you guys are going to be the Carver Conference track champs. Now notice I didn't say Franksburg or Webster. The jocks from Franksburg drink too much beer and the Webster fieldmen use Kotex. Now I don't see any nose warmers today so since you guys seem to know where a jock strap goes, I suspect I've got a genuine group of guys ready to kick ass."

Coach O'Reilly started to stroll again. "I've got one problem. No, WE have one problem. There's a chasm between potential and champions. A deep hole. I'm here to guide you across it. Coach DeAngelo will help me. Hard work will be our bridge. We're going to work you boys hard, harder than in past seasons, because this team has potential."

Several runners glanced at DeAngelo beseechingly, asking with their eyes if Coach O'Reilly was going to bust their buns worse than the year before. The young assistant calmly let Coach O'Reilly have the stage.

When Coach O'Reilly approached Mark Perkins, he stopped. "I can guarantee that our practices won't be the reason we don't win the conference," he said. "It's after practice I worry about. I hear of any of you drinking or smoking, you'll be off this team so fast your jock strap will be chasing you home." He stopped in front of Dave Wilson. Dave looked straight ahead. He had already lived through two seasons under Coach O'Reilly.

"And lay off the girls. They distract you. Sap your strength. I catch any of you daydreaming about girls instead of this championship, I swear I'll become your worst nightmare. Because nothing is going to keep that trophy from resting in our awards case if you focus. It's all mental, boys. I'm telling you that we can cross that chasm if you believe. I believe. Do you all believe?"

"Yes, sir!" they thundered in unison to Coach O'Reilly's first direct question.

Coach O'Reilly nodded. "Right answer, boys. Let's get started right now." He looked around at the surrounding walls. "Thanks to our glorious weather we're stuck inside today, so John here will take the runners. Fieldmen, stay with me," Coach O'Reilly said.

He turned to assemble those who broke ranks to follow him, then stopped. "One more thing. Joe Mitchell here just joined the team. His dad needs him for farm work, so he'll be cutting out of practice at 4 o'clock every day. He's still running home, mind you, so he'll do his miles. But that's my only leniency for the season. Anybody else looking to miss practice, it better be your mother or you who is dying, because I won't budge."

DeAngelo peeled himself off the wall. Only then did Joe notice his lithe movements. He treaded lightly across the parquet floor like a cat. His five o'clock shadow gave him a criminal look, which his protruding brow accentuated. In contrast, his eyes held the fire of a zealot—incredibly blue and piercing.

When all the runners had surrounded him, DeAngelo said, "Okay, listen up. Dash men, you stay with me. We've got wind sprints to do. Mark, you've been through the drill. Lead these future Olympians through our hallowed halls. Fifteen minutes at a steady jog, and then come back here. Pace yourselves, boys. You have hundreds of miles to run to reach that trophy."

Released at last, about 15 runners followed Mark up the corridor from the gym. They clomped up the narrow stairs and veered right down the wide, central hallway of the school. Mark set out in an easy gait, his black hair a bobbing beacon. His charges followed like a herd of wildebeests, their tennis shoes squeaking and leaving scuff marks on the polished floors. The former basketball players and wrestlers, still in shape, stayed on Mark's heels. Joe and the other runners struggled to keep pace. Mark led them up more stairwells and down the second and third floor halls. They roared past rows of lockers like rioters, and then funneled down the three flights of stairs and returned to the gym. Mark preceded them all. He ran in place along the netting, talking to Greg Harrington through the mesh. When the last of the stragglers arrived, he led them on another loop.

By the end of the fourth loop, most of the runners were exhausted. A few desperate souls tried to hide behind the rolled-up wrestling mats near the locker rooms. Mark, the veteran, had strategically positioned Scott Hamre at the back of the pack for this very reason.

"Hey Mark, we've got some slackers here," Scott yelled.

Mark stopped the pack at the base of the steps. His nostrils flared from effort and delight. Joe saw how much Mark was in his element. He liked leading them.

"Keep on running," Mark commanded his charges. "You all know the route now. I've got a lesson to teach."

To his surprise, Mark found Crazy Nolan among the three deserters. "What gives, Craze? You can't be tired."

Crazy climbed out from behind the mat, as skinny as a cornstalk, along with Peter Bilik and Kurt Wuamett, two other sophomores flushed with fear.

"Not tired, Mark. Bored. I've been logging miles since Christmas."

"Well, then, you are crazy. But you know the rules. Scott, go get Bobby."

Like vapor, Scott vanished down the corridor. He reappeared as quickly, with Bobby at his side.

"Ready for a ride, Bobby?"

"Always," Bobby bubbled.

"Then mount up, cowboy, and don't spare those spurs," Mark said.

Mark and Scott easily placed Bobby onto Crazy's back. Crazy accepted the weight without complaint. "Up and down the steps three times, Craze."

"Oh, man, we were only kidding around," Peter whined as he watched Craze begin his climb with Bobby hugging his back like a second skin.

"One more whine and you'll carry Bobby the whole circuit. Make sure they do the task, Scott." With that Mark sped after his other charges.

On the third floor, Joe found himself falling further behind the lead runners. Only another senior, Tom Woodard, and two juniors named Wheatley and Evans, ran doggedly along side him. Joe felt hot and flushed. Despite his daily chores, he seldom ran. While his leg muscles felt strong, his wind was failing him, and he panicked a bit when he heard footsteps. Mark loomed large behind the four lagging runners. They sped up to avoid his chastisements. He overtook them easily, and assumed their gait. To their surprise, he encouraged them. "Hang in there, guys, this is the last loop before stopping."

They collectively wheezed grateful thanks. Joe tried to smile through his rapid breathing. Mark gave him a sideways stare, the same sizing up look Coach O'Reilly had directed at him the previous day. Joe's absence from athletics and school events made him a mystery. Then Mark's expression changed. He leaned in and spat out a warning. "Stay way from my girl, Mitchell."

The remark startled Joe. He viewed himself the rival of no one. Yet Mark now ran backwards, glaring at Joe to make sure the message had been fully delivered. He unexpectedly came to the end of the corridor and, spinning around to make the turn, plowed into a group of startled girls. They all screamed and catapulted their books skyward. Advanced Calculus and American History rained down with hard-cover damage. Joe reached a shaky Annie first, while Woodard and Evans bent to help Betty Carlson and Maggie O'Leary.

"You guys nearly scared me to death," Betty gasped, her hand over her heart.

"Oh, crap, my glasses are broken," Maggie added, squinting. She held the wire frames in two pieces before Mark's face. "You're going to have to pay for these."

"I'm sorry, it was an accident," Mark replied sincerely.

"Yeah, I guess accidents will happen when you're running BACKWARDS," Annie scolded. She moved to console Maggie, who rubbed the bridge of her nose and checked for other injuries.

"Why don't you set a better example?" Annie snipped. "You're the co-captain you know."

Mark's ears burned. It was bad enough that Annie wouldn't take his calls, and chided him in private. This public belittlement made him irate.

"You okay, Maggie?" he asked, ignoring Annie.

"I'll live. But what about my glasses? My mom will have a fit."

"Don't worry. Tell me the cost. My old man will cough up the dough." He turned privately to Annie and whispered harshly, "Don't mock me in public, Annie." Without waiting for a reaction, Mark said, "Let's go, guys. DeAngelo will wonder where we are."

Joe heard the whisper, and saw the slight flush in Annie's cheeks. While the others trotted after Mark, Joe reached out and touched Annie's arm.

"Are you okay?"

"I'm fine. Just a little jostled." She smiled then, clasping her books to her bosom. "I'm glad to see you're on the team. Are you going to be around after practice?"

"No, I had to strike a deal with my dad and Coach O'Reilly to even get on the team. I have to take off each day at 4."

"That's too bad," Annie said.

"Mitchell!" It was Hamre, down the hall. "Let's go."

Joe hesitated. Annie seemed in no hurry to leave either. Although he thought it impossible, his heart raced faster. "*Go, ahead, ask her. Do it. Do it!*" his inner voice shouted. It was the same bold being that spurred him to ask George and Coach O'Reilly to get on the track team.

"Say, Annie, uh, I was wondering," he stammered, "are you busy Saturday night?"

"No, I'm not."

"You're not? That's good. I mean, would you like to go to a movie or something?"

Annie smiled. Behind her Betty and Maggie giggled. Annie turned and shushed them. "Yes, I'd love to go."

"You would? Great." Joe grinned sheepishly. "I'll talk to you tomorrow," he said as he started to sprint after the others.

"Call her tonight, Joe," Betty hollered, causing Joe to blush. Annie shushed Betty again, but then joined her friends in animated conversation as they continued down the hall.

Joe was a mere four blocks from school when he realized he had run too hard in his first practice. The three miles that lay before him seemed an impossible distance. Joe gingerly jogged down Main Street, the pack carrying his school clothes bouncing on his back. The ashen March snow melted everywhere around him. Side alley tributaries converged into frigid ponds at the bottom of the downhill streets. Those puddles soon left his shoes and socks sopping. Joe slowed to a walk as he passed St. Lawrence's Catholic Church. Its steeple gargoyles grinned down at his labors. His wind restored, he jogged through the yellow of the town's lone stoplight and drew even with the Red Rooster Café, where curious diners, mostly retirees this early, craned their necks to follow his path. Parts of Troy's business district floated by. The Sears Outlet store where Ruth did her Christmas shopping by catalog. The brick post office, which dated back to 1911, and allegedly contained bullet holes from John Dillinger's revolver. Joe saw the holes, circled in white paint. Then past Lil's Flower Shop, its front window displaying Easter lilies. The town's sidewalks soon ended. Joe swung over to the frontage road. Here, Troy's few industries flourished. Gallagher's Millworks provided cabinetry, doors and window sashes for much of the county. Joe whiffed its sweet smell of lathed oak and stained pine. Next door, Henson's Grain & Feed—that of the dreaded duck promotion—anchored the rest of the double block.

Joe eventually hit Highway 17. He picked his way through the potholes to the gravel roadside, and braced himself against the traffic. The oncoming cars sprayed him mercilessly. He reached the edge of town (Troy, Population 1,857, A Centennial Town, the sign said), and decided to run cross country to avoid more soakings.

On the first gravel road bisecting the blacktop, Joe headed east until he found the field road. Barely visible beneath the patches of snow, it consisted of parallel paths stretched as wide as the John Deere combines that traversed it. This rural alleyway ran straight south for two miles. To the east and west, red barns and silver-domed silos stood like paintings in a white-walled gallery. In the distance, peeking over a rise and next to a patch of evergreens, Joe spotted the rooflines of their farm.

Although he was tired and his feet were wet and cold, the freedom of the field road stoked his spirits. He forgot about the drudgery of his waiting chores and entered his daily dream world. His daydreams were specific now. The foggy apparition of a fantasy cheerleader appeared clearly as a cherub-faced girl named Annie with heavenly eyes beneath neatly plucked eyebrows. And here he was, slogging through slush and matted weeds, mud splattered in a stripe up the middle of his back, bearing down on an imaginary finish line to impress her. Still, no daydream could deaden the growing pain in his left leg, and Joe came up favoring it three-quarters of a mile short of the farm. Looking at his watch, he fretted over his slow progress. These were no six-minute miles, he told himself.

The low moan of a train whistle blew over the fields and Joe watched a Burlington Northern locomotive and boxcars emerge from behind the Garth's farmstead to the east. The grasshopper green cars carried wheat and corn to waiting barges miles away on the Minnesota River. They rumbled on tracks that ran parallel to the gravel road in front of the Mitchell farm. Joe caught a glimpse of those tracks now, glinting gold in the low slant of afternoon sun. The rails split the last quarter-mile he would be crossing daily for the next two months. Joe hoped the train ran regularly and on time. If it did, he vowed to use its daily position to measure his improvement.

The train crossed in front of him again the next day. Only Joe was far off his day-earlier pace, and much closer to another blowup with George. The night before, George chided him when Joe started his chores at 4:50 p.m. To make amends, Joe worked late, lining up musty hay bales by the chute in the overhead loft for George to feed to the livestock the next day when Joe was away at school. That and offering to wash the milking machines guaranteed dried-out pork chops for supper, but a slightly pacified father. Joe crawled into bed at 10 p.m., exhausted.

Only seconds passed, Joe was convinced, before the alarm barged through his dreamless sleep and started his morning routine again. Joe found he could barely move. Muscles ached and rebelled. Red-hot needles of pain punctuated his every move. Even his toes, staring up at him from the floor like sleeping trolls, made him wince as he bent to dress.

"What's the problem this morning?" greeted him as entered the barn 10 minutes later.

"I'm sore from running," Joe answered. He limped his way toward the feed room to throw down the morning's silage.

"Sore or not, you need to get your chores done before school," George yelled toward Joe's turned back. "You know the conditions."

As Joe worked, his body limbered up but he felt devoid of energy. He skipped breakfast in order to finish his work. Ruth flagged down the school bus and pleaded with Mrs. Zimmer, the driver, to wait while Joe hobbled down the drive late. He began day two of practice in agony, but eventually the hard exercise worked out the kinks. Now, approaching the tracks, Joe's legs felt like he, and not the Burlington Northern, was hauling North Dakota durum. And it was only Wednesday.

Drawing close to the farmyard, Joe spied George crossing the yard. A bale of bedding straw hung from a pitchfork balancing on his shoulder. George walked unevenly under the weight, resembling a grotesque hunchback.

What a life, Joe thought, as he jogged ever nearer. Every day George slogged through mud and manure that sucked at his boots like something alive. Working 15-hour days so he could eat a meal he was too tired to taste. Then to the rocking chair with the oil spot that marked where his head sank back nightly as he fell asleep, newspaper crumpled in his hand, not even the headlines read, until Ruth roused him for bed.

Why didn't his father work at something else, Joe wondered—a trade of some sort. Maybe a cabinet-maker like Roger Gallagher's father. Even Jim Kuhn, who worked for the county plugging potholes and scraping road-kill off blacktop, made more money.

Joe realized again he was ashamed of being a farmer. The profession for Joe carried no connotation of stewardship, no sense of the nobility that George touted. Joe desired nothing more than to disassociate himself from it. He had a sudden impulse to turn and flee. Instead he plodded forward, like his father before him, on the obedient path he knew. Later, as he pulled on his tattered work clothes and manure-encrusted boots, he vowed for the thousandth time to leave.

First Loves

The first spring rain fell as if the heavens were melting. Cold and heavy, it assaulted pockets of snow like a scrubwoman. Soon countless rivulets of melting snow converged on the farm's low ground. There, March's migrating mallards, blue-wing teal and coots filled the temporary ponds.

Joe sat in the bathtub, thankful for the rain pelting the window. It enabled George to help with the evening chores. They started milking early and then George agreed to finish. Joe drained the water and refilled the tub a second time. He rubbed his skin raw to remove the stench of the farm. Drying in front of the mirror, Joe tried to see what Annie saw. His eyes were deep-set and lamb's ear green, his nose a bit crooked, and his mouth, like his father's, a bit too thin. His blond hair, cropped short, lacked its field-bleached summer glow. Nothing exceptional. But small children don't flee from me, Joe thought inside his good mood.

While he questioned his looks, he admired his body. The only benefit of working on the farm. His sculpted muscles carried neither the excess bulk nor bulging veins of a weight lifter, or the Dachau appearance of a marathoner. The proportions and tone seemed natural and right, like those of a gymnast. He flexed his arm muscles, and made them dance.

Joe covered his muscles with new blue jeans and a cream-colored fisherman's knit sweater. An extra splash of English Leather assuaged any lingering fears of barn odors. Loafers, a gold windbreaker, a quick good-bye to Ruth (*"Let me know when you get home, Joe, even if I'm asleep"*) and Joe found himself nervous and excited behind the wheel of his parents' '65 Chevy Impala.

George watched Joe drive away through the open north door of the barn. The rain had abated into a fine drizzle, and the freshness of the thawing earth rose like percolating coffee. George breathed in this earth reborn, hoping it would enliven his spirits. It didn't work. His melancholy mood remained.

George felt burdened by his extra work. He also envied Joe. First track and now a girl. The next thing Joe would be falling in love, drifting further and further from his side.

A rooster pheasant cackled from over the knoll, and George sought him out. In the gathering dusk, he could make out only the tops of the pine beyond the tracks. Then there it was again. Another male declaring spring, marking his turf. There were other sounds that carried easily across the languid landscape. The twill of returning redwing blackbirds, the surprising drone of frogs from Becker's marsh, and the first chirps of robins.

A movement near the road caught his eye. In the dusk, he first thought it was O'Leary's collie, trotting home from frolicking with one of the neighborhood's bitches. Then he realized it was Ruth, bent over and pitching the snowplow's wintry deposit of stones back onto the gravel road.

"Ruth, for Pete's sake. I told you I'd get to that."

Ruth turned, a mere silhouette before him. "That's what you always say, and then things don't get done. I'm not keen on breaking a lawnmower blade."

"You won't be cutting grass for two months," George said, annoyed.

"Well, there'll be raking and burning off the lawn sooner than that."

George shook his head. Ruth stacked projects before him like pancakes, and he could never digest them in a timely enough manner to suit her.

"Ruth, go in the house before one of the neighbors sees you," George scolded now. "I'll get to them damn rocks tomorrow."

"You've got seed corn coming tomorrow." The voice came back as territorial as the pheasant's.

"Well, then, suit yourself. I've got cows to milk," George said in resignation. Out of Ruth's sight, he spat a circle of irritation into the lime on the barn floor before sidling up to Carrie. George silently fumed while he affixed the milker. He had thought freeing Joe for track would relieve the growing tension between them. Instead, it exacerbated things. Joe could have gotten to those rocks if he weren't out running, George thought, and shifted his anger toward his son.

"Damn you both," he said into Carrie's side.

With Joe gone, he listened to polkas on the radio to calm his nerves. Instead, the bouncy music reminded him of distant courtship days. Ruth and he never quarreled back then. The onus of work had not yet cleaved their marriage. And if Joe left, it would just be Ruth and him. His melancholy worsened as he envisioned Joe gone. It would be as if he had lost an arm. What would he do? He wondered how he had suddenly found himself at this juncture, unprepared and desperate. Somewhere along the line his life had been reduced to chores, eating and sleeping. Conversations with Ruth had become estranged. Too many nights in bed ended in turned shoulders. Usually, in the spring, he grew excited about planting. Turning the rich slivers of soil over, watching the blue-black grackles fill the fresh furrow behind him like gliders—those things renewed him. This year, with Joe running, that task would likely transpire under the dim glow of tractor lights.

George could not shake his gloom. It was as if he had been unknowingly standing in quicksand for years, and now, today, he had lost all buoyancy. Too much of him lay beneath the sucking silence. He had acquiesced to Joe's request as desperately as he would have grabbed a vine to pull him free of the muck. He did it to please Ruth. Now he wrestled with the fact that he had endangered their livelihood to hang onto the remnants of their marriage.

A milker across the way gasped, and George hopped across the floor, emptied the milker and affixed it to another cow. Like a county fair carney, he deftly worked his merry-go-round of machines. In time, he forgot about the rock-throwing Ruth, and remembered another.

It was about this time 20 years ago that he had been smitten like Joe. In fact, it had been a March Easter. All the Catholic women were bedecked in their pastel garb and white shoes for St. Lawrence's high mass, but none wore a hat like Ruth's. Red and festooned with woven flowers, the hat looked like a swatch of someone's flower garden scooped up and plopped on Ruth's head. She walked down the aisle to turned heads, snow melting off the hat's broad brim. George watched her throughout the service, or her hat rather, as it rose like an umbrella for the Gospel and Apostles' Creed, and dropped when Ruth knelt for the Consecration. When she left the Communion rail, George caught her reverently bowed profile. Her hands, folded in prayer, led her back to her pew.

After Mass, George followed that island of spring outside. A blustery wind whipped the newly fallen snow. Ruth was supporting her mother, Margaret, down the sidewalk when a blast of icy air snatched her hat. It careened across the snow toward George. He reached for it but another gust sent the hat swirling, first this way and then that.

"My hat, please catch my hat!"

George thought how appropriate Ruth's choice of the word "catch," because the hat, for all its maneuvers, mimicked a Bandy rooster. Twice George lost his footing and went to his knees in the snow. For a moment, the wind abated and the hat nestled several yards from the slush of the street. As George reached for it, the wind again sent it skimming. Before thinking, George planted his size 10 Sunday Oxford on the garden plot.

Ruth reached George as he stooped for the crumpled hat. He rose as crimson as the bonnet. George handed over the trampled remains. Ruth inspected the hat slowly while George felt the snow in his shoes begin to melt.

To his surprise, Ruth began to laugh. A dainty chuckle at first, but then a hearty, tears-in-the-eyes roar. George grew redder still as he noticed a flock of parishioners staring at them over Ruth's shoulders.

"Well, I have to applaud your gallantry," Ruth said, between sighs and wiping her eyes. "Mr. Mitchell, isn't it?"

"Yes, George Mitchell."

"Yes, George, your efforts were gallant, but your methods leave something to be desired."

"I'm so sorry," George blurted out. "Maybe I can fix it." He started to reach out for the hat, but then withdrew his hands. The hat was totally demolished.

Ruth started laughing again, then, worse, to sing. "Easter, Easter bonnet, with George's shoe upon it."

George wondered how much more crimson he could get, because his ears seemed capable of melting snow. "I'll buy you a new hat, Miss Hampton."

Ruth raised a fine pair of eyebrows. "So you know my name?"

"Just the last name, like you know mine. It's a small county."

"Well isn't that the awful truth," Ruth said. "I'm Ruth. I had to go all the way to the cities to find this bonnet, George. Would you go all that way to Minneapolis for me?"

"Tomorrow if you like."

George thought he noticed a slight blush rise on Ruth's cheeks, as if his boldness had transferred some of his hue to her. It could have just been the cold and his wishful thinking. But he meant it. He had never seen a more attractive woman, except in the movies, maybe. The blowing snow peppered her blond hair, and caught on her eyelashes in perfect dewy stars.

"That's very nice of you to offer, George," Ruth said, demurely. "But I don't think any hat you buy will have the impact this one just did in its short life." She rotated the hat and plucked at some shredded daisies. "I will miss the flowers though. Of course they're fake, but with this endless winter, it's so long before real bouquets. Snow's fine for Christmas, but I'm ready for the colors of spring." She seemed lost in thought, as if trying to conjure up real daisies in her mind. "Well, my mother needs me, George. Thanks for rescuing my hat." She giggled again. "Maybe I'll see you next week in church."

George did not wait a week. He drove home through the unabating snowfall. Several times he had to buck the Dodge through the drifts. Once home, he stopped only to change out of his Sunday clothes. Normally, he relaxed Sunday afternoon. This day, he never unfolded the thick Sunday paper. Instead, he headed straight to the tool shed. Amongst a pile of boards and busted wicker chairs, he found a cornerpost to an old bed. He worked the afternoon in the cold shed with lathe and knife until he emerged, dusted with wood shavings, with an elegantly sculpted wooden rose. It wasn't until after milking cows that he sanded the petals into silk. The next day between his chores he spent in the basement. Barn paint kissed a blush of red into the rose. Green porch trim brought life to the flower's slender stem.

The rare Easter blizzard clogged the road for two days before George heard the county's snowplow rumble by as he finished breakfast. Before the grader returned for its westward swipe, George had traded his barn clothes for his town coat. In his '47 Dodge he sped down the plowed half of the road until he reached the highway.

Mrs. Hampton gave him a stare colder than the March day when he arrived at her doorstep and asked if her daughter were home. Ruth appeared in a maroon house dress and white apron, with flour on her hands.

"Why, George. What are you doing out in this weather?"

George stood awkwardly in the doorway, Sunday hat in his callused hands. "I've been thinking about your bonnet, and what you said about there being no flowers this time of year."

"And you drove over here to tell me that? Come in out of the cold," she said, letting him into the warmth of the kitchen. Small scallops of unused dough lay scattered between a jar of flour and a rolling pin on the table. He smelled pie apples and cinnamon.

"We decided to bake with the roads closed, but I guess they're open now," Ruth offered.

"Highway's cleared. But I wouldn't venture out. Snow's fence post deep."

"You did. You ventured out."

George looked down, then askance to Ruth's mother. Ruth's eyes followed his. "Mother," she said, simply, and Mrs. Hampton knowingly left the kitchen.

"I drove over here to give you this," George said. He reached inside his coat and lifted the rose delicately, as if it were fresh cut and had needed his body's warmth to survive.

Ruth looked at the scarlet rose, then at George, then back to the flower.

"Take it. It's not real. It's wood. I made it for you."

Ruth wiped her hands on her apron and accepted the rose. She stroked the smoothness of its petals. She acknowledged its perfection by smelling it.

"George, it is absolutely the most wonderful gift I have ever received." Then she pecked him on the cheek.

For his wedding gift to her, George carved a dozen roses and a wooden vase to hold them. Upon their receipt, Ruth hugged him tighter than ever before. Her love almost crushed his ribs. Now, the wooden bouquet stood faded and dusty on Ruth's hope chest in a corner of their bedroom.

The tears rolling down his cheeks and spotting his rubbers brought George's thoughts rushing forward two decades. Where had it all gone? The love. The sense of joy. There were more than the miscarriages to blame. Somewhere, for some reason, out of fatigue or self-absorption, they had quit giving. The night with the ice cracking on the roof, George had hoped part of the ice between them might also crack. They had mutually agreed to let their son start tasting a life they themselves were all too close to losing.

George wiped his tears on the back of his worn sleeve. These emotions were long buried. They scared him. Like a cold engine cranked into action, he shuddered when his heart started working again.

It took him longer than he expected, three evenings on the sly. The end result was cruder than he would have liked. He prayed that it would have some magical effect, though. Prayed like a man with quicksand tickling his chin. Still, he hesitated outside of the tool shed, rose in hand, wondering if he could convey what weighed so heavily on him, wondering if it was too late. A desperate need propelled him forward. He opened the screen door and entered the kitchen. Ruth stood behind the ironing board, busily pressing his Sunday shirt, the long-neck Budweiser bottle converted into a sprinkler moistening the way for her iron. George walked to the ironing board and, without fanfare, handed the rose across it.

"Happy spring," he said. Then he leaned over his shirt, careful not to touch the delicate white with his unwashed hands, and kissed her.

Ruth put the iron on end and caressed the rose with both hands. She marveled at its beauty. George had chosen yellow for the petals, and they shone like a sunrise. "Thank you, George," she said, touched. She could barely hold his eyes. "You haven't carved me a flower since our wedding."

"I know."

"Why now, George? What does it mean?"

George winced slightly. "It means I still love you, Ruth."

Ruth reached across the ironing board and stroked George's hand. "I know you do, George. I love you, too."

George pulled back, as if Ruth hand still held the iron. "Not like that," he said, irritably.

"Like what?"

"I want more," he said blindly. "I want us to be like before. When you couldn't wait to see me." He bowed his head slightly. "When I carved you roses because I was nuts about you. And you kissed me instead of patting me."

George felt his eyes misting again—the thing he had feared outside the tool shed—opening the gate. "That's what it means. I want to be nuts about you." George paused then and took a deep breath. "But I'm not, and I don't know what to do about it."

He looked beseechingly into Ruth's eyes, his shame visible.

Ruth stood as stiff as her ironing board. Her hands moved unconsciously, smoothing the shirt before her. Ruth shut her eyes and stayed closed behind them a long time. Then, slowly, her composure returned. Once more she reached for his hand.

"Let's sit down, George," she said, soft but controlled. They moved as a unit to the kitchen table. The fresh breeze coursed through the screen and over their clasped hands.

"Are you saying you don't love me anymore?" Ruth began cautiously.

"I said I still love you."

"But not as much as at one time?"

"No, not as much."

Ruth mulled this over as if only hearing it twice made it real.

"The same goes for me."

George's eyes saddened more. He had long known the truth behind Ruth's words, but spoken they cut like his bone-handled knife.

She leaned into George then, so that their foreheads touched. They stayed that way, each unknowingly closing their eyes to the other. "It's been 20 years, George. The passion ebbs. But I still love you."

George took a deep sigh, and moved his hands onto Ruth's shoulders.

"I don't feel very alive anymore, Ruth." There was desperation in his voice, a yearning of years. Yet the words came out a whisper, like a last dying breath, afraid to be spoken less his life be extinguished.

"What brought this on?" Ruth whispered back.

"I don't know."

"Yes you do. You've already told me you don't love me as much anymore. You can tell me anything now."

George's thoughts traced back to the cackling pheasant, Joe driving away, and the freshness of that night. All was spring and youth and courtship outside. Yet there he had knelt among his cows, a machine moving machines. All alone.

"It's Joe. Him going out the other night."

"And you were wishing we were young again and you were courting me?"

"Something like that."

Ruth slowly rubbed her forehead across George's for several moments. "Oh George, oh George," she whispered. She raised her head and kissed his forehead.

"I wish, I wish . . . ."

"What George?"

"I wish . . . we could start over, without all the bad luck."

Ruth crawled onto George's lap, put her arms around his neck and kissed him deeply. He slumped thankfully into her embrace. George rocked her in silence for a long time.

Ruth whispered into his ear. "Well, then, if you want to start over, why don't we?"

No, Elaine hadn't married the creep, and now she and Ben sat at the back of the bus, with no idea where it or they were going. As "The Graduate" ended, Joe, too, questioned where he and Annie were headed. Several times during the movie he wondered which was make-believe—the images on the screen or Annie next to him. While the credits ran, Annie slipped her small, warm hand into his, and chased his doubts away.

The storm had regained its fury. They ran through torrents of rain to the Impala. Inside, they laughed at their drenched appearance. "Mrs. Robinson, are you trying to seduce me?" Joe said, impersonating Dustin Hoffman.

"Just stay away from my daughter," Annie laughed, playing along.

They chatted about the movie as they drove south from the city toward Troy. Just north of town, Annie said, "Turn here."

Joe veered off the highway onto a gravel road dimpled with puddles.

"Where are we going?"

"Haven't you ever been to Fiedler's Meadows?" Annie chided.

"Can't say as I have."

Annie laughed gleefully. "Joe, you're so innocent."

Hurt, Joe focused on the road. It was true, yet he didn't want Annie to think of him that way.

"I said I haven't been there. I know its purpose, though."

"Oh, Joe, don't get upset." Annie slid a bit closer, reached out and stroked the back of his neck. "Don't you want to go there?"

"Of course I do, it's just . . ."

"Just what?"

"I didn't think you would." Joe bit his lip.

"Why not?"

"I don't know."

"I'm having a great time, Joe," Annie said. And, to her mild surprise, she was. That first night she had sought only a ride home. But from the moment Joe rubbed her cold shoulders, and then ran to get her door outside of Mel's, she realized he was a gentleman. She liked Joe even more for having the nerve to ask her out, as shy as he was, and right in front of Betty and Maggie, no less. All through the evening, he made her laugh. She was quite happy when Joe listened to her directions and drove the car to a stop under a huge oak looming out of the darkness.

Joe killed the car lights and let the engine run beneath the thumping of rain on the roof.

"Well, here we are," Joe said, sweeping his hand over the dash to encompass the meadow before them. "It's not much, but marry me and some day this will all be yours."

Annie laughed and played along again. She scanned the meadow, which fell away from the tree line. Flashes of lightning revealed thick grasses matted by the winter's snow and occasionally broken by Black Hill spruce. Behind it, a woods of massive oak and maple rose in charcoal shadow.

They sat watching the rain run in rivulets down the windshield.

"What do you think happened to Ben and Elaine?"

Joe pondered the question while he punched buttons to find a better song. When the Bee Gees started in on "Massachusetts" he said, "I think they lived happily ever after, or at least until they ran out of bus fare."

"I'm serious, Joe. They were so impulsive."

"They just knew."

"Knew what?'

"That they had found the one."

"Just like that?" Annie snapped her fingers.

"Just like that."

"But how can you tell that fast? They hardly knew each other."

"Hey, I'm not a scientist. I'm just a romantic."

"Well, what about us? Do you know, just like that?" She snapped her fingers again.

Joe squirmed. He knew he would likely marry the first woman who would have him. "Won't know until after at least one kiss."

"That's fair," Annie said, but she remained seated by her door. The song ended, and the DJ's overbearing enthusiasm thrust itself between them. Just as quickly, the opening refrains of "Faking It" by Simon and Garfunkel poured out of the radio.

"I wonder if you're still hung up on Mark. That maybe he's your Ben," Joe ventured.

"I don't think so," Annie said. Seeing Joe's reaction she added, "Mark's like a street light, you know. All bright and showy. Up close the light gets harsh."

"Then why did you date him for so long?" Joe pressed.

"I don't know. He was nice to me. He's tall, dark and handsome as they say. He took charge."

"Where does that kind of confidence come from? I mean," he said, leaning toward Annie in the semi-darkness, "are you just born with it or can you learn it?"

"I think you're born with it. Some people are so at ease while the rest of us get cursed with inadequacy. Or a witch's wart on our nose."

"Your genetics seem top of the line," Joe said, playing with the steering wheel.

Annie groaned. "I've got my flaws like anybody else."

"Name one," Joe said, not believing any could exist.

"Well, for starters I can't tolerate anything ugly."

Joe laughed. "So slugs aren't on your list of favorite things."

"It's more than that." Annie tugged at the ends of her hair. "It's more the opposite of what I just said. I love only beautiful things. That makes me a perfectionist. I expect a lot of myself and others. Maybe too much."

Annie shook her head to end these self-reflections, then slid over next to Joe. He could smell her damp hair and dimly see her open smile.

"What about you, Joe? What's your cross to bear?"

Joe wavered between just kissing her then—she was so close—or answering. He answered because nobody had ever asked him before.

"Sainthood."

At that instant, a bolt of lightning unzipped the darkness. It cracked thunderously close and lit the car's interior. They paused momentarily, looked at each other's ghostly pallor, and laughed.

"Better whisper," Joe said, assuming his comfortable role as jokester, "I'm not suppose to share that news with mere mortals."

"Be serious, will you?" Annie squealed. "I can never tell when you're serious. Now tell me, truthfully, what's your burden?"

"I AM serious. I've been burdened with sainthood all my life."

"That's a cross?"

Joe realized only a litany of facts could explain. "Take parochial school," he began. "Man, I was such a Holy Roller. My classmates voted me to play the Christ child in the temple in the Christmas pageant. Next, I was named Savio of the Year."

"Good lord, what's a Savio?"

"Dominic Savio, the patron saint of boys. He was a 16th century Italian canonized by Pope Pius the XII in the '50s—I think because he froze to death waiting to serve Mass outside a locked church."

Annie looked at him incredulously. She saw no lies in his face. "Oh my God, you ARE serious."

"Yes," Joe said excitedly, "of course I am. I even have a relic of his."

"Here we go again. What kind of relic? Remember, I'm Lutheran."

"I have a piece of his sock in a holy card. That's why he froze outside that church, I think. Because he forgot his socks."

"Enough," Annie said, pounding on his right arm playfully. "Were you really the Savio of the Year? Did you knit a pair of socks to win?" Annie laughed at her own joke.

Joe peered beyond the St. Christopher medal where more lightning stitched through the rolling clouds. "To win, your classmates had to vote you most like St. Dominic."

"That IS a burden to live with," Annie teased.

"You're telling me," Joe said, unfazed. "The bad thing is, it stuck. I don't do it consciously, but I don't do anything considered sinful."

"Oh come now, you must have some vices," Annie probed. She sat forward and removed her light jacket. "Don't you drink when you play cards with the guys?"

"I rarely go to play and then maybe one beer if no parents are around. I wouldn't think of it at home."

"Steal a cigarette? Swear? Gossip?"

"Not really."

"Masturbate?"

"Annie!"

"I see your cross is real. Maybe I can help. Would you like to do something St. Dominic would think was terribly, terribly wrong?" Annie said seductively.

"Depends. Will it knock my socks off so they can become a relic someday?"

Moving closer, initiating, Annie whispered, "Do you like to steam up windows?"

Joe pulled her to him at last, with none of the awkwardness Annie half expected. His hard muscles surprised her, while Annie's warm, full lips were how Joe had imagined. When his own lips welded a hot seam the length of her cool, white neck, Annie shivered, drew back and looked into Joe's eyes.

"They never taught you that in that Savio Club."

Joe was lightheaded from the smell and touch of her. He smiled. "No, and I'm not twelve anymore, either."

CRAZY NOLAN

Joe felt a buoyancy in his stride the following Monday in practice. He didn't know if he could attribute it to thoughts of Annie, the much-needed weekend break, or the fact practice moved outside. The brisk March air filled his lungs while he and his teammates exercised in the school parking lot. Snow lined the roadways, and patches of the melting slush still lay claim to the practice fields. But they were outside.

After calisthenics, the fieldmen plodded through the snow and puddles to the west end of school where no one minded where their discuses and shot puts landed. Hurdlers busied themselves spacing hurdles across the lot. The coaches gathered the rest around them.

"Okay, boys," Coach O'Reilly said, "We've been pussyfooting inside the gym for a week. And now," he said, holding up his stopwatch, "it's trot and slot time. Time to see who the miler is and who's a quarter man. And who's got that little extra and can handle one or the other in a pinch."

"So let's start with a quarter," Coach O'Reilly continued. He pointed down the long school driveway. "I've marked off 220 yards from the school flagpole. You can see those cones up there." He wagged his finger at them, two short orange specks at either edge of the blacktop. "That'll have to do until we can get on the track. I want you all to spread out and run to the cones and back here as fast as you can. Just let it out and see what kind of times we get. First one back here doesn't have to run the next quarter. Okay, line up."

The runners shed their sweat pants and pressed shoulder-to-shoulder to fit across the drive. Coach O'Reilly hustled to the side, set himself, and raised his stopwatch. Joe stood along side Hamre, knowing the co-captain ran the 440. He looked down the long line of his teammates, and noticed their winter-white legs. He was staring at his own pale kneecaps when Coach O'Reilly yelled, "Go!"

Scott bolted like a greyhound. Joe accelerated to catch up. Unimpeded by tight hall corners, the runners blazed down the asphalt. They "just let it out." For the first 100 yards they ran tightly as a line, the only sound the rhythmic slapping of their shoes on the pavement. Just before they reached the cones, the group started to splinter. The first runners to reach the cones skidded to quick stops in the driveway grit, then reversed their direction and dodged back between the slower, oncoming runners.

Joe turned among the leaders, and almost ran smack dab into Crazy Nolan. Joe veered at the last moment as Crazy grinned, and again pursued Scott, Mark and others. Coach O'Reilly loomed before them. He held onto the flag's rope with one hand and waved with his stopwatch hand for them to hurry.

But Joe couldn't. A mysterious quicksilver seemed to pour down his legs and turn them wobbly. His heart pounded, and he ran with his mouth wide open to suck in air. As he labored more, his stride shortened. It was as if July had arrived, and the asphalt beneath him boiled in a gooey, constricting mess. Until the last 50 yards, only Mark, Scott and a few others outpaced him. Then Reynolds sped past, followed by Jim Nelson and Danny Probst. When Joe finally reached the finish line, in the middle of the pack, he grabbed his sides and bent at the waist like the other runners. Slowly walking with their heads down, white legs and all, they looked like wading egrets.

Joe hung his head in discouragement. Then he felt a hand on his back.

"Not bad Mitchell." It was Coach O'Reilly. "You ran that first 330 well." Joe eyed him beseechingly. Coach O'Reilly gave him a wizened grin. "Unfortunately, a quarter mile is 440 yards. You're built like a sprinter. You've got well-proportioned muscles. But as quick and powerful as you are, you're pretty short to ever win the quarter. It's really a full dash, and that requires stride, strength and speed. I'll keep you in the back of mind if I ever need an extra 440 man, but let's put you in the 880 or up for now."

So Joe became a distance man, but not before he ran four more 440s and heaved some color into the gray snow lining the road. He was thankful to see 4 o'clock arrive. Pitching silage seemed heavenly compared to running past the dreaded cones one more time. They began to resemble the fiery gates of hell. Joe was so tired that he walked a good share of the three miles home.

The week progressed. Joe now ran distance, which meant he daily heard Coach O'Reilly say "go run somewhere and come back in an hour." For Joe, this became a blessing. He lit out with the rest of the group, and if Mark or Tom Woodard chose that particular day to run south, he simply grabbed his backpack at the start of the run and continued home when his teammates headed back to school. Joe found the long runs much more to his liking. He didn't lack strength—the farm took care of that. The miles he racked up circling the town conditioned his heart and lungs. He soon moved up to sixth in Coach O'Reilly's daily obligatory 440.

In the distance group, Joe often found himself alone. Mark and Tom outpaced him by 70 yards. Crazy Nolan fell next in line. Keith Paluska, the son of one of the only pig farmers in the township, and several juniors, trailed Joe. He heard their shoes slap on the sidewalks. The soon-to-quit sophomores were further back, out of earshot. It didn't matter. Only Crazy Nolan talked in the group. No one else had the breath for it. Nolan apparently possessed the lungs of a Tahitian pearl diver. Plus his legs seemed to start at his Adam's apple, giving him a tremendous stride. The only reason he trailed the leaders at all was because he liked to explore the terrain.

One day, they spooked a big yellow tabby that flattened its ears and hissed as they approach. Crazy chased it down an alley. They heard trash barrels overturning and Crazy loudly meowing before he caught up to them minutes later, the swipe of the cat's claws visible on his hands. Another day he vanished, only to appear blocks later with a pint of ice cream and a plastic spoon.

Crazy Nolan alighted next to Joe in similar fashion another day, startling Joe so much that he almost leapt off the sidewalk in front of an 18-wheeler.

"God Almighty, Craze, what are you doing?" Joe scolded.

"What a day for a day dream," Crazy Nolan said. "Custom made for a day-dreamin' boy."

Nolan was called Crazy for many reasons, but this penchant to mouth the lyrics of popular songs, or entire scenes from movies, made the name stick like glue. On this particular day he favored the Lovin' Spoonful.

For reasons Crazy Nolan would not reveal, perhaps because he could find no song lyrics to properly convey them, the gangly sophomore took Joe under his wing. Crazy had been running since the eighth grade, a future phenomenon, and already a veteran. Crazy could sense when Joe struggled with a kink or a cramp, as if he possessed a medical monitoring device. Like today. Joe labored past the parochial school of his Savio days, suffering from an excruciating side ache. He ran clasping his side, waiting for Crazy to come up with the appropriate healing lyrics. Instead, Crazy started to hum "Classical Gas" by Mason Williams. After a few bars, he actually spoke non-lyrically.

"Side hurts like hell, doesn't it?" he asked, rhetorically.

"No," Joe panted, "I'm just resting my right arm."

"Ever notice that side aches are always on your right side?" Crazy persisted, ignoring Joe's retort. "Why is that do you suppose?"

They reached Troy's lone stoplight, thankful that it shone green. Joe smiled through his pain. Joe liked Crazy, found him refreshingly offbeat. Like the other runners, he teased Crazy mercilessly, but Crazy could tell there was no meanness behind Joe's remarks.

"Because that's the side you're on," Joe offered.

"No, it's where the small intestine empties into the colon. Last porthole before dumpsville." Crazy floated easily at Joe side. "You're suffering from *Cafeterius colitis* or else it's trots from trotting. Since we had chili for lunch, I bet it's a bad case of gas."

"Any known cure?"

"Run bent over and let it rip."

"What?"

"Like this." With that, Crazy bent over in full stride and blasted away like a dragster. Joe followed suit and found himself jet propelling forward and painless inside of 30 yards. Both laughed until they collapsed on the stoop of somebody's house.

"You were right, Craze," Joe said. "I feel much better."

"You learn a lot running as much as I do," Crazy replied.

Joe eyed Crazy's ragged running shoes. "How many miles do you figure you've run in your life so far?"

"More than a thousand."

Joe whistled. So many miles, he thought. And he'd logged less than 40 to date.

"Why do you run so much?"

Crazy scizzored his legs in the air. "My dad says I'm built like a daddy longlegs spider. Says I'm built this way to run. I run so he doesn't ride me."

Keith Paluska and three sophomores herded by, huffing and puffing, prompting Crazy and Joe to their feet. They settled into a swift jog to catch them.

"How about you, Joe? Why are you out here running your balls off?"

"Just because, I guess."

"That's lame. Come on. I answered you."

The reasons were too numerous to count. Joe felt he couldn't explain, and, besides, he didn't know Crazy that well.

"I'm trying to find a new life," Joe finally said as vague as possible. "Running seems the fastest way to get there."

Crazy cast an inquisitive eye in Joe's direction and then shook his head. "And they call me Crazy," he said, and let the matter drop.

RECONNECTIONS

The request flabbergasted Joe. With spring blowing in, George and he busied themselves removing straw bales from the house's cracked foundation. The bales had served their insulating purpose, but now, with a winter's worth of moisture, they lay heavy and rotting. The savvy farm cats sat by, waiting for dislodged mice. Between tossing the sodden bales onto the wagon, George popped the question.

"Joe, can you finish the milking this Saturday night?"

"How come?"

"Because I'm wanting to take your mother out to dinner. Maybe dancing, too."

Joe's mouth dropped. He couldn't recall the last time his parents had gone on an actual date.

"Is someone getting married?"

"No, it's just me and your mom."

"Is something wrong?"

George held a bale in mid-heft. The cats stared hungrily up at it. "Now why would taking Ruth out mean something's wrong?"

"I don't know. It's just been a while."

"You're right about that," George said. His forearm muscles bulging, he completed his toss. "There, that's the last of 'em and I'm still waiting for an answer."

"Well, sure Dad."

"Good. Take these bales to the spreader. They're nothing but mush now."

Agreeing to George's weekend request meant canceling his own plans with Annie. The news upset her. Their first date had gone remarkably well. They craved a reprise. In the end, Joe convinced Annie that freeing his folks for a night on the town was the right thing to do.

This time, Joe stood in the frame of the barn door as his parents' car turned onto the country road in a wide arc. He smiled, conscious that St. Dominic Savio, his recently resurrected childhood saint, would have been proud of him.

Troy offered few social outlets. No movie theater graced its short main street, or that of any of the surrounding towns. Anything special required driving to the city. Thankfully, the rural community required little—a place to gather and plenty to eat sufficed for most. Troy Community Hall provided that venue. Under its high-arched ceiling, vendors hawked vacuum cleaners and encyclopedias at the Carver County Fair. Princess Kay of the Milky Way contestants promenaded across its stage. And its hardwood dance floor and attached kitchen attracted numerous wedding parties.

On most weekends, though, the hall served up fried fish and dancing. George picked it because, on such short notice, he could think of no other place to go. Besides, Ruth liked to dance. He liked fish.

They drove to Troy in self-conscious silence. The carved rose had opened up a long-locked portal, yet, in the days that followed, they struggled to pass through it. They were cordial, visibly affectionate, but to both of them it felt forced.

Walking through the double doors of the Community Hall, they still presented a striking couple. George wore his dark gray suit and Ruth sported a new navy blue skirt and a white blouse patterned with blue flowers. A steady drone of conversation greeted them. Roughly 25 tables draped with paper cloths and encircled by folding chairs filled half of the hall. Townspeople and their rural neighbors already filled a good share of the rounds.

"Why don't you check our coats while I go freshen up in the ladies room," Ruth suggested.

George obeyed, passing the heavy coats to the sour-faced girl behind the half door. He dropped his claim checks into his suit pocket, patted them, and ambled back to the front of the hall. Waiting for Ruth, he scanned the room for known faces. He spied Curt Post, a dairy farmer still stubbornly married to purebred Guernseys when the whole county had switched to Holsteins. Sheriff Ed Hansen, looking much thinner without his revolver and uniform, carried two drinks to a crowded table. Most were mere acquaintances, neighbors beyond the fence; he had few true friends.

"Well, George, haven't seen you here in a coon's age." The voice preceded the slap on the back. Turning, George faced Terry Birkhahn, Troy's banker. A square-faced man with jowls pinched by his starched collar, he grinned drunkenly at George. "How'd you get away from those cows of yours?"

"Joe's handling it tonight," George said.

"Well, good for Joe. Always been a good kid as I recall. Not like my Bill. Christ, I couldn't trust Bill to watch my business. He'd clean the vaults," Terry snorted. "That wouldn't look very good to folks, now would it?"

"No, can't say that it would." Terry's hand still rested on George's shoulder. He wished the banker would remove it.

"Course, some don't have much in the bank, so less skin off their noses if Bill were to pilfer the dough, right?" Terry snorted again, digging his collar deeper into his fleshy neck. "Take for instance, you George. When you gonna put some more money in my bank to pay off some of them loans?"

George stiffened. "You know I just bought seed and fertilizer. Your checks come steady, with interest paid."

"I know George," Terry said, changing his tone. "Don't get me wrong. I'm just a concerned banker. And neighbor. I've seen it too often the last few years. Corn prices plummet. Guy gets over-extended. Next thing I'm getting 50 cents on the dollar at his bankruptcy auction." Terry pawed at him as if George were a long-lost friend. "So you take care, George. You're a valued customer. Hope you have a bumper crop, come fall."

Birkhahn departed with a waddle as a beaming Ruth returned to George's side. "Eugena Hansen was back there. I haven't talked to her forever. She plans to come pick strawberries in June." She squeezed George's hand. "Thanks for bringing me, George."

George commandeered an empty table and awkwardly pulled Ruth's chair out. Ruth accepted the gesture graciously. A beefy but cheerful young waitress—Ruth told George later she was one of Edith Clanton's girls—took their drink and food orders—a Black Russian for George, a Rusty Nail for Ruth, and fish platters for both.

George sat close to Ruth on his folding chair. He watched the young waitresses hustle from the tables through a set of swinging doors, and heard the cacophony of kitchen noise rise and fall as the doors swung back and forth. Birkhahn's insinuation clung to him like wet toilet paper. The gall to suggest that he was going under, George thought. He was thankful when Edith's daughter brought their drinks. The Black Russian sweetly and swiftly calmed him.

Ruth sipped her drink and soaked in the surroundings. She loved to socialize, and found herself waving at people she usually only saw at church or the grocery store.

"Look at Helen O'Donnell," Ruth said, leaning into George. "She's lost so much weight with the cancer." Helen seemed to sense Ruth stare through her graying flesh, and waved across the tables. "The doctors in the city think they got it all with the mastectomy. Dear God, I hope so."

"She had a mastectomy?" George asked, leaving thoughts of Birkhahn behind for good.

"George, where have you been? I told you that months ago."

George looked at Helen. She had certainly wasted away from her previous self. Her bare arms were as thin as hammer handles and her dress hung flat across her chest. George found the sight disturbing. Increasingly their acquaintances were contracting diseases or dying. Just the previous November Joe Kayne keeled over from a heart attack while deer hunting. Then, in January, the city doctors had opened Vance Degner and sewn him right back up with snug stitches and a cancerous death sentence. George wondered if Helen or Vance would be their next funeral.

"At least her hair looks nice," George said.

"George, that's a wig."

"Christ," George said. "Let's talk about something else."

Ruth latched onto George's arm in response. "When's the last time we did this? Not for a wedding or relatives, but just the two of us?"

"I'm ashamed to say I can't remember."

"I know. It was our 17th wedding anniversary—almost two years ago."

"I'm sorry for that, Ruth." He patted Ruth's hand.

"Hush. We're here now." Ruth squeezed his arm tighter. "Will you dance with me later?"

"I don't know if I remember how."

"Yes, you do. You've always been a good dancer."

George smiled, munching on a filbert and feeling the assault of the Cossack. "These make me graceful," he said, hoisting his half-finished drink.

"Drink makes dancers of all men."

"That's clever. Who said that?" George asked.

"I guess I did."

They both laughed. Ruth could light up a room with her vivacity, and now she beamed above her Rusty Nail. She took another sip, leaving a lipstick smile on her glass.

"Well, if you expect me to dance, I'd better order another."

"Order another for me, too."

Their second drinks arrived, and they were on the road to serious ruin when Edith's daughter mercifully brought two plates stacked high with fried filets, and a steaming baked potato. A separate plate of hot rolls and butter, and chive-sprinkled sour cream, followed. The green salad with French dressing added the only vibrant color to the table. George surrounded his plate and ate ravenously, almost two hours behind his normal suppertime. Ruth took time to savor someone else's cooking.

"Look, there are the Osters. Let's invite them over," Ruth said.

George waved and Nick and Irene Oster nodded back as they checked their coats, and soon pulled up chairs next to Ruth. Nick had a pinched rat face leathered by years in the sun. He wore the dark pall of a chain smoker. Irene, in contrast, looked starchy white, her plumpness pushing outward against her skin so she appeared without wrinkles. They ordered food and drinks simultaneously, and talked while Ruth and George ate.

"I seen your Joe running down my field road the other day," Nick said. "You punishing him or something?"

"No, he's on the track team," George answered.

Nick gave George a disapproving frown. "The track team? What about your farm?"

Ruth looked at George, and then stated to Nick. "We're managing."

"Well, it's probably good for him," Nick said, leaning back and scratching his thinning hair. "Sports were good for Frank."

"Is he here?" Ruth asked.

"Yeah," Nick said. Without turning, he added, "Up at the bar."

The rest of them looked toward the entrance of the hall, where a makeshift bar was tucked near the kitchen door. Frank Oster stood at one end, talking to the bartender.

"How's he doing?" Ruth asked with neighborly concern.

"Same as always," Nick said. "Drinking too much. Helping when he's sober. We'll be fine if we get past spring. This is his hard time."

"Oh, you be quiet, Nick. Frank's been fine. He likes the spring after the long winters," Irene said, giving Nick a hard stare. When she turned back to them, George heard her girth slide softly against her tight dress.

"We're surprised to see you here," Irene said. "Who's doing the milking tonight?"

"Joe," George said.

"Now that makes sense," Nick cackled, slapping his knee as if before that comment he considered George plumb loco. "You let him run all day so you can run around all night, is that it?"

"I never looked at it that way, but it worked out tonight," George said.

George took another swig of his drink. Maybe Nick's right, he thought. Maybe I could do this more often. If Joe stays, we could split the milkings. Get some time off. He smiled inwardly, feeling the glow of the alcohol.

Edith's girl brought the Osters' drinks. Nick turned his back to the bar and furtively took deep draughts of beer. He cradled the glass in his lap and licked the foam from his lips with a satisfied sigh. Seeing the rest of the table watching him, he said, "Sorry, I don't get to drink at home, cuz of Frank."

They all turned again to the bar, where Frank animatedly ordered another drink with his good arm. The image sobered George, and he returned to his plate instead of his glass.

They chatted through the meal on the things, mundane and critical, that shaped their lives. Bill Stancher's upcoming auction. Nick said his combine was worth a look. Irene complained about St. Lawrence's Church, which had published the amounts of money each parish family had tithed the previous year. It made them look cheap when they gave all they could afford, Irene said. Most of the talk centered around money, for they possessed little.

"Every year, Pioneer raises its prices as if we was planting diamonds instead of corn," Nick said in his turn on the subject. "Hell, we never know till October if we're looking at six-bit or $2 corn. I told Charlie Wharton that I might switch to DeKalb unless he could do me a better price. You should, too."

"Ah, Nick, Charlie won't budge and you know it," George advised. "Pioneer's got him by the short hairs, too. Besides, why plant something you've got no experience with when you're investing so much money and labor in a crop?"

"Used to be we had more of a say in these things. Farming's getting too big, and we little guys have to band together."

The women tired of the farm talk. They got that in spades over every supper. They sought a different plane. Irene filled Ruth in on Eileen Herman leaving her husband, Roy.

"For a younger man, after 18 years of marriage, mind you," Irene chirped. Ruth nodded but understood poor Eileen's decision. Roy drove semis, and often left Eileen alone for a week at a time.

"Oh, and did you hear that Jake and Marie's boy got killed in Vietnam?" Irene asked.

"You mean Gary? Oh no," Ruth said sadly.

"An army officer from Ft. Snelling drove down to bring her the news two days ago. I hear Marie just crumbled right there on the kitchen floor."

"Gary was only two years ahead of Joe," Ruth said, reflectively. Below the table she twisted her napkin. She thought of poor Marie. Better to have lost them stillborn than raise them to that end.

"How did it happen? When?"

"During that Tet offensive that's plastered all over the TV," Nick chimed in. "Westmoreland got caught with his pants down. Enemy right in the streets of Saigon. Wouldn't be this way if we were serious about winning, right George?"

They all waited for George, the veteran, to respond. He had followed Hannibal's route in reverse during World War II, from North Africa through Anzio and Rome and onto the Alps. He had seen little action, but enough.

"It's a different kind of war. It's hard to fight when you don't know whose friend or foe," he said with solemnity.

"You saying we should pull out?" Nick challenged.

Nick was starting to annoy George. He had come to woo Ruth, and now Nick was questioning his farming practices and his patriotism.

"All I'm saying is I'm not sure why we're over there in the first place."

"Well, whatcha gonna do when they want Joe to go over there?" Nick continued.

George bristled. He looked to Ruth, who had the same concerned thoughts.

"No way I'm letting Joe go over there," George declared with a square jaw. "Besides, he's our only child. Don't that mean he's protected?"

"Might be, but I don't keep up on these things since we only got the girls and Frank," Nick offered. "But you know this Tet stuff will escalate things. They'll be drafting more, and soon."

At the far end of the cavernous hall on the raised stage, Phil Dobson and his quartet tuned up. The interruption was welcome. Ruth used it to visit the restroom. George was done talking for awhile, and used the arrival of the Osters' food to graciously hide the fact. He rotated his chair to face the band.

Its members wore maroon sports coats, ruffled white shirts and black bowties. Not many bands still played polkas and waltzes with the teen music changing things. The Troy Boys found a sanctuary in the hall. Their white-haired patriarch, Phil, draped his squeaky accordion over a chair to help his band arrange the drum set, and position chairs for the clarinet and cello players. He checked each microphone with individual taps, alerting the waitresses to clean up dishes and take more drink orders because at 8:30 sharp the hall lights would dim and the Troy Boys would begin to play.

Phil started with a polka, and the diners let the band play almost the whole song before a few couples ventured onto the floor. The level of dancing competence noted, more pairs joined in. The women, feeling their drinks, looked lustfully at their husbands. The men, still a drink short, concentrated on their feet and wrestling the lead away from their wives. Soon the pulsing music freed even the shiest among them, and the dancers whirled across the floor as wild as they dared under neighbors' scrutiny.

Upon Ruth's return, George led her directly to the dance floor. Soon he was freely swinging her around. He downplayed his skills, but he could dance. Without a good three-step, farm boys didn't find wives, their mothers warned. So they learned early, tucked in the corners of church basements at relatives' wedding. They watched the adults, and practiced their first steps with cousins. The boldest boys left the shadows as teenagers, and grateful girls left the punch bowl and buzzed around them like bees. In time, they left the fringe and danced confidently in the center of the floor.

In their courting days, George required little prodding to the dance floor. Ruth remembered those days as Phil slowed the pace and played Moon River. The Mancini melody wafted over them. George himself floated on a river of moonshine, swept along by the waves of music. Both stripped him of his awkwardness and sour mood. He smiled into Ruth eyes, and realized how sorely he, too, missed some romance. This is what I want, he thought. A change. Love. Life.

"What are you thinking about right now?" Ruth asked.

"How good this feels," George said.

"Yes, it does. Does it make you love me more?"

"I'm sorry I said anything the other day."

"No, you were being honest. We need to be honest, don't we?"

The dancers pressed tighter, and George maneuvered Ruth through them like a New York cabby.

"We need to be honest, even if it hurts, or else we don't talk, and that's the worst thing of all."

"I'm scared about Joe."

"So am I," Ruth said, moving protectively against his body. "Why are you scared?"

"Because I can't see how I can run the place without him."

"The farm. Sometimes I wish we could leave it." Ruth startled herself in saying it, but the alcohol loosened her tongue, too.

"And do what?" George asked harshly.

Ruth felt him tense against her. She laid her head against him. "This."

"Now that makes no sense," George said, peeling her off his chest. Phil and the Troy Boys finished Moon River to loud applause. Sensing the crowd's mood, Phil steered the group into "The Very Thought of You." Ruth re-embraced George.

"You know I love farming," George said, calmed by Ruth swaying silently in his arms. "Don't get me wrong. I like this, too. I like it a lot. I was thinking, if Joe stayed, we could do this more often. Not during the busy times like planting and harvest, but in the winter. We could even take a vacation. Go up the North Shore after the oats are in, or even to the Black Hills. Joe's capable of running things for a couple of days. And probably would be willing if I threw some real money at him."

"That's a nice dream," Ruth said. "But Joe won't stay."

"Has he said something?"

"Can't you see it, George?"

They danced silently for several moments. The song reminded them of when they still believed in happily ever after, and thought they would never struggle so. That God would bless them with a bevy of boys and girls with black curls and white souls.

"I'm worried about losing Joe in a different way," Ruth said inside the music.

"Don't worry, I'd send him to Canada before Vietnam," George said.

"No, George. I'm not afraid of Joe leaving us. I'm afraid of him not coming back."

George slowed. This was a new thought.

"I don't understand."

Ruth placed her head on George's chest. She shunned his eyes.

"What reason have we given him to stay? What reason to come back once he leaves?"

There it was in a nutshell. The prospect of another lost child after so many dreams and so much labor. Not a physical death, not a Gary Tomkins in a flag-draped coffin, but a departure—spiritual and emotional, torturous and final—nonetheless.

"Let's make a pledge, George," Ruth said, picking up her head. Her eyes implored him intently.

"What kind of pledge?"

"Let's not worry about things till school's out." George sensed the hope in her voice. "Let's vow to make this the best two months we've ever had—as a family. Let's try to be happy. Let's help Joe chase his dream." She returned her head to his chest. "Maybe helping him will sweeten him some on staying. Maybe him chasing his dream will help us. Help everything," she murmured. "Let's pledge."

She squeezed him again, and kissed his lips right their on the dance floor. George checked to see if his fellow dancers had witnessed the kiss. In the next moment, he didn't care. Here was the audacious bride of his wedding night, the one he tried to conjure up with a yellow rose. He had made another pledge to her years ago. A husband's pledge—different and stronger than the Christian one he made before God and neighbors at the altar. The pledge said, "Forever."

"I pledge, Ruth," he said. "I pledge."

AFRAID OF HEIGHTS

The March thaw continued, the snow giving way to black soil as if God poured oil across winter's white shroud. Joe now contended with slippery mud instead of grainy slush. Regardless, he grew stronger with his daily runs. His legs quit aching, and by Friday of the following week he ran completely home from school without stopping. In the evenings, late, he called Annie to say what grew in his heart. Joe longed to return to the shaded oak. He thought about their first night together constantly. Annie was everything he desired, but not what he expected. Until their long conversation during the storm, he had thought her above him. But in his arms, Joe found Annie strong-willed and vulnerable, a perfectionist too hard on herself, but caring to a fault for her friends and things of beauty.

Now, on Saturday morning as he mucked out a calf pen, he looked forward to the evening. A party at Nancy Jones' house. George had granted Joe's permission for part of the night off without complaint.

Joe picked Annie up about 7:30. For the first time he met Donna and Harry Jensen. They invited him into their living room while Annie finished dressing upstairs. Joe took the offered easy chair, sat forward and straight on its cushion, and grinned uncomfortably. Harry and Donna sat on the edge of a plush blue sofa across a coffee table from him. Copies of *Life* and *Business Week* magazines partially covered its glass top. The narrow room was tastefully done. Its light wood furniture seemed new; at least, it carried none of the scratches and dents of his parents' living room set. The cream carpet lay newly vacuumed, with his fresh footprints visible. The coordinating-colored drapes, combined with the blue of the sofa and other room accents—a Monet print, the lamp shades—gave Joe the impression of a wheat field under clear August skies. Against the far wall, an upright piano sat like an altar in front of pictures of the Jensen family. Annie as a homecoming queen candidate. Annie and her older sister's senior pictures. Harry at a function with the governor. The four Jensens posing together in a family portrait.

"Do you play, Joe?" Donna inquired, seeing him eye the piano.

"No. I wish I could. I love music," he said politely.

"Then you should learn. Desire is half the battle," she said.

Joe thought about telling her his family couldn't afford a piano. Anything beyond a harmonica, or even a comb wrapped in cellophane to make a poor man's kazoo, would be a stretch. He didn't wish for them to know his background. Unfortunately, that was Harry's purpose for inviting him in.

"Annie tells me you live on a farm," Harry said, his inquisitive stare like a laser. He towered above his stout wife, and Joe realized Annie received her fine features from him.

"Yes sir. My folks have a small dairy farm about three miles south of Troy."

"An honorable profession, farming," Donna said. "No one works harder."

"Yes, where would this country be without the farmer," Harry chimed in. "The plight of the farmer is what caused the Great Depression, you know. It wasn't a bunch of New York rich losing money on the stock market. No, it was the Dust Bowl of the early '30s. Cut our farm production. We had no exports, so the economy collapsed. The whole country was agrarian back then."

Joe nodded and said nothing. He rarely heard someone use the word agrarian, but he was still pretty sure the Jensens knew as much about farming as he knew about nuclear physics. Joe wished Annie would hurry. In the silence, he noticed the grandfather clock for the first time, its brass pendulum swinging like a hangman's noose.

"What are your plans after graduating?" Donna probed. "Are you staying on the farm?"

"No, I've been thinking about a junior college or trade school," Joe replied.

Donna seemed relieved. In the off chance this romance went further, she could be assured her daughter's future wouldn't be agrarian.

"Annie says you're on the track team," Harry said, taking another turn.

"That's right."

"What event?"

"Looks like the half mile or mile. Coach O'Reilly says my stride's too short for the dashes."

"Another Jim Ryan, huh?" Harry said. He leaned back into the sofa, leaving Donna the only one on the edge anymore.

"I wish," said Joe, meaning it.

"Then you might run against Mark," Donna said. "Mark Perkins."

"I guess so," Joe said, "unless Coach O'Reilly puts me in the 880. Next week will tell. We've got our first meet, finally."

"Mark's a good runner. Let's hope you're a half-mile man," Harry said.

"I'm ready," Annie said from the top of the stairs, heralding her entrance.

Joe looked up and drank in the vision of her. Annie beamed upon seeing him smile, and her brushed hair framed her face like a glowing fire. Her clothes announced the arrival of spring. She sported a short-sleeved red top with a modestly scooped neckline, and tight new jeans that complemented her slight figure. As she bounced down the carpeted stairs, the thin gold chain around her neck danced and caught the light. They rose as one to meet her.

"Are you going to be warm enough?" Donna asked disapprovingly.

"We'll be indoors, Mom," Annie said, slipping a bold hand into Joe's sweaty one.

"Take a sweater just in case."

"Mom," Annie moaned.

"Don't 'Mom' me," Donna said, and Annie reluctantly headed back up the stairs.

"What time will you two be home?" Harry asked.

"I'll have Annie home by 11:30, Mr. Jensen."

Harry liked the response and tone.

"11:30 is fine. Be careful driving. Bye angel," Harry said as Annie bounced back beside Joe.

Freed, they hurried out to the car. "Did I pass?" Joe asked as they closed their respective doors.

"I'll find out tomorrow morning, "Annie said. "That's when I'll get grilled." She snuggled close and pecked him on the cheek.

They arrived at Nancy's house in short order. A copy of Annie's house, it stood well lit against the shadowy woods behind it. Mrs. Jones, nervous and loud, greeted the guests as they arrived. As with the others, she laid down the rules of the house to Annie and Joe. Any signs of alcohol, the party's over. Any second calls from the neighbors, the party's over. Nancy rolled her eyes in embarrassment behind her mother. As the three of them headed for the basement, Joe surveyed the house. A chandelier hung in crystal opulence in the entryway. A huge TV console and adjoining stereo in the living room were centered before a high-backed sofa and two leather chairs. Ceramic and metal sculptures swept upwards from end tables and the fireplace mantle. Mostly he noticed the floors, in part because the music from below pulsed through them despite the fact the carpet was as thick as a ewe's winter coat.

Descending into the throbbing noise, Joe was again taken aback. He had never seen a finished basement quite like this. More carpet, a wet bar and refrigerator to their left at the bottom of the stairs. The basement opened up from there into a huge rec room. An octagonal poker table, sleeved in plastic, held pyramids of sandwiches, bowls of chips and iced sodas. At the opposite end of the room, most of the guys surrounded a pool table, the click of careening balls punctuating their conversation. Along the wall to their left, another honeycomb of electronic gear hummed.

"They've got two TVs," Joe said to Annie.

"Hey, Joe, good to see you man," Dave said as he rose from one of the folding chairs and clasped Joe's hand. "Annie, how you doing? Come sit with Betty and me."

Annie and Betty hugged and then they all sat in a tight circle. Talking above a Rascals' song, Annie told them that Joe apparently passed muster, because her folks had let them out the door. Joe explained the types of questions Donna and Harry asked, and said he didn't consider it a grilling.

"Oh, they're grilling you, all right," Dave said. "Every time I've dated a girl for the first time it feels like the Inquisition."

"Every time?" Betty piped in. "How many times are we talking about?"

"Well, there was one time, two years ago when I was a sophomore," Dave began. "I'd just gotten my driver's license, and I asked Alice Dornburg out."

"You dated Alice? You never told me that." Betty cuffed the back of his head.

"Let me finish," Dave said, ducking an expected second blow. "Bell bottoms had just come in, and I had a pair of maroon hip-huggers held up by a big buckled belt. I wore that and a green paisley shirt to pick up Alice."

"You still haven't learned how to dress, have you Dave?" Annie teased.

Dave ignored her. "On the way, the muffler fell off my folk's car. I didn't think, and tried to pick it up. It was hotter than hell, and burnt my hands but good. I drove up to Alice's house with the Pontiac sounding like a tank. When I rang Alice's doorbell, her father answered. There I stood, looking like Sonny Bono, my hair messed, the worst of my burnt hands wrapped in my handkerchief, smudge marks on my face. 'Can I help you?' he asked through the screen. 'I'm here to pick up Alice,' I replied. Then he looked me up and down and said, 'You look like Jack the Ripper.' I said, 'I'm not. Jack's just a distant cousin.' He slammed the door. So I never did date Alice."

"That's not an Inquisition," Joe laughed. "That's self-preservation."

"He asked me a question, didn't he?"

"Why did you say you were related to Jack the Ripper?" Annie asked.

"Hell if I know. It just came out. Anyway, if I hadn't, I probably wouldn't be here with Betty."

"Ah," the rest of them sighed in unison.

"You're such a catch," Betty added. "Why don't you prove it by getting us something to drink?"

When Dave left, Annie and Betty started chatting amongst themselves. Joe turned to the TV. Danny Probst and Steve Kennedy, dateless, were watching Mission Impossible. All his classmates talked about it, but he had never seen it.

Unable to follow it, Joe perused the room. Mark Perkins and Greg Harrington were competitively engaged in a game of pool. On the edge of this group, Scott Hamre stood with one arm around Maggie O'Leary, who wore his letterman's jacket despite the room's heat. She sported new glasses and a smile.

"Here are your Cokes," Dave said, sitting back down. Joe marveled that the chair didn't collapse under his weight. Dave's success on the basketball team stemmed from his sheer bulk. Opposing centers couldn't move his 215-pound frame. With curly black hair and his jocularity, he resembled an immense teddy bear.

"How are those cross country runs going, Joe?" Dave asked.

"Actually, they're getting easier. I'm finally making it home without stopping."

Dave popped open his Coke, and took several quick gulps. "You know, some of us think you get to the edge of town and have your folks pick you up."

"There have been days I wish I had."

"We're also wondering how you convinced O'Reilly to spring you." Dave suddenly belched.

"Dave!" Betty scolded.

"Jeez, that felt good," Dave said, tapping his chest. "You're not the first to try, you know."

"Shows you how desperate he is to win the championship, I guess," Joe said.

"Oh, enough of sports. That's all you guys do all week. That's all you talk about," Betty said. "Is there any other dimension to your lives?"

Dave and Joe exchanged glances. Dave winked. In unison they said, "No."

They teased some more, then distanced themselves from athletics and conversed about their upcoming graduation. The four of them stayed on the surface of things, like children on March ice, knowing how tenuous and untested were their future plans.

The boys moved through the basement's toys in rapid fashion. When their interest in pool waned, they moved to the stereo and jockeyed to play their favorite song from their favorite artist. Most were too cool to turn to the TV, so they checked out the recesses of the room for something else of interest, but Mrs. Jones was a tidy sort. Food became the next attraction, and the pyramids crumbled to their foundations in short order. Soon, boredom wedged its way into the party.

"Hey, Nancy, is this it?" Scott yelled above the noise.

"What do you mean?" Nancy replied.

"What's next?" Scott yelled in return.

"There's cake coming," Nancy said.

The room laughed as one, and Nancy blushed.

"Is someone coming out of the cake?" Mark asked, and more laughter erupted.

"Oh, leave Nancy alone, you guys," Betty said. She joined Nancy in the middle of the room. "She was nice enough to have this party."

Mark tapped his chest with a mea culpa. "No offense. The natives are restless. They grow tired of watching me beat Greg in pool."

"You're only up three to two, asshole," Greg retorted.

Nancy pulled a sweep of hair back behind her right ear, and glanced at Betty for ideas. Betty shrugged. Someone turned the music down, drawing more attention to her. "Do you want to play charades or something?" she asked in growing desperation.

"No," the group shouted. The partygoers stood like children, demanding entertainment.

"Well, it's awfully cold outside, but there's the trampoline . . ."

"You have a tramp?" Mark said excitedly. He didn't wait for an answer. Both he and Greg tossed their pool cues onto the felt table and, in a flash, led the partygoers outside. They found the circular trampoline framed in the muted glow of the house lights. Mark and several others immediately vaulted over its springs onto its taut surface. They began to jump independently and soon shot up and down like car pistons.

"There's too many of you on there at once," Nancy yelled, seeing the tramp sag.

Scott immediately shoved Greg over the edge, and the free-for-all was on. Those on the grass scurried back for safety. The boys bounced like ghoulish shadows, frantic in their desire to fling a friend earthward, or escape a similar fate. Joe heard heads knock and subsequent groans of pain. Annie leaned into him, shivering, and he put his arm around her. Together, they watched the group whirl until only two shadows remained.

"I figured it would be you, Dave," Mark said, and all around knew the final combatants. Mark breathed rapidly from his exertion, and hugged the edge of the tramp furthest from the hulking darkness that was Dave.

"Ditto," Dave said. "Prepare to meet your doom."

"Why don't we just call it a draw?" Mark implored.

"Squash him like a bug, Dave," Greg prodded.

"Don't listen to him, Dave. He's sore because I beat him in everything. I can beat you, too. But I like you. You're not a piss ant like Greg. How about it, Dave? A draw, we both win."

"You want a draw because you know there's no way you can push me off of this tramp."

"You're right, Dave. I can't budge you. You're a behemoth. A colossus. An eclipse. But I can get you on the ground."

With that, Mark back-flipped off of the tramp. He landed squarely on his feet, a perfect dismount. In the same instant, freed of his weight, Mark's side of the tramp lifted, sprawling Dave backwards into the howling crowd.

"Betcha didn't see that one coming," Mark hollered in elation. "Brains vs. brawn always wins."

Dave sat in momentary embarrassment. Then he saw the cleverness in Mark's action, the playfulness in his tone, and he began to chuckle.

"Where'd you learn to do that," Dave said, rising to applause.

"The back flip? In 10th grade phy-ed. Remember? When Sanders broke his foot?"

"I remember Sanders falling off the high bar. I don't remember old man Kaufold teaching us what you just did." Dave brushed himself off as Betty appeared at his side.

"Mark, you could have seriously hurt Dave by jumping off."

"I can't help it if he weighs 300 pounds," Mark said playfully.

"215," Betty interjected.

"You would know best, Betty," Mark parried. The crowd tittered. They were enjoying themselves again. "215 or 300 pounds, I still won."

"Well, not actually," Joe began, and then wished he hadn't. Mark moved into the dim light.

"Go on," Mark said, frowning.

"Dave was the last to leave the tramp, is all."

"That's right," Greg popped in. "You bailed. He sailed. But, technically, he was the last man standing."

Others among Mark's basketball teammates chimed in, just to get his goat. "Greg's right. You outwitted yourself," they bantered.

"Ah, crap, you guys. I won. You're just sore because Dave or I tossed you off." Turning to Joe, he said, "I don't even remember seeing your smart ass up there."

"Let it go, Mark. Like you said. It was a draw," Dave said.

"Draw, hell," Mark said, growing more infuriated. "I can best anyone here, in anything."

"Big whoop," Scott said.

"You don't believe me?"

"We just don't care, Mark. It's childish."

Mark couldn't believe Annie spoke those words. His eyes trailed from hers to the tramp again, and the woods behind it. A single tree formed out of the diffused light, and the huge oak with its gnarled branches gave him an idea.

"Some of you guys help me pull the tramp over there," he said, pointing.

"I don't think my folks are going to like this," Nancy fretted.

The boys ignored her, and dragged the tramp across the lawn. Someone handed Mark a flashlight and he bounced its beam from tramp to tree, calculating height and angle. "Someone take the light," he said, and Joe, being closest, grabbed it. "Shine it on the trunk. Scott, boost me up."

"Mark, don't you dare!" Nancy said.

"Yeah, Mark, you'll get hurt," Annie said.

"Do it," Greg said.

Scott cupped his hands and Mark propelled off his right foot to capture the lowest horizontal branch. It had the girth of a beer keg, and he swiftly straddled it. From there, he maneuvered through the labyrinth of branches, directing Joe to move the light to guide his way. Nancy kept up a constant wag of warnings, but she knew only her parents could stop matters and she wanted the party to continue. While Nancy watched, Mark positioned himself on a limb about 20 feet above and to the right of the tramp.

"You want us to move the tramp closer?" Greg asked, nervously noting the vast distance.

"No, this is fine. This is just perfect."

Joe watched Mark in the halo of light. He looked like a circus trapeze artist—lithe and fearless. Below him, his audacity hushed the crowd. He released his grip from the upper branches, bounced with the give of the limb, and sprang outward from the tree. Joe's light could barely follow his arc. It missed Mark's tuck and roll, but framed Mark as he landed squarely on his back dead center on the tramp. His impact lifted him straight up, and for a moment he seemed to be sleeping on air. He plopped back onto the tramp, and on his second bounce brought his legs beneath him. Just like that, he stood before them.

"Match that, any of you," Mark dared. He couldn't see them, squinting into the flashlight's beam. "How about it, Dave? Or you, Joe, all wise and knowing. And where's Greg, he of the loud mouth."

"I'm here," Dave alone answered.

"Well?"

"No way I'm letting you do that, Dave," Betty said. Joe's light followed the voice, and framed the couple. "You'll break your neck."

"I doubt that," Mark said from the dark. "Dave's so big he won't get up into the tree."

"Get that light out of my face, Joe. Some of you guys help me up this oak."

Dave had a much harder time of it, as did Greg, Danny and Scott, who struggled beneath Dave's weight. At last Dave pulled and shimmied his way onto the lower limb.

"You think the tree can hold him," Danny laughed from a prone position.

"Shut up, Danny," Dave said, and Joe noted a tinge of anger and fear in his friend's voice. Regardless, Dave cautiously made his way down the same lit trail to the launching limb.

"Oh, Dave, please be carefully," Betty said with true concern.

"Just don't fall on one of us," Mark added.

Dave stood a long time on the branch. Below, the crowd remained quiet.

"Shine the light on the tramp so I can see where I'm going," Dave commanded. Joe shot a shaft of light horizontally across the tramp's black surface. Above, they heard Dave breaking small branches as he took his final position.

"Yahoooo!" roared above them. In the next second, Dave entered the light, hands and knees first. He hit the tramp at an angle, and then, almost in the same instance, he was gone, catapulted into the darkness.

"Dave!" Betty screamed and bolted around the tramp.

"Bring the light, bring the light," someone yelled.

They found him in a heap next to the patio. Flat on his back, with one leg twisted under the other, he appeared dead.

"My God, he's hurt. My God, Dave." Betty knelt over him, looking for some sign of life. "Dave, are you all right? Oh, my God, someone call for help. Dave, say something!"

"Your knee . . . is on . . . my crotch," Dave said, one eye now peeking up at Betty.

"Oh, you bastard," Betty said, and slapped him.

"Now I need a doctor," Dave said, and the crowd burst into relieved laughter. His friends helped him to his feet as Betty stormed away toward the basement.

"You're okay, then?" Joe asked, not believing Dave could have survived such a fall.

"Soon as I swallow my liver I'll be right as rain," Dave said.

Mark appeared into the circle. "I didn't think you would do it, Dave."

"Guts I got." He reached for his lower back. "Now can we quit this crap?"

Mollified, Mark put his arm around Dave's neck, and the two strode back toward the tramp.

"Are you going to try it Joe?" Annie asked as the crowd gathered once more.

"No," Joe replied. They stood in the dark now, Joe having given up his flashlight.

"Let's walk and you can tell me why not."

Annie took his hand, and they slipped away from the crowd unnoticed. She seemed familiar with Nancy's yard, which was ample, and guided them in the dark toward the neighboring house.

Joe was relieved. He, too, had suffered through the two weeks of gymnastics two years earlier in phy-ed. With his upper arm strength, he excelled on the pummel horse and vaults. The trampoline and high bar were a different story. Mr. Kaufold, the phy-ed teacher, forced all the sophomores to do a backward dismount off the high bar. It consisted of sitting on a narrow, 8-foot-high bar, letting go with one's hands, and falling backwards. The high bar was suppose to catch the back of the student's knees until his weight and momentum worked like a pendulum to swing him around to a height where he simply dropped his legs and stood up.

On his dismount, Bruce Sanders broke his toe. Fearing a similar injury, Joe froze during his turn. They had to get chairs and pry his fingers off the bar to get him down. By the time his turn on the trampoline rolled around, he was near panic. The encouragement of others turned slowly to teasing and then indifference as he bounced safely and softly in the middle of the tramp. No flips, forward or back, for him, no daredevil stunts. It had been two years earlier, but Joe experienced the shame all over again when he watched Mark expertly master the tramp and the crowd.

They stepped from grass onto patio brick, and Annie said, "There should be a picnic table here somewhere."

"Ouch," Joe winced, bumping into it.

"Ah, you found it. Let's sit."

The second they did, Annie's arms encircled his neck. He pulled her to him in a deep kiss, feeling the swell of her breasts against his chest.

"I've missed you, Annie," Joe said. "I've missed this."

"Me, too," Annie said, and kissed him again. The kisses were more passionate than their first date. Instinctively, he moved his right hand until it rested on her left breast. She did not brush it away. They continued fondling until their growing excitement made Joe conscious of their surroundings.

"Don't you think we should be careful?"

"Of what?"

"Someone's likely to come looking for us."

Annie nibbled on his ear lobe. "I'm not embarrassed if they find us."

Joe's nervousness was real, though, and broke the spell. Annie nestled into Joe's arms, and they faced back toward the trampoline. They saw Scott silhouetted high in the tree.

"So why won't you jump?"

"I'm afraid of heights."

"Really?"

"Yes."

Scott jumped, chased by the flashlight's beam. A thunderous roar followed.

"Would you jump if I asked you to?"

"Yes, if you asked me."

"Would you do anything I asked?"

Joe gulped at the realization. "I'm afraid, so."

"There's that word again. Afraid."

"Heights and you. They both make me dizzy."

"Nice recovery," Annie said. She kissed him again, affectionately.

"Aren't you afraid of certain things?" Joe asked.

Annie settled back on his chest and sighed. "Only of not getting what I want out of life."

"What is it you want?" Joe asked curiously.

"Everything."

"Who wants cake?" they heard Nancy yell from the basement door.

"Cake! Nancy has cake!" someone sounding like Greg yelled in mock enthusiasm.

"CAKE! CAKE! CAKE!" the group took up the chant, and made a mad dash toward Nancy that made her scream and scramble inside.

"Do you want to go get some cake?" Joe asked.

"I'd rather stay here with you," Annie said, and began making out with him again.

From dark shadows, Mark watched. He had seen Annie and Joe slip away, and bided his time to evade the throng as well. In the darkness, he could see little, but heard much. His blood rose in hurt and anger. He knew the lips Joe kissed, the curves he caressed. He was on the verge of rushing in and pummeling Joe when Nancy intervened.

"Mark, Joe and Annie, are you guys out here?" she yelled from about 50 feet away.

"We're here," Annie said, only after Nancy edged ever closer to them.

"What are you two lovebirds up to?" Nancy asked rhetorically.

"Three guesses," Annie said.

"Seen Mark?"

"Not since Dave jumped," Joe said.

"Oh. Must have overlooked him inside. Come on in. Everyone else has."

They followed Nancy, who continued to look for Mark. No one had seen him, and all assumed he had left. After cake, couples started to leave, seeking an hour of privacy before curfews. Joe and Dave stayed until the end as Annie and Betty helped Nancy clean up the mess.

In the car in the Jensen's driveway a half an hour later, Joe and Annie necked again. The same window curtain was pulled back as on their first date.

"They really do keep an eye on you, don't they," Joe said.

"Yes they do," Annie answered, perturbed. "I can't wait to get away."

"Me neither," Joe echoed.

Joe walked Annie to the door and kissed her a final time. "Goodnight Annie."

"Goodnight, my Joe."

Joe left floating on a cloud of love. His thoughts returned to the picnic table, and he felt himself aroused again. He wanted to remember everything about the night. What Annie said, how her breast felt in his hand. He rolled down the window and let the cool breeze inside. Smells of spring mingled with Annie's perfume on his clothes, and he breathed them in. "How Can I Be Sure" by the Rascals came on KDWB, and Joe cranked up the sound. He sang along happily as the moon rose and brought form to the countryside. Its pockets of woods and expanses of fields suddenly seemed like Eden through Joe's love-struck eyes. Driving under the railroad trestle near to home, he even smiled at the graffiti-covered cement. Its crude messages suddenly seemed youthful and life-affirming.

It came as a surprise, then, when the headlight-less car appeared in his rearview mirror. Despite Joe's speed, the car came rushing up to his tail lights. Joe hit the accelerator, and the phantom car sped up in turn. Joe tapped his brakes, and in the red glow of his lights tried to see the make of car. He had expected to see an Impala, but he knew Mark's, and this car was a blue Ford. Joe saw the emblem until it disappear beneath his car's trunk as the car edged closer.

"Are you crazy?" Joe yelled out loud.

Fearful, Joe floored the accelerator, laying rubber. The Chevy fantailed until Joe wrestled it back under control. He roared down the highway, doing 70, then 80 mph. His pursuer kept pace. They took the curve near Becker's farm dangerously fast, both cars' tires squealing. Then, just as quickly as it had appeared, the car eased back into the blackness. Joe slowed as he neared the turn-off road to his farm. Pulling onto the gravel, he slammed the car to a stop and hopped out. He heard the pursuing car glide past on the highway.

A minute later, Danny Probst shifted through gears. He had turned in a farmyard, and he and Mark were driving north on the highway now, back toward the gravel road.

"You think he knows it was us?" Danny asked, glad to be using his headlights again.

Mark saw the beams of Joe's car headlights. They bore through the evergreens and onto the adjoining field like ivory chopsticks. Pulling even with the side road, they spied Joe standing by the Chevy's open door.

"Nah, he'll think it was me. He doesn't know your old man's car. And now I know where he lives."

THE TOUCH

Joe's absence became painfully clear to George the following Monday. Rita, one of his best Holsteins, was calving. After two hours of labor, only two glistening black hooves protruded from her uterus. George had fashioned his slipknots carefully around them, but pulling on the rope produced no calf—only exhausted moans from Rita. Doc Harvey was on the other side of the county, his receptionist told George. Joe was the answer, but Joe was off running under the security of the pledge.

The Pledge. It had seemed so right to vow. They came home from the dance and fell into each other's arms. George awoke refreshed, despite the late night and early morning, as if a yoke had been lifted from his shoulders. Still, a gauzy veil of self-consciousness hung between them. One night did not restore years of love's erosion. Despite himself, George wondered if Ruth opened herself out of love for him or for Joe.

A test case stared him in the face in the form of the Holstein's heaving sides. George needed Ruth's assistance. To give it, Ruth would have to break another pledge—to never to enter the barn.

George tracked her down in her garden. Ruth was gleaning bits of garden trash degorged by George's recent plowing—the spidery roots of the previous year's sweet cornstalks, and chunks of rotted pumpkins protruding like pottery shards from the soil.

"Ruth, I need you in the barn," George said matter-of-factly. "I've got a cow down, and if I can't deliver her calf, I'm likely to lose her."

Ruth straightened up. She unconsciously clutched at the front of her dirty sweater. Her expression acknowledged what was left unsaid. Pledge against pledge, one made because of a dead son, one made to help another.

"There's no other way?" Ruth asked after several long moments.

"Not really. Otherwise I wouldn't have come."

will be issued for (i) purchases made by check less than 7 days prior to the date of return, (ii) when a gift receipt is presented within 60 days of purchase, (iii) textbooks returned with a receipt within 14 days of purchase, or (iv) original purchase was made through Barnes & Noble.com via PayPal. Opened music/DVDs/audio may not be returned, but can be exchanged only for the same title if defective.

<u>After 14 days or without a sales receipt</u>, returns or exchanges will not be permitted.

Magazines, newspapers, and used books are not returnable. *Product not carried by Barnes & Noble or Barnes & Noble.com will not be accepted for return.*

Policy on receipt may appear in two sections.

Return Policy

<u>With a sales receipt</u>, a full refund in the original form of payment *will be issued* from any Barnes & Noble store for returns of new and unread books (except textbooks) and unopened music/DVDs/audio made within (i) 14 days of purchase from a Barnes & Noble retail store (except for purchases made by check less than 7 days prior to the date of return) or (ii) 14 days of delivery date for Barnes & Noble.com purchases (except for purchases made via PayPal). A store credit for the purchase price will be issued for (i) purchases made by check less than 7 days prior to the date of return, (ii) when a gift receipt is presented within 60 days of purchase, (iii) textbooks returned with a receipt within 14 days of purchase, or (iv) original purchase was made through Barnes & Noble.com via PayPal. Opened music/DVDs/audio may not be returned, but can be exchanged only for the same title if defective.

"Doc Harvey . . . ."

"Over on the Ralsch farm on the other side of Franksburg, dealing with pseudorabies. Won't make it in time. Neither will Joe."

A full 30 seconds passed. Ruth shut her eyes and breathed deeply. Her hand dropped from her sweater front to her side in surrender. "Do I need to bring anything?"

"Gloves. You'll need leather and latex ones. I'll grab them for you," George answered.

They walked together to the house for the gloves, and then resolutely to the barn. Ruth paused once inside, adjusting to decade-old sights and memories. George granted her the time, though a look down the manger to Rita's tortured face told him to hurry. The cow's head lay twisted at the bottom of the stanchion. Her breathing was short and labored. What scared him the most were Rita's eyes. When he had left, they had bulged like cue balls in panic and pain. Now they seemed submerged and defeated.

"What do you want me to do, George" Ruth implored. She struggled to move forward on her own.

"I need you to help me pull," George said, leading Ruth by the arm down the barn floor behind the cow. The rope still dangled from the minute hooves on the loose straw George had strewn to receive the calf. "Here, put on these gloves, and when I say pull, pull slow and hard and steady."

Ruth maneuvered behind George. Gloved, she clasped the rope. She avoided looking at the struggling cow. When George wound the rope around his hands for a better grip, she followed suit.

"Slowly, now, pull."

Rita came alive in her pain. The Holstein attempted to rise, and collapsed back onto her side. She gave out a wet, gurgling bellow as they tugged. The calf's legs emerged almost to the knee, but no further. They pulled and pulled until Ruth's arms ached.

"Stop. It's no good," George said releasing the rope.

"What do we do?"

George took off one glove and massaged his temples. "It doesn't make sense unless the calf's head is twisted," he said. "She's had plenty of calves, big ones. And those are front hooves sticking out."

"We have to help her. She's in so much pain," Ruth observed.

"I know. I'm thinking. Let me think."

"What would Doc Harvey do?" Ruth pressed. "You must have seen something like this before."

"A couple of times. Once he did a Caesarian."

"The other times?"

"He repositioned the calf in the birth canal."

"Let's do that." There was growing desperation in Ruth's words, and justifiably so. Rita lay as if dead, her whole back end awash in the blood and fluids of birth.

"I've already tried that. My hand's too big."

Ruth understood immediately. "That's why you brought the other gloves."

"I'm sorry. I hoped the two of us pulling would be enough. I don't think there's any other way."

"What do I do?" Ruth asked, reaching hesitantly inside her sweater pockets for the rubber gloves.

"I'm going to try to push the legs back a bit. Probably won't work. The calf's on its way. Regardless, you need to work your hand inside. Follow along the legs. See if you can feel the head. It should be down on its front legs like someone diving. Tucked in like. If it's not, that's the position we need to put it in."

Ruth removed her sweater and tossed it on the grimy floor. Donning the right-hand glove of the pair, Ruth bent down behind the cow. George knelt in the straw next to Ruth, and noticed her arms were shaking. George pushed. Rita bellowed. The legs barely budged.

"You'll just have to try to go around them," George said.

Ruth leaned forward. She gingerly tried to find a crack, an entrance, between calf and cow, but the flesh was unyielding.

"You can't be gentle, Ruth," George instructed. "We're way past gentle."

"I can't do this, George."

"Yes you can. You have to do this or the calf will die. The cow might die."

"I can't get in."

"You must do this. We've lost too many unborn already, you and me."

Ruth spun her face around. George looked at her intensely. Ruth began to breathe more rapidly. She began to nod. Tears welled in her eyes, and she bit her bottom lip. Then she ripped off the glove as if it were an annoyance. She leaned right on top of the cow's haunches, and plied the uterus with her fingers. She squeezed and curved and worked her hand slowly inside. The fluids and smells and Rita's awful noises hurtled Ruth to the edge of gagging, but she persisted. Her hand inched along the calf's wet legs, past knee to shoulder. Ruth felt the cow's contractions along her forearm. Suddenly, she touched the calf's head. Reflexively the calf moved. Ruth screamed and half retracted her blood-stained arm.

"What's the matter?" George yelled, clamping down on Rita's arched back.

"I felt its head. It moved."

"Which way is the head turned?"

Ruth gathered herself, and plunged back inside. She reached the head again, felt the calf's eyelashes blink against her fingers.

"Its head is facing away from us."

"Can you turn the head?"

Ruth tried. "There's no room."

"Try to grab its nose. Get your thumb and finger in its nostrils. Don't be afraid to hurt it to get a good grip. I'll push again. When I do you pull its head around."

George braced both feet against the gutter. He grabbed hold of the twin hooves. "She might try to stand up on us, so be careful, Ruth."

"I will."

"On three."

George counted, and with a mighty heave worked the calf back several inches. Rita lashed out feebly with her right rear leg, but enough to knock George into Ruth. He righted himself and leaned forward again.

"Now Ruth, pull!"

Ruth's hand engulfed the small nose. All was unseen and viscous, a wet pulp of mystery. Ruth yanked for all she was worth. Yanked to save the calf. Yanked for her sons, alive and dead, and for George. And the head turned.

"I did it!" Ruth yelled. "I turned it."

"Hurry, let's pull before it gets twisted again."

They both scurried to their feet. They pulled the rope taut on George's signal and, with steady pressure, resumed their tugging. The calf's knees soon appeared, and then the tip of its black nose, as round as the end of a baseball bat.

"It's coming Ruth. Don't let up."

The head emerged and, seconds later, the long black body swooshed out on a tide of fluid into the yellow straw.

"We did it. We did it George!"

George moved quickly over the quivering calf. He stuck his fingers into its nostrils, clearing them of fluid and mucus. Then he pulled the calf further from the gutter. Leaving it, he hustled up the walkway and released Rita from her stanchion. The weary cow miraculously rose and backed slowly out of her stall. The sight of her calf seemed to revive her. She sniffed it from head to tail, and then began methodically to lick its matted hair.

"She's doing that to get rid of the afterbirth," George said, showing off his animal husbandry. "They've long been domesticated, but in the wild, cows had to get their calves clean and walking fast to avoid predators."

The comments floated right past Ruth, who stood agog over cow and calf. She had seen many calves born, yet she had never helped birth one in such a fashion as today. It left her shaken but ecstatic. The calf displayed beautiful markings. Shoe-polish black from head to tail and far down her sides and legs before hitting stockings of snowy white hair. A nova of white on her forehead shone like Venus on a February night.

"Look at us," George said. "We're quite the sight."

And they were. Ruth's blouse was soaked through in parts, and blood and pieces of straw festooned her pants. Her slender right arm looked like a barber's pole, and her hair stuck to her sweaty forehead. The front of George's bib overalls was equally drenched. He reached in his back pocket and withdrew a dry red kerchief and began wiping Ruth's face.

"Thank you, Ruth."

"It's okay."

"I know you want to leave. You can whenever you want. I've got things under control."

"I think I'll stay a bit and make sure he's okay."

"Fine, but he's a she. Just big, is all. That was part of the problem."

An idea popped into George's head. "Why don't you name her?"

"Me?"

"You're the reason she's laying there. Pick a good one. I've got to go call Doc Harvey's. Tell Margo to tell Doc he doesn't need to come."

George departed. Ruth stood alone and watched Rita mother her newborn. The cow's tongue rasped its way through the calf's coat, so long and strong it moved the calf's body with each lick. If the calf bawled, Rita went immediately to its head, sniffing and mooing, as if speaking to the calf. In time, the calf attempted to stand. At first, its legs seemed as wobbly as hoses, and the calf plopped back into the straw. Rita was there to nudge her back up. Finally, the calf stood up, her legs aslant like those of a sawhorse. Her first steps were an adventure, and Ruth was glad to witness it. She rubbed the star on the calf's forehead, and dubbed her Venus.

It's strange, Ruth thought, watching Venus try to suckle minutes later, how basic life is, stripped down. Procreation summed it up. Wasn't this her sole purpose, too? To ensure Joe stood on steady feet, with the strength and skills to attract his own wife, and thus continue the cycle? Their pledge to Joe took on new meaning with these thoughts. The Pledge suddenly morphed into everything.

George carried his own unspoken thoughts through the rest of the day. His focused not on the calf, nor Joe, but on Ruth. He was virtually abuzz with the hope that Ruth would again partner with him in the dairy, not only in spirit but toil, as she had done early in their marriage. Hadn't she broken her pledge of some 15 years for him? If Joe left, but Ruth helped with the chores and milking, he could reduce the herd size and maybe keep dairying in some fashion. All through chores and milking that night, he watched Joe and saw Ruth in his place. He would have to carry the milk and do the heavy lifting, but Ruth could swab an udder and scoop feed the same as Joe. The longer he dwelt on the possibility, however, the more doubts surfaced to nibble at its corners. George soon convinced himself the afternoon's events were a one-time concession by Ruth. An emergency only—one that left her no choice. It had nothing to do with their night of passion, or his random yellow rose. He envisioned that his plan of requesting Ruth's help would blow up in his face.

It was late when George came up from the barn that night. Joe had preceded him and was sprawled out on the linoleum floor in front of Ruth's feet watching TV. George washed up slowly and entered the living room.

"How's that calf of ours doing?" Ruth asked, looking up from her needlepoint.

"Fine. She ate well tonight. What's on, Joe?"

"*The Plainsman*, with Gary Cooper."

George sunk into his rocker. "That's a favorite of mine. They don't make movies like this anymore. How much is left?"

Joe checked his watch. "About an hour. It goes till 10."

"Maybe I'll watch."

Ruth laughed into her pattern. "George, you'll be asleep in 10 minutes and you know it."

"Well, maybe not tonight." Ruth's words were so true. He knew he always fell asleep. The dairy routine deprived him of sleep. If Ruth helped more, he could gain an hour here and there. Maybe actually finish watching a program. These thoughts raced through his mind as Gary Cooper, as Wild Bill Hickock, raced across the black and white plains.

"George, wake up. It's time for bed."

It was Ruth, waking him. Wild Bill was dead and Joe upstairs. George rubbed his face. "You coming up?"

"Soon," Ruth said. "I want to catch the weather first."

"Goodnight," George said, rising from the chair and pecking her on the cheek.

"Goodnight, George."

He wandered upstairs and plopped on the bed facing the wall. Normally, he would have dropped off in seconds but, the downstairs catnap behind him, he contemplated anew on Joe's expected departure. What would make him stay? Out of this worrisome goo, his deepest fear emerged like a phoenix. What if after the Pledge was fulfilled, Ruth left, too? Was she only staying with him because of Joe? That's why he carved the rose. He believed Ruth alone loved him, but how much love was contained in "not as much?" George knew he could be stripped of his pride, even his livelihood. He could be maimed like Frank Oster. In the end, in his heart, he knew only one thing. He treasured Ruth above all else.

Ruth came down the hall. Before entering the bedroom, she switched off the hall light so as not to wake him. So many nights ended like this. George asleep first and Ruth coming up in the dark. George feigned sleep as he heard Ruth undress. He felt her weight transfer through the mattress as she climbed in bed. From her breathing, he knew Ruth was awake and staring at the ceiling. Still he faked sleep, even tossing in a muffled snore.

And then it happened. Ruth, thinking him asleep, reached out and caressed his back. Leaned over and softly kissed his shoulder. "I love you, George," she whispered to the night.

BERTHA

On Holy Thursday, Joe ran swiftly on a hardened field road, equally upset with Mark Perkins, his parents and Jesus. Mark had denied everything about the car chase, calling Joe paranoid. "Call my folks if you don't believe me," he had said. Still, Joe could discern the lie. He had the farmer's eye and ear for honesty.

Of more immediate concern were his parents. Devout Catholics, they declared the weekend holy, and forbade him from taking Annie to the movies. He argued briefly, saying Jesus wouldn't mind him dating on Holy Saturday. That garnered him his first scolding in more than two week, so Joe decided not to further disturb the calm that had recently settled over them.

His news upset Annie because the farm increasingly occupied his weeknights. She told him that she wanted to see him more, not less. When he promised Annie two dates the following weekend, it did little to appease her. She said she didn't understand, and said goodbye, frustrated. Joe wondered, sacrilegiously, if his suffering was any less than a crucified Christ's.

Eventually the brilliance of the day dabbed at his imagined stigmata. The whole land reverberated at last with spring. Along the fence line marking the Oster farm, Joe noticed lime green asparagus spears piercing through the thatch. Stripped gophers appeared like miniature periscopes along the field road. When Joe thundered down on them, the gophers waited until the last minute before flattening and scurrying toward their holes.

Mourning doves cooed in the still bare branches of the box elder trees. Not to be outdone the year's first warblers—yellow rumps and palms—flitted on a stretch of barbed wire fence. They composed a musical score with the twitching of their tails, or a hop to a higher strand of wire.

Near the clump of pine that marked the end of Becker's farm, Joe spied another harbinger of spring, a female fox and three young kits. Their orange coats gleamed like Christmas presents beneath the evergreens. His spirits rebounded further when the Burlington Northern train roared into view. His conditioning brought him much closer to its daily crossing time before his home.

Entering the kitchen minutes later, he found Ruth humming as she peeled potatoes for supper.

"Hello, Joe. You're home before 4:30 again," she said, turning on her stool and eyeing the kitchen clock. She continued to talk as she tossed cubes of potatoes into a yellow bowl on the counter. "George will be pleased. He's anxious to start plowing with this weather."

"Saw some asparagus along Oster's fence line, Mom."

"Ready to pick? That's early."

"Not yet, it's just peeking through."

"Good. Don't forget to pick it next week when you're out running for the roses," Ruth said, somewhat distracted.

"Mom, that's the Kentucky Derby."

"What is?"

"Horses run for the roses, Mom."

"I must have roses on my mind. Well, just don't forget it when you're chasing whatever you're chasing," she said, returning to her slicing. "You better hurry up and help your father."

Joe feigned leaving, then looked back around the kitchen door. The window near the sink was cracked open, and the sweet smell of earth seeped through the screen. The breeze lifted the curtains. The lace seemed to rise and fall with Ruth's humming, as if she orchestrated its movement. He could not remember his mother humming, not in recent memory, anyway. The sound was soft and private. It reminded him of Friday nights when, with a strong north wind, he faintly heard the Troy marching band during a football game three miles away. Not the collective horn and drum, but a delicate, indecipherable whisper of melody rolling over the quaking cornstalks.

The soft notes took control of him. They made him forget Mark and Jesus. An unfamiliar happiness suddenly abounded all around him, hatched by Annie and track and spring and, now, his mother, and he didn't know how to deal with it. So he went to Ruth's side and kissed her on the cheek.

Ruth turned to him unstartled and smiled. She raised her left hand and stroked his upper arm. Her look said, "Yes, something good is happening." Then she returned to her paring.

"Don't forget that asparagus, Joe."

On Good Friday, the three of them quit their respective chores at 3 p.m. They knelt on the linoleum floor in the living room, their elbows on the green sofa, and stared up at the crucifix. The Palm Sunday frond wrapped around it was already yellowing against the patterned wallpaper. Ruth led the fifty Hail Marys while George and Joe droned their responses into the sofa cushions.

On Holy Saturday, they joined their neighbors in the long confessional lines inside St. Lawrence Church. As they snaked ever closer to forgiveness, Joe contemplated his relationship with Annie. In his St. Dominic Savio days, he believed an impure thought alone smudged his soul. How blackened must his soul be now as his relationship with Annie grew more physical? When he entered the darkness of the confessional and heard Father MacDougall sliding back the small, wooden window, he faltered. The priest's narrow face loomed dimly from the shadows behind the mesh.

"Bless me Father, for I have sinned. My last confession was two months ago," Joe began. He then entered into a litany of safe sins—pride and envy, forgotten prayers, and taking the Lord's name in vain.

"Is that all?" the priest asked when Joe finished.

"Yes, Father."

"Have you gone to Mass every Sunday? Kept the sacraments?"

"Yes, Father.

Joe heard Father McDougall slide closer. "How old are you, my son?"

"Just 18, Father."

"Are there no girlfriends in your life?"

"I wish." Joe gulped, and prayed Father McDougall hadn't heard his lying Adam's apple.

"God only forgives the sins we confess. You know that, don't you Joe?"

Joe froze. He had been recognized. How? His altar boy days? He felt his lie about to be exposed to God, Father McDougall and, worse, his mother kneeling in the adjoining confessional. But in his heart his thoughts of Annie, his searching mouth or his hand cupping her breast—these were not sins. These were beautiful things, natural things. Things his Jesus would not condemn.

"Yes, Father."

"Good, Joe. For your penance say three Our Father's and three Hail Mary's, and, during Easter Mass, pray to remain holy so you can some day be with the risen Christ." Father McDougall broke into Latin then, passing the Lord's forgiveness through the screen in a foreign whisper. Joe waited until the window slid shut, and then left the confessional, pure again in God's eyes and his own.

The next morning the Mitchells donned the best that their closets offered and sought spiritual rebirth at Easter High Mass. Sunday awoke as chilly as a tomb, but the cloudless morning convinced the Catholic women of St. Lawrence's parish to forsake their winter coats. Walking up the broad steps and through the propped open doors into the church in their pastel finery, they reminded Joe of the recently deceased red and green ducklings.

George and Ruth exchanged wedding vows in St. Lawrence's. The gothic structure looked as much a fortress as a place of God. Today, the church's well-worn bells peeled for the parish, much to the dismay of the steeple's pigeons. They darted between the church and parochial school, like gray and white cherubs heralding the Resurrection. Inside, the recently painted arched ceilings and plaster walls presented a bright, refreshing contrast to the church's somber exterior. Through the stained glass windows, the April sunshine shot muted shafts of color over the filling pews. The entire church took on a heavenly glow, as if Christ had risen from its very altar. On the supporting pillars that ringed the interior of the church hung paintings of Jesus going through the Stations of the Cross. The Mitchells always sat on the left-hand side of the church, near the tenth station showing Jesus being crucified. With Christ over their shoulders, Joe daydreamed, and Ruth snuck more money in the collection basket than George would ever have allowed if he had been awake. Their rituals fit snugly inside of the bigger pageantry of the Mass. St. Lawrence clung to the Latin service. Its holy inflections reverberated around the pillars as priest and parishioners and choir exchanged their Dominus vobiscums and et cum spiritu tuos.

Being a High Mass, the choir was in top form, and the smell of incense drifting over the parishioners like God's blessings. All around the church, the black shrouds that had covered the statues of Mary, Christ and St. Lawrence on Holy Saturday had been lifted. Sin had been overcome, folded and tucked black into lower drawers in Father MacDougall's chambers for another year.

Father MacDougall's sermon centered on how Christ's resurrection meant eternal life. His wired exuberance blasted through the church speakers so loudly that even George roused. Joe looked over at his parents during the sermon and saw them holding hands. Things *were* changing.

Easter didn't change everything. Joe still entered his dream world. Now it was a new dream dipped in possibility. In it, he defeated Mark in the mile with a last-second burst. Past the finish line, Annie caught his spent body with open arms and adoring love. George put his huge hands on Joe's shoulders and said, "Son, I'm proud of you." Ruth kissed him, tears of happiness in her eyes, before embracing George and forming a unit of parental pride. And, from out of the frenzied ring of his adoring teammates, a tall man in a double-breasted blue suit handed Joe a crisp, white document and said, "Son, you're a hell of a runner. Sign here and you've got a four-year scholarship to the University." In this dream, George said, "Go ahead, Joe, you've earned it."

Suddenly the congregation stood for the Apostle's Creed, shaking Joe from his make-believe world. He mumbled through the well-known beliefs, and slid back comfortably into the ritual. He knelt and stood, sang his hosannas and amens, watched God's body and blood turned into bread and wine. Walking down the aisle for communion, he wondered how deeply Annie clung to her Lutheran religion. His parents wouldn't approve of a mixed marriage. They believed Martin Luther a heretic, worst than Lucifer himself. Father MacDougall preached that entering a Lutheran church was a mortal sin for a Catholic. It could only be outright damnation for a former Savio of the Year.

A slot opened up along the communion rail. Kneeling, Joe shut his eyes as Father MacDougall and the altar boy approached. He felt the paten slipped under his chin and touch his throat. At the words, "Body of Christ," he received the thin and tasteless wafer of salvation onto his tongue. As the host dissolved on the roof of his mouth, a flush of warmth passed through him. Many times he questioned his faith, but when the host dissolved and sought his soul, then he truly believed.

George, Ruth and Joe carried the Lord home with them in the Impala. Anyone doubting HIS existence had to but look at spring's rebirth along the gravel road—the returning flocks of starlings like a black, flowing river in the blue sky above, the chorus of frogs rising from thawed ponds, and the maroon branches of budding dogwood in the hollows.

Joe loved Sundays. While not a governor's reprieve, it passed for a prisoner's stretch in the exercise yard. Even George rested on the seventh day, at least from mid-morning until late afternoon chores when the dairy ritual began again. After church, Joe ran to the mailbox. He plucked out the Sunday paper, as colorful and compact as a rooster pheasant. He soon nestled into George's rocker, discarded the front page with its Vietnam headline screaming at him, and spent the next 20 minutes reading every article, caption and box score on the Minnesota Twins preseason game. In the kitchen, Ruth browned chicken while shortcake awaited strawberries on the counter. Joe later laughed through Lil' Abner and was reading the second panel of Prince Valiant when George stormed into the house.

"Joe, get your work clothes on, quick," he yelled from the kitchen.

"What's wrong, George?" Ruth inquired.

"Bertha's busted through the fence and is headed for Randolph's." Then to Joe, "Get a move on, Joe, before the rest of the cows get out or cut up their udders on the barbed wire."

Joe scurried upstairs and changed out of his Sunday clothes. He slipped on his running shoes rather than work boots. Poor, miserable Bertha, he thought. Less than a week ago she had dropped a chunky bull calf. Within two days it developed scours and soon was too weak and dehydrated to rise. Mercy for the calf came on Good Friday, but unlike Christ, the calf hadn't risen.

There was no mercy for Bertha. She kicked at George when he tried to milk her swollen udder, and bounced side to side in her stall. When George let the herd outside, she butted the other cows and pranced along the length of the fence, her udder swinging and spraying milk from all teats. For two days, Bertha mooed for her lost calf. Joe wondered if cows grieved as he ran back down the stairs. He decided they did. Why else would Bertha plunge headlong through barbed wire?

Outside, he found George running helter-skelter, trying to cut off the escape routes of a dozen or so Holsteins that had wandered through the narrow gap punched through the fence. Instead of joining George, Joe ran for the pickup. In seconds, he wheeled it up to the feed room door. There he furiously filled two bushel baskets with ground feed and tossed them in the back of the truck. Hopping back behind the wheel, he rolled down the window and then roared out along the cowyard. He barreled across the bumpy oat stubble toward his father. The escapees turned curious heads in his direction. George waved his hands frantically, trying to stop Joe.

"For Pete's sake, what are you doing? You'll spook the rest of them to kingdom come."

"I didn't think the two of us could round them up on foot," Joe replied. "Besides, if we try to chase them back through that busted fence, they'll get all cut up. I figured it might be better to lead them than chase them."

George stood there looking at Joe, his hands on his heaving sides.

"Okay, spill a little out, then pull ahead another 10 yards and dump some more," George instructed, taking charge as if the feed were his idea.

Joe poured an arrow of ground feed into the stubble and then pulled the pickup ahead before stopping and dropping another mound. Cindy, an old matriarch, bit first. Soon other Holsteins fell in line along the traveling trough. Once inside the fence, George and Joe easily chased the jail breakers back into the barn, where they obediently sniffed out and entered their individual stalls. When all were locked in their stanchions, George and Joe turned their attention to Bertha.

They heard her before they saw her. Coming over a slight rise in the field road in the pickup, they caught a glimpse of the cement silo and gray roof of Randolph's dairy barn. When the whole farmscape fell into view, they spied Bertha looking over Randolph's cowyard, where 60 of their neighbor's disinterested Holsteins lay on the ground and chewed the cud of their Easter hay. Fifty yards from Bertha, George killed the engine. The dying ticks of the engine mingled with Bertha's bellows.

"Got a plan, Dad?" Joe asked.

"Yeah," George said, "but I forgot the 20-gauge and I don't think we could lift her carcass onto the truck bed anyway."

Joe eyed George with surprise. Every cow carried a dollar sign. George rarely joked about his herd.

George looked out the window and surveyed the situation. Pulling his head back inside, he asked Joe, "How fast can you run and for how far?"

"I don't know how fast, but I can run to Troy and back if you want."

"No, back to the barn is all. If I can get Bertha spooked with the truck and get her headed northward, maybe I can keep her from cutting across the fields on one side with the pickup. But that means you've got to keep her from going left. We've got to form a moving corridor. So, can you keep up with Bertha?"

"Probably for a short ways. But I don't think I'll be able to spook her if she turns on me."

George snorted. "Hell, she'll trample you if you get in her way. No, I just want you to run and yell while I honk and drive. Maybe it'll be enough to move her. She gets it into her cockamamie mind to go home, she'll run on her own. If this plan don't work, then you can run and get the shotgun."

Joe positioned himself about 20 yards off the road onto last year's soybean stubble and inched his way toward the fence. George approached Bertha with the truck lumbering in first gear. He reached the fence line to Bertha's left and was almost upon her before she acknowledged the pickup. She turned, revealing a scarlet necklace of blood where her chest had bested the barbed wire. Lowering her head, she bolted across the 10 yards that separated them and rammed the grillwork with a powerful thud. The charge jolted the pickup back a good half foot. Bertha arched her head and rolled it back over a shoulder, one eye bulging, and the other wincing from the blow. It seemed to have knocked her half unconscious, and she staggered in a circle away from the fence, kicking up old corn stalks on weakened knees. George seized the opportunity and drove the pickup against her haunches. He literally pushed her across the field road before turning the pickup straight on that path parallel to her.

Bertha stood frozen, head bowed. George pumped the horn, which elicited a glazed stare. Foam hung from Bertha's mouth, and the end of a bellow squeezed off a wet chunk to the ground.

"Now what?" Joe yelled, feeling exposed and insignificant in the open expanse.

"Let's see that fine pitching arm of yours."

"I don't pitch. I run."

George nodded, even smiled slightly. He made a circle with his hand out the cab window, indicating, "Let's go."

Joe scooped up some dirt clumps and let them fly. They exploded into dust against Bertha's flank. She didn't flinch.

"Next idea."

George inched the pickup up alongside Bertha. She noted his presence with a long, low moan of such utter despair that for a second George thought the 20-gauge might be the best answer. Instead he grabbed her tail and twisted it with all his might. The tail seemed to come alive, writhing between hand and rump like a snake as Bertha tried to free it. George squeezed harder. Bertha finally leaped forward, and they were into it.

Joe sprinted along Bertha's left flank, surprised at the speed of a one-ton cow. Thoughts of domesticated animals vanished with the black hulking blur to his right. Bertha seemed more a runaway locomotive than a Holstein. Powerful strides. Determined strides. Hooves that could kill him if he wasn't careful. They cut deep scallops into the black soil, spraying both Joe and George with dirt when she rambled their way.

George stayed tight on Bertha's right flank, honking if she slowed and speeding ahead when she tried to skirt around the cab. They had rumbled a good hundred yards before Bertha suddenly veered in Joe's direction. Joe yelled his most blood-curdling scream. This momentarily spooked Bertha's down the moving corridor. They traversed another 50 yards when Bertha again turned toward Joe, this time bearing down on him.

"Watch out Joe!" George yelled, turning the pickup in a tight arc after Bertha.

Joe altered his course slightly but kept running. He prepared to dive sideways into the dirt when he realized Bertha wasn't intent on trampling him. She didn't lower her head. Her eyes were glazed. It was as if she saw through Joe, thinking back on her dead calf, grieving again. Or else she was still knocked daffy from the grillwork.

Joe leapt onto Bertha as she rumbled by. He flung his arms around her thick neck as if he were bulldogging a rodeo steer. Only Bertha was no little dogie. Her head alone was half Joe's size. She carried him into the adjoining alfalfa field. The young growth tugged at Joe's dangling feet, and the sweet smell of shredded clover perfumed the unfolding drama.

Raising his legs, Joe hung on for his life. Bertha plowed ahead, oblivious to him. Behind him, Joe heard George's voice and the horn, but he could not make out any words. He pressed his head harder against Bertha's neck and heard her breaths climb up from her labored lungs. His arms grew numb from trying to keep his lower body away from Bertha's thundering legs. Joe felt his grasp slipping. Out of desperation or defiance, Joe used his remaining strength to climb higher on Bertha's neck until her leathery ear flapped against his face. Freeing one hand, he seized the black frond and bit into it.

Bertha reacted as if Joe's bite were a cattle prod. She jolted to the right, then whipped her head back to the left, and threw Joe somersaulting into the alfalfa. He scrambled to his feet and waited for the charge that didn't come. Bertha continued to run full bore for the cowyard. George yelled a quick "Are you all right?" Joe didn't feel any broken bones, but the fall had knocked the wind of him. He couldn't speak, so instead gave a quick wave and nod, sending George in pursuit of the fleeing cow. His breath returned about the time Bertha pranced back through the hole she had punched through the fence. Joe watched George drive right behind her up to the barn door to cut off any possible retreat.

As Joe trotted toward the cowyard, Bertha reappeared in the barn doorway. Joe heard the pickup's blaring horn, and then watched Bertha clamor over the cab. There was another sound of breaking glass, then hooves skidding on metal. A final lunge put her over the pickup's end-gate, on the ground and on a direct line toward Joe. He sought refuge behind a solid fence post. Bertha thundered by and headed again for Randolph's.

When George didn't emerge from the cab, Joe sprinted through the muck, worried. Reaching the cab, he thought he heard George crying. Pulling the door open, he found George laughing. Glass from the left front windshield was strewn across the cab; the right side glass remained intact, a cobweb of cracks emanating outward from Bertha's hoof print. George, covered in shards, looked at Joe and howled louder.

"Are you all right, Dad?"

George slid off the torn vinyl seat, chuckling. "Oh, sure, I'm fine. Don't I look fine?"

"I don't see what's so funny."

"I was just thinking," George said, shaking inside his overalls and sending small bits of glass down his pant leg, "that I haven't had a female that big in a pickup cab since I dated Leroy Hawkin's daughter, Maureen, long before your mother. Where's our girl, now?"

"Half way to Randolph's again," Joe said, motioning to the south.

"Well, that means we go to plan C."

"The shotgun?"

"No," George said. Another grin split his face. "That was plan B. Plan C is where we save the shells and you simply pull Bertha down from behind and go for her jugular. Whatever got into you to take a chunk out of her, Joe?"

"I don't know," Joe said, suddenly amused with himself. "Must be lunch time."

They both laughed. Then yet another curious thing happened. George put his arm around Joe's shoulder. "Lunch time," he laughed, holding Joe close. George started them toward the house.

"What about Bertha, Dad?"

"Let's save her for dessert."

THE FOX

Annie sat brooding in the Adirondack chair. Easter had dawned serene and pastel, like the decorated eggs nestled in the huge basket on the dining room table. Her yellow dress shone equally as bright. She received many compliments on it at St. Mark's Lutheran. Her family's annual Easter brunch followed, made special because her sister, Beth, was home from college. Now, though, her father slept off the heavy meal of ham, potatoes and gravy, Donna was reading, and Beth was somewhere visiting old high school friends, leaving Annie alone, wrapped in a sweater and boredom. The promise of a gorgeous day stretched before her as inviting as the greening lawn, but instead she sat watching a female robin hop across the grass with makings for a nest in her beak.

The robin knew it was time for courting. That's what Annie's friends were doing today. Going to the movies or bowling, driving around with their boyfriends, or simply walking together, in pairs, into the blossoming spring. Why not her and Joe?

Something else beyond Joe's absence gnawed at her. Prom lay only five weeks away, and Joe hadn't asked her yet. She had certainly sent him the right signals at Nancy's party. Now time grew short to shop for and alter a gown before May 15. In her mind, she couldn't afford to lose another day. With Joe's chores and his parents' Holy Week dating ban, she hadn't seen him in four days. Joe had shied from asking her over the phone the night before. He had seemed on the verge, but Annie heard "Gunsmoke" on the TV, and assumed Joe lacked privacy.

Thinking about that call, Annie tried to imagine Joe's house. She had never been on a farm, and could only think of the huge, square houses she saw from driving country roads. She imagined them filled with tribes of children. With kitchens half the size of a gymnasium, rows of canned corn and green beans in

Mason jars in an adjoining pantry. Porches both front and back of the house, one a handshake to visitors, the other a refuge from them. Outside, majestic oaks and cottonwoods, nearly a century old, shading chickens that scratched for insects and seeds in patchy lawns.

This state of half worry and half imagination finally spurred Annie into action. The Catholics couldn't send her to a worse hell than the one she currently experienced. She rose from the deep scoop of the Adirondack, sending the robin chirping to the trees. Then, armed with her mother's permission and the keys to the Buick, Annie went in search of the Mitchell farm.

From Troy she drove south on Highway 17. Here the freshly plowed fields stretched flat in every direction. After a mile, the blacktop curved around a lowland marsh where mallards swam in pairs. Turning the radio down, Annie heard the trill of red-winged blackbirds as she sped by. The road straightened and Annie again passed farms with half-empty corncribs and run-down outbuildings. She knew Joe lived east of the highway, but the number of the county road, if Joe had ever mentioned it, escaped her. With no cars tailing her, Annie pulled off on the shoulder of the highway as she neared a crossroad. She was deciding whether or not to turn when something in the distance caught her eye.

A quarter mile away, raising a cloud of dust, a familiar dark green pickup hotly pursued a cow. Lagging behind but giving chase, a lone figure ran. Turning off the car engine, Annie heard the pickup's horn and then laughter. The cow stopped until the pickup butted it into motion again. The pickup fanned a tail of topsoil into the air as the cow suddenly lunged to the left. She lost the whole scene momentarily in a cloud of dust. Based on their direction, however, she turned down the adjacent gravel road toward the nearest farm.

As Annie had imagined, an ancient cottonwood did rise to the west of the farmhouse, its age revealed by the girth of its trunk and a quadrant of dead branches 70 feet up. The dirt driveway looped around it. The house appeared appropriately large and square, too. But it, and the rest of the farmstead, didn't match her image of pastoral bliss. The two-storied house's front porch sagged, and fist-size holes pocked its screens. Rust from the screens stained the porch's siding in vertical veins of orange. Peeling paint hung in blistered scallops on the house's west side. The farm buildings seemed in worse disrepair. The barn's weathered wood carried the hue of sunburned skin, and black blotches on the roof demarked where shingles had been patched with tar. Several windows contained cardboard panes. Only a huge garden, the black soil recently turned, seemed alive.

Annie curled around the cottonwood and pulled to a stop in front of the farmhouse. The smell of the barnyard assaulted her as she strolled to the porch door. She entered, noting that the screens on this porch were intact. She reached to knock on the inside door when Ruth opened it.

"Yes?"

Ruth's sudden presence startled Annie, and, for a moment, she couldn't speak. "I'm looking for Joe Mitchell. Is this the Mitchell farm?"

"Yes, it is. I'm Ruth, Joe's mother." Ruth looked over Annie's shoulder toward the fields. "Joe's not here right now. He and his father are trying to round up a loose cow."

"Yes, I know. I saw the pickup. I'm Annie Jensen, by the way."

Ruth's eyebrows arched. "So you're Annie." She made a mental note to tease Joe on his good taste. "Well, where are my manners? Come in and have something to drink. Joe should be in shortly."

Ruth shut the door behind them. "Burr. Still too cold out there," Ruth said, rubbing her thin arms. "Is Joe expecting you?"

"No, I don't think so," Annie said vacantly.

She was busy taking in the kitchen. It, at last, lived up to her expectations, almost matching St. Mark's church kitchen in size. Knickknacks—mostly porcelain chickens and cornhusk dolls—gazed down from the tops of cupboards. Tin canisters containing flour, sugars—cane and brown, and salt formed a cityscape along the far countertops. A lace doily lay beneath a chipped bowl that held waxed fruit on the massive white freezer beside her. Newly washed dishes dried in a plastic rack by the sink. An egg-shell white hutch set off its contents of rose-patterned china, the cups suspended proudly from little hooks. A dried-flower arrangement adorned the kitchen table.

"Have you eaten?" Ruth asked. "I've got strawberry shortcake. The berries were frozen from the patch last year, but they're still tasty and the whip cream is fresh."

"That sounds wonderful, thank you."

"Sit yourself, then, while I dish it up."

Annie looked around further while Ruth pulled a bowl of strawberries and whipping cream from the refrigerator. Through the doorway Annie saw the living room. A huge oil-burning stove the size of a bank safe loomed along one wall. Colorful afghans covered most of the low-backed green couch, and the Sunday paper sat in a nearby rocking chair. The furniture stood worn but solid. The whole house had a just scrubbed scent.

"Here you go," Ruth said. She placed a huge wedge of shortcake in front of Annie, the berries half buried beneath an avalanche of whip cream. "Would you like some milk, coffee?"

"Oh, this is fine, really," Annie said.

"Oh, how about some milk to please a dairyman's wife. It's creamy, not like your store bought."

"Yes, then, please."

"That's better." Ruth returned to the refrigerator for milk. On the way, she ignited the burner beneath the still warm coffee pot on the stove. Annie noted Ruth was still dressed from church, and the apricot-colored dress revealed her sculpted figure. The build was a female version of Joe, as was Ruth's blond hair.

"You have a lovely house, Mrs. Mitchell."

"Call me Ruth, and thank you. I do try to keep it nice, but it's hard." She surveyed the kitchen and noted both its tidiness and age. "A farm's a dirty place." Ruth chuckled. "But don't start complimenting this old place too much or I'll take you into the basement. We've got mushrooms growing out of the dirt floor down there."

"I didn't mean any offense."

"I know. I'm teasing. Besides, I don't think you're here for a house tour."

Annie blushed, a tone midway between the whip cream and red berries before her.

"I'm curious about Joe, is all," Annie said, shrugging her shoulders. "How he lives. He doesn't talk much about home."

Ruth moved to answer the percolating coffee pot. She secured one of the china coffee cups from the hutch. Easter Sunday and a guest warranted her best.

"No, I don't imagine Joe would."

"Why is that?"

"Well, he's anxious to get away from all this." Ruth paused, coffee pot in hand. "A farm's a lot like a marriage. It's great if you're in love, but no thrill if it's been prearranged."

Ruth poured both cups to the brim, set the pot down and joined Annie at the table. She scooped a teaspoon of sugar and eddied it carefully into the steaming liquid. "Some people are determined to work at it once saddled, but Joe's doesn't want any part of it."

"Does that disappoint you?" Annie asked.

"Heavens, no. I'm glad he's got choices. I wish he would stay because I love him, and if he leaves, well, that presents a hardship for George and me. But you young people have different dreams these days."

"Do you know what Joe's dreams are?"

"My, you get to the point. You're the one he's in love with. I thought you could tell me."

Annie blushed a second time.

"Oh, I'm being a mother hen. Forgive me," Ruth said. "I'm really not sure. We don't share as much as we should in this family." Ruth caught herself. "My goodness, I'm telling you things not even my sister knows. Well, I've started. We're kind of a quiet family. A bit closed."

"Why is that?" Annie asked with true curiosity.

Ruth shrugged.

"What would Joe do if . . ." Annie hesitated, "he left?"

"Oh, he'll leave someday soon," Ruth said, a glimpse of sorrow escaping from her eyes. "Only duty keeps him here now. And then? Then he should do something to help people. Joe's got a kind heart. He's willing to give so much, and hopefully the right person will recognize that. That's what I hope for him once he leaves here."

Ruth sipped her coffee. "What about you, after graduation?"

"College. I'm waiting to hear from the University. And Mankato State."

Ruth tried to imagine the life in front of Annie. "We never had such opportunities when I was your age. Now girls like you think nothing of it."

The whine of an engine cut the conversation short. Ruth stood up to see the pickup. George was quite visible through the missing section of the windshield, but the shattered glass on the passenger side blocked Joe from view. Both emerged from the pickup, doffed their hats, and laughed as they swatted the dust off their clothes.

Joe's smile disappeared when he saw Annie. He had wondered whose car was parked in front, but figured it was one of Ruth's friends. Now, here he stood, blackened from the chase. The dirty side of his life he never wanted to show to Annie. He felt like a turtle out of its shell, incapable of moving.

"Hello, Joe, bet you didn't expect to see me here," Annie said.

"No, I didn't," Joe answered, looking plaintively at Ruth for an explanation.

"Well, I don't even know who you are, but I'm glad you're here," George said, stepping through the awkwardness. "We could use another body to round up Bertha."

"Dad."

"Oh, George, hush. Annie, this is my husband, George, as you might have guessed. George, this is Annie Jensen, a friend of Joe's."

"Pleased to meet you, Mr. Mitchell." Annie reached to shake his hand.

"Oh, you don't want to grab onto my hand till it's washed," George said.

Annie withdrew her hand. "Who's Bertha?"

"Bertha's the cockeyed cow that Joe and I have been spending the better part of this Easter Sunday afternoon trying to corral."

"She's still out there, then?" Ruth asked.

"Somewhere between here and the Iowa border by now," George said. "Don't worry. She'll get hungry soon, and probably lope into the barnyard on her own."

"In that case, you're probably through with Joe for a while. Joe, why don't you show Annie around outside?"

"I'd like to change, first, Mom." Turning to Annie, he said, "I'll be right back."

Annie chatted with Joe's parents beneath the sound of shoes dropping on the floor overhead and then running water in the first floor bathroom. Shortly, Joe emerged in faded jeans and a navy T-shirt, his hair wet. He took Annie's hand, but said nothing as they walked out the porch.

"Joe, are you mad at me for coming?" Annie asked when they reached the drive.

"Not mad. Just embarrassed." They were by the garden now.

"Why?"

Joe waved his arm around to encompass the farmstead. "Just look at this place."

"I would like to."

"What? This pig sty? It's just crumbling buildings and cow shit."

"It's your home, Joe," Annie said, reclaiming his hand. "Come on, I've never been on a farm. Show me what goes on here."

"You're serious," Joe said, slowing shaking his head.

"Yes, I am. Show me what the other part of your life is like."

Reluctantly, Joe agreed. They crossed the wide lawn toward the barn, walking parallel to Ruth's clothesline. Inside the barn, the stench of the cows greeted them. Annie wrinkled her nose slightly, then smiled at Joe to lead the way. He started with the nearby generator, which, he explained, ran the vacuum system that helped suck the milk by machine from the cows. They walked deeper into the barn. For once Joe was glad for his father's fastidiousness about cleaning, for the alleyways and main floor were swept smooth. He worked an empty stanchion so Annie could see how the cows were penned and released. Next he explained that cows had four stomachs and chewed their regurgitated food, or cud. He turned Annie to face Sally, and pointed at the cud rising visibly up her throat like an underground mole. The Holstein chewed her cud for about a minute before reswallowing.

Annie seemed genuinely enthralled with it all, and asked countless questions. How do the cows remember which stalls were theirs? By smell initially, then memory. What would happen if you didn't milk the cows for a day? They would first leak their milk and eventually "dry up." What happens to the calves? The heifers are raised to enter the herd, the young bulls are castrated, raised as steers and sent to the slaughter house at about 700 pounds. Annie grimaced at the mention of castration and slaughter.

As they walked down the middle of the barn, Annie's presence spooked several of the cows. They rose agitatedly in their stanchions. Two raised their tails and either sprayed copious streams of yellow urine onto the floor or plopped manure into the gutters behind them. Annie backed away.

"See what I mean?" Joe said, witnessing Annie's revulsion. "I spend every day in this. I clean this up."

"It's nothing to be ashamed of. It's what you were born into."

Her honesty disarmed him. Still, he didn't want her to associate him with the task of cleaning out gutters. "Why don't we get out of here," Joe suggested.

"No, it's all right," Annie said, believing she had somehow offended him. "I'm just not use to any of this. It's really quite amazing." She looked around the barn. "Do you have any calves?"

At the south end of the barn, in small square pens, the newest crop of calves frolicked. The youngest was Venus. Joe grabbed a nippled bucket from the adjacent feed room. He took two scoops of powdery white milk replacer and plopped it into the bucket. Then he filled the bucket half full with water and mixed the powder by hand into a creamy slurry before handing the bucket to Annie.

"Annie, meet Venus," he said. "Annie, Venus is hungry."

Annie eyed Joe inquisitively.

"Go on. She's ready to be weaned, so if she's hungry enough she might take the nipple."

Annie hefted the bucket, stepped gingerly into the manger at the front of the pen, and held the bucket firmly. Venus stuck her head through the manger's restraining slats and flipped the rubber nipple back and forth with her black nose. But Venus wouldn't suck.

"Take a little milk on your finger and get Venus started there first and lead her to the nipple," Joe encouraged.

"You're kidding, of course," Annie said.

"No, it'll work. Give it a try."

Annie dipped two fingers daintily into the liquid and held them out. Venus sniffed Annie's dripping white fingers and then began to suck them, first tentatively, then with vigor. Annie let out a shriek that sent Venus spinning around the pen kicking her hooves in the air.

"That a girl, Annie," Joe barked. "A few more screams of encouragement like that and we'll have this calf weaned in no time."

"It felt so strange. Its tongue is so rough. I thought it was going to swallow my hand."

"Try again," Joe chuckled. "Only this time put your fingers *under* the nipple."

"You're sure she won't hurt me?"

"I promise."

This time, Annie approached the pen with death-row prisoner wariness. She didn't retreat when Venus again came searching for the milk, however. As Joe instructed, Annie wet the same two fingers, this time resting the bucket's nipple on top of them. Venus took Annie's fingers with the same relish, her raspy tongue encircling them as if they were her mother's teat. Annie allowed Venus to suck her fingers until the nipple, too, was wrapped by that tongue, then she deftly pulled her hand away. Venus seemed momentarily bewildered, stopping in mid-suck. Then she chewed away on the fake rubber nipple, swallowing the milk in huge draughts.

"She's eating, she's eating," Annie said, holding the bucket steady. "Look at her go! Good girl, Venus."

Joe watched Annie lean into her task. Her urine-spotted tennis shoes stood in stark relief against the manger's dark cement. She cooed encouragement as Venus slowly drained the pail, her delicate features alive with amusement. Her hands dripped with milk. A smile wider than Venus' crossed her face, and Joe knew he was hopelessly in love.

Venus, with a white ring of froth around her greedy mouth, gave the pail an unexpected butt. The remaining milk sloshed upward, splashing Annie full in the face. She shrieked, startling the five nearest Holsteins to their feet. Joe leapt to her rescue, offering her his shirt to dry her face while Venus tried to pull the dropped bucket through the manger slats.

"Are you all right?"

Annie started laughing. "That little pig," she said. Then looking down at herself, she added, "I'm quite a pig myself."

"Do you need some dry clothes?"

"No, I'm fine, but maybe I've seen enough of the barn."

"I think so, too. Let's go outside."

In the next 15 minutes, Joe found himself explaining more about the farm than he thought possible. Annie asked him why nothing grew in the field adjacent to the cow yard, and Joe explained that corn had indeed been planted two days earlier, but had not yet burst through the soil. Planting any earlier, he informed, might expose the seeds to a killing frost. Joe stooped in the field to unbury a kernel, and found himself explaining that the kernel was pink, not yellow, because it had been treated. He rolled the kernel over in his palm to show the first protruding hint of germination at its apex. He did not feel foolish explaining all this. Nor did he know if Annie was simply being polite or expressing genuine interest. He felt surprisingly proud of his knowledge.

Their walking classroom took them down the field road behind the farm buildings. There were no attractions to point out, no agronomy lesson to expound upon with the gray fields disked and barren around them. So they strolled along the windbreak of jack pine west of the garden until they reached the gravel road. They were about to turn back toward the driveway when Joe stopped dead in his tracks. He pointed like a setter over the road.

"Look, there's a fox," he whispered. Annie strained to see it by looking down Joe's extended arm. She saw only some railroad tracks running parallel to the road.

"I don't see anything."

"By the tracks, right in front of us. Look at the dead pine and come this way," he said, directing her with his finger. "It's lined up right with it."

Annie spotted it. A splash of orange beside some brush, stepping lightly along the edge of the rail bed where the gravel apron met the weeds. It was closer than she had thought, no more than 40 yards. While Annie watched, the fox crawled almost imperceptibly ahead, ears back and plumed tail flat.

"What's it doing?" Annie whispered.

"Hunting. There's a cottontail on the rail about 20 feet to its right. See it?"

Annie followed the rails. Only its twitching ears revealed the rabbit.

"Yes! Joe, it's not really going to kill that rabbit, is it?"

"If it's clever enough it will."

Annie did not want that to happen. Rabbits were cute. Besides, it was Easter.

"We've got to stop it. Let's yell or something."

"The fox has to live, too," Joe said harshly. "Let's watch and see what happens."

"Joe, please!"

Joe grabbed Annie's arm. "Be quiet, I said!"

Hurt, Annie watched the ancient ritual unfold. The fox flattened ever lower to the ground, moving one foot closer, and then another. The rabbit nibbled on the grass sprouting between the rail timbers. Soon fox and rabbit drew almost parallel, with only a slight rise and the steel rail separating them. The rabbit's ears twitched and it half turned, sensing danger. For a brief second, nothing moved. The fox crouched so still it seemed frozen. Then the rabbit resumed eating. In a flash the fox leapt for it. As if spring-loaded, the rabbit bounded forward with a crazy, twisting motion. All was blurred motion for a moment, with both animals scrambling for the advantage. The rabbit shot down the tracks. In hot pursuit, the fox sprinted over the timbers, its plumed tail twirling like a propeller. The fox was no match for the cottontail in a game of misdirection. But the rabbit seemed bewildered. As if in a flume, it declined escape over the rails, and hopped pell-mell down the center of the track. With a quick swipe, the fox knocked the back feet from under the cottontail, and in the next moment, sank its sharp teeth into the rabbit's rump. The rabbit squeaked, but then the fox moved quickly up its body, releasing rump for neck and finishing the kill with a quick chomp.

Annie turned away. She had never seen anything killed before. The brutality disturbed her, and she suddenly wanted to be away from the place.

"Are you all right, Annie?"

"No," she answered angrily and yanked her arm free of Joe's grasp. "Why didn't you stop it? I asked you to stop it, and you didn't."

"Why should I have?"

"Why? Because you could have saved that poor rabbit."

"So you want me to save the rabbit and let the fox die, is that it?" Joe asked, nonplussed.

"It's just that the rabbit didn't have a chance. And I asked you to stop it."

Joe turned from Annie back to the fox. It bounded with conviction toward the evergreens, the rabbit dangling lifeless from its mouth.

"Annie, come with me," he said gently.

"Why?" Annie said, still hot. "I suppose you want me to watch it eat the damn thing, too."

"Not her. Them."

"Them?"

"Annie, come with me, please," Joe beckoned, tugging at both her hands.

His soothing overtures convinced her to follow. They walked in silence across the rail bed, and followed the fox's path toward the edge of the pine. Occasional streaks of red blood appeared on the new growth alfalfa, marking their way.

Despite the fact they had not spoken for several minutes, Joe raised a finger to his lips and signaled for Annie to be quiet. They had crossed several hundred yards of open field, and now stood on the south side of Becker's woods. Together, they bent under the canopy of spruce branches. The stand of pine had been planted, part of a DNR conservation effort during the Depression. Joe's course took them perpendicular across the rows. They slowly brushed aside branches. A rusty carpet of pine needles cushioned their steps. Joe slowed their pace, and they skulked forward together. Several times Joe stopped completely. He checked the wind, which blew softly in their faces and gently swished the pine boughs. Then he would commence again, each time reminding Annie not to speak by raising his finger to his lips. They traveled about 100 feet this way. It took many long minutes.

A squeeze of her hand alerted Annie to stop. Joe signaled her to her knees. Imagining and dreading what she was about to see, Annie hesitated, then complied. She crawled by Joe's side, and suddenly realized they were hunting in the same fashion, at the same pace, as the fox had the rabbit. They approached the edge of the stand. Only two rows remained before open field. Annie saw the blue sky. Softly but with purpose, Joe touched Annie's shoulder. He did not have to point. There, on a nearby dirt mound, no more than 30 feet in front of them, stood the fox. At her feet lay the rabbit, and three fox kits. With a bloody nose, the fox dipped into the rabbit to tear off a chunk of furry flesh. The three kits were obviously new to this meal. Although they snarled and nosed at the flesh, they consumed none. One kit left the meat and tried to suckle at the visible teats on the female fox. She nipped at the kit and sent it rolling with a front paw. By then, its siblings had caught on. They ripped tiny bits of meat free, and chewed awkwardly, discovering at last a purpose for their jaws. Soon they growled and tugged over the stringy sinew.

Satisfied with the lesson, the female fox consumed part of the rabbit herself. Then she hauled the remains of the carcass into the field and covered it with dirt. Only then did she return to the lair and let the kits suckle. While they churned away at her belly, she licked their bloody faces. The task eventually finished, she yawned and looked around her. Her gaze settled on Joe and Annie.

Annie marveled at the sight. The fox shone an even brighter, richer orange in the shadow of the trees. Her ears were black-tipped, her snout regal. Annie lay close enough to see the fine, long whiskers fan out from it. There was no sound save the slight moaning of the wind in the pines, and the kits' faint smacking. The fox did not rise in a panic. Several minutes passed, eyes never leaving eyes. Finally, the kits slowed in their nursing. The vixen rose and slowly nudged them, one by one, into the hole of the den. Like a sentinel, she stood above the hole in the earth, looking at the two intruders. Then she slipped beneath the earth.

"Time to go," Joe said. Slowly they rose, turned and walked away without looking back. Soon they reached the other side of the stand of trees.

"Do you understand now?"

"Yes," Annie said.

THE FIRST RACE

Mark plopped into the bus seat, raised his aviator sunglasses and tossed his spikes to the floor. Like the rest of the team, he was excited about this first meet. The weeks of conditioning were a burden to be endured, like taking driver's training when you had been laying rubber and parallel parking blindfolded for years. Mark suffered less in training than many because he came directly off four months of basketball. He never pushed himself to the gut-retching state the sophomores did to please Coach O'Reilly. No, he did as he pleased, and it pleased him to work hard but never that hard.

That tact seemed totally acceptable to Mark because he rarely lost. He loved winning and usually did on sheer natural ability. Plus, he entered every competitive contest believing he would win. When he lost, he didn't curse or sulk. In fact, he quickly congratulated the winner, both out of amazement that he had been bested and because he desired a closer look at his better so he could fixate on him until their next meeting. He stripped any loss down to its bare bones. Did someone box him in? Did he start his kick too late? On the rare occasion that, after his dissection, he determined the other runner was just plain swifter, he would then train with a vengeance. With a rematch, Mark invariably won. To his coaches' frustration, however, Mark's defeats usually came during the final conference meets or at the district level, where no chance for a rematch existed. No amount of preaching about how he had to run against time vs. opponents ever worked. Mark required a living, breathing target to focus on. When one surfaced, he attacked it full bore.

The season's first meet gave Mark a gauge on the year's competition. Had someone else spawned a Crazy Nolan, who apparently possessed the lungs of a pearl diver? Had a star transferred from another school into the conference? Franksburg, today's competition, lacked lung-men, according to Coach

O'Reilly. Mark knew he would win today's mile, just as sure as he was that this seat would be waiting for him on the team bus.

Mark's seat sat six rows back, right side, aisle. Far enough back from the coaches so he could goof off. Far enough back not to be associated with the goodie two shoes behind the coaches—simple Bobby Thorton, Crazy Nolan, Jack Deiter, Tom Woodard and Joe Mitchell sat well in front of him. Yet close enough to the coaches to acknowledge his role as team co-caption. And not so far back to acknowledge the existence of the sophomores and senior retreads bolting down the backseats. They were nothing to him, guys trying to letter out of sheer perseverance. No, the front/center/right side of the bus was the place to be, between the axles for a smooth ride, away from the exhaust, and protected from the sun. Surrounded by a few select runners he either liked or respected. Scott Hamre, his co-captain and their top 440 man. Danny Probst, because they were drinking buddies. Henry Thompson because he was black, and Mark thought that having a black friend was cool indeed in rural Troy. From aisle seat, row six, right side, Mark felt he commanded the best spot on the bus.

Mark found himself in a similar position during the second lap of the year's first mile run. Sixth runner behind the pacesetters. Inside lane to run the race in the fewest steps. Far enough ahead of the dregs to avoid getting trapped, and close enough to the leaders to pounce once they tired.

Runners always went out too fast in the first meet, Mark knew from experience. The first real race negated all the coaches taught about pacing. Adrenaline blasted the anxious runners off the starting line. Mark hated an early fast pace because he was not a good sprinter. In fact, that prompted his switch to the mile. Coach O'Reilly believed Nolan the superior sprinter, which became more important in a shorter distance race. Mark won distance races on a constant, smooth gliding gait—a necessity for the 1,000+ steps required to circle the quarter-mile track four times.

Despite the fast-opening pace, Mark felt invincible. The early April winds made stripping out of his warm sweats difficult, but in the heat of the race the breeze served as a coolant. He started the third lap passing a tiring orange-jerseyed Franksburg runner.

"Go get 'em, Mark," he heard Danny Probst yell from the track infield.

Five yards in front of him, bunched together, ran Franksburg's two legitimate milers, followed closely by Tom Woodard and Joe Mitchell. Woodard he had counted on, but Joe surprised him. But then, Joe kept surprising him. A month ago, Mark viewed him only as an annoyance, like an ugly pimple that surfaced and would soon disappear. Mark initially wrote off Annie's coolness as spite. Now he knew Annie spurned his advances because of Joe. Since the night Mark caught Joe and Annie necking, he had vowed to break the code of Annie's attraction.

At the moment, he tried to break down Joe's strengths as a runner. Mark lacked an accurate gauge because Joe spent his practices racing fence posts. Closing the gap rapidly between them, though, Mark spotted his flaws. Joe virtually sprinted to keep pace, his arms flailing wildly. His stride was too short because his legs were too short. Another runner trying to make it on heart, Mark thought to himself. He waited until the start of the backstretch before he blew past him. Both runners exchanged sideways glances, and Mark suppressed a comment when he saw Joe struggling. No need to mock.

The nearest Franksburg runner, a skinny, red-headed kid with back acne peeking over the neckline of his jersey, fell next to Mark's surge. Woodard entered his sights, and Mark prepared to gobble him up. Instead he waited until they rounded the track in front of the bleachers. Might as well get some cheers, he thought, and sure enough, the few diehard fans and girlfriends who followed the team to Franksburg cheered his advance.

With one lap left, Mark concentrated on Number 23 in front of him. This was Stockland, Franksburg's best miler, the one O'Reilly earmarked as Mark's competition today. Stockland was only a sophomore. Mark had yet to run him into the ground. Today was the day.

With 330 yards to go, Mark moved into lane 2 to pass Stockland. Determined, Stockland tried to pull away. From across the track, it looked like a gazelle trying to elude a cheetah. Both were obviously gifted runners. For 40 yards they ran parallel. They became one blur driven by four legs. Finally, Mark inched ahead and slipped into the inside lane. The move seemed to suck the life force out of Stockland. He looked over his shoulder for more challengers. Reassured, he gladly assumed a second-place pace.

Mark broke the tape 20 yards ahead of Stockland. Coach O'Reilly only briefly congratulated him, however, before rushing back gleefully to the finish line. Mark turned to see the cause of this fuss, and witnessed Joe nipping Woodard for third.

"Way to go, Joe," Coach O'Reilly said, holding his tired runner upright. "You've just earned your first point toward lettering."

All Joe wanted to do was collapse, but Coach O'Reilly kept pummeling him on the back. He had not counted on Joe "on paper." And now, in his first race, Joe surprised him, surprised them all.

Mark turned away, displeased. He passively accepted his teammates' congratulations, then stretched out in silence, removed his spikes, and walked barefoot to the bus. He plopped down, fuming. Suddenly, row six, right side, aisle seat, lost some luster. Even in winning, Joe stole his thunder. Mark wanted to lash out at him. But pummeling him now would be the end of Annie. He continued to seethe as the last two events ended noisily somewhere behind him. Soon the happy Troy thinclads boarded the bus, their first win of the season tucked convincingly away.

"Really a great race, Mark," Bobby Thorton said admiringly as he walked down the middle of the bus. Mark ignored him. "You hurt or something? You need something?" Bobby asked.

"Nah, just leave me alone Bobby," he answered dejectedly, wedging his bare feet into the back of the seat in front of him.

Joe, the only new senior on the team, accepted lots of congratulations on the bus and, later, at his locker. He beamed under the praise. The race had unfolded like a dream. Joe really had no concept of what to expect or what pace to run when the race started. He simply followed the leaders the first two laps. He felt weightless in his spikes and thin uniform, and didn't tire until the final lap. Then, near the end of the race, he saw Woodard faltering, and realized he still had a kick. Now Tom stood among those shaking his hand, and Joe felt a deeper friendship spawning.

Into these happy thoughts, he heard Crazy Nolan's cries of protest. It mixed uneasily with laughter from the toilet area. Joe shot a quick glance toward Coach O'Reilly's office. He apparently heard Crazy's cries, but ignored them. Already, he was busily recording everyone's performance.

"Don't worry," Dave Wilson said, shedding his tank-top down the locker row. "It's just an initiation into the team. If you win a race as a sophomore, you get a swirly. Coach approves of the practice. He says it binds us as a team. Let's go watch."

Dave lifted Joe off the bench by the arm and hauled him into the john. There, in the narrow room, Mark and Danny Probst held Crazy over a toilet. No one could see Crazy, except for the top of his legs above the stall wall, unless they stood right outside the stall's door. Those privileged few saw Crazy's spidery arms and vise grip fingers clasp the porcelain, and keep Mark and Danny from plunging his head into the just-flushed bowl.

"Don't flush until his head's down. Now we have to wait," Mark said.

"I thought he was down. He's got the arms of a gibbon," Danny retorted.

"Hey guys, I'm really not into this," Crazy protested fruitlessly.

"Well then you shouldn't have won the 880, Craze," Danny said in a brotherly tone. He adjusted his grip on Crazy's legs. "Quit wiggling and make it easy on yourself. It's tradition. We'll be quick."

The blood rushing to Crazy's head and looking at his teammates' crotches upside down drained his resistance. "Okay, then, but wait a minute. I'll tell you when," Crazy said.

"Well, hurry up. We can't hold you all day," Mark said.

Crazy collected himself. "Can I say some final words?"

"Sure, but like I said, do it fast."

The two seniors struggled with Nolan's long legs as Crazy composed himself. A calm settled over his face and his arms relaxed.

"You've lost that loving feeling. Oh, wo. That loving feeling," he said slowly.

"Flush and dunk," said Mark.

"You've lost that loving feeling. Now it's gone, gone, gone."

And Crazy was, down into the bowl, the rest of the Righteous Brothers' lyrics disappearing below the water line. One quick dunk and they pulled Crazy back. He gasped, but when they put him down and he emerged from the ordeal soaked from the neck up, he smiled to the approving roar of his teammates.

"That was fun. Who's next?" Mark inquired from the open stall door. "Any other sophomores rise above dog meat today?"

"Craze was the only one," Dave said.

"Ah, nuts," I was just starting to enjoy myself." Mark scanned the faces in the cramped room. "How about a new rule? Anyone "new" to the team this year getting a point gets a swirl."

Joe instantly knew Mark meant him. Before he could escape, the mob sided with its co-captain. Only Joe was twice as strong as Crazy. He grabbed the doorframe and proved immovable until they pounded on his fingers. Joe released his grip, and his world turned upside down. He repeated Crazy's handstand on the stool. His tank-top fell over his face, blinding him. He felt Mark's and Danny's strong grip around his calves and ankles.

"It's no use, Joe," Dave said from over the wall. "Might as well give in."

"It's not so bad, really," Crazy chimed in.

"Yeah, Joe, we'll be gentle," Mark said.

Reassured by Dave, and wanting acceptance by the team, Joe quit resisting. "Okay, but . . ."

Before he could finish, they plunged him into the bowl. More like dropped him, as Joe's head banged on the porcelain. His mouth opened in pain, and he gulped water. Joe panicked when his captors made no move to lift him out. He kicked out with his feet, freeing himself but falling on his knees on the tile floor. Joe choked and gasped for breath. A small gash beneath his scalp trickled blood over his left ear. Crawling outside the door, the first drops of his blood spotted the tile.

"What do you think you're doing, Mark?" Dave shoved him roughly against the wall.

"Hey, he slipped. Okay?"

"Slipped, my ass. You dropped him on purpose."

"Back off, Dave, or you'll be next."

"Yeah? You and whose army is going to pick me up."

Mark put his hands around Dave's neck. Dave reciprocated. For a moment, they twisted in the room like two Greco wrestlers.

"What's going on in here?"

They turned to find Coach DeAngelo glaring at them.

Dave released his grip. Mark more reluctantly broke his.

"We were just giving swirlies to today's first time winners," Mark said first.

DeAngelo eyed them suspiciously. "Dave?"

Dave remained quiet, trying to calm down. He liked Mark enough to not rat him out.

DeAngelo noticed the blood on Joe's face.

"What happened to Joe?" he asked the room. Again, silence.

"I slipped. They were holding me for a swirly, and my hand slipped off the toilet."

Mark and Joe exchanged glances, but neither said more.

When no other explanations came forth, DeAngelo dropped the issue. "Joe, let's see about that cut. The rest of you, let's not ruin a good day. Go shower and go home."

The room emptied, leaving DeAngelo and Joe alone.

"Is that what really happened? You slipped?"

"Close enough," Joe said, wincing as DeAngelo dabbed at his cut with a paper towel.

"I don't think you need stitches. Head wounds always bleed worse than the damage. You feel woozy?" He continued to dab as the cut began to clot.

"No, I'm fine."

"Well, if you're still hurting in the morning, go see Doc Crow."

DeAngelo threw the bloody towel into the trash. "You ran a good race today, Joe. You've got potential. Like I told the rest. Go home and savor it."

"Thanks, Coach."

DeAngelo, too, departed. Joe examined the top of his skull as best he could in the mirror. Then he stripped out of his uniform and let it fall wet to the floor. Bobby was there in a flash, retrieving it.

"You okay, Joe?" Bobby asked with concern.

"Thanks, I'm fine, Bobby, really."

Joe walked to the showers, and stood with others under the soothing warmth of the nozzles. He let the pulsating spray clean his scalp. Looking across the shower past the naked torsos, he spied Mark beneath a steamy spray. Mark caught his gaze and leered back. Mark turned off his shower, pointed his finger like a pistol, and mock fired.

THE ATOMIC SIT-UP

Coach O'Reilly's good mood from his first victory disappeared early the following morning.

Taking the trash out in the pouring rain, he discovered the tops of his garbage cans welded shut. One of his industrial arts students thanking him for a third quarter D, no doubt. He spent the better part of the morning trying to figure out which one of society's future tradesmen had permanently raccoon-proofed his cans. Through the day's shop classes, he ogled his students like the Gestapo to uncover the smirk or red face that belied guilt. Eventually, he deduced that Pat Spalding was the culprit. Another farm boy, Pat earned his D not for incompetence, but sloppiness. Pat argued at length that a job was good enough when Coach O'Reilly demanded perfection. In Pat's world of busted combines and twisted axles, perfection mattered little. Getting back to work did. Coach O'Reilly resented Pat for his belligerent attitude and frequent disruption of class. He gave Pat a passing D based solely on his welding skills. Pat could spot a bead better than anyone.

Coach O'Reilly hovered around Pat the whole hour. He noted Pat's furtive glances in his direction as his other charges learned that a carburetor was as intricate in its compartments as the human heart, and that a 350 V8 was one big honking engine. When beads of sweat appeared on the back of Pat's neck, Coach O'Reilly set to bounce. Just then, a jack slipped and a '61 Buick Skylark came down on Pat's right foot. Despite two smashed toes and a shoe filling with blood, Pat seemed relieved. Instead of expelling Pat, Coach O'Reilly hustled him to Doc Crow's in his station wagon.

Coach O'Reilly had not returned from his ambulatory run when classes ended and the track team meandered into the gym. The baseball team simply scrapped practice with the spring torrents. The track team could still run the halls. Coach DeAngelo, unaware of O'Reilly's emergency, left school at the bell for a scheduled dental appointment. Word of the shop accident and Coaches O'Reilly's and DeAngelo's absences passed through the team faster than any baton exchange. Most of the team wanted to split. They turned to their co-captions for direction. Perkins and Hamre conferred, and decided they should spend a half-hour on calisthenics in case Coach O'Reilly returned. They didn't want to invoke his wrath. The team groaned, but obeyed. They watched the large black hands on the gymnasium clock crawl slowly toward 3:30 p.m. as they stretched, did crunches and pushups, and ran wind sprints. As the half-hour expired, several began jogging for the door.

"Hey, hey, hey, not so fast," Mark yelled. The deserters stopped in their tracks, and reluctantly returned to the group. Mark eyed them all mischievously. "Before we go, we're going to see who's the toughest guy on this team. We're going to see who can do an atomic sit-up."

"What the hell is that?" Danny Probst asked. He leaned like a prostitute against the gym wall, impatient with having to remain.

"Something my brother in 'Nam wrote me about. It's a sensory deprivation thing. The Marines use it with Viet Cong prisoners. When they keep Charlie blindfolded and plug their ears with mud and lay them flat on their backs, the platoon hardly has to watch the VC at all," Mark said, enjoying the rapt attention his references to Vietnam received. The war drew nearer for the seniors. They hungered for true pictures of the soldier's experience, and seemed to like this one, which showed the VC vulnerable.

"The reason was, with their senses impaired, Charlie couldn't sit up," Mark continued.

"Save it for the sophomores, Mark," Danny said, speaking for the group.

"It's true. My brother doesn't lie. You don't lie when you face death everyday. You don't believe it, I dare you to be the first volunteer."

"You're on," Danny said without hesitation, unhinging himself from the wall.

"Bobby, go get us something that will work as a blindfold. And find some chewing gum in O'Reilly's office," Mark commanded. Bobby Thorton scurried toward the door on his short legs. In a short time he returned with a baseball jersey and a double pack of Juicy Fruit.

"I'll let you chew the gum since it's going in your ears, Danny," Mark said. "And while you do that, here's how an atomic sit-up works." They all closed in now, starting to believe. "We tie this jersey around your eyes till you can't see anything, and I mean anything. Then you cram the gum in your ears. If you can hear a little, that's fine. Your equilibrium will still be off. Then you lay down, hands behind your head, legs extended. "I'll count real slow to three. You'll hear me 'cuz I'll be yelling LOUD," Mark said in a rising voice. "On three, try to sit up. A six-pack says you can't."

Danny sat down on one of the basketball court's free-throw lines. The rest of team formed a semi-circle around him. Bobby handed him some gum, and while Danny chewed, Mark tied the jersey tight around his eyes. Danny blew a gigantic gray bubble before sucking the gum back and biting it in two. Rolling each half into balls, he shoved them into his ears. Then he stretched out on the parquet floor.

"Can you hear me?" Mark yelled close to Danny's ear.

"Yeah, barely. Let's do this nuclear thing."

Mark motioned the circle back. "Give him some room, boys, in case he surprises us all and does it. Okay, on the count of three, try to sit up. One. Two. Three!"

To everyone's amazement, Danny jerked both his feet and head off the floor about three inches, only to collapse back. He tried again, his neck veins bulging above his jersey from straining. After many contortions and grunts, Danny relaxed as if someone had suffocated him with a pillow.

Mark came forward, removed the blindfold, grabbed Danny by the hand and lifted him from the floor. Danny seemed woozy and disoriented.

"I'll be a son-of-a-gun," he said, getting his bearings. "It really works. I couldn't do it."

Mark surveyed the rest of them. "Any other takers?" None stepped forward. They all seemed ready to concede that such a thing as an atomic sit-up really existed, since Danny was as strong as any two of them combined.

"Joe, how about you?" he challenged. "You're tougher than Danny here, aren't you?"

"I'll pass," Joe said, raising his hands in concession.

"Bucckk, bucckk," Mark made the sound of a chicken. Still Joe declined, his increasing mistrust in Mark galvanizing him to the floor.

"Let me try," Bobby Thorton shouted.

Mark found Bobby among his teammates. He stood near Dave, who dwarfed over him.

"Nah, I don't think so," Mark said, shaking his head.

"Please?" Bobby squeaked in his tiny voice.

"Come on, let Bobby try if he wants," Joe said, knowing how much Bobby adored Mark. Bobby would have grown the trees to make the gum needed for the experiment if Mark had asked.

"Okay, Joe, if you insist. Front and center, Bobby."

Bobby stepped forward with a grin Mark could barely cover with the jersey.

"New gum," Mark ordered, reaching his arm out like a surgeon for a scalpel.

Bobby quickly moistened another two sticks of Juicy Fruit and wedged them deep inside his pointed ears. He lay down and stretched his arms back. At their feet, he looked no larger than a catfish pulled from the nearby Minnesota River, yet he gritted his teeth with fierce determination as Mark meticulously checked his hearing and his vision. When Mark was satisfied, he yelled, "Okay Bobby, just like Danny did, on the count of three, try to sit up with all your might."

"Okay," Bobby said.

On "One," Mark straddled Bobby, his back to Bobby's face.

On "Two," Mark dropped his shorts.

On "Three," Bobby Thorton exploded off the floor with such force and precision that for a moment his face buried itself deep between Mark's exposed white cheeks.

Bobby recoiled as if snake bit. In disgust, he whipped off the jersey and wiped his face. He rose red-faced and defiant, only to be beaten down by the cascade of laughter. Bobby hung his head and ran from those he admired and served.

Joe instantly sprang at Mark and shoved him to the floor. Mark slid backwards with an audible squeak across the parquet. "What the hell was that, Perkins?"

Mark was too deep into his practical joke to care. He laughed heartily. "Danny and I meant to get you, farmer Joe, but you wouldn't bite. I got you anyway. Bobby thinks you're in on it, now.

"Screw you, Perkins. You're a hopeless case," Joe said, retreating after Bobby. Joe found him standing deep in the uniform room with his back turned, reaching high to hang up laundered track uniforms. The locked lower half of the equipment room's door protected him from more physical abuse.

"Bobby, are you all right?"

Bobby hung up Number 33, and checked a line on his clipboard. He sniffled and said nothing.

"Bobby, you've got to know this. I didn't know what was going to happen. I wasn't in on it, really. You've got to believe me."

Bobby remained turned away. "I believe, you," he said, his voice barely a whimper. "What he did wasn't right." Bobby said it slowly, as if it had taken him this long to pull Mark off his pedestal and acknowledge his idol was capable of such a demeaning act.

"You're right. It was awful. But he didn't do it to get you. He was after me. You just got in the way." That thought grew within Joe, turning the act even more heinous.

"I want to get even," Bobby blurted out, looking at last over his shoulder. His beady eyes glared red from crying, and a bubble of saliva balanced on his lips. "I'll put liniment in his jock strap, or loosen the spikes on his track shoes, or something," he said.

"You do and Mark will know it was you and he'll do something even worse. I don't think he's above that."

"Then what?" Bobby whined. He paused, as if the answer might materialize if he waited just a bit longer. "I've got to do something. I've got some respect, too, you know."

Bobby Thorton, slow, diminutive son of a grocer, destined someday to polish floors and clean urinals in the midnight hours, had feelings, too.

"Leave it to me, Bobby," Joe said. "I'll think of something."

Joe figured out how to avenge Bobby Thorton three nights later. With the April showers abating, George let the cows sleep outside. The Holsteins now spent their days in sprouting pastures. They loved the succulent young grasses after a winter of stale silage and moldy hay, and they ate to excess. The result—50 cows with the runs. Each time one lifted its tail, a fetid stream of brownish green manure shot into the gutter.

With milking almost over, Joe told George he would finish, then wash out the milking machines and let the herd out so George could get an hour of planting done before dark. George hastily accepted the offer.

After Joe finished his routine tasks, he secured several large, black garbage bags from the milk house. He lined one inside the other until the bags stood almost thick enough to stand. Then he inserted them into an old five-gallon grease bucket, and draped the piled plastic over the edge. With a long-handled shovel, he scooped out the near-liquid manure from the gutter and filled the bag half full. Then he added a small pail of water to the stinking brew. While tightly tying off the top of the bag, the stench almost overcame him. Even though a moat of manure surrounded him each day, the combination of plastic and bubbling waste emitted the most lethal odor Joe had ever smelled.

He waited until the sun set before leaving the barn. Then, spying through the house windows to make sure Ruth wasn't watching, he carried the bag gingerly to the far ditch across the road and hid it in the weeds.

The next morning he waited for the school bus. When Mrs. Zimmer cranked open the bus door, Joe told her he had forgotten something and not to wait. He would catch a ride from his folks. As the orange bus pulled out of sight, he slid into the ditch, hoisted his treasure carefully and headed across the fields in the reverse direction of his afternoon runs. Joe walked slowly and carefully, cradling the bag in his arms as if it contained the head of John the Baptist and Salome awaited him. Unconcerned about the time, he rested when his arms tired. He needed to arrive at school after classes started. The forged excuse note, for which he would pay later, rested in his pocket. That was in the future. Presently the thought of revenge for Bobby Thorton sloshed through him as fluid as the cold manure he felt through the layers of plastic. Consequences, however severe, would pale in comparison to winning back Bobby Thorton's respect and getting even for Mark's recent hostilities.

No one stopped him or seemed remotely curious as to what he carried as Joe strolled through Troy's small downtown. He made his way through the side streets and approached the school from the back side. Unnoticed, he cut across the school's baseball field toward the student parking lot. Luck shone brightly as he noticed Mark's car faced away from the school.

Mark loved his car almost as much as he loved himself. It showed. Jacked up, souped up and paid up, Mark scrubbed and polished the 1964 burgundy Chevrolet Impala convertible more often than Father MacDougall did his communion chalice. Mark wouldn't permit anyone to drink or be drunk in the car, for fear of vomiting. He didn't drive it on rainy days. Or if he drove and rain threatened, he carried a canvas in the trunk to cover the convertible.

Today was a fine, clear day. The first dandelions dotted the grass like egg yolks. The temperature was rising by the minute. Another good sign, Joe thought as he popped the latch and lifted the Chevy's hood. He whistled audibly as he viewed the immaculate engine. Recently power hosed, the engine block and all its appendages gleamed silver in the morning sunlight. Joe stole a furtive look toward the school and then set to work. He lifted the bag and draped it gently and strategically into the folds of the engine. It rested there, looking everything like a living bladder in the intestines of a robot. And this bladder was looking for a way to relieve itself. Joe figured that out, too. He hoisted the bag slightly and shifted it forward about three inches so that one sagging, bulging, black corner rested contentedly against the blades of the radiator fan. From under his shirt Joe pulled out a note sleeved in plastic and taped it to the underside of the hood. Checking twice for clearance, Joe gently eased the hood back down until the latch clicked. A final look under the chassis revealed no leaks. Feeling everything like a terrorist, he entered Troy Senior High School with no remorse for what was about to happen.

The subject was income taxes, and Mr. Carter elaborated on what things a citizen could list as deductions. As he scanned the room to see how many seniors daydreamed, Mr. Carter thought it ironic that these students would be on the streets in 50 days without a clue of how to make a living, but by God they would know how to pay the government its due. He discovered early in his 20-year career how futile it was to try to teach seniors anything when the Minnesota weather hit 70 degrees outside. He himself struggled when the windows were cranked open like today and the sparrows chirped and courted in the ground-floor viburnum bushes.

Mr. Carter didn't shake the seniors from their dreams for one other reason. His audit. In two decades of studying the federal tax system, the Minnesota tax code and more, he knew every possible loophole that existed. Or so he thought until the plain white envelope with the deadly words "Internal Revenue Service" crossed his desk in late January. The IRS sequestered his financial records and his dignity. His students impudently asked him daily just how many dependents he had, or if his church donations actually paid for that new mission in New Guinea. He lost their respect and didn't care. All he cared about now was not losing his life savings to the IRS.

Like much of the class, Mark half listened and pretended to take notes. He concentrated mainly on doodling around the name "Annie" written in his notebook. The longer they were apart the more he realized his loss. The lovemaking was only part of it. Mark missed their conversations, her laughter. He missed the comfort of her. He knew he wouldn't find anyone better than Annie.

The bell rang, pulling Mark from his brooding thoughts and out into the hall crowded with students. Lunch hour. Time to grab Harrington and take a spin around town. It was a fine day. He would take the top down on the Impala.

Greg stood at his locker putting on his letterman's jacket.

"You won't need that today," Mark said. Greg pointed to his arm. A new "conference champs" basketball patch rested below other symbols of his athletic prowess.

"Got to. This patch will be worthless in a few weeks," he replied.

Together, they weaved their way through the masses and out the front door. Most of the other students opted for the outdoors as well on such a fine spring day. Two of them, Joe and Bobby Thorton, leaned against the school's flagpole and tried to look inconspicuous.

Mark ran his hand along the Impala's shiny finish when he reached the car. He thought he felt the Chevy shiver beneath his touch, as if it were alive. Sliding into the driver's seat, he leaned over and popped the far lock for Greg. The car's black interior burned through their pants.

"Crank the top down and open some vents. I'm roasting here," Greg demanded.

"Then take off that jacket," Mark said, flipping open the vents and unlatching the convertible top. With the push of a button, the hydraulics kicked in and the white top accordianed back behind the rear seat.

"Say, what's that smell?"

Mark noticed it, too. "Smells like plastic melting or something."

"Smells more like afterbirth. Or a taco fart. What did you have for breakfast?" Greg pulled out his lighter and flicked it on. "Want me to light the next one?"

"No flames in the car," Mark warned. "You know the rules."

"Yeah," Greg said, slipping the lighter back into his pocket and easing himself deeper into the folds of the seat. "Unless you want to see Valhalla, don't mess with my Impala," he mimicked.

"That's right," Mark said, emphatically. "Nobody messes with this car and lives."

With that he pumped the accelerator once and turned the key in the ignition. A sharp rapping sound commenced as the busted bag instantly wrapped around the fan belt and blades. There was a veritable explosion of manure under the hood, coating the metal and hoses, seeking every orifice. The shocked engine seemed to cough for relief, and some of the wettest, foulest, greenest slime in the history of Carver County shot through the dash's air vents and into their shocked faces.

"Shit!" they yelled in unison, which was a mistake, as a second volley of slime found their open mouths. But what else could they yell but "shit," as that's what it was. So they yelled it and yelled it as if it were their mantra, hopping from the car, circling this suddenly diarrheic monster.

The students in front of the school came running. Behind them, Bobby Thorton whooped and shoved his fist in the air. He gave Joe a joyous hug.

After he cleared most of the manure pack from his face, Mark approached the front of his car and wrenched open the hood. The greenish-brown manure, mingled with bits of shredded black plastic bag, covered every square inch of the engine. He surveyed the damage in horror. Then, looking up, Mark saw manure dripping from a plastic sleeve taped to the underside of the hood. He seized it angrily and wiped it reasonably clean on his pant leg. The scrawled message read:

> *Those who respect the Atom,*
> *Know it can be split.*
> *Those who toy with the Atom,*
> *End up eating shit.*

Mark moved like Moses through a parting sea of students who backpedaled either from the smell, or the tire iron in Mark's hand. The smell of a fight overpowered the musk of the manure, and the swelling ranks backfilled behind Mark as he strode toward the only two figures standing their ground.

Bobby peeked behind Joe, fidgeting with fear.

"Just stay back, Bobby," Joe said, trying to hide the tremor in his own voice, "unless Greg gets involved."

Mark never slowed, and when he was within 10 feet of Joe, he lunged with a roar, the tire iron raised. Joe moved simultaneously, diving low for Mark's knees. He felt the piercing blow of the iron across his lower back and buttocks as he rammed his head into Mark's midsection. They both sprawled onto the pavement, Mark trying to deliver more blows, but doing so ineffectually because he could get little leverage with them locked in a bear hug. He let the tire iron clang to the blacktop, and pummeled Joe with his fists. Joe did the same, landing solid punches to Mark's face. Soon, Mark used his size to roll Joe over, and delivered rapid blows to Joe's face, bloodying his nose. Joe's world turned blue and black. He heard the nervous screams of the girls as the fight turned bloody, and yells of encouragement from the boys, but he didn't know for whom they rooted.

He opened an already swelling eye to see Mark rear up to deliver the coup de grace. Only it never landed. Bobby pounced on Mark's back, choking him around the neck. Mark rose and tried to spin him off, but Bobby locked his short legs around Mark's waist and squeezed for dear life.

"Nuclear war, nuclear war!" he hollered.

The crowd contracted and expanded as Mark and Bobby veered this way and that in their whirling dervish.

"What the hell is going on here?" It was Mr. Varness, the principal. The fire in his eyes and the command in his voice quieted the students.

Bobby released his grip and Mark shoved him off with disgust. Bobby scurried over near Joe while Mark put on an air of bravado. "Nothing's going on, Mr. Varness."

"Don't lie, Perkins," Mr. Varness warned. "Who started this?" he continued, seeing several students helping Joe to his feet, a borrowed, bloody kerchief pressed to his nose.

"Ask Mitchell."

Mr. Varness prided himself on keeping order. A seasoned administrator, he did not tolerate disobedience. One had to stomp hard on it whenever it raised its head. For a second, he thought about expelling Perkins and Mitchell on the spot. When he spied the tire iron, the sentence actually poised on the tip of his tongue. But the end of the year rushed toward them, and the school wasn't so big that he didn't know a track championship could rest on Perkin's legs.

"Everybody who's not covered with shit, get inside. Now!" he finally bellowed. The students reluctantly herded toward the school. "Perkins, Thorton, Mitchell, and, you, Harrington," he said, eyeing another encrusted compatriot, "stand by the flagpole until I get back."

"What did I do?" Greg protested.

"I don't know, but I'll figure out what it is."

While Mr. Varness secured the students back inside and made his phone calls, Joe, Bobby, Mark and Greg encircled the flagpole. Joe dabbed at his nose and said nothing. Mark spewed out a steady stream of threats and insults, but Joe only paid attention when he heard the occasional "kill" or "maim." Bobby still fidgeted beside him, but a smile beamed across his silent lips. While they hurled insults, Mark and Greg had enough sense not to touch the shit bomb terrorists.

Mr. Varness reamed them out individually, taking each to the end of the parking lot and threatening them with expulsion while they leaned tamely against the backstop of one of the softball fields. While Joe received his dose, he heard his dad's Dodge pickup approach. Mr. Varness heard it, too, and released Joe to what he assumed would be far worse punishment than he could dole out.

Mr. Varness had informed Ruth who informed George of the nature of Joe's crime by phone. Still, George was taken aback by Joe's appearance as his son slid bruised and reeking into the cab. Joe's left cheek glowed an eggplant purple. The front of his shirt—between the manure stains—revealed rusty dried blood. George noticed Joe's scraped and bloodied knuckles. He said not a word as he spun the pickup around the parking lot and headed back up the hill. To the right George noticed a shirtless student bent over the engine of a car while another wiped at the sleeves of his letterman's jacket. He turned onto the highway.

Above the chug of the pickup's engine, he finally asked with feigned anger, "So what was the fight about?"

Joe's face turned a red that complemented his wounds. As they passed Henson's Grain & Feed, their neighbors busily picked up anhydrous fertilizer or herbicides on a day meant for farming, not fighting. *Ramifications*, Joe thought. *They're on their way.* He plowed forward nonetheless, honestly telling George the story of Bobby Thorton and the atomic sit-up. And then of his retaliation.

Silence returned to the cab until George downshifted and pulled over onto the shoulder near the railroad trestle. He hopped out of the cab and ran to the back of the pickup, and Joe assumed something had flown out of the truck bed. Sure enough, checking his side mirror, he saw George bent over, hands on his knees, as if searching for something lost in the gravel. When he rolled down his window to offer help, however, he heard George laughing uncontrollably. Joe rolled his window back up, leaned back into the seat, held the rag to his left eye, and smiled.

Foxes Revisited

By the time the story of the fight wove its way through the halls and underwent numerous translations, Annie believed Joe lay dying somewhere, his skull crushed by a tire iron. She tried calling him from school, but no one answered at the Mitchell's. She endured afternoon sessions of Speech and Advanced Algebra, and the bus ride home before she finally got through to Ruth, who told her Joe was fine except for a black eye, scrapes and bruises. No, he couldn't call now, he was doing chores. But she would be sure he called at suppertime.

Joe didn't call then, however. Lots of her friends did. "Did you hear what Joe did to Mark's car?" "I hear he was standing up for Bobby Thorton." "I hear he pinned Mark to the ground before Mark bashed him with a tire iron."

She worried about Joe, but she was glad he had challenged Mark. Joe certainly knew how to get revenge. Annie envisioned Mark at some power wash in the cities paying good money to salvage his prized convertible. Knowing Mark, the car would be ruined for him even if it again glided spotless and odorless down Main Street. For a moment, she felt sorry for Mark's loss.

Much to Annie's mother's relief, Joe called at 8:30 p.m.

"Joe, are you all right?" Annie asked.

"I'm fine."

"Did you really pour manure all over Mark's car?" She wanted to get the inside story.

"I supplied the fuel," Joe answered, "but Mark brought down the fall-out on himself."

"The fall-out?"

"Never mind."

"You sound funny. Are you eating?"

"No, it's hard to talk with an icepack to your face."

"Oh, no, Joe, are you sure you're all right?" Annie grew worried about Joe's condition again. Then another thought worried her. She hesitated to ask, knowing how small it seemed compared to Joe's injuries. "Prom's only four weeks away. Will your bruises be cleared up by then?"

Joe laughed, and winced from pain as he did. "I guess that's your way of asking me if I'm taking you."

"Are you?"

"If you would so honor me, yes."

"Of course, Joe." Annie paused. "I love you."

Joe let the words sink in. No girl had ever said them to him before.

"I must see you. Can we meet at your locker first thing tomorrow?"

"Can't. We've been kicked out of school for a day until our parents meet with Varness."

"Well, then, can you pick me up tomorrow night?"

Joe looked to make sure his parents weren't eavesdropping. Ruth was watching "Big Valley" in the living room. George was asleep in his chair.

"I can't do that, either, Annie. My parents grounded me. My dad nearly split a gut laughing when I told him what happened, but my mom didn't like it one bit. You must be a bad influence on me because I've never been grounded before."

"Can you have visitors?" Annie asked, and Joe noticed frustration crackling through the line.

"I think so."

"I can get my folk's car on Saturday. Can I come over then?"

"That would be great. My folks have a wedding. They'll leave by noon and be back late for chores and milking."

"Daylight is better," she said. "I want to see the foxes again. See you at noon."

Farm weddings united more than bride and groom. They pulled together lifelong neighbors in an affirmation of their rural roots. Everybody knew everybody, from bassinet to the altar to the grave. They knew the groom, Larry Achison, since he was born. Knew his mother Ethel drove him to the emergency ward when Larry was clipped by a car when he was 10 years old. Knew Larry still couldn't hear out of his left ear because of that accident. Knew Cynthia Gorsham won every 4-H county fair ribbon for sewing. Knew, thank God, that she would stay on the Achison farm and help Larry like a good daughter-in-law until Jerry Achison deeded it over to them in 20 years.

Other things united the neighbors, things deep in the earth, like the shared aquifers that filled their wells and the property fences that stitched their farms together. Ancient, basic things. The unspoken things that rallied them together to raise a new barn, or take turns filling one another's silos in the fall.

The things that said this is how life should be—tied to the earth, centered on family, and moving slowly to God's other Eden. They brought these beliefs to every wedding. They showed off their own long marriages to the newlyweds as proof that their way of life pleased God.

Cynthia Gorsham waited appropriately until after Lent to marry Larry Achison. This pleased the Holy Catholic Church, but irked the area farmers. The fine spring day beckoned them to the fields as surely as Larry would beckon Cynthia to his bed that night. The farm wives always persevered in these matters, however, so George, looking handsome in his blue suit, and Ruth, wearing her Easter dress and matching shoes, left promptly at 11:15 a.m. to get a strategic pew.

Joe waved as his parents left. The dust from the Chevy had barely settled before Joe ran in the house. There, he furiously scrubbed off the smell of barn. He donned a cream colored, long-sleeve turtleneck and blue jeans, and dabbed some English Leather on his newly shaved face. He was combing his still damp hair when he heard Annie's car on the gravel drive.

She entered the kitchen in lavender brilliance, the soft color of her blouse a bloom of lilacs. At the kitchen table, she fussed over Joe when she saw his discolored face. Joe winced with real pain as Annie traced his bruises with a cool finger. He detailed the whole story of the atomic sit-up, Bobby's grief and the manure-in-the-engine revenge down to the smallest detail. Annie gasped and laughed throughout the telling, as if in hearing it she became a co-conspirator.

When the story played out, an awkward stillness fell between them. Something electric pulsed through the air. It reminded Joe of the calm before an approaching August storm. Rolling purple clouds moving toward a sea of golden oats. Then through the silence, a whoosh, as if the earth itself exhaled. The golden stems, with their clusters of bearded grain, bent and swirled and undulated as if the field were a giant animal, and God's invisible hand stroked its thick fur. Still there would be no sound, only the smell of dust outdistancing the rest of the storm, until finally the wind reached the big cottonwood near the house and shook its branches violently.

Joe sensed such a storm brewing inside Annie. It radiated through her eyes. He leaned kitty-corner across the kitchen table, kissed her and waited for the rustling of cottonwood leaves.

"Do you think the foxes would be out right now?"

"It's afternoon and sunny, so I'd say not likely," Joe said, wanting to kiss her again.

"Let's go check anyway," Annie implored.

They walked toward the pines, hand in hand, under a brilliant sky. A John Deere tractor put-putted in a distance field. Joe and Annie crossed the railroad bed, remembering the fox kill, and then stepped carefully over newly sprouting corn and then into alfalfa.

Annie had to see the foxes again. Viewing them the first time, she had experienced nature in an entirely new way. Something basic and essential. Since that day, she had realized Joe carried the same traits. He lived in a world abounding with life and death. He was part of nature, not just a viewer like herself. And being part of it, he played no games. He didn't know how. The foxes and Joe possessed some sort of feral beauty that deeply affected her.

Annie thought about the foxes often. She wondered about their life underground in the den. The thought of the young foxes suckling in the black womb of the earth comforted her. Safe from the storms above. Communicating by whiskers and whimpers.

With Joe, she felt like one of those fox kits. Protected. Nurtured. His strength, his sense of right and wrong evidenced in his defense of Bobby Thorton, had stirred new thoughts. She felt unafraid to share her fears and aspirations. To whimper. Safety and warmth lay in his arms.

When they reached the woods, Joe took the lead. Since the wind wasn't a factor, they walked with purpose far down a row between the pines. Then Joe turned and cut across three rows of conifers. One row from the open fields, they moved slowly over the rust-colored pine needles. Annie saw why Joe had chosen this route. The pine row petered out before the others, giving way to a lush green thicket of grass. Too close to the trees to get plowed, it butted up to the edge of the den mound.

They finished the last 10 yards under the trees on their knees. Joe put his finger needlessly to his lips. It took a full minute to traverse the final 10 feet before they laid down a scant two yards from the back side of the den. They watched its earthen rim, shoulder to shoulder on their stomachs. Joe felt the sun warm his back. Annie's perfume mingled with the smells of the verdant vegetation, making him lightheaded. He lowered his eyes and watched a tiny red spider scurry down a lime green shaft of grass. This close, the short hairs on the grass stood visible, as were the spider's legs.

Joe felt Annie's hand squeeze his, and looking up he saw the female fox peering out of the hole. It stayed only a second, just long enough for them to capture the wariness in its eyes, and the glint of its teeth. The fox retreated as if sucked backwards into the earth.

Annie's heart pounded in her ears, and she looked over to Joe, who grinned broadly beside her. He leaned over and kissed her cheek in the joy of their good luck. As he pulled away to look back at the den, Annie reached over and softly touched the back of his neck. Joe turned and looked deep into her eyes. They danced with excitement. Annie's hand still rested on his neck, stroking the edges of his hair softly, and then she pulled him to her and into a deep, hungry kiss. Her lips covered his face, stopping only when, from somewhere beneath them, they heard the muted yelps of the fox kits.

"Make love to me, Joe."

Joe hesitated. He had never made love before. Hadn't yet even kissed a naked breast. His mind exploded with a thousand thoughts. Of his parents and their disapproval and disappointment. Whether or not he would be committing a mortal sin. Whether he might get Annie pregnant. And if it was Annie's first time, too. And if not, did it matter?

Ultimately, nothing mattered but the miracle in his arms. He roughly fondled her breasts, softly biting her neck. He disengaged himself from Annie's desperate grasp and started to remove his shirt. Annie followed suit, first with the lavender blouse, then her bra, and, finally, she slid out of her jeans and panties. Joe watched her as if in a trance as she lay back white in stark contrast to the lush green grass. The same gold necklace, that of their first date, smiled at him from her neck. He could hardly get his pants down over his erection, and was momentarily embarrassed by his nakedness.

Annie held out her arms. She took the lead, and Joe found himself again in her embrace, her nipples hard and brushing against his chest, her breathing rapid in his ear. All doubts vanished as he caressed this new naked world. He sought her lips, her neck, and her small breasts. He quivered as she directed his hand to her sex and felt, for the first time, the coarseness of her hair, and the warm dampness within. She moaned ever so softly, and Joe felt himself about to explode. He moved between her legs and Annie guided him inside her. She kept whispering, "I love you, Joe."

She meant it. Joe's initial awkwardness touched her. But his lovemaking was so like him. He thought of her pleasure first. His movements were rugged and passionate, yet caring and protective with the way he held her, with his words and kisses. She feared nothing in giving herself to him. Joe would not hurt her. She felt safe in their little world on a grassy knoll next to a fox den.

For Joe, all was pleasure and wonder. He moved deep and steady inside her, and his senses focused there, yet, on the edges, he grew conscious of other sensations. Annie's hands pressing against the small of his back. How the long lashes of her closed eyes fluttered ever so slightly. How her breathing accelerated in his right ear. All too soon Joe felt himself exploding into thunderous pleasure. Annie felt him shudder in her arms, felt his heart beating against hers. He continued to move slowly inside her. She held him close until his breathing slowed, making circles on his back with her fingers.

"I'm sorry, it was so quick," Joe finally said.

"You never have to apologize to me, Joe."

"It was my first time."

Annie smiled. "I know," she said, wincing. "It's my first time in a field."

Joe pulled himself away from her. "Are you uncomfortable?"

"Just a little. And a bit cold, too," she said, sitting up and hugging herself.

Despite their shared intimacy, in the daylight they both suddenly became aware of their nakedness. Joe handed Annie her clothes and turned his back to don his own. When they were clothed, Annie settled intimately between Joe's legs, leaning against his chest and facing the fox den.

"I wasn't the first, was I?" Joe asked.

"No," she said, reaching back to stroke his face. "Mark and I dated for almost a year. But it doesn't matter. It's you now. You're the one who's captured my heart. You, your foxes and this day."

She turned back into his arms and he kissed her as deeply as he could to thank her for her gift. They talked for the next hour, oblivious of the foxes, which never appeared. In their conversation they shared an intimacy deeper than sex—their dreams. Awkwardness vanished between them.

Annie came again on Sunday, this time with a picnic basket, a blanket and a camera. Joe told his folks about the foxes, and was relieved when George acknowledged that Bill Becker, too, had seen the kits. There was enough truth in Joe's lie about Annie wanting to photograph the foxes that he could tell it straight-faced. Their plans carried too much audacity for his folks to suspect their true intentions. Despite another sunny day, this time they wrapped their lovemaking inside the thick blanket. The foxes became an afterthought. This day, Joe applied a Sunday's pace to his lovemaking. He took time to survey and explore Annie's exquisite body. He grew comfortable kissing the small breasts which only days before he had fantasized over. There was time to count Annie's heartbeats as they slowed after lovemaking, time to get used to the smell of their union.

For Annie, Joe became her wild fox. A sentinel watching over her. Protective in how he curled around her. Lean and hard and sure in strength and heart. When she searched his eyes for judgment, she found none. His smiles, peaceful eyes, and laughter flowed genuinely from his heart.

As they finished dressing and left their food for the foxes, Joe drew Annie to him for another deep kiss. He had already decided he would marry her to remove the mortal sin from his soul. Letting go of her delicate hands, he slipped off his class ring and slid it easily over her finger. Annie rubbed it.

Joe held both of her hands and said, "My bounty is as boundless as the sea. My love as deep. The more I give to thee, the more I have. For both are infinite."

"Joe, that's beautiful."

"It's Shakespeare. The only thing I remember from Romeo and Juliet."

"No, Joe, it's you."

A DASH MAN

On Tuesday, George drove Joe to school, where Joe apologized for his actions before father, principal and flag. His expulsion had been short, likely because of the triangular track meet scheduled for that night. Not for his role, but for Mark's.

Leaving Mr. Varness' office, George donned his Pioneer seed cap and then extended his hand. Joe looked dumbfounded.

"It's to shake. Men do it."

Joe shook his father's hand for the first time in his life. It was huge, warm and callused.

"The day of the fight, I never told you that I was proud of you," George said, still hanging onto Joe's hand. "Not for the fighting. Your mother and I don't condone that. But for how you stood up for someone less fortunate. You took on a bully near as I can tell, and that's all right in my book. Now be on your guard, because bullies don't like to be made out for a fool. Anyone who would come after you with a tire iron isn't through with you."

George smiled and started to walk toward the door. While Joe watched, George stopped and added, "Of course, this guy has to be a little worried, too, seeing what you did to his car." George continued out the door, laughing at his son's unique form of vengeance. He would never have been so brazen in his day.

While the handshake surprised him, it paled in comparison to his classmates' reception. Many stopped whatever they were doing and cheered upon his arrival. While he worked his combination lock, a chant of "Atom Ant" filled the corridor. On the outside of his locker, Dave Wilson had taped a picture of Charles Atlas with a nuclear symbol drawn on his bulging bicep. Joe responded with a face the color of Florida sunburn. Inside he glowed.

His intentions had been only to right a wrong, and he had not thought of the consequences beyond the expected beating at Mark's hands.

Dave came up and draped his arms around Joe. "Hail the conquering hero. Created quite a stir haven't you," he said as the first hour bell rang and sent students scattering. "This thing is huge," he said excitedly as they walked together into English class. "The whole school's buzzing. Everybody thinks what you did was great, even the teachers. Betty says the yearbook staff got pictures of Mark's car and they're going to try to sneak it by Mrs. Newman. That gets in, you're immortal." Dave squeezed Joe's neck before taking his seat. "Watch your backside, though."

Friends, and even underclassmen he didn't know, congratulated him throughout the day. Bobby Thorton, apparently, was now revered and untouchable. When Bobby sought out his benefactor and hugged him openly in the halls, more cheers erupted. Even DeAngelo smiled at Joe several times during Advanced Algebra.

Twice Joe saw Mark during the day. Mark scowled but took no action. It pleased Joe to see that Mark carried the yellow tattoo marks of his fists.

Through all this adulation, however, Joe's thoughts returned constantly to Annie. He relived ever minute of the weekend. Pictured her again naked and wanting against the green grass. Sometimes, the memories became so powerful that he found himself aroused. At lunch, he sought out Annie, which did little to squelch his sexual tension.

Joe might as well have not been in school at all that day. He fluttered between classes in a dream world. Not until 2 o'clock did Joe start to focus on the track meet. They came frequently now in the short season. He foresaw another duel with Mark, another defeat. But Annie promised to come, and he wanted to make a good showing. He also planned a new strategy—to stay on Mark's back tighter than Peter Pan's shadow.

The triangular meet in Elbow Lake took the team bus lumbering south on Highway 17. Joe scanned the all-familiar countryside. It shone under another gorgeous day, a continuance of the unseasonable warm spring, and farmers crawled over the fields turning over bottomland or completing their soybean planting. The splash of green or red in the otherwise brown palette revealed each farmer's loyalty to either John Deere or Farmall machinery. Stronger than the divisions between Catholics and Lutherans, or Ford vs. Chevy owners, farmers stood by their tractor lines. They considered these iron horses part of their genealogy. Sheriff Hanson frequently broke up skirmishes at the county fair because a discussion about the attributes of either tractor brand could end in fisticuffs.

Looking east out the window as they neared his farm's crossroads, Joe spotted George a half-mile away. By the cloud of dust engulfing the tractor, Joe deduced George was dragging, the last step in preparing the soil for planting. Sixteen-feet across with eight rows of six-inch spikes, the drag coifed the field into a fine grit that was likely powdering George's face. As a child, Joe thought the wind devils that spun brown and gritty across such open fields were tornadoes. George told him they were God stirring the soil with his finger, and Joe believed this for years until George also told him that thunder was the sound of God and the Angel Gabriel knocking down 10 pins. Still, Joe saw distant tractors kick up cyclones, and thought again of God stirring the world lazily.

The Mitchell farm disappeared, replaced by other dairies along the road, each with their bullet-shaped silos and breadbox barns in various stages of deterioration. Most of farms sprung up after the First World War. Returning soldiers believed once again in peace, and built these rural monuments as a sign that life must begin anew. New paint signaled where the farmer's wife ruled the roost, as was the case at the Murphy farm. There the window trim on the huge, two-storied farm house came from the same gallons of red paint that made their barn shine crimson in the late afternoon sun.

Highway 17 continued its long curve around Elbow Lake. The sun caught the spires of the Christ Lutheran Church and the hamlet's water tower, and reflected them obliquely in the lake. The farmsteads fell behind, replaced first by a trailer park, and then farm implement and car dealerships. A few station wagons, with children running from their open doors, surrounded the town's Dairy Queen.

The Troy bus turned right off the highway at Elbow Lake's only stop light and drove under the main boulevard's branches just turning a katydid green with new buds. Another left turn brought them along side Elbow Lake High, a dark-bricked, three-storied old school from which newer, one-story additions extended like opened bureau drawers. The cinder track encircled the football field on the south side of the school. The Lakers and non-conference Plainview teams already dotted the field in their respective gold and green uniforms. The distance men jogged in the outside lanes while the hurdlers perfected their timing and strides. The fieldmen stretched and chatted.

While he limbered up, Joe still couldn't shake thoughts of Annie. The sweet smell of the grass and the warmth of the sun on his bare legs reminded him of the fox den. He was hopelessly in love. He remembered reading once that one didn't fall in love with another person. One merely found a person who accepted you as you were. That acceptance let you fall in love with yourself. Therein lay the ecstasy. Joe smiled inwardly. Someone else could define love. He just wanted to taste more of it.

The meet progressed the way Coach O'Reilly expected. Wilson heaved the discus flat and far. Thompson won the high jump, leaping like a frog over the bar that his opponents continually clanged off its posts. Crazy Nolan quit voicing song lyrics long enough to win the 880. The Trojans stood within 2 points of where Coach O'Reilly had plotted them prior to the meet when, during the 440 yard dash, a Plainview runner caught Scott Hamre' heel with his spikes. Scott sprawled headlong into the cinders. The Plainview sprinter promptly spiked Scott in the shoulder in a failed attempt to leap over him. He, too, plunged into the tearing grit.

"Foul, foul!" Coach O'Reilly yelled sideways at the timekeeper as he ran across the infield. Scott writhed on the track holding his ankle. While Coach O'Reilly genuinely cared about Scott's well being, especially when he saw the bloody gash, he worried equally about Scott's five points lost.

"Looks like a trip to the ER," DeAngelo said, coming up quickly behind Coach O'Reilly. DeAngelo applied a white towel to Scott's wound.

"How bad is it Scott?" Coach O'Reilly asked.

"It hurts like hell, Coach," Scott winced. His face was white, scraped and dotted by bits of black cinders. The pain in his ankle was real, because he ignored the bloody punctures on his shoulder until DeAngelo dabbed at those, too.

"Let's see if you can put some weight on it," Coach O'Reilly said.

Both coaches lifted Scott to his feet, and to Coach O'Reilly and Hamre's joint relief, Scott put his full weight on the ankle.

"Looks like it's not broken or sprained. But you'll definitely need some stitches," DeAngelo said, peering beneath the bloody towel. "You're in luck since you're in the one town in the county with a hospital. Ken, I'll run him over to Emergency while you finish the meet. Hey, someone find me Scott's sweats," he yelled.

Bobby Thorton had already taken charge of that task, and Maggie O'Leary, concerned etched across her face, stood by with her car keys in hand. Together the three of them helped Scott into Maggie's car.

Coach O'Reilly turned back to the meet. He sought out the other coaches to disqualify the Plainview runner for interference. They agreed. Still, Coach O'Reilly remained unmollifed, because on paper Scott earned a first place—or no worse than second—and now his points had vanished in a bloody towel. Moreover, he had no one to fill Scott's leg of the mile relay that concluded the meet.

"Who can I plug in there?" Coach O'Reilly said out loud as the runners assembled for the next event, the mile run. He spied Mark and Joe circling the starting line, pumping their legs to relieve pre-race jitters. Joe, Coach O'Reilly immediately thought. A fourth-place finish at best in this mile competition. Good for one point, maybe. What was his time in the 440? O'Reilly couldn't recall, and wished DeAngelo hadn't fled so quickly. Probably just barely a sub

60-second 440 man, he figured. Still, with Kennedy, Reynolds and Simkas, Mitchell might be enough to secure at least second place in the relay. It seemed the smartest route.

"Hey, Harry, wait a second," Coach O'Reilly yelled to the Lakers' coach, who stood poised along side the milers, starter gun in hand. "I've got to pull one of my guys to fill in for the relay man I just lost. Joe, you're out."

Joe looked bewildered. He wanted to challenge Mark. He and Bobby Thorton had discussed the continuation of their cold war before the meet, and now Bobby frowned at him from the infield.

"You'll have to eat my cinders next go-around," Mark volleyed as Joe hustled off the track.

Coach O'Reilly steered Joe away from the milers as they tensed for the crack of the pistol. Harry held them a short time before pulling the trigger and releasing them off the starting line.

"Sorry, Joe, but this gives us the best chance to win this meet," Coach O'Reilly said. He perused his clip board as he spoke. "You've run enough quarters in practice to have a good feel for the pace, and I know you can help us place at least second. We've got about 20 minutes before the relay, so find Kennedy and practice some baton hand-offs." Coach O'Reilly turned in mid-sentence.

"Hey, Steve, grab a baton and get over here pronto," he yelled. "Now the hand-off, Joe, that's where you'll make or break us. The key is to gauge how fast Steve is approaching so you're at the same speed when he slaps the baton into your hand.

Steve Kennedy, one of the relay runners, appeared. "There you are. I was explaining to Joe the art of baton passing. You take over. Run him through a few until he gets it. Not too many times, though, or you'll both be fagged by the time the relay starts."

With Joe penciled in on his sheet, Coach O'Reilly left to follow the progress of the mile run. Joe glanced dejectedly at the milers as they neared the end of the first lap. Mark held a three-yard lead over a thinning clump of runners.

"Okay, Joe, let's go," Steve said. A floppy-haired, big-eared, three-year letterman, Kennedy talked like he ran—at a peppered clip. He began to put Joe through the paces, showing him how to extend his arm and offer an open hand so the baton could be plopped into it like a hotdog into a bun. Once, as they practiced, Joe dropped the baton. Steve promptly explained the seriousness of his action.

"A slow hand-off is better than no hand-off. Retrieving a dropped baton can take precious seconds, seconds you don't have." Steve held the hollow tube between his two hands a foot from Joe's face. "Think of the baton as a stick of dynamite that will blow if it hits the ground, and you'll do fine."

They ran four more exchanges to gauge speed and distances, and then reversed roles so Joe learned how to properly hand off the baton at the end of his lap. Satisfied that they were somewhat synchronized, Joe and Steve turned together to watch Mark cross the finish line a full 20 yards in front of Elbow Lake's best miler. No other Trojan miler placed, but Mark's victory gave Troy five points.

"Well, that helps," Steve said. "Takes a little pressure off us. We don't have to win the relay to win the meet. Okay, any final questions about the baton pass?"

"None there," Joe replied, rubbing the aluminum cylinder between his hands. "Just a question on pacing. How do I make sure I don't go out too fast and burn out before I pass the baton to Simkas?"

Steve laughed. "You can never start out too fast in the 440. It's one l-o-n-g sprint. The way I set my pace, see, is I think I've just been told my girl is about to be murdered, but that I can save her if I reach her in time. Now, I don't know how much time I have—only that I have to get there as fast as possible." Steve tensed in the telling, his eyes vacant as he imagined the scene. "Not fast enough and she's dead. Gone. Forever. And my life is over. Kaput. Any questions?"

"No," Joe said, amazed at Steve's intensity. "And let's never double date, either."

Joe took Steve's advice literally. As he later waited in position between Kennedy and Simkas on the track's edge while Reynolds ran the first leg of the relay, he envisioned Annie screaming in the arms of an abductor. To make it real, so he would not waver during his leg, Joe made Mark the villain. In Joe's mind, Mark dragged Annie toward a deep chasm, bent on revenge for her dumping him. She resisted furiously as Mark jerked her along. Joe could not determine how long before Mark would reach the precipice, but he focused on believing that, if he ran fast enough, he could stop Mark. The image became so real, the terror in Annie's imagined voice so clear, that Joe almost panicked.

To Joe's right on the track, the second relay man from each of the three teams started to sort out lanes. The first Elbow Lake runner held a narrow but clear lead over Reynolds, so Steve shuffled over into lane two and awaited the baton exchange. Reynolds approached in a rush, and made a clean pass to Steve, who pursued the Elbow Lake runner like a banshee. Joe wondered what imaginary peril Steve's girlfriend faced, and then remembered Steve had no girlfriend.

By the time Joe stepped out onto the track, he had convinced himself he would lose Annie unless he gave Simkas the lead for the final lap. He pictured the baton as Annie's lifeline, a glass vial of antidote for some dreaded disease, to be delivered intact and on time.

The lane positioning remained unchanged as the runners neared the end of the second lap. O'Reilly and the other coaches yelled out instructions, but

Joe hardly heard. He focused on Steve's tortured face as the tiring runner approached. Steve's eyes seemed to roll back into his head as he strained the final yards. His hair flew back from his flushed face. Joe suddenly worried about the exchange as he saw the baton pump rapidly up and down in Steve's hand. They had not practiced an exchange at this speed, under these jostling conditions, with Steve gasping for air.

Someone yelled, "Go," and Joe surged forward, eyes on the track before him, right arm back, waiting for the slap of the metal baton. When it came, it resembled a French kiss, snuck unexpectedly and smoothly into a willing portal. Armed with Annie's hope, Joe sprinted toward the cliff. No. 26 of Elbow Lake led by two yards to start the lap, but the sprinter's bolt after the exchange quickly increased that to four yards. Joe sped up to close the distance in an all-out sprint. This was a foot race. No time for plotting strategy or to get into a runner's rhythm. No time for his mind to wrestle with the thought of slowing down or speeding up as in the mile. This race mirrored the fox after the rabbit on the railroad track. The feral feel of the chase enlivened him and, for a moment, he decided his survival, not Annie's, rested on him catching the fleet-of-foot runner in front of him.

Entering the backstretch with still two-thirds of his lap to go, Joe pulled right behind No. 26. Joe was now so close that he could see the frayed edges of the number 6 on his opponent's jersey, a sliver of a scar on the back of his right calf. Turning a determined face over his shoulder toward Joe, No. 26 defiantly quickened his pace. Joe surged forward to draw right behind once more. Down the long backstretch, to the cheers of the small pockets of fans, they ran in tandem. When they entered the final curve, Joe wisely tucked behind No. 26. Running in lane two would add a yard to the distance Joe had to cover. Plus the Laker bore the brunt of the headwind that swept west to east the length of the track. With 100 yards to go, Joe veered into lane two and pulled even with the Laker. The hollow baton whistled with each pump of his right arm, but Joe could more clearly hear the internal pounding of his heart. Annie again materialized at the edge of the precipice.

For a moment, Joe thought he might faint. The sky went black one second and then exploded back like a violet nova. He heard the crowd cheers. Joe tried to focus on delivering Annie's salvation, but he could no longer hold the thought. The baton now became simply something to get rid of so he could quit running and lie down and die in peace. Then an excited Simkas yelled, "Go, Joe, Go." Joe somehow moved the baton from his right hand to his left, something he realized he should have done right after receiving the baton. He lost a valuable fraction of a second in the switch. Just when Joe thought he was going to run right up Simkas' back, Simkas shot ahead like a bullet train. Joe feared he might pull away, leaving him like a decoupled caboose. Somehow, Joe slapped the baton audibly into Simkas' hand, and Troy's top 440 man sprinted quickly into lane one and the lead.

Joe teetered off the track and collapsed in the grass. Annie lived. The vile Mark had been thwarted. Good had triumphed! Dave Wilson and Crazy Nolan came to his assistance with strong arms and pleasing praise. As they lifted him to his feet, Joe saw Annie waving from the stands. For the first time, he began to believe his legs, and his heart, could win all he desired.

BERTHA BLUES

Spring fieldwork ebbed into its last week. George nightly left Joe in the barn to finish the milking, and drove the noisy Super M into the gathering dusk. The colors of day seeped back into the soil as the sun sank, and George switched on his lights. They cut a rectangular swath of light before him. At nightfall, the starlings and grackles held fast to their perches in the trees or in the rafters of the distant farm buildings. The only winged creatures occasionally dipping into the light were small bats. They snatched fluttering insects, disturbing George with their darting, furry bodies. One night he spied a raccoon at the edge of his vision, its eyes ghostly circles reflected back in the halo of lights. The size of a small dog with its thick coat and arched back, the bandit rubbed his gloved hands together before high-tailing it into the shadows.

George didn't mind the night plowing like he had expected. He was happy again. The rift between Ruth and himself closed daily under the glow of the Pledge. Together they plotted out small ways they could stay on top of the farm work and still spring Joe free for track. Ruth began driving Joe to school to gain 15 minutes of bus time. She washed the stainless steel milking machines morning and night, and the bulk tank on days the Land O'Lakes truck came and drained it of its volumes of milk. She drew the line on entering the barn, however, unless it was to check on Venus. Still, Ruth's milk house chores gained George 30 minutes a day.

When he came in as black and dirty as the night from his fieldwork, Ruth usually had cooked something special. Some nights, he wondered if she didn't watch him in the distant fields, awaiting the tractor lights to turn at last up the field road and home. By the time he washed up, his fresh food lay steaming hot at his solitary place setting.

Other things in his nights became hot and steaming. It occurred first the Saturday night Joe took Annie to a party. After his bath, Ruth led him upstairs. They stayed awake until Ruth began to worry Joe might come home and hear them. George suffered greatly the next day from lack of sleep, but he thanked the Lord in church on Sunday, and begged God's forgiveness as he used his sermon sleep to recover.

Ruth was the most thankful among them. She blocked the future and lived happily in the moment. In this fabricated Eden, George doted on her again. Conversation returned to the dinner table, and made cooking a joy. She felt younger and happier than in years. Mostly she watched Joe. He smiled constantly. At dinnertime, he talked animatedly about Annie, unashamed of his obvious love for her. Each track meet brought stories of his small victories. Even when Ruth scolded him for the nuclear war incident, she could barely maintain her pride. Standing up for the underdog. Joe, her hero. Her track star. Again her happy son.

In these warm spring days, Ruth planted her garden. She dug and hoed and seeded, enjoying the hot sun on her back and the cool black soil in her hands. With the sharp edge of her hoe, she etched neat, straight rows across the garden, and laid down sweet corn, peas, carrots and bib lettuce, folding the soil over the seeds like molding a loaf of bread dough. She randomly buried the pumpkin and squash seeds in their allotted space, knowing in four months their ripening gourds would rise like small houses in the tangled neighborhood of vines.

Ruth planted something new in her garden this year. Hope. How could she not believe it would sprout with her family truly happy for the first time in years? She prayed to God to protect this fragile familial crop. She thanked Him, too, for Annie, who frequented the farm on weekends. Sometimes Annie and Joe walked the road or went in search of the foxes when George could spare him. Annie walked to the fox den alone if Joe were occupied. Other times the two women visited in the kitchen, Ruth happy for the company. Annie pried her for stories of Joe as a child, and Ruth quickly complied.

One day Annie brought snapshots of the fox kits. Annie had learned her stealth lessons well from Joe, and caught two of the foxes sleeping at the foot of the mound. Her camera clicks awakened them, and Annie's camera caught them yawning.

"They really are precious when they're small," Ruth said over the photos. "They remind me of Joe's kittens."

"I didn't know Joe had kittens."

"Oh, not now. This was when Joe was about 11. It's kinda a tragic story, really. One of the farm cats, a gray and white Joe dubbed Sissy, gave birth to a litter of kittens. For two days, Joe searched for that cat, wondering where she had hid her young."

"What do you mean, hid them?" She sat across from Ruth in the living room, legs curled beneath her in George's rocker.

"Farm cats are about as wild as tigers when it comes to their kittens," Ruth answered. "They'll find the darkest, safest corner to bring them into the world. Joe was persistent. He found them, meowing deep in a corner of the hay mow. Joe knew enough to let them be for a while. About a week later, Sissy started mousing in the barn again."

Annie tried to envision Joe back then. A blond, curious child, alone on the farm, his life for a week revolving around the birth of the kittens.

"Joe wanted to see those kittens something fierce by then, so he started unstacking bales of hay," Ruth continued. "Took him a long time, him being so small. In time, though, he dragged a whole bunch of bales out of the way. With a flashlight, he eventually spied Sissy nursing her litter. He watched them for hours, never doing them harm or spooking them. Sissy got to the point she trusted him. The next thing I know, Joe's bringing up one of those dear kittens, its eyes still closed, meowing so softly if seemed like it meowed through gauze. He stroked its gray head, and kissed it. Even though he was only 11, that kitten barely filled his hand."

Ruth sighed audibly into the room.

"Then Sissy got run over. We don't know by whom. Probably the milk truck. Joe found her. We buried her together south of the steer shed. 'What about the kittens, Mom?' Joe asked me. Well, I didn't know. We got an eyedropper and some cow's milk, and soon Joe was feeding those kittens. Their eyes opened about then, and they took Joe for their mother. They followed him everywhere." Ruth laughed at the remembered sight. "In time, Joe got tired of them tailing him, and he would run across the yard to escape, and those kittens lit out after him. Once I saw him through the window, two or three of the kittens hanging by their claws from his jeans. George took to calling him the Kitten Kid. Joe complained about the whole fiasco, but the next minute you'd see him on the ground, letting those kittens crawl all over him."

"That seems so much like Joe. He's kind."

"Yes. Yes he is," Ruth answered. "But there's another side to him, too. I saw that with the kittens as well."

"What do you mean?"

"Well, a stray tomcat came into the yard one day. As George parked the car after Mass, that tom sauntered right off the porch stoop and to my car door, purring all the time. He was an enormous cat, black and gray with sorta tufted ears. Found out later he was part Maine coon.

"Most of the time a stray's just a cat from the next farm, but you don't know. It was tame enough. So Joe asked me to get it some milk and bread. He fed it right out on the porch. Wasn't more than a half hour later though, that Joe came running to the house in tears. 'That tom killed my kittens. The tom killed my kittens,' he cried."

"Oh no," Annie gasped.

Ruth nodded in understanding. "We climbed up into the hay mow together, and there they were. Four tiny, dead gray kittens, each with a bloody red throat where the tom had done his deed. Joe was beside himself as you can imagine. I tried to explain to Joe that's what toms sometimes do—kill the young of other cats. It's to bolster their own line. Lions in Africa do the same. I saw it on TV."

"What did Joe do?"

"He cried hard, then he gave those cats a proper burial. Four separate holes and crosses made out of string and twigs right next to Sissy. I thought that was the end of it."

"It wasn't?"

"No, the next day George came in from the shed. 'Joe hung that tomcat,' George said."

"He killed it?"

"Well, at first I couldn't believe it, either. Not my Joey. I followed George to the shed, though, and that tom hung stiff as a starched shirt from a piece of baler twine swung over a rafter. We questioned Joe about it at lunch. He said something like, 'I don't care about lions in Africa. What that tom did was cruel. He killed my kittens, so I killed him.'"

"I can't believe he would do that," Annie said

Ruth nodded. She remembered how Joe's righteousness seemed so out of place in one so young. It left George and her silent. They knew from Joe's expression that he felt no remorse for the execution.

"I know. I know. But that atom bomb thing at school? It didn't surprise me one bit. That's just Joe evening out the cruelty he sees in the world. He's quick to decide what's right and wrong in his mind."

Later, Annie took this new knowledge and walked toward the field where Ruth said Joe was plowing. Joe was nowhere in sight, so Annie leaned against a box elder tree and waited. It fit, in a way, Joe hanging the cat, she thought. It put his nonchalance toward the death of the rabbit into perspective. Annie found any death unsettling, and murder unconscionable. At the same time, Joe's strong sense of right and wrong intrigued her. A bit too black and white for her, a product of his farm upbringing, she imagined. But then, she thought, as she saw a tractor top a ridge in the field and approach her, she might have hung that stray tom, too, if she had seen those poor kittens.

The April Saturday bore a bit of a chill. Nonetheless, Joe rode toward Annie shirtless in a vane attempt to jumpstart his tan. Annie noted he needed the color, as his skin resembled that of a cadaver. Regardless, Annie marveled at his upper torso, carved by his daily hard labor. As he pulled the tractor to a stop before her, he reached for his shirt.

"You don't have to put it on for my account," Annie said flirtatiously.

Joe hesitated, smiled, and pulled the blue work shirt on. "What are you doing here?"

"Came to see my beau." Annie said it in a sing-song little girl's voice.

"Well, you've seen him."

"Came to see if my beau would let me ride on his big red tractor. Annie's never been on a big red tractor before," she cooed. Joe laughed, and made Annie happy.

"Well, come on up."

Joe put the tractor into neutral and idled it at its lowest speed. He helped Annie climb up the back of the Super M, and instructed her to sit on one of the huge curving wheel well fenders on his right side.

"Now you hold on tight, Annie. This really isn't the safest place," Joe said as he returned to the tractor seat. "You fall off, and this plow will run over you. That can kill you. Do you understand? Promise me you'll be careful. It's the only way I'll let you stay up here."

"I'll be careful," Annie said, suddenly frightened. She gripped the fender with one hand; the other she latched firmly to a horizontal headlight bar. Her fear heightened as Joe lifted the plow blades with a push of the hydraulic lever, put the tractor in gear and wheeled 180 degrees. He lowered the plow blades into the furrow, pulled the throttle back, and headed down the field. As the plow first ripped the soil, the tractor bucked, and Annie hung on tight.

The tractor engine whined so they could hardly converse, but Joe answered Annie's questions about the various instruments and what action they initiated. They rode in silence for awhile as tractor and operator eased into the long quarter-mile furrow. Bits of dirt, churned up by the tractors wheels, stung them in sudden gusts of wind. Grackles and starlings flocked into the newly turned soil for grubs and earthworms. Annie became conscious of the overpowering pungency of the earth. Turned over from a foot deep and a winter's sleep, it smelled of the ages.

"Exciting, isn't it?"

"Yes, very."

Joe laughed. "I'm kidding, this is the most boring thing on earth."

Annie laughed, too. "It IS boring. I was trying to be nice."

"You won't hurt my feelings," Joe yelled above the tractor noise. They hit a slight rise, and the plow struggled, so Joe yanked the throttle back two more notches. The tractor belched blue smoke, and they surged ahead again. "I don't mind it when the weather's good. Mainly I daydream."

"About what?"

"You, lately."

She dared to free one hand to rub his arm.

"What about before me?"

"Leaving this place. But, really, lately all I do is think about you."

"Ditto."

They reached the field's end, and Joe pushed the throttle forward, eliciting an enormous backfire from the tractor's muffler.

"Is that suppose to happen?"

"Nah, I'm just showing off."

Joe repeated his actions from the other end of the field, and soon they were traversing back toward the homestead. Annie grew accustomed to their movement, and her fear disappeared. She took the opportunity to survey the farm, since she rode in the middle of it. There was an overpowering sense of openness, the horizon unbroken in all directions save for the random farmsteads surrounded by green-treed windbreaks. The fields themselves lay as proper and colorless as Quakers.

"Want to drive?" Joe asked, leaning into her.

"Me? No."

"Come on, your friends will be impressed."

"Which ones?"

"Come on."

"I don't know how."

"I'll help. I'll even let you sit on my lap."

"So that's what you want . . ."

"No, seriously, come on over. It'll be fine. Promise."

Annie crossed over the space between the wheel well and seat. Joe helped her get positioned between his legs on the foam rubber seat.

"Now take the wheel," Joe said. "I'll help."

Annie grasped the black metal steering wheel and squeezed it so tight that Joe saw her knuckles whiten. She felt the tug of the narrow twin front wheels reverberate all the way up the steering column and into her fingers as they bounced and jerked over the uneven soil.

"It's a lot like a really big motorized tricycle, don't you think?"

"Hardly," Annie said, still wrestling with the two-ton machine.

"Now you've got to watch your wheels," Joe said. He no longer needed to shout. His lips moved mere inches from Annie's ears. "Keep the right tractor wheel on the edge of the furrow and check the rear plow wheel, too. You've got to keep the plow straight."

"What's the furrow?"

"It's this little gully we're driving down."

They continued another 50 yards or so. "There, you're doing great," Joe said.

"Ah, ha," Annie let out a little triumphant scream. "I'm plowing."

At the end of the field, Joe partially took over, but he still let Annie hydraulically raise and lower the plow, pull back the tractor throttle, and send them on their way again. Joe leaned in and kissed Annie's inviting neck.

"Don't, Joe," Annie said hunching her shoulders. "I can't concentrate when you're nibbling."

Joe backed off and looked over Annie's shoulder as she kept the tractor true. He noticed the blond hairs on her arms in the sun, and the same soft down behind her cheekbones. Above the earth's aroma, he still breathed in her perfume.

"I'm really glad you came out today," he said, rubbing Annie's shoulder.

"I am, too."

"I love you, Annie."

"I love you, too, Joe," she said, freeing one hand to reach back blindly to caress his face. He grabbed and held it a moment, until the jolting tractor demanded its return. Annie started to laugh.

"What? It's funny that you love me?" Joe teased.

"No, I was just thinking I'm in love with a cat killer."

"Huh?"

"Your mom told me about Sissy and the kittens. And the hanging."

"That stray deserved it."

"It's okay," Annie said. "I was thinking earlier if I had seen those dead kittens, I might have helped you."

They reached the field's far end once again. "That was a long time ago," Joe reminisced. "It was hard hanging that cat. But it was the right thing to do."

"Would St. Dominic have approved?" Annie asked. "Or did he come later?"

"It wouldn't have mattered. Growing up on the farm, I've seen plenty of births and deaths." Joe grew reflective. "I used to name the bull calves. Apache. Chunky. We'd feed them for a year or so, and then the next thing I know I'm eating one of them at Sunday dinner. That's the farm, though. That's the life I know. It's kind of hard to explain."

Joe corrected Annie's steering. She concentrated less with his talking.

"Take my Dad. One summer he's cutting hay and comes upon a pheasant nest. That hen is sitting there, ready to be sliced in two rather than leave her eggs. So Dad backs up and goes around. He didn't cut that little stand of alfalfa until August. By then those chicks stood a foot tall and ran every which way through the hay. Come fall, though, there was my dad with two of our neighbors hunting, walking that hay field stubble, knocking down those same birds with shotguns. For him, I don't think the two acts were connected. That's sorta the way it is with me. The farm's molded me, too."

"It's sounds like a strange way to grow up."

Joe shrugged. "It is."

As they neared the farm buildings, Joe spied Ruth standing by the barn. She frantically waved a white dishtowel.

"Something's wrong. Hang on, Annie," Joe said. He stopped the tractor and raised the plow, then quickly shifted up through the gears. They bounced around at a higher speed until they hit the flat field road. Joe locked the left brake and they spun 90 degrees in a split second. Joe craned his neck to discover what put Ruth into such hysterics. She still waved the towel wildly. But he saw nothing. A hard right brake sent them barreling toward the barn. There, Joe noticed a new gash in the fence. He slammed on his brakes short of his mother, and had turned off the tractor and was on the ground before the Super M quit backfiring.

"What's happened," he asked, grabbing both of Ruth's arms.

"It's Bertha," she said, trembling. "She busted out again. George tried to stop her but she ran him over."

"Is Dad okay?" Joe blurted out.

"Yes, just a few cuts and bruises. But, Joe, Bertha's broken her leg. George's beside himself. He can't put her down. Someone's got to."

"What's wrong? What's happened?" Annie said, reaching their side. She saw Ruth's pale expression, the hint of tears in her eyes.

"Why don't you take Annie inside, Mom." To Annie, he said, "I've got to help my dad."

Joe turned and ran to the house ahead of the women. He heard Bertha bellowing now, back by the soybean bins. He didn't see her, but spotted George sitting in the grass by the pump house. Inside the house, he went into the small office off the living room where Ruth did the bookkeeping. A cheap bookcase lined most of the room's west wall. Bending down and pulling out the "G" encyclopedia from the bottom row, Joe found the gun case key.

Unlocking the glass door, he first reached for the 16-gauge shotgun, but he couldn't find any slugs in the bottom drawer of the gun case. Buckshot wouldn't do. He opted for the automatic .22, a small caliber rifle but capable of delivering 15 shots. In the drawer, the Remington hollow-point shells stood upright in their box like miniature missiles. Joe carefully inserted 15 shells into the rifle, worked one shell into the chamber, clicked the gun safety on, and strolled past an astonished Annie in the kitchen.

Joe marched purposely toward his father, the .22 automatic swinging freely in his right hand. George didn't move the whole time Joe approached him. Rounding the pump house, Joe finally caught sight of Bertha. She leaned heavily against the wire frame of a corncrib, the bin's protruding yellow cobs poking her in the side as her left hind leg stuck out like the kickstand of a bike. The bone glistened white through a mass of bloody pulp at the hock. Bertha tried to hobble forward, snot dripping from her nostrils. Another bellow and a snort blew the snot into mist. Bertha tried to kneel and collapsed awkwardly and heavily to the ground.

George wasn't aware of Joe until he felt Joe's hand on his shoulder. He turned to reveal a fresh red wire welt across the left side of his face, a mark of his futile attempt to contain Bertha in the cow yard. A silent communications passed between them. For all his gruff and fence-post stubbornness, for all his dogged determination to dominate the undulating fields, George hated killing things unless it was to feed his family. Especially something he helped bring into the world.

"It's okay Dad," Joe said. He continued to touch his father's shoulder. "Why don't you go call the rendering company?"

"Randles won't come. It's Saturday," George said, rubbing his welt. His voice was hollow, defeated. Bertha bawled again. George grimaced and rubbed harder.

"I know it's Saturday. You can call now, though, so they come first thing Monday. That's best."

"She shouldn't be suffering. All she was trying to do was find her calf. I should never have thrown the damn thing back here in the weeds. She must have still smelled it."

"Go call Randles, Dad."

George rose with great effort, looked blankly into Joe's eyes before sauntering toward the house where Ruth and Annie waited inside.

Joe turned to the task at hand. For all the talk of tomcats, killing wasn't his forte, either. But like with the legless ducklings, when something was dying and needed to die quicker, Joe could dispatch it swiftly. Bertha seemed to sense this and tried to rise as Joe neared. Her busted leg prevented her, and she moaned heavily back onto the ground.

Joe squared himself in the weeds, raised the rifle and looked down its short blue-steel barrel at the middle of Bertha's forehead. He clicked off the safety. Bertha glared at him, as if declining a blindfold. Did she know she was about to die? Joe wondered. Can cows sense such things? He had never killed anything so large. A chill down his spine caused him to shiver, and Joe suddenly wished

George would return and do this dirty job. His resolve weakened, the barrel dipped slightly in his hands. He wondered if he should call Doc Harvey and let the vet end Bertha's misery.

Bertha swung her huge head around and tried to lick her bloody leg. She failed, the effort too great. A throaty bawl escaped her frothing lips, and she rolled her gaze back to Joe. His trigger finger ignored the "no" in his mind, so the sharp retort of the gun startled him. The bullet pierced Bertha's skull with an audible pop. But the .22 caliber shell, so capable of cutting a barn rat in two, wasn't meant to drop a full-grown Holstein with a skull the consistency of petrified wood. What Joe thought would instantaneously kill Bertha jolted her upright on her three good legs. Joe fired again and again. Pop, Pop, Pop, into Bertha's skull as she half lunged, half hobbled toward him. The seventh shot sent her back to her knees, where her massive frame quivered before she collapsed. Only then, in the throes of death, did Bertha's dark blood start to ooze from the Orion's belt of small round holes across her white face.

From the living room window, with the lace curtain lifted aside, Annie watched the execution. She saw Joe's hesitation, his cheek raise up from the rifle stock and return again. Then the slight kick of the gun against his shoulder; then a steady stream of rifle hacks until Bertha's head entered her field of vision. Annie gasped as she watched Bertha drop a scant two yards from Joe's feet. Although Joe could now stretch out the gun barrel and touch the dead cow, he had never jumped back. Annie turned away and let the curtain fall.

The executioner stood over his handiwork, sickened by the blood that pooled into the green vegetation before him. Bertha's body twitched, and he debated whether he should fire some shots through her eye. He leaned forward, though, and saw death reflected back hauntingly from Bertha's bulbous eyes. Joe stopped shaking. He ejected the remaining live shells and stooped to pick their golden casings out of the grass. Behind him he heard the screen door slam, then, seconds later, Annie's car kicking up gravel down the driveway.

THE MEADOWLARK

George always said that Congress created daylight savings time for farmers. Changing the solar timetable enabled them to work late into the evening when fields were long dried from morning dew. George drove the Super M tractor into this extended dusk. The farm's last strip of untilled acreage beckoned him. In the corner of his 160 acres, where a creek bubbled into marsh and cattails and formed a natural boundary between the Mitchell farm and O'Leary's and Randolph's, the black soil gave up winter frost last. For that reason, it became the planting ground for George's sole cash crop. Everything else—the corn, alfalfa, soybeans and oats—became fodder for the dairy cows that generated the monthly milk check.

This year George planned on vegetable peas. Green Giant paid an attractive price for the crop, and provided the harvesters, too—enormous green combines that cut swaths through the tangled pea vines like a sperm whale slicing through a sea of plankton. The roving combines spit the harvested pea vines back onto the field as they churned ever forward. George then baled a small portion of the vines for cow feed. Unlike alfalfa, which dried into a musty and scented hay, the pea vines quickly rotted. For three or four days, however, the Holsteins stampeded to the hay bunks for this rare feast.

George's thoughts floated far from peas, contented cows or the July check from Green Giant. As he hitched up the three-bottom plow, Bertha weighed on his mind.

Randles had arrived at 10 a.m. that morning, the rendering truck mud-splattered from its frequent treks down rural roads and into pens to pick up the victims of animal husbandry. Young red and black Duroc hogs that died following castration, calves that died of scours and dehydration, and, as happened one stormy June at Stoebels, half a herd of bloated Holsteins, struck dead when lightning zapped the sole oak under which they sought refuge.

Jerome Randles had been the local renderer for 20 years. In that time, the causes of deaths seldom varied. The way he collected the farm dead did. A motorized winch replaced manual block and pulley. His truck's loading ramp now extended hydraulically.

A jolly, red-faced man despite his morbid profession, Randles efficiently performed his mortuary tasks. Once he knew where the corpse lay, he maneuvered his truck adroitly in reverse. Randles could hop out of the idling cab and lower the manure-splattered tailgate faster than most rodeo stars could lasso and hobble a sprinting steer. Most amazing was the way he wielded the rusted 100-foot chain. Randles unraveled it quickly from the back of the truck. Together, they snaked into the bowels of barns and sheds where the lives of animals ended. Randles could still deftly loop the chain around a stiffened leg or a bloated neck and notch it securely with the claw-like hook at the chain's end. He knew the proper tightness and logistical placement required to tug a 1,500-pound Holstein down a white limed barn floor, or a 300-pound sow out of a sucking wallow of mud.

Randles enjoyed his job, too. Farmers, so often reticent, opened up to talk about their animal losses, as if they were at a neighbor's wake. They spoke of the dead by name, speaking of their virtues or faults. Randles formed a kind of bond by sharing stories of other neighbors' losses. He became a traveling animal obituary for the county.

Of late, his stories sparked keen interest among the dairymen. Some still favored a bull to service their herds. Most others had progressed to artificial insemination. Both camps eagerly listened to Randles' stories of the deformed calves this new science occasionally created. Just last week, Randles visited the Crosby's farm for a calf borne with no eyes and an elongated alligator-like head. And in January, the Randolph's called Randles to pick up the pieces of a stillborn calf that Doc Harvey had quartered during a cesarean to save its mother. While its head loomed gargantuan, its rear legs shriveled into hoofless stumps. These tales of deformity garnered knowing nods from those farmers who believed that tinkering with genetics was not only risky but against God's laws. Randles had no opinion either way, but he gladly shared these stories.

A visit to George Mitchell's farm promised no freaks of nature, because George's bull, Manfred, still patrolled his own pen on the south side of the barn. Today's visit suggested the unusual, however, because George didn't drop whatever he was doing to chat. Instead, George simply signaled from the barn door for Randles to go behind the pump house.

Randles punched the rendering truck into first gear and drove under a box elder tree in search of his quarry. He soon spied the dead cow next to a corncrib, stiff from rigormortis with a hind leg perpendicular to her body as if saluting him.

Slipping the truck into reverse, Randles backed around a rusted trash barrel until Bertha's body half disappeared under the truck in his rearview mirror. Randles hopped to the ground, rolled the tailgate down hydraulically and switched on the winch. It played out the cable with a whine. Grabbing the hook and looking for the best place to enwrap Bertha, Randles saw the cause of death. The wounds resembled a series of commas across her massive head, the round bullet holes having each dripped their serifs of blood. That explained why George stayed away, Randles knew. If farmers regarded their livestock like family, and Randles' visits like church wakes, George was in mourning. Obviously George or someone ended the cow's life. A mercy killing, no doubt, but something harder to swallow than a bolt of God's lightning or twisted DNA. Likely a great story, Randles thought. It might sustain him and his patrons for weeks. He vowed to get all the gory details before he left.

Randles hung his makeshift noose around Bertha's neck and scraped her massive carcass through the weeds and up the ramp and into the coffin of his truck. There Bertha joined an ancient Guernsey, its carcass so emaciated that its ribs visibly protruded against its brown hide.

George stayed in the milk house until he saw Randles truck lumber back across the ruts he had created in the search for his prize. Ruth emerged from the porch, checkbook in hand. Only then did George venture towards the cab.

"Must have been a hard one for you," Randles said imploringly down to Ruth and George from his rolled-down window.

"What do we owe you?" George asked matter-of-factly.

"$27 should cover it," Randles said, disappointed. He watched Ruth rest the checkbook atop the truck's hood and scrawl out the amount. Randles tried again.

"How long she been dead, in case they ask?" "They" being the rendering plant. A Buchenwald-looking building near the stockyards by the river where animals like Bertha were eviscerated, torn of their hides, and summarily poked, stewed, trimmed and processed until they were "rendered" into animal byproducts. Hooves and ears were processed into dog chews, the smooth hide of the underbelly cured to make baseball covers.

"Saturday about 2 o'clock," Ruth answered, handing the blue check to Randles. He accepted it crisply, then doffed his hat and began to wipe its sweat-soaked inside brim with his handkerchief.

"She busted her leg and Joe shot her with the .22."

It all came together at last for Randles. Another tale to tell, maybe embellished in the process with the cow so riddled full of holes. "Sorry to hear of your bad luck," Randles said, tugging his hat back on and giving a tip of its visor. "I best be going. Becker's lost a fresh cow to milk fever last night. One of his best milkers, I hear. Not a good day in dairy land"

With that he waved and rumbled down the driveway. George was relieved that visible signs of Bertha vanished forever.

Now, tugging the plow and Bertha's loss behind him, George headed down the lane that divided his fields in neat quadrants. Past the cow yard and to his left, this year's alfalfa stretched like a long green throw rug, first down into a hollow, and then up an adjoining hill to the county road. To his right, his earlier planted corn rose in neat rows like green herringbone stripes in a new black suit.

The lane ran east for a hundred yards before taking a right turn into the heart of George's 160 acres. The machinery-compacted lane rolled beneath George in a new growth of dandelion, thistle and milkweed. To the west, the sun floated earthward, promising George an hour till dark. Enough time to unfold half of the 20 acres decreed for peas before he would need his lights. George pulled back the Super M's throttle, and sped faster down the lane. He jounced in the seat and lifted his Pioneer Seed cap to let the wind breeze through his thinning hair. He startled a pocket gopher scooping out dirt from his newest mound of underground excavation. Otherwise, he was alone.

Despite his melancholy mood, George looked forward to reaching his last stretch of untilled soil. It was his favorite field. Away from the roads, at the very junction where his land abutted at right angles with Randolph's and O'Leary's, the field came as close to a sanctuary as George could find. It sloped out of sight from the farm's buildings as gradually as the curvature of the earth. George found solace atop the black soil of this rounded shoulder of his domain.

Tonight was no exception, as he lowered the shiny blades of the John Deere plow into the edge of the field. The roots of last year's corn crop popped audibly as the plow blades cut like a surgeon's scalpel into the loamy soil. George set his sights on the distance fence line a quarter of a mile away, and made his first long, straight incision. The Super M struggled through the soil at only a few miles per hour, as the underground mangrove of corn stalk roots clung tight. The plow rolled over a five-foot swath. If a jetliner had been overhead, the triad of George, tractor and plow would have resembled a caterpillar slowing chewing its way through ochre vegetation and leaving a trail of black refuse in its wake.

Nearing the end of the field, George first heard then saw the meadowlark. Muted against the graying sky except for its mustard-colored breast, the meadowlark tipped back its head and warbled a claim to his homestead among the blackberry bramble and emerging foxtail that edged the field.

Every year George longed to hear a meadowlark more than any other bird. The cardinal, a yearlong resident, started singing in early February when his scarlet jacket held easy dominion over the dull gray snow. Mourning doves cooed as early as March, but George considered them mournful indeed, and rather stupid looking, too, with their pea-size heads bobbing above pear-shaped bodies. Robins owned April. Like the rain, they were too commonplace. The meadowlarks awaited the warmth of late April, when insects hung in the air like floating buffets. This meadowlark sang like an Italian tenor—proud and well rehearsed. George pushed the tractor throttle forward and turned off the Super M to enjoy the performance. No other sound existed beyond the measured trill of the small bird. It flitted from post to wire, working the fence like the frets of a guitar. Its same song proclaimed, "I'm here, I'm forever here."

The meadowlark reminded George of himself. Forsaking the forests for the tranquility of the open prairie the same as George shunned the bustle of the city. Driven by instinct and southern winds to the same dip of land each spring as surely as the season sent George crisscrossing this very field. Shy and skirtive one moment, but driven in defense of its domain the next.

George savored its song. The sheer beauty of its arias this April evening helped block Bertha from his thoughts. For the past three weeks, he had lived the life of his dreams. Thinking of his happiness, George wondered what lay beyond the Pledge. Joe stood a scant month away from graduation. Then what? They were just eking by. George paid Joe a measly $50 a month for his 150 hours of labor. No hired man would set foot on the place for 10 times that amount. George suddenly realized why he was so blue. He knew he couldn't continue farming without Joe, not only for his lost labor, but for the purpose he gave George to farm in the first place. A reason to toil. To raise a good son and have a good family life. Could Ruth and he survive as a couple without Joe at their center?

"Damn," George said aloud, and shook his shoulders to free the grip of these thoughts he had successfully buried until Bertha's death. He pressed the rubber starter with his thumb. The Super M belched back into action, spooking the meadowlark from its perch. George completed the last 100 feet of the first furrow before raising the plow blades, turning left and following the fence line south until he reached the edge of the marsh. George wheeled tractor and plow parallel to the marsh to start a new furrow heading east. In this way, he marked the edges of his field. The soil here rolled off the blades in thick clods as black as used motor oil. Heavy with lowland moisture, the land abutting the marsh produced a copious growth of foxtail, velvetleaf and cockleburs every summer. Despite his cultivating, they choked the neat rows of corn or beans with their unbridled growth. This refuse of weeds and withered corn stalks bunched over the plow blades, at times reaching high enough to tickle the plow's long, straight green shaft. The slick soil, too, sucked at the Super M's massive rear wheels, and, for a second, George debated whether he should raise the plow, head home and let the field dry out another day. Instead, he pulled the throttle back. The Super M lunged forward, its wheels spitting up globs of dirt and roots.

A quarter of a century earlier his father probably faced the same scenario, George thought. A field too wet to work, but the press of the season requiring that he push on. Then, two colossal Belgian horses, Queenie and Maude, dragged the plow.

George remembered them now. Magnificent bronze beasts standing nearly six feet at the shoulders, with manes and tails the color of August oats. John, his father, could curlicue the reins over their rumps to slap their shoulders, and Queenie and Maude responded as one to unearth a stubborn boulder or rotate a harvester's swath. What George remembered most was their agility despite their size. Freed of their harnesses except for the sweat shadows they left, the two horses often frolicked in their paddock. They glowed with the low sun as they chased each other around in the confined space, their manes and tails flying. Later they rolled on their backs in the dust, their hooves airborne and as big and round as cymbals.

While they ate hay from their feed bunk, George would climb onto Queenie's back. Maude would buck, but Queenie ignored him except for sending an occasional rolling quiver down her spine as if George were a gnat she could simply flick away. George let the quiver flow through his legs. He leaned forward, grabbing Queenie's mane, and pretended he was Red Rider or Johnny Mack Brown. He loved those horses.

Then one day John drove up the long drive with a new red Farmall tractor as ominous as blood. The Farmall "H" pulled a two-bottom plow with ease. And with its external drive shaft, it easily ran the black, belching threshing machine at oat harvest time. The retired Queenie and Maude languished in their paddock, and only cocked an ear when the Farmall roared into action. Their retirement seemed harsh to George, but Queenie and Maude reveled in it. If an apple tree fell in the orchard, or sometimes out of nostalgia, John would hitch up the team to give them a workout and himself a chance to again feel the leather reins looped around his hands. Sometimes, in the frigid winter, the tractor wouldn't start, its battery frozen. John reverted back to the Belgians to spread the barn manure, or pull stalled cars out of the drifted snow along the highway. In time, the horses aged to the point John had to choose between glue or burial. Always frugal, John sent Queenie and Maude to the rendering plant. Following the memory, George realized it was the first time he had met Jerome Randles. That took him all too quickly back to Bertha. And Joe. Like George's father, Joe could be an executioner. Joe lacked George's years, and the tiredness that came with many deaths and the struggle to beat nature's odds on the farm. That would soften Joe's ability to kill in time.

George also dwelt on the financial loss with Bertha. Joe blew away $1,200 with his mercy killing. Bertha's dead calf meant he lost a future replacement heifer. Neither boded well when stacked atop the monthly bills for feed, vet services, machinery repair or other necessities for the farm—5-gallon pails of grease, tightly wrapped rolls of twine, propane to warm the house. Springtime brought huge seasonal expenses for fertilizer, fuel and seed. Each year he pulled loans from the Troy First National Bank as fast as a gambler pulled markers in Vegas. And, like a Blackjack player holding 16, he sweated for seven months to see what weather card the dealer rolled over.

Drought or too much rain, corn boring insects or hail—any or all of them could descend upon his crops and deplete the harvest he needed to feed his dairy herd. After 20 years before the green felt gambling table that was his farm, George still rolled the dice. He put his faith in God to provide. Especially out in this corner pocket of the farm, where the sky seemed biggest and the land the gentlest, he felt God's presence. Here he took his communion.

The lane appeared suddenly, startling George from his thoughts. He repeated the same mechanics the end of the field required. The hydraulic whined, the muffler putt-putted, and the engine hummed with the plow free. He turned left for his counter-clockwise consumption of the field.

George thought again of his father and his own unending loyalty to follow John Mitchell on the farm. John died tossing hay bales off a wagon, a heart attack at age 76. He gripped George's hand as he lay silently dying against the wagon wheel. George felt the same quiver through John's hands as he felt upon Queenie's back years earlier, and then John was gone. Everyone understood George would take over the farm. He did it proudly. Joe felt no such loyalty. George recalled the mantra of farm ownership: "The father breaks the ground; the son works it; the grandson sells it."

Being honest, George knew the farm held no future for Joe. Today, his 160 acres produced barely enough to feed his Holsteins. With deflated milk prices, George borrowed against his land to continue farming. The Troy First National owned nearly half of everything if George quit today.

At the same time, the thought of Joe leaving angered him. Today, his son, His Son, could end his livelihood. He lashed out at this thought, not so much due to Joe but because 20 years of farming found him in this predicament. He had been too cautious. Never expanding while his neighbors gobbled up acreage, or modernizing while others mechanized their operations with electric silo unloaders and milk lines that pumped milk straight from the cow's udder into a bulk tank. Never trusting the new genetics that helped his neighbors boost their cows' milk production by 30%.

Instead, he clung to his father's ways. Afraid of borrowing, experimenting, and failing. Afraid, afraid, afraid. George turned on the tractor's lights as the tilled and untilled soil blended together in the gathering twilight. He caught a glimpse of a bird he assumed was the meadowlark as he again neared the western edge of his land. The sun gone, the bird no longer sang, its breast no longer shone.

Nearby, Joe left the gravel road for the fields. A cottontail parted the ditch grass and, with rapid bounds, leapt for the culvert that ran beneath the road. The rabbit had spooked him. It was just such events, plus the prospect of twisting an ankle in the dark, that Joe tried to avoid on these evening runs. But he worried about falling behind his teammates. In the fading light, he gingerly stepped over the sprouting green corn as he made his diagonal course home. He liked crossing the rows because they forced him to stretch his stride, and the tilled earth was soft and giving beneath his feet. He felt different muscles at work, different tendons loosened.

Coming up over a rise in the field and nearing the field lane, Joe first heard the tractor then saw telltale belches of black smoke in the purple glow of the western sky. Both signaled trouble. Joe changed course and jogged southwest. Soon he spied George. Stopping 25 yards away, Joe crouched and saw his father throw up his hands, put the tractor in park and climb down to the plow.

George tipped his cap back and inspected the compacted mess. Even with the plow blades raised to their zenith, they were almost engulfed in a weedy wallow 10 yards from the creek's edge. With mud half way up the calves of his OshKosh overalls, George struggled to dislodge the pile of dirt and weeds that imprisoned the front half of the plow.

Joe listened in shadow to his father's curses. They punctuated the running conversation George held with the plow. Tugging on the labyrinth of stalks, a few broke free and sent George sprawling backward into the muck. George hopped to his feet quickly, a fighter too feisty to stay down for the count. He approached the plow again, and kicked rubber tires and metal alike. In resignation, he remounted the tractor and buried his head in his arms atop the steering wheel. Joe heard George mumbling and, embarrassed, realized George was praying.

"I have to get this done, Lord," George lamented. "I'm dead in this seat, so give me this. Bust up this clump. Send a bolt of lightning or just wink at it, but get it done and me home to supper." George stopped as if he thought the skies might actually part. Nothing happened, and George again buried his head.

Joe knew George believed in the power of prayer. Still, from the look of things, Joe figured it would take a month of rosaries to raise the plow from the quagmire. Not wishing to hear more and ashamed of his spying, Joe faked breathing hard and ran forward. Startled, George looked down at him from atop the tractor.

"Looks like you've got problems," Joe offered. George had removed his goggles. He looked the reverse of a raccoon, a flesh-colored eye mask stood out from his dirty face.

"I'm glad all your schooling has improved your observation," George chided, glad to see Joe. "I can't work the hydraulic, rock the plow and attack the damn clump at the same time, so an extra set of hands would be appreciated."

"Do you want me on the tractor or working on that plug?"

"I'm already dirty, so you climb up. I'm going to find something to pry with," George said, hopping down to the ground. He wiped his muddy hands on the front of his bibs as he walked to the nearby fence line. Joe had barely settled into the Super M's seat before George found a post frequented by the meadowlark. Rotted at ground level, it was easy to dislodge. George hefted it and trudged back to the plow. Climbing onto the plow's spine, he directed Joe on the course of action.

"I can't rip this clump apart with my hands, Lord knows I've tried. And I can't come at it from the bottom. So I'm going to try to cleave it in two from the top," George said, straddling the middle of the plow. "Keep the tractor in neutral and work the hydraulic up and down. If that and this post don't work, I may have you rock things back and forth. But do it slow and careful, and listen for my signals."

Joe fired up the tractor. He maneuvered the hydraulic lever slowly up and down. Behind him, growing fainter in the ebbing light, George probed, scooped and bashed at the main clump.

"There's no place for this damn ball to go. Not enough space between it and the ground," George yelled. He looked around for a better angle or some way to use the post as a fulcrum, and came up empty. "Try to pull ahead a bit. Maybe that will give me more room."

Working the hydraulic, the clutch and throttle in unison, Joe coaxed the tractor forward against its earthy constraints.

"Keep doing what you're doing, it's helping," George commanded as he peered down into the coagulated blob.

Getting into a rhythm between first gear and reverse, Joe turned in the seat to watch George. His father stood silhouetted against the dusk, the plow beneath him a defused, colorless blur of shadows. For a moment, with the post hoisted in two hands and plunging into the ball's flesh, George reminded Joe of Captain Ahab. Only his obsession wasn't a white whale, but a cursed beast as black as the gloom around him. Down rammed the harpoon, seeking the beast's heart and an end to this twilight madness. Now and then George managed to hack off a chunk of the refuse. Or sink his post into a fissure that sucked and gasped when he wiggled the harpoon back and forth.

"We're getting there, Joe! Slowly put some more torque to her," he said, leaning his full weight into a new fissure that promised to crack open the clump.

The beast struck back. Joe pulled the throttle back a few more notches. That and George's furious workings suddenly meshed to split and roll half the clump away. Tractor, plow and riders bolted forward. George followed his post straight to the ground, where the freed plow blades carved their way over him.

"Dad! Are you okay? Oh my God!" Joe yelled hearing George scream.

Joe pulled the tractor ahead to get the plow off George and in one swift motion leapt to his side. George lay half submerged in the mud. The weight of the plow blades and wheel had pressed him into the soft folds of the wallow. On hard ground, the blades would likely have cut his legs clean off. As it was, the blades had sliced into both of George's thighs. Even with all the mud and darkness, Joe knew by its warmth that the surrounding wetness was blood. He brought a sticky finger to his tongue to remove any doubt. George spooked him by suddenly trying to rise. He fell back with a roar of pain.

"Dad, Dad. Is it more than your legs? Christ, Dad, I'm sorry!" Joe looked around in panic, seeking he knew not what.

George moaned. Joe put his ear close to George's lips.

"My legs," George gasped. "The left one . . . the left one I think is broken. Jesus, it hurts. Help me, Joe. You gotta help me."

"Dad, you're bleeding bad," Joe said. "I've got to stop the flow."

Joe ripped off his sweatshirt to make a tourniquet but, in the dark, he didn't know which leg to bind or where to apply the pressure. Tucking his sweatshirt into the side of his shorts, he tried to pull George out of the hole. He dragged George about six feet before George's shrieks stopped him. He laid George back onto the ground and sprinted to the tractor. Uncoupling the hydraulic hose and unhitching the plow, he hopped into the seat. Locking the right brake, he spun the tractor 180 degrees so that the Super M's lights framed George.

In the light, George's wounds made Joe gasp. Shredded denim, mud and blood coalesced in ragged gashes. The left leg was mangled the worst and oozed blood freely. Joe stifled an urge to gag, and now seeing clearly his task, encircled the upper thigh with his sweatshirt. Crossing the sleeves, he made the tightest knot possible. George's loud scream momentarily silenced the frogs. They began droning again as Joe examined George's other leg. This one revealed a cleaner gash, and not as deep, but it, too, bled freely. Joe unbuckled George's belt. Encrusted in mud, it felt like a cold snake in his hands. He slid it under George's right leg and fashioned it into another tourniquet with a slipknot.

The pain in George's legs throbbed through his whole body. He watched Joe working over him. In the harsh light, Joe looked like an angel. St. Joseph with his strength. When the belt tightened on his second leg, George thought of Bertha, and how Joe had taken care of that cripple. He reached out and grabbed Joe's naked shoulder with a muddy hand.

"Joe, you've got to go get help. This is no good, this is no good."

"I'm not leaving you, Dad," Joe said. There was good reason. He didn't think George would be alive by the time he got back, with all the blood he had lost. "We're going home together."

Joe climbed aboard the Super M again. This time he steered the tractor until its rear stood a yard from where George lay. He needed a rope or something. "Think, Joe, think, or Dad's going to die," he gasped out loud. Then he remembered the hydraulic hose. One end still dangled from the back of the tractor. About 8 feet in length to reach from tractor to plow, it would suffice. On the ground again, Joe propped George up and slipped his arms under his armpits. With all his strength, he dragged George to the tractor and, taking another breath, hoisted him with a grunt onto the tractor's low u-shaped hitching bar. He ignored George's now barely coherent pleas for him to stop because of the pain. Resting George against the inside of the right wheel well fender, Joe yanked the loose end of the rubber hose across George's torso and over his shoulder. Joe looped it through the coils of the tractor seat and pulled it taut. He tried to slip his hand between George's chest and the hose. Satisfied he couldn't, he tied it off.

George screamed in protest as Joe started across the field, for his feet still dragged on the ground and every bump jiggled his wounds. Joe blocked the screams out, and drove as fast as his lights allowed. Night had truly fallen now, and the farm's yard light shone like a beacon 500 yards away. The drive seemed forever. George quit screaming and Joe hoped he had only passed out, and not died. Nearing the turn in the lane that ran parallel to the cow yard, Joe suddenly saw his lights reflected in a dozen pair of eyes. By the time the rest of the ghostly images of the pasturing cows materialized, they were turning, their udders swinging as they charged away. About 100 yards from the house, Joe started pounding on the tractor's anemic-sounding horn and yelling with all his might. He was almost to the barn when the front porch light flashed on and Ruth came running out the door.

HONEYMOON IN TAHITI

The surgeons worked to save George's legs until 3 a.m., setting bones, mending muscle and sewing shredded veins. The lead surgeon, Dr. Baker, a tall, balding man with a beak for a nose and a nasal voice, told Ruth that Joe's quick actions saved George's life. Dr. Baker droned on about unknown nerve damage and how well the muscle fiber would mend. Ruth heard talk of pins and 60% or 70% use of the right leg through a fog of exhaustion. All she could think about was that, barring unforeseen blood clots, George would live.

Joe slept in the corner chair in the waiting room, wrapped loosely in a powder blue hospital gown. He had remained shirtless and muddy until the nurses led him out of the emergency room and into a vacant room with a shower. The pulsating water and a sedative ensured he didn't pace during the five-hour surgery.

Ruth left Joe sleeping and called John Franksmeier to fill him in on the accident and garner his help for one morning to handle the milking until Joe returned. Then she followed Dr. Baker down the quiet halls to the intensive care unit.

"He's still heavily sedated and I don't expect him to rouse for several hours," Dr. Baker said, stifling a yawn. "But you can sit here awhile if you want."

"Thank you, Doctor, for all you've done." Ruth shook his manicured hand.

Ruth pulled an armchair along side George's bed. Its wooden armrests were worn from many late night vigils. George laid there, tubes coming out of his nose and an IV dripping clear liquid into his right arm. Plaster encased his entire left leg, and Ruth ran her hand down the hard shell. The right leg lay in heavy bandages. Ruth watched the faint rise and fall of George's chest and let her hand settle there. She felt his pulse through the thin flannel gown. Her mind drifted to the countless times she had found solace on George's chest.

Solid and smooth-skinned, it was broad enough to pillow her sorrows or cradle her joy. Tears in her eyes, she focused on the latter.

St. Patrick's Day in 1949. An arctic blast swept out of Canada, dumping unexpected knee-deep snow and bringing -30°F below wind chill. Drifts clogged the rural roads. Pheasants roosted in the evergreens. Without cars, without movement, a silvery silence settled over the farms. The land simply shut down, waiting for the road plows. The two-bedroom farm house they rented that first year of marriage shook with the wind. Cold air seeped in around the plastic-covered windows and wisped its way across the linoleum floors. George, unable to get to his job at Shell Oil, ate a leisurely breakfast with Ruth. Then he announced he was going to fill a 5-gallon pail with fuel oil from the raised tank 25 yards from the house.

"George," Ruth pleaded, unable to even see the tank through the blowing snow, "you're not going out in this blizzard. We've got enough fuel until this storm ends."

George ignored her, buckling up his black rubber boots and putting on enough layers so he could barely move his arms. "Not enough fuel for what I have in mind." Turning to go outside, he said through his scarf. "Don't worry. I'll tie a rope around me in the garage. Even if I get misdirected, I can always pull my way back."

Not mollified, Ruth wrapped on her own winter coat and scarf, and donned her fur-lined Sunday boots, and stood in the garage while George trudged into the drifts. Within seconds the whiteness swallowed him up. Ruth watched the constant movement of the rope to assure herself that George made progress. The rope suddenly went slack and Ruth panicked. She yelled his name above the howling wind until she realized the slack rope meant George was filling the oil can. Sure enough, about three minutes later, the rope came alive again. Finally George emerged from the swirling snow, as white as powdered sugar, and they both hurried back inside. Climbing out of their overcoats and boots, they let the snow melt on the floor mat. George hefted the can and filled the stove's reservoir to within an inch of the top. Setting the can down, he hunched down and turned the burners wide open. The flames jumped bold and blue behind the stove's tempered glass.

"George, what on earth are you doing? It'll be 80 degrees in here inside of 10 minutes."

A grin crossed George's face. "You're right; it'll probably be too hot to even wear clothes."

"George, you're a devil."

When he reached out for her, though, Ruth hurried into his arms.

"Let's pretend we're richer than the Rockefellers and honeymooning in Tahiti." George kissed Ruth full on the lips. "Why don't you make yourself comfortable, and I'll get us some cold beer."

They drank three beers apiece, and made love after each. By 2 p.m. they slept naked on top of the quilt on their bed. Ruth awoke later sweating in the dark. She grabbed her robe out of false decency and scurried downstairs to lower the temperature on the stove. Looking out the west window, she saw no lights on the highway. They were still socked in. Upon her return to bed, George sat up, his hair disheveled.

"Is it morning?" he asked groggily.

Ruth cast her robe aside and lay down beside him. "No, it's still our honeymoon."

MOHAMMED ALI

"It's a hard thing you will be asking of Joseph," Bill Becker told Ruth as he stirred another spoon of sugar into his cup. They sat in the mid-morning quiet, a slight breeze whispering through the screen door and slanting the steam from their coffee.

"I don't know what else to do," Ruth said. She, too, stirred her coffee, but without purpose. "The doctor said George will be in the cast for at least two months. Then there's physical therapy. When he comes home he'll insist on at least doing the tractor work, but he can't handle the milking."

"Some of us neighbors can help out from time to time," Bill offered. He sat stiffly next to Ruth, his straw hat on the table next to his cup, a balding German immigrant with a dirge of a voice. A good neighbor, like all the other farmers who surrounded the Mitchell's place. They all gave of their labor, but this seeking of advice on somebody else's family matters rubbed Bill like a hair shirt.

"Thank you, I know you will. But you've got your own herd to milk, and you're doing it twice a day, same as us."

"Ach, that's true, Ruth," Bill said. He rubbed the crease his hat had made across his forehead, not knowing what else to say. Ruth spoke the truth. Like children, the cows had to be fed and tended to throughout the day. They had to be stripped of their milk every 12 hours. Every dairyman wore a mantle of relentless responsibility.

"The good thing is school ends in a month or so and Mr. Varness the principal said Joe could make up tests throughout the summer," Ruth said. "More coffee?" The German shook his head.

"Do you think Joseph sees this coming?" Bill saw the anguish on Ruth's face. If he had not been German, a farmer and a neighbor, he would have reached out to console her. But he was all three, and sat quietly.

"Yes," Ruth said.

Coach O'Reilly excused Joe from track practice following Ruth's call. Joe had already spent two long days milking and caring for the dairy herd alone while the doctors observed George's legs for blood clots and infections. At each day's end, almost too weary to converse, he fielded Annie's calls. Joe explained the situation, saying it was temporary, and that Ruth was seeking help from neighbors so Joe could resume classes and, more importantly, he told Annie, their relationship.

Ruth finally approached him in the hay loft. Joe noticed the bales stacked to the ceiling to his sides and behind him, and thought how tactically his mother had cut off his options to flee.

"Joe, we need to talk about the farm and your dad," Ruth began, climbing up a few rows of bales. Joe removed his leather work gloves, hesitated briefly, and then hopped down beside Ruth. He looked straight ahead, not facing her.

"The doctor says George needs to stay in the hospital another week. And once he's at home, he must stay off his left leg completely for another three weeks."

Joe remained silent. He looked at the square of blue sky through the hay shed door and awaited the blow.

"There's no easy way to say it, so I'll just say it. I need you to drop out of school until George is able to help again."

Joe felt gut-punched. "What about graduating? And track? And Annie?"

"I've talked to every neighbor, every farmer I thought might be able to help us out. I've racked my brains since this happened to find another way," Ruth said sincerely. She picked at some hay stems protruding from a bale. "I know you have, too. Have you found a solution?"

Joe slowly shook his head and cast his eyes downward. He had thought about it on and off for three days. "No," he mumbled. The despair at accepting reality rushed over him.

"It isn't fair, Mom," he said angrily. "Just when I was finding some happiness. Just when I had found someone. And now you want to ruin it. All because of this damn farm."

"Joe, don't swear. I can't help it your father's lying in the hospital. So I have no choice. You want to know what we owe Wharton's for seed and fertilizer this spring? $2,000. And to Henson's for our dairy feed each month? $500. The only thing that offsets those bills is the milk check. We're just getting by. If we don't manage the herd, we're finished."

Ruth continued more steadily as if her explanation resolved the issue. "I've talked to the principal and your teachers and they say you can make up your lessons later this summer and graduate. By then, George will be on his feet."

"And what about after that?" Joe asked hotly. "I'm not staying around this hell-hole after this summer. How are you going to manage then? Whatever you were planning for next fall why don't you do it now?"

"I can't think that far ahead, Joe. Right now I've got to make sure we survive the next month. My heart aches for you, believe me. I just don't know what else to do. There's not enough money to hire someone for two months, and even if there were, I don't know who it might be."

Ruth turned away and fought back tears. Joe didn't know what to do. Already thrust into the role of dairy manager, he balked at assuming George's role of comforting Ruth. Still, he reached out his right hand and touched her shoulder. Ruth grasped his hand and gave it a sideways tug, but remained facing away.

"I'm sorry, so sorry, Joe," she whispered.

Joe leaned back against the bales, and felt their prickly jabs. He squeezed his leather gloves, looked where the shirt sleeve of hay dust ended on his wrists where he had pulled them off.

"So am I, Mom," Joe said. "So am I."

"What do you mean you're going to miss school for a while?" Annie said into the phone, bewildered. Over the line, Joe tried to explain that milking on his own took nearly twice as long. The daily chores that combined took George and Joe three hours to complete now fell solely on Joe's shoulders. And although all but the pea crop nestled in their seed beds, Joe still faced some field work. He informed Annie he would miss the rest of the week of school, maybe more.

It made no sense at all to Annie. Her father worked for Data Systems. Harry always had backup. They lived in the suburbs. Their evenings were free. Farming remained as alien to Annie as life in China. And like many other things foreign, she rejected Joe's excuses.

"Well, then, I'll hardly get to see you at all. Can you still make it to Betty's Saturday?"

Joe wanted desperately to say yes. Even if he finished milking by 9:00 p.m., though, it would take a half-hour to scrub off the barn stench. Yes, he could arrive by 10:00 p.m., but he was so exhausted that the idea held no appeal, no matter how much he missed Annie.

"I don't think so."

"Joe, please, I want you there. I miss you."

"Maybe I can see you Sunday afternoon."

"What will I tell the guys when you don't show up at Betty's?"

"Tell them the truth."

Joe waited for a reply but only heard Annie's soft breathing over the line.

"How long does this have to go on, Joe?" The voice was fraught with frustration.

"My dad can't do anything for at least a month, so it's going to take me right through late May," Joe said weakly. "I'm sorry Annie."

"What about prom? That's May 15th." Another pause. "You're not telling me you can't even go to the prom?"

"Don't worry, I'll figure out a way to take you, Annie. I'll have my mom find some neighbor who can help out that one night."

"You'll be able to go on the picnic on Sunday, too, won't you?"

"Sure, by then I can. Please be patient. I have no choice."

"Okay, then, no party Saturday. I'll call you tomorrow."

Joe cringed at the disappointment laced in Annie's voice.

"I love you, Annie."

"I love you, too," Annie said, and hung up.

Joe sat numbly at the kitchen table. He thought about calling back, but he had nothing new to offer. No new hope. Morning for him now came at 4:00 a.m., so he plodded wearily up the steps. He fell quickly into exhausted sleep.

Ruth overheard Joe's conversation from the living room. It pained her to see his first real relationship floundering. She knew how lucky they were to have Joe, how willingly he made the sacrifices required by the farm. At the same time Joe's deep sense of duty seemed unhealthy. Part of her wished Joe would shed the shackles of her request and walk away. Saying "no" would force George and Ruth to face the reality of their future. Instead he sacrificed. Joe's recent enthusiasm raised their spirits. They marveled at the freed bird. Now she was returning him to his cage.

BRANDY MANHATTANS

Frank Oster swirled the remainder of his second brandy Manhattan around the bottom of his glass, then sucked down the amber liquid with one gulp. He liked his drinks sweet, like his women, he was wont to say, although there were no women.

"Rich, one more," he said to the bartender, the only other person in the VFW at this early hour. The VFW was a dingy rectangular room with dark wood paneling from floor to ceiling. Equally dingy small square tables filled two thirds of the room, each with a red votive candle wrapped in glass and mesh plopped in the middle for atmosphere. Narrow windows near the entrance let in minimal light. They illuminated the Trojans' basketball schedule, the scores of each game written in by magic marker pen. Calendars from several of the town's small businesses graced the walls. In one corner, covered by tables for the noon crowd, lay a rectangular wooden dance floor. The bar dominated the north side of the room. Its lip showed the wear of thousands of elbows. If he weren't already an alcoholic, the place probably would have driven Frank to drink.

He was especially thirsty today, having walked the three-and-one-half miles from his parents' farm into town. They had revoked his driving privileges, which didn't seem possible to Frank since he was 32 years old. In their case revoking privileges simply meant stealing Frank's keys from his pants pocket after he passed out on his bed. Although his actions warranted the revocation, it still left Frank boiling. Nick, his father, made the rules when it came to the farm work, and commandment number one said, "Thou shall not operate farm equipment drunk." Frank disobeyed, and didn't think leveling the apple sapling should constitute a violation.

Rich set down the third Manhattan and made change out of the $20 bill Frank placed flat on the counter. Frank picked out the maraschino cherry with his left hand and rolled it around his tongue for several seconds before tugging the stem between his teeth as if de-pinning a grenade. He squeezed the cherry against the roof of his mouth, and awaited yet another little explosion of sweet escape. Problem was Frank had been trying to escape for 15 years. Escape was as useless as his right arm.

Frank pitched for the Troy baseball team those many years ago. A lanky kid, he had long sinewy arms and a high kick. The afternoon his fastball tore the webbing out of Gary Snyder's catcher's mitt his teammates named the pitch "The Frankquilizer" because it silenced opponents' bats. A scout from the Minneapolis Millers even came to watch Frank pitch. Frank promptly threw a two-hitter, fanning 11. There was talk of a tryout and a possible minor league contract.

The accident happened after school ended. Nick cut the first crop hay. The next day Frank raked the green stems into neat, tubular rows. He later sat on the John Deere tractor, which pulled the baler, while Nick used a baling hook to pierce the hay bales and lift them off the baler's chute onto the wagon for stacking. The baler churned rhythmically as its toothed auger ingested the alfalfa. It was a mindless job and one that let Frank daydream about baseball contracts and a future that had previously seemed beyond his grasp. With the wagon loaded, Nick hollered for Frank to kill the power take-off—the cylinder that revolved at more than 500 rpms from the back of the tractor and turned the internal gears on the baler—and unhitch the baler from the tractor. Only Frank remained rooted in a ninth-inning fantasy. Jumping down, Frank's open shirttails brushed the spinning power take-off rod. Instantly, it tore off his shirt. The bunching of it in the gears mercifully clogged the cylinder to a stop, but not before Frank's arm partially wrapped around the cylinder. Nick rushed to turn off the power take-off. But from just above his elbow to his finger tips, Frank's arm was crushed around the metal, white bone protruding where the elbow separated, sinew and muscle stretched and bunched into unnatural configurations.

The doctors said it was a miracle Frank's arm hadn't been ripped off. That brought little consolation to Frank, whose reconstructed arm allowed him to fill out a sleeve but little else. In time, he regained some use of his right shoulder and upper arm, so he could use it as for leverage when lifting or driving. He grew adept at using his left hand.

Frank fell into a dark depression. Incapable of helping on the farm, he spent the winter indoors. In the spring, Nick coerced Frank to try pitching left-handed. Southpaw pitchers were rarer than 100-bushel-per-acre corn, he explained. He bought Frank a glove for his deformed right hand, and kept it in place with a band of rubber looped around Frank's elbow. Frank tossed a rubber ball off the red barn door onto which Nick had chalked a white batter's box. Frank's erratic throws careened every which way off the barn. He couldn't field well with the glove because his useless hand couldn't squeeze the leather tight. When Nick realized his efforts caused his son only sorrow, he painted over the chalk lines so that section of the barn door sparkled an unblemished apple red again.

Nick and Irene did everything within their means to help Frank find a one-arm job. Searching through the vo-tech school offerings, they quickly nixed most trades. Frank's grades ruled out college. Nick eventually landed Frank a job as a car salesman at Brickman's Buick. There, Frank's right arm remained hidden inside his suit coat sleeve. His left hand could still open a car door, pop a hood and sign a contract.

Frank's bouts of depression kept returning, however. His worst spell followed a poor fall harvest two years after his accident. Frost-damaged soybeans nipped the local farmers' dreams for a new LeSabre. In the showroom, WCCO radio broadcast the sixth game of the Braves-Yankees series. The teams entered the eighth in a pitchers' duel. Eddie Matthews fouled off pitch after pitch hurled by Whitey Ford. Without warning, Frank picked up a black 8-ball paper weight from his desk, executed a jerky windup, and tossed it left-handed right through the "O" of the "New Skylarks On Sale" sign painted on the show floor window. Frank stood marveling at his uncanny accuracy for a full minute before he walked across the shattered glass into his manager's office and quit.

Frank returned to driving truck during harvest for Nick, and, eventually, climbed up onto a tractor again. The tasks were mindless; they required only a strong sense of alignment and enduring patience. Frank plowed, disked and dragged all of the farm's 320 acres, planted the oats, corn and soybeans, and replowed the reaped fields in the fall. He shied away from the hay baler and combines. When he finished Nick's fields, he hired out cheap to the glee of neighboring farmers.

No one knew, however, the dark thoughts that Frank pulled down those endless rows. Blacker than the soil he turned, they clung to him like May mud. He took to the fields because inside the barn or sheds, his eyes wandered to beams. On a tractor, with the nearest buildings or roads hundreds of yards away, he felt safer.

On his 21st birthday, he drove to the Troy VFW. By 10 p.m. on the first day of legal drinking age, Frank stood heaving his insides out next to the trash barrel the club used for burning cardboard boxes. A pattern emerged. When cloudbursts turned acres into quagmires, or when he couldn't chase nightmares away, Frank found his way to Troy. He became a VFW regular. Nick's protests ended when he observed Frank, half in the tank, conversing easily with the other farmers, truckers and store clerks. Frank connected with some of his old teammates, and, miraculously, got to the point where he watched them play American Legion summer ball. In time, he helped umpire games. Frank found his balance in a bottle. His moods still went up and down as often as the beer bottles he hoisted, but, three years after almost losing his arm, he found equilibrium.

The night before he flattened Irene's apple tree, however, some truckers hauling diesel started calling him "Lefty," then "Left-Out" and, finally, "Left Nut." They were deep into their multiple Budweisers, looking for amusement at the end of a 400-mile day in their rigs. One, named Cliff, a skinny man in a mustard-colored chamois shirt and black suspenders, with a dirty mustache flecked with bits of beer foam, asked Frank what happened to his left arm. Frank stayed mute, sipping at his Manhattan.

"Hey, farm boy," Cliff pressed. "Just curious is all. Looks like you tried to twist that arm through a lead pipe. Me and Pat here would just like to know what happened."

Frank had almost reached his happy place. The brandy tunneled through his capillaries to tingle his cheeks and numb his fingers to the point he could barely discern the coldness of his drink glass. He took another sip.

The truckers continued to taunt him, but Frank remained sipping and silent until they grew quiet. Once he heard their rigs churning onto Highway 17 to deposit them at their $28 rooms at the Truckers' Chateau, Frank paid for his drinks and left. The cool April air pouring into his open car windows kept Frank awake while he weaved his three miles home. He passed out as soon as his head hit his pillow. A hangover woke with him the next morning; the apple tree became its first victim.

Now he rolled the cherry stem around his tongue, wondering if there were any way to get home without walking. Looking at the clock he realized it would be an hour before anyone in the lunch crowd might offer him a ride.

Into his malaise stepped Ruth Mitchell. She entered the darkness of the tavern and stood still while her eyes adjusted. They eventually settled on Frank. She approached the bar with purpose, and hopped up on the round stool next to him. She wore a red and white checked gingham shirt, a jean skirt and a serious look.

"Morning, Ruth," Frank said, surprised to see her. "What brings you into this fancy joint so early?"

"I came to see you, Frank."

"Really? Now why would you come looking for me?"

"I came to ask for your help."

"How long is the asking going to take, because if it's going to be a while, I'm pretty thirsty." Frank raised his near-empty glass.

"Give him whatever he wants," Ruth instructed Rich with a smile. Rich approached from behind the bar, a fresh Manhattan in hand. Then he plopped down a napkin in front of Ruth. "No, thanks, nothing for me," Ruth said. Then burrowing into her worn purse, she drew out her red billfold and then a crumbled $5 bill.

"Thank you," Frank said, not believing his good luck. "I suppose you're here because of George getting hurt. I heard about that. How is he?"

"He'll be fine, only it's going to take months for his legs to heal so as he can work again."

"Well, your crops must be in by now. We finished yesterday," Frank said, grabbing his new drink. He saluted Ruth and his good fortune.

"You're right," Ruth offered. "What's not planted won't ripen before frost at this point." She fidgeted with the bill, as if she couldn't afford to part with it. Then she laid it folded on the counter. "Except peas," she said, remembering the unplanted cash crop.

"You need me for planting peas?"

Ruth didn't answer.

"That is what you're here for, isn't it? To ask me to help in the fields till George gets on his feet? If so, you know the answer is yes."

Ruth hesitated. They had jointly arrived at the issue quickly. Ruth had anticipated more small talk, more time to get her courage up.

"No, not really. I want you to help us milk our cows instead."

The rim of the glass froze inches from Frank's lips. His eyes went wide, his body stiffened. What, is Ruth crazy? he thought. Can't she see my arm dangling between us? He set his drink down, and leaned forward on his stool.

"Ruth, I can't milk a cow. You know I've got this." He held up his mangled right arm, revealed by his twisted hand and the looseness of his shirtsleeve. "I've got hardly no real feeling in my hand," he continued, oddly wiggling one withered finger. He shook his head. "I'm sorry, but the last time I checked, milking was a two-handed job." He picked up his Manhattan again.

"It is," Ruth said. "That's why I'm going to help you."

"Ah, that's just crazy. What the heck are you talking about?"

Ruth took a deep breath, and prepared to continue. Instead she turned to Rich. "I've changed my mind, I'll have what Frank's drinking." She reached for her billfold.

"You've got enough out already, Ruth," Rich said, finally taking the $5 bill.

Frank took another sip of his drink and waited.

"You see, Frank, it's like this." Ruth's voice came out high-pitched and uncertain, as if she, too, believed what she was about to ask were too far-fetched. "Things haven't been the best on the farm. We just get by. It puts a lot of stress on us. We're not a real, well, happy family all the time."

Her drink arrived. She sought fortification from it, and coughed after swallowing a big gulp.

"That's a sipping drink, Ruth. You don't want to waste it," Frank said. "I do know that an unhappy family can drive you to them. Cheers," he said, and Ruth clinked glasses with him.

"It's not so much that, but that it was getting better. A lot better," Ruth said, happy for Frank's empathy. It opened her up. "It started when Joe went out for track. He became so happy. He's done really well, Frank. Placed in a couple of races. His happiness has been infectious. George and I, well, it's been good for us because it seems we have something to rally around. We even made a pledge to help Joe finish the season." She let out a small sigh. "It's made us a family again. Now, with George hurt, Joe has to miss track and much of what's left of the school year. And I can't stand it. I can't go back to the way we were before."

Ruth sniffled, and dabbed at her eyes with her drink napkin. Frank saw the strain she was under, even through his fog. When he lifted his left arm to console her, she sniffled and regained her composure.

"No, I guess I can stand it. I have to stand it. And that's why I'm here. I've racked my brains trying to think of how to let Joe truly enjoy the last weeks of his school year. Can I hire good help? Are there any of the neighbors who could help? But we're all running dairies, so there are no extra milkers around. Except for you and me."

"You're sorely mistaken, Ruth," Frank said. Now it was his turn to take a gulp. He felt the brandy slide hot as blast-furnace steel down his gullet. "Sure, I help out anyone when they want plowing or disking done. Hell, when your corn's up, I'll cultivate it for nothing. Beans, too, after that. But you're talking about a real physical chore. And something you have to do morning and night."

"Joe can still help out real early every morning, and after supper when he doesn't have meets. I can help prep the cows for milking. I just can't handle pulling off the full milker and dumping the milk into pails. That can weigh 40 pounds. So you could lift with your good arm and I could help tilt the milker and together we could pour."

"There's a lot more to it than that and you know it," Frank said testily. The fourth Manhattan on an empty stomach had his head buzzing. "There's cleaning the barn. Three times daily feedings. Moving bales. Pushing shovels and brooms. You must have livestock to feed besides what's in the barn, too."

"Yes, there's that and a dozen other things you'll think of if we sit here drinking. But will you do it? I'll pay you what I can, now, and the rest in the fall. If you don't, well, then I just don't know."

Ruth dabbed at her eyes again. Frank turned away from her. Damn, I can't stand to see a grown woman cry, he thought. He desperately wanted to get control of the situation. Here was someone who wouldn't accept his handicap, who didn't realize that he wanted, more than anything, to be left alone. Hadn't he, as recently as March, when the gray pallor of winter hung on like a death sentence, contemplated gassing himself in his folks' enclosed garage? Did Ruth know he was all wasted inside, and that's why he tried to fill the void with alcohol?

The VFW door opened again, and in walked Tim Cofty from Henson's Feed. His curly blond hair stuck out from under his cap. Approaching the bar, he nodded his greetings to Frank and Ruth. Frank noted the fine mill dust even clung to the hair on Tim's arms. His two good arms.

"Frank, Ruth," he said. To Rich, "I'll have a Bud tap." Tim turned back to Ruth. "Heard about George. Sharon baked a casserole. I'll bring it out with me on Friday with your feed."

"It's appreciated. Tell Sharon thanks for me."

"I'll do that," Tim said. He grabbed his glass and sauntered over to a corner table.

"Hear that, Frank. Everyone's helping. That's how neighbors get through tough times."

"You want a casserole, I'll bake one. You're asking the impossible."

"Almost. But will you do it?"

"How can I?" he finally asked softly.

"I just told you how. I'll be there right beside you."

"It's not that. It's that I'm more than handicapped," he confessed. "Ruth, look at this drink. It's my fourth and I want more. It's what gets me through lots of days. You can't afford a drunk."

Ruth reached out and took both of his hands. Frank tried to pull back but her grasp held firm. Besides, no one had intentionally grabbed his mutilated hand in years.

"Frank, I thought a lot about that before I ever came looking for you. How do you think I found you? Your folks told me you would be here."

She didn't release her grip. Her hands were rough, the long fingers newly callused from spring gardening, the nails broken. She rubbed his withered hand without revulsion.

"I thought a lot about why you drink and, with your life since your accident, you more than anybody else in the county has a right to drink as far as I'm concerned. Then I thought, there's also nobody in the county who would understand more what this means to Joe. You see, you never got your chance. Never went pro because of that baler. And there was nothing you could do about it."

Ruth watched Frank's face. It remained closed.

"This sounds corny, but maybe this is how you win some of that glory you missed. Coach O'Reilly says the team has a real good chance to win the conference, and he's counting on Joe for a point or two in the mile. Coach O'Reilly says it will be that close between Troy and Webster. Maybe you helping us will make the difference."

It did sound crazy, but Frank was remembering how many nights, early on in his years of regret, that he fell asleep pitching with the Braves or Reds, his right arm snapping off curves that seemed to roll off a table, or throwing the Frankquilizer, his arm nothing but an arcing blur. A fluke farm accident tore away his youth. Now, George's accident was crushing Joe's chance at glory, too.

"If you saw him run, once, you would do it," Ruth pressed. "He runs after milking. During chores. He runs everywhere."

"Ruth, I don't know if I can give up the drink," Frank said plaintively.

"Then don't. Drink after the evening milking. Just so you can get up the next day and function. I'll even drink with you, if that's what it takes." She let go of his hands, picked up her Manhattan, and took another gulp. Again she coughed.

"You're right, it is a sipping drink." Ruth continued smiling. "What do you say, Frank. Will you do it? Will you give Joe his chance?"

Somewhere in the back of his mind Frank pitched that World Series game of long ago. He stood tall, young and whole on the mound, and let the cheers waft over him like Christmas Eve snow. It was an odd memory, and, surprisingly, not unpleasant.

"How early do I have to get up?" he asked.

Ruth had described the routine accurately, although even she didn't envision how much work she had signed them up for. Frank arrived blurry eyed at 5:10 a.m. on Thursday. Ruth led him through the yard light-lit dawn to the barn. Joe had already forked down the silage for the morning feeding.

Enthused by the prospect that if Ruth's plan worked he could return to school the following Monday, Joe already had two milkers stationed at the far end of the barn. Alongside them, he lined up the milk pails, the bucket of antiseptic wash water, and the long leather milker straps.

Joe refreshed Frank on the rudiments of milking, something Frank did before his accident. It was not a difficult task. Joe reached the strap around the first cow, a docile old Holstein named Gerty. He caught the strap's metal bar, which ended in a hook, and pulled in underneath Gerty's belly. He fit the hook through one of the strap's metal lined holes. Grabbing the washrag from the hot antiseptic water, he then cleaned the dirt and manure off of Gerty's teats, tossing the rag back into the pail with a splash. Then he retrieved one of the milkers, stepped across the gutter and along Gerty's right side.

The milker looked like an upside-down wood tick, with a bulbous tank and four elongated cups affixed to it by rubber nozzles. A hose extended from the other end of the machine. This Joe inserted over a metal tube that connected perpendicularly with the vacuum line. Turning a nozzle above the tube created a vacuum within the milker. Joe hung the milker on the metal strap, and then, kneeling, inserted each of the four cups around Gerty's teats. The pulsator inside the milking machine, created a mechanized squeezing and releasing on each teat.

With the first milker working on Gerty, Joe repeated the routine on Linda. All the cows had names, Joe told Ruth.

"Which one is named after me?" she asked, knowing George all too well.

Joe smiled and pointed down the line. "Third one from the end on the left, before the walkway. You'll have to go around front to see why he picked her. She has a pretty face."

While George was adept at working three milkers at once, Joe recommended two for Frank and Ruth. Joe reasoned Ruth could wash and strap the cows while Frank handled two milkers and helped carry pails. At either end of the milk transfer—emptying the milker's liquid into the pails or emptying those pails into the milk house bulk tank, Frank could lift with his left hand and Ruth provide direction and finesse for pouring.

Later, Joe showed Ruth how to release the cows from their stanchions. When they all stood outside, he scrapped manure off the barn floor with a long-handled shovel. Taking lime in a bucket, he walked the length of the floor, strewing the moisture-soaking white pellets before him. Excess lime bounced into the gutter straw with a hiss. This, he told Ruth, is now your twice-daily task.

The motorized barn cleaner emptied the gutters. Frank agreed to pull the manure spreader into position, but he refused to haul the load to a fallow field because of the spreader's power take-off. This task fell to Ruth. Joe never thought he would live to see such a sight. She sat atop the tractor with the back spiral teeth of the spreader spewing chunks of manure and straw in a continuous brown arc. She surprised him again, later in the barn, when she helped bed the cow stalls with fresh straw. By 10:30 a.m., Joe, Frank and Ruth had completed the morning chores. Frank left for lunch. Ruth collapsed on the couch. The whole process lay ahead of her again for evening chores and milking.

Somehow the unlikely trio got through Thursday and Friday. Frank agreed to help Ruth and Joe on the condition he got weekends off. He promised he'd stay reasonably sober during the week, but Saturdays remained sacrosanct for drinking at the VFW. He needed Sundays to recover.

Ruth, although she could barely climb out of bed Saturday morning, grew adept at washing udders and tossing chunks of hay into the mangers. She and Joe handled all the chores alone on the weekend, and still found time for church and a brief visit from Annie Sunday afternoon.

"How do you think we're doing?" Ruth asked with a tired smile as the two of them ate a Sunday supper of roast beef sandwiches and reheated potatoes.

"Better than I thought we would," Joe said.

"Same here. I think we'll be all right, if Nick stays sober." Despite her exhaustion, she was pleased with herself. She had risen to the task, both physically and maternally. The struggle drew her closer to Joe and made her appreciate George more. She felt connected to her family and the farm again. It gave her a greater sense of purpose, and she liked it.

"Thanks, Mom," Joe said with real gratitude as if reading her mind.

The two of them fell into their respective beds three hours later. Six miles away, Annie lay awake in her own bed. She floated between excitement and disappointment. Joe had told her earlier in the day that Ruth had found a way for him to return to school. But he added that he couldn't get weekends free. When she visited that night he rehashed his weekend regimen necessitated by Frank's alcoholism. Trying to improve Annie's mood, Joe turned on the TV and they began watching an old movie. Joe soon fell asleep next to her on the couch. She saw the exhaustion in his face. The shadows under his eyes mirrored the gray of the film classic. Annie let him sleep, and hid her disappointment as he apologized profusely when she left.

Joe's explanations brought no relief from her growing restlessness. Only five weeks of her senior year remained. Joe had promised he would find some way to take her to the prom, but now he informed her that the post-prom Sunday picnic with the other seniors at Taylors Falls wasn't likely. She had hedged her final high school memories on Joe, and now faced the prospects of graduating in some kind of dating nightmare.

Annie rolled over. She flipped her pillow to find a cooler surface. Then there was Mark. Aware of Joe's situation, he had approached her Saturday night at Betty's party. He looked sleek and handsome in a cream Polo.

"Where's Joe?" Mark had asked.

"He's still covering for his dad and couldn't get away," Annie replied.

"Pretty frightening, huh, what happened. Tourniquets out of belts and stuff. I don't know if I would have had the wherewithal to save my old man like that if he were bleeding to death."

Annie eyed him suspiciously. "That almost sounded like a compliment."

"It was. Joe's all right."

Annie's heart skipped. She wanted Mark and Joe to be friends.

"Even after what he did to your car?"

Mark chuckled, but a faint look of sorrow belied his pain. "Man, if it had been done to anyone else, it would have been the greatest stunt ever."

Mark looked around. The basement was half empty. Many of the party-goers had either left or roamed around outdoors.

"Annie, could we talk?" Mark said softly.

"Sure."

"Not here, outside, where we can be alone."

Annie had barely said okay before Mark gently guided her into the yard. A three-quarters moon lit their way. The yard sloped up to a thicket of trees, and Mark directed her there. They sat down and faced the house. The shadows of other roamers and lovers occasionally shuttered the basement windows. The night was brisk and, despite her sweater, Annie began to shiver. Mark put his arm around her.

"Only for warmth," he said. Annie didn't pull away.

"What do you want to talk about?"

Mark took a deep breath. "Lots of things. First, I want to apologize for what I've been doing to Joe. It's just, well, I see him as the reason we're not together, so I'm lashing out at him. You see, I'm still in love with you, Annie. The more we're apart, the more I realize it."

Mark looked over at Annie, but she remained silent. He stared back toward the house.

"I know I'm the reason we're apart. And I know your feelings are for Joe now. I just want you to know I accept that. I just want to be friends, is all, to quit our fighting."

Annie lapped up the words. This was Mark's gallant side, the one manifested during their early dating days when she could think of no one else.

"I want that, too, Mark," she whispered. In response, Mark leaned over and kiss her platonically on top of her head.

"Good, then. Let's talk as friends. Bet you got a big charge out of the car bomb thing, huh?

"Yes and no. I mean it was funny, and from what I heard, deserved. Why'd you have to pick on Bobby?"

"I was after Joe, for the reasons I said. I screwed up."

"Well, I was happy and sad. Bobby got his revenge but I know how you love your car. I felt sorry about that."

"My car?" Mark exclaimed. "What about me? Have you ever tasted shit?" He began to laugh again. "Man, that Joe's a clever guy."

Annie leaned into him. "You, too. I felt sorry for you. But it was hilarious."

They both laughed, and then reflected back on the incident individually. Any one paying attention would have seen their smiling faces reflected in the light.

"So Joe can still take you to the prom?"

"I hope so."

"You don't sound sure."

Annie frowned. "Everything's up in the air, day to day with Joe's dad and their farm."

"Well, if it gets down to the day, and Joe can't take you, I'll escort you."

Annie looked up inquisitively. "I thought you were taking Nancy?"

"No, I was just using her to get to you. Like I said, I'm trying to stop being such a jerk, so I'm not stringing her along anymore. I told her Thursday."

Annie ruminated on his offer. She was torn. This was the Mark she had loved. If he could have remained this person, she wouldn't be involved with Joe in the first place. Plus she wanted to go to the prom. She could say yes to Mark, on the condition it was as friends only. Besides, she told herself, Joe would keep his promise. She had no intention of hurting Joe, and if things worked out Joe need never know Mark and her had the conversation.

"As friends?" she asked.

"Sure."

"I'll think about it. If something goes wrong between Joe and me, then maybe. But not a word that we discussed this, okay?" Annie warned.

"Scout's honor," Mark replied, removing his arm to cross his heart. His hand went from his heart and tousled Annie's hair. "Like I said, I'm growing up. I won't do anything to hurt you again."

They rose together and Annie brushed off her jeans. She stood on tiptoes and kissed Mark on the cheek. "Thanks Mark. I'm glad we're friends again."

The whole conversation seemed to make sense as they parted. Now, a night later, she remembered Mark's darker side. The times his barbs struck hard enough to leave internal scars. What if he blurted out in school tomorrow that he was taking her to the prom? Dark Mark wasn't above that. Joe wouldn't be so trusting, then. Why had she been so stupid? Or was Mark really changing? And why did Joe have to be the son of a dairy farmer? That created the problem in the first place. Her mind raced between the Joe naked at the fox hole, cool and white and loving in the April chill, and the other Joe—the one tied to the farm and ready to kill.

Until recently, Annie could always extract Joe mentally off of the farm. He escaped it easily enough before his father's accident. Now she saw him intricately connected to it, and it tarnished her image of Joe for the first time. There were two Joes—the one who treated her with more respect than she had ever known, and the foreign executioner, blasting holes into dying cows without hesitation. And now there were two Marks tossed into the stew.

No wonder sleep escaped her. Part of her wanted to rush to Joe, to work by his side if necessary because, in just a short time, she believed she had come to love him. Now a new thought tugged her toward dreams. She and Joe came from very different worlds. Events were creating a riff between them. Did she love him enough to close it?

SETTING THE PACE

Joe returned to school on Monday as excited as a puppy. Annie stole a quick kiss by his locker. Crazy and Dave slapped his back and asked how the week's vacation had gone. Betty and Maggie gave hasty hugs. Everywhere there was concern for George, admiration for Joe's heroics.

Joe's joy ebbed during the day as he realized how far behind he had fallen in his studies. When last he left Social Studies, Mr. Carter concluded his dissertation on the federal tax system by boldly sharing his IRS audit. Now Mr. Carter rambled on about the role of the electoral vote and its importance in the upcoming Presidential election. Joe sat fearfully through the class. In some strange way, he had been able to think about school totally devoid of academics. While slaving away at home, the thoughts of school were thoughts of flight. Of Annie. How did homework fit into the picture? It caught him off guard. In fact, he found himself saying it didn't matter. Hadn't he just spent his recent days doing the work of an adult? Hadn't he learned to love in the last month? Kill? Compromise? What did the electoral college have to do with anything happening in his life?

For the moment, Joe decided, nothing. Despite a twinge of Catholic guilt, he laid out a plan to leverage his absence as long as his teachers would allow. He believed they would grant him a long grace period to catch up. He could graduate in July. Or the following July, for that matter.

Instead of listening to Mr. Carter, he watched Annie across the classroom, and prepared mentally for the day's race. The minute Frank's ability to milk guaranteed Joe's return to the team, Joe had checked the yellow mimeographed track schedule taped to the side of their kitchen cupboard. A non-conference meet against Warring and Comley was slated.

Joe worried about his absence from practice. Sure, he ran like a madman through his chores. Still, he never pushed himself the way Coach O'Reilly could.

He also worried about his lack of sleep. Even now, as Mr. Carter explained why Bobby Kennedy wanted desperately to win the California primary, Joe caught himself nodding off. He dug his fingernails into his thighs to stay awake. In desperation, he turned to Dave behind him.

"Hey, Dave, can you do me a favor?" he whispered.

"Sure. What?"

"Every minute or so, jab me with your pencil so I don't fall asleep."

"What makes you think I'm awake?"

A half hour later, with a likeness of the Andromeda constellation tattooed in graphite across the back of his shirt, Joe escaped Mr. Carter's class and headed to the locker room. Coach O'Reilly greeted him with enthusiasm, still hopeful of the points Joe might contribute to the conference finals. Crazy Nolan made Joe's return official by mouthing the words from a Doors song. Other teammates picked up the refrain, and Joe headed to the track underneath a deadpan recital of "People are strange, when you're a stranger."

The song seemed appropriate, because Joe felt strange and detached from the team, as if his absence had severed his right to walk among them. Even his attire felt foreign. His spikes made him feel weightless after nearly two weeks of slogging in heavy work boots. His shorts felt loose in the waist. He had shed a few pounds. He had not thought that possible as thin as he was already.

One thing remained familiar—the butterflies on speed in his stomach as the voice through the megaphone announced the mile run. He noticed Annie, Betty and Maggie sitting together in the stands, forever the loyal fans. Annie waved. Joe acknowledged her with a slight nod.

Mercifully, the high-hurdle heats finished. The runners from the three teams hurriedly removed the white barriers from the track and stacked them neatly in rows along the fence. The milers assembled. Joe drew lane two. Mark landed behind him in the second row. In all, 11 runners awaited the starter's gun.

Mark nudged Joe in the back and said, "Welcome back, Joe. Sorry about your dad."

"Thanks," Joe said, confused by Mark's friendliness.

Joe turned back to the race. He leaned forward, as did the rest of the milers, poised for the report of the gun. Joe didn't plot much strategy, because in his mind the mile came down to which runner had the biggest lungs and the strongest legs. Joe's goal today centered on finishing somewhere better than last.

Joe relished the brief seconds before they all hurtled down the track. With the gun raised, his worrying stopped. He connected to the track by crushing out an imaginary cigarette in the black cinders. He listened for the beating of his heart. He tensed, like the lion beside the water hole, its eyes on an unsuspecting gazelle. Joe sensed the primitive rush of it. Felt its raw importance, when running fast meant live or death. For that reason, he wished the mile were strung out straight instead of around an oval track. On a track, he could monitor his performance. He could grow complacent or demoralized, knowing almost to the exact yard how far he had run and how far ahead or behind he was. On a straight fly, on a stretched-out path ending at some unknown distance on the horizon, such knowledge disappeared. He could run listening only to his own internal rhythms and frantic mind, not knowing how far he had still to run. He could run on sheer guts, on sheer will. Joe envisioned the track today in this fashion. He stripped it of lanes, stopwatches and yelling coaches. He simply wanted to do what he lately had decided he was born to do. Run.

Joe bolted with the bang of the starter's pistol. He set a fast pace, denying runners angling from the outside from gaining the cherished inside lane. He leaned into the first curve, and glided swiftly forward. He had never set the pace before. Never led the caravan of runners. Never entered the backstretch without someone's bouncing jersey blocking his view. He heard clearly the commotion behind him, though. The crunch of the cinders sounded like a giant chewing glass. He didn't need to glance over his shoulder to determine who dogged his heels. Mark was there.

Joe hurtled down the backstretch, his mind alive with thoughts. He had recently done the work of two men and certainly three Marks. For 10 days he experienced no school, no sitting, studying, or reading. Instead he lifted, shoveled, carried, pushed, dumped and threw tens of thousands of pounds. He bent, climbed, ran, squatted and twisted through his days. And although his labors sent him whimpering to bed exhausted every night, they fortified him as well. He felt sleek and powerful.

A new sensation passed through him. Confidence. With each step in the lead, he let this embryo grow. Mentally he no longer believed Mark invincible.

Invigorated by this heady stuff, Joe fended off Mark's attempt to take the lead at the quarter-mile mark. When Mark sprinted, Joe sprinted. When Mark eased off, Joe slowed. Joe forced Mark to stay on his shoulder. They ran around the north bowl of the track the second time in this fashion.

"Get out of my way," Mark shouted between rapid breaths. "You're pissing me off."

Joe didn't reply. Answering wasted a breath. Maybe cost him a stride. And every stride had to count. That's why he kept Mark in lane two. He also knew his silence irked Mark. While vanity wasn't a trait Joe possessed, Mark wore it tighter than his jock strap. Sure enough, he tried to pass Joe before the end of the backstretch.

Joe fought him off a second time. He heard a "Goddamn you" as Mark eased behind him to avoid wasting energy around the curve. The Mark Joe knew had returned. Joe closed in on the halfway point of the race relishing his lead. He heard Annie's and Betty's voice from the stands, and a "Go get him'" from a smiling Wilson near the shot-put pit. Coach O'Reilly simply looked bewildered by Joe's pace.

DeAngelo yelled out the leaders' times as they passed the half-mile mark. "2:16, 2:17, 2:18" they heard until they flew out of hearing range. Way too fast for me, Joe thought. Yet he didn't slow. His lungs already began their pleas of mercy, and Joe knew the race would soon be lost. But until that moment, Joe claimed victory with every front-running step.

Down the backstretch a third time—a thousand yards into the race—Joe savored the view for posterity. He framed the parallel lanes etched in white chalk as they disappeared around the track's curve. Behind the football scoreboard the green grass climbed over the hills, invaded by patches of yellow dandelions as defiant as Joe. The sky shone robin's egg blue. He took it all in. He looked down at his own churning legs. White pistons, left, right, left right, left right, gobbling up ground.

Joe wished for that straight-line race now, because the upcoming curve signaled that the race was two-thirds done and Joe was three-quarters spent. Mark surged by him, curve or no curve. Joe struggled to catch him, but his legs didn't respond. His stride stiffened and slowed his pace. Feeling light-headed, Joe plowed valiantly forward. Soon some of the other milers he had long since forgotten taught him that strategy did play a part in the mile run. Fortunately, not all the milers knew strategy, either. Joe's early pace burned up six of them. Two Warring and one Comley miler ran their own race. All finished in front of Joe and one Warring running came perilously close to beating an exhausted Mark.

When Joe finally crossed the finish line, Coach O'Reilly didn't even let him collapse. He pulled Joe onto the infield, away from his teammates.

"And what the hell was that suppose to be?" he hissed.

"What was what suppose to be?"

"Don't give me a stupid act." Coach O'Reilly continued to squeeze Joe's arm. The scalp under his short-cropped hair shone red. His eyes darted with hostile intent. "You almost cost us this race. Your fast pace almost burnt Mark up. That was five points on the line, and what are you doing? Trying to set some new land speed record."

"I was just trying to win the race, Coach," Joe said in shocked defense.

"Trying to win the race, my ass. You're showboating for a girl. Or did one of those cows you've been milking actually kick you in the head. Is that it Mitchell? Is that why you ran such a dumb race? It better be, otherwise I might not let you run in the next meet. Tell me it was a cow that kicked you."

Joe looked down and remained silent.

"Yeah, you let it sink in," Coach O'Reilly said, nodding. He released Joe's arm and pushed him away with disgust. "I've bent over backwards to accommodate your schedule and your farming. Because, despite today, I think you can get me a point. That's what I want from you. One point in the conference championships. Fifth place in the mile. I've got you penciled in for one point. Tell me I won't see a display like this again and that I can count on one point from Joe Mitchell."

Joe raised his head. He held Coach O'Reilly's challenging stare, trying not to tremble, searching long for the right words. "Forget the pencil," he said. "Put it down in ink."

Coach O'Reilly harrumphed, and walked away. But he wasn't finished. Next, he tracked down Mark, who leaned against the wire-mesh fence surrounding the field. Mark's throat felt raw and abused, and his heart still pumped rapidly—otherwise, he would have fled. Instead, he stood like a dazed and battered bull waiting for the matador's plunge.

"Do you want to explain what was going on out there, Perkins?" Coach O'Reilly seethed between his teeth.

Mark shrugged. "I won the race."

Coach O'Reilly grabbed him by the jersey, and pulled Mark to his face. He was in no mood for this sass, first from Joe and now Mark. He kept his back to most of the team and fans. Mark smelled the snuck cigarette on O'Reilly's breath.

"Yeah, you did. Not because you were smart, but because we're running against a bunch of yokels. They don't know how to run a race, but you do. We run it by quarters, remember?"

Mark felt faint this close to the Camel breath. "Yes, coach, you're right."

That appeased Coach O'Reilly. Releasing Mark, he emphatically nodded his head up and down. "That's right. We run by quarters. And we time them. I call out your times as you pass, and you know how you're doing. Let the Mitchells of the world burn themselves out like Roman candles. They don't know what they're doing. You must run under control. You have to run your race."

Mark nodded. Coach O'Reilly continued the lesson. He wanted to ensure they didn't repeat this near disaster at conferences.

"So what's between you and Mitchell? Is it that he shit-bombed your car or is there more?"

Oh, there's plenty more, Mark thought. He's taken my girl and embarrassed me in front of the whole school. He's causing this current agony—being berated by my coach in front of my teammates.

"Yes, it's the car. I've taken it to three professional cleaners and I swear I still smell shit."

Remembering the incident suddenly struck Coach O'Reilly as funny. It was the most audacious act ever committed at the school. He tried to stifle a chuckle, but Mark noted it.

"That was quite a prank. I can see why you're still pissed," Coach O'Reilly said. "But, look, Mark, you get even on your own time. And after the conference meet. I'll not tolerate this type of behavior on this team. I expect the most from you. Christ, you're team co-captain. Are we understood?"

"Yes, Coach. It won't happen again."

After his own scolding, Joe headed straight towards the school. Even if he could have stayed, and he couldn't because his nightly chores beckoned, he would be walking this same path. Joe was furious, in part because Coach O'Reilly had denigrated him in front of everyone, but mostly because Coach O'Reilly was partially right. Joe's personal vendetta against Mark had eclipsed his duties to the team. Still, he resented his treatment, as if he had no right to win. Joe, the one-point man. Joe, the set-up man for Mark's victories. Why couldn't he challenge Mark? It wasn't his fault, anyway. Mark followed him blindly on a vendetta of his own.

A worse truth quickened his departure. He couldn't beat Mark. Never could. He left his new-found confidence somewhere back on the track. Would he ever be more than a one-point man? How could he become more, straddled with the farm and his parent's needs? It all seemed terribly unfair. He felt a prisoner of responsibility, and resented that others around him had no concept of the word.

We'll lose everything, our livelihood, Ruth had said among the bales, unless you help. Atlas carried less weight. What did Mark know about sacrifice? What did Annie? Or Coach O'Reilly? None of them knew what he was going through. And he certainly couldn't explain it. Joe's was a vanishing world on the cusp of social change. Most of his generation was born into post-war radiance, breast fed on great expectations and raised on space-age dreams. They peered confidently forward and saw a future of hopefulness and opportunity. In contrast, Joe was tethered tighter to the 19th century, with its agrarian roots, manual labor and familial codes.

Coach O'Reilly felt magnanimous accommodating Joe. He discounted the fact that, in addition to practice, Joe put in six hours of physical labor every day, and more in George's absence. Joe humped bales while Coach O'Reilly still lay in bed dreaming of his conference championship. Humping bales and toting pails. They gave him the shoulders of Hercules, but not enough self worth to knock the chips off of them.

Annie chased after Joe across the practice fields. She caught him behind second base of the baseball diamond. He jerked when she touched his shoulder, so withdrawn was he in his self-loathing. Joe gave her a pained look and turned away. The late-afternoon sun forced both of them to look down as they plodded toward the school.

Annie understood Joe's silence. She and anyone else within 100 feet of Coach O'Reilly overheard the chastising of the two milers. She wanted desperately to comfort Joe, but didn't know where to begin. She had never seen Joe so distraught.

"I think Coach O'Reilly was way out of line back there," she finally blurted out, trying to keep pace with Joe's determined gait across the infield gravel. "I mean, you were winning for a long time. It was exciting."

"Coach doesn't want me to win," Joe whined. "That's reserved for Mark."

"Well, that doesn't make sense."

"Yes, it does," Joe spat. His words came out deliberate and believed. "It's not my place. I'm just a one-point man."

"Oh, stop that, Joe, it's not true."

"Yes it is, Annie," Joe said, suddenly stopping and turning toward her to deliver the point emphatically. "Yes it is. Remember our first ride home, when you told me that some people were born with a cocky gene and some with a loser gene? It's the silver spoon thing. I didn't get one."

Annie remained unfazed by this defeatist tirade. She believed Joe's mood was the culmination of weeks of frustration with his family and the farm. But she was tired, too. She looked to Joe's humor and optimism to lift her spirits every day. She struggled now with their roles reversed. They walked further in silence. Joe kicked up white dust as he shuffled across the third base chalk line.

"So maybe you didn't win," Annie offered. "You're still doing really well. Placing in the conference will mean you're one of the best milers in the district. And it hasn't been handed to you. You've worked harder than anyone for it."

Joe stopped again. "Yes, I have," he said. "But not anymore. I'm going to quit and O'Reilly can find someone else to win his glorious point."

"You can't do that, Joe," Annie said, "track means so much to you."

"Meant. Meant," Joe said with finality. "Maybe I'll quit school, too. I'm so far behind now that I'll never catch up in time to graduate in June anyway. I'll go to summer school once my dad gets back on his feet."

"But what about the prom?"

Annie said it innocently, the first thing that crossed her mind. But it came out petty and inappropriate. Joe took it like a slap. A look of disbelief crossed his face. He slowly shook his head back and forth.

"That's rich," he said, hurtfully. "I'm trying to keep from flunking and all you can think about is a stupid dance."

"Joe, you know I didn't mean it that way. It's just I've been looking forward to going to the prom. It's our senior year. I want to go with you."

"You just don't have a clue about what life's really about, do you?" Joe sneered.

"Joe, stop, you're being mean."

"So what? It's who I am. I just hide it from you."

"I know that not true. I know the true you."

"No you don't."

Joe felt sick over his comments, but he couldn't help himself. His dreams unraveled by the minute, spurred by each new misguided sentence. He couldn't beat Mark, so his dream of glory—gone. He couldn't catch up in school with only five weeks left and George disabled. Hopes of a good finish to school—shattered. So Annie was right. Only she and the prom promised to brighten the end of his senior year. Even that seemed tainted somehow. The other components of his three Gs—glory, girl and graduation—were being stripped from him. He felt cheated.

Joe hated his life and himself at this moment. He didn't want Annie to see him in this state. His self-loathing squeezed him like a python. It hissed in his ears, and told him he didn't deserve Annie. It said trying to hang onto her with the rest of his world crumbling was futile. Reaching the school, Joe turned and leaned his back against the cool steel door. Annie waited for him to speak.

"This just isn't going to work," Joe said, flatly. "Why don't you find someone else to take you to the prom?"

Annie looked at him, stunned. Joe wore his executioner's face—all tight lips and dead eyes.

"I don't want to go with somebody else. I want to go with you."

"Well, I don't want to go with you," Joe said icily.

Annie reached for him, tears welling up in her eyes.

And then he pushed her. He didn't mean to push so hard, only to keep her from saving him when all he wanted was to wallow in self-pity. But he did push. Annie, caught off-guard, fell backward onto the entryway. She landed hard, scraping her elbows on the cement. She looked up at him with disbelief. Joe reached quickly to help her up, but Annie scrambled to her feet on her own and pushed him away before running around the corner of the school. Joe didn't follow. Instead, he turned and slammed his fist into the metal door. He wanted something to hurt worse than his heart.

REFLECTIONS

The minute Ruth left to get groceries George took action. He had been home three days, and all he did was lie on the couch and watch game shows. "The Price Is Right." "Concentration." He could only stomach so much of that. How was he supposed to know the price of an electric can opener? He itched to get back to work, but like the itch inside his cast, he couldn't scratch it, at least not with Ruth around. She hovered over him like a mother hen, bringing him lunch, massaging his still swollen foot, and flipping the TV channels. Plaster encased George's leg from groin to ankle, and where the break had been most severe, steel pins pierced the white cast so that his right thigh looked like Sputnik.

George's mood the past 10 days ranged from black depression to black, fathomless depression. Ruth, Joe and a half-sober Frank Oster somehow managed the milking. Until he got back on his feet, Ruth said. The doctor's departing advice as they wheeled him out the hospital door—his left leg extended like a battering ram—torpedoed his spirits. Two months in the full cast. Then six months of rehab to strengthen the leg. Able for hard, physical labor—the type the farm required—maybe by Christmas. Even then, Dr. Baker droned, be prepared for pain, stiffness, occasional swelling, arthritis in time, and a permanent limp. The only consolation came when Dr. Baker informed George that he could likely sit on a tractor if he could somehow brake without using his damaged right leg. So the farm stood perilously at risk unless Ruth, Frank and Joe could continue their current arrangement into the fall, and if Joe could handle the summer work of baling hay and combining oats. How could Joe manage that, though, single-handed?

Christ, George thought, as he lowered the folded wheelchair a step down into the vacated garage. If Joe even stays. He reached for his straw hat as he hopped carefully about on his right leg, and finally grabbed his brown spring jacket. Hopping down into the garage and opening the chair put him into a shaky sweat. He rested a minute before centering himself between the footrests and collapsing backwards into the wheel chair. In agony, he lowered the footrest, and gingerly eased his left foot against it. Next came the jacket, which he draped over the bare foot.

The wheelchair wasn't designed for navigating the rutted driveway. Too much in a hurry, George now wished he had grabbed his leather baling gloves because his sweaty hands kept slipping on the steel wheels as he rolled over gravel. He toiled with no plan in mind. He simply wanted to feel the sunshine warm his shoulders through his shirt, to smell and see his farm again.

George's meandering path took him toward the barn. He circled around the puddle formed by the frequent visits of the Land O'Lakes milk truck. The season's first barn swallows glided over its murky water. One passed so close that George ducked and cursed. He followed the swallow's path and saw the muddy foundation of its nest forming like a turret beneath the milk house eaves.

Looking past the milk house, he scanned the newer part of the barn. Straight-line winds took the wood roof and most of the original structure in '55. George and his neighbors used the occasion to extend the barn.

George recalled its construction as one of the highlights of his life. So much productive work. The sound of 20 happy hammers punctuating the conversations that ran the length of the barn. The farmers walked the scaffolding like Iroquois. Those below T-squared and sawed the lumber into various lengths, sweet sawdust encircling their high-top shoes. When a heavy beam needed spotting, the men in blue overalls quit their individual tasks and stretched as one body to hold it steady.

His favorite memories of that week of barn building centered around the lunches. The men gathered beside their old Dodges and Chevrolets parked on the edge of the lawn. Ruth, and Marie Becker, she of the wide girth and grin, and Alice Brennan, too, cooked together all morning. At precisely noon they carried out the feast, each woman wearing flowered aprons that lifted in the wind. They hefted full platters of fried chicken, potato salad, and thick-cut bread across the yard and placed them on three card tables. A second trip brought plates burdened with corn on the cob and sticks of softened butter, and sweating pitchers of milk and lemonade. As the men dug in, Ruth made the final trip with the desserts of the day. Sometimes lemon bars and Devil's food cake. The next day apple pie and brownies. On really hot days, a case of beer appeared. The workers used their car hoods for tables, or leaned hobo-like against the car doors, nestling the long-necked beer bottles carefully in the grass to avoid spills.

It was about as close as one could come to a party on the farm. By nature, they were all reticent men. Yet, they all sensed the goodness of their Samaritan efforts. That, the beer, and the sweet smell of Bill Becker's pipe tobacco turned them downright giddy some days. Dick Cordelle was the worst. Cordelle, the comedian.

One day he told them that at the last county fair, he got locked in the semi-trailer that served as the stage for the girly show. Everyone knew what he was talking about, the 60-foot trailer furthest back on the fairground property, against the trees and away from the lights, and garishly painted with pictures of buxom women across its entire length. All denied to their wives of ever going in, though most had. Everybody lied, that is, except Cordelle.

Cordelle said he paid his $3 dollars and climbed through the trailer's side door with about 20 other curious men—all that could fit on the folding chairs in the elongated rectangle. At the other end, a small stage aglitter with tinsel rose a foot above the floor. The stage's colored lights pulsated in greens and reds. The men sweated in the trailer's muggy air, but they sat still and waited patiently.

It was the night's last show. So as the last of the dancers gyrated to a scantily-clad halt, Cordelle decided to stay behind. He wanted to see what happened at closing. Short and sinewy, he wedged himself behind one of the massive loudspeakers that anchored the corners of the trailer behind them. Cordelle held his breath and waited.

Sure enough, the barker chased the salivating farmers out the door without realizing Cordelle remained inside. Peering from around the speaker, Cordelle watched in amazement as five of the dancing girls shed all their dancing garb and began to dress into their street clothes. They chatted as easily as women after church as they hooked their bras and hitched up their panties and jeans.

"I've never seen so many naked young breasts in my life," Cordelle said. "They were all kinds of different shapes and sizes." George could see all the farmers back then, leaning in so Cordelle didn't have to speak in a tone that the wives might overhear. "Then my manhood started to grow and it got real tight behind that speaker."

George remembered Leroy Bauer had shot some beer out his nose on that comment. George himself chuckled at the memory.

"Anyway, I found myself in a very uncomfortable position. I didn't want to be discovered because I was enjoying the show. Yet I swear my Johnson moved that speaker the more I watched. I had to duck back out of sight to abate my arousal." Cordelle always talked like that, using unusual combinations of words, as he alone among them had finished high school. "Then the next thing I hear is a door slam and a padlock shut. There I was locked in one of Satan's semis, with Maureen expecting me and the kids home in 15 minutes."

"Ach, what did you do?" asked an enthralled Bill Becker.

"What did I do?" Cordelle echoed. He waited till he had them all on edge. "I conjured up those naked women in my mind, re-aroused my arousal and used my Johnson to drill my way out."

Oh, those were grand times, George thought. So many strong, virile men with young dreams and new wives. They planned to build their lives the way they raised the barn—on a strong foundation, surrounded by friends, reaching skyward.

Where was Cordelle today? Sold out and ran the Land O'Lakes Creamery plant south of Elbow Lake. More money than dairying, Cordelle told George, and no weekend work. "It's get bigger or get out, these days," Cordelle had said. "Two hundred acres was all right for farming a decade ago, but it's a turd in a toilet nowadays."

Cordelle was right, George thought to himself, rotating the wheel chair and rolling it past the peeling paint of the feed house and the steel-girded silo. He glimpsed Manfred in his corner pen, frisky with the cows in view. Beyond the bull's pen, George scanned the cows through the barbed-wire fence. They lay on the ground in pinto pockets as they chewed. The wires in front of him sagged a bit. Wasn't it just three years ago that Joe and he stretched that wire taut and silvery in the sun? He remembered it had been beastly hot that day. They couldn't pick up the wire stretcher or cutter without gloves lest they burn their hands. It had taken only three years for the cows, stretching through the wires to snare some green grass with their serpentine tongues, to slacken the whole line. It was hard to keep ahead of the work.

George struggled through more ruts passed the corncribs. He had shot many a rat off their foundations over the years. A match for the farm cats, they thrived. These vile rats alone gave him a twitchy trigger finger. They devoured his corn, chewed away at his livelihood. So he split them in half with .22 hollow-points every chance he got.

He neared the farmstead's southern windbreak of ash and box elder trees. Their first leaves, almost lime green in their newness, unfurled like butterflies from their chrysalises in the late April breeze. Decades earlier, his father used their trunks as posts for another wire fence, and in places George could see where the trees had grown around bits of rusted wire, the bark swallowing up the thin cords, and gnarled scar tissue now protruding like pursed lips.

George reached the field road. Before him the churned up soil prevented him from advancing in the wheelchair. The corn sprouts stretched out before him, row upon row of green two-inch "Ys". Puffy white clouds floated over the planted field, casting the new corn in and out of shade.

God, I love the fields. I love watching things grow, George thought. What am I going to do?

No answers came rolling over the flat land. George hoisted himself out of the chair. After steadying himself, he hopped on his good right leg a few yards down one of the corn rows. He sat with great effort and stretched out his more seriously injured leg on the soil. This is better, he thought, placing his hands on the warm dirt. He dug his hands deeper, and found the cool blackness that protected the corn's roots. Such a simple thing, dirt. Yet so complex. Like a woman, it needed nurturing. You had to listen to it, respect it, give things back to it, or it could grow barren and useless.

City folk don't understand that, George thought. You had to be a farmer. You had to sit in dirt, work it with your fingers, crumble it, to know that clay soils meant you planted a different corn hybrid, and that sandy loams meant you terraced your fields. You had to forget fall plowing, no matter how much of a head start you wanted in the spring, or else your topsoil blew to Ohio.

George let a stream of powdery dirt funnel from one fist into the cistern of the other. The wind caught the overflow and blew it away.

What am I going to do?

He let the remainder of the soil sift through his hand. He fell into a general malaise—just the type he hoped to avoid by making the trip to the field. There were deeper issues to explore, just like the cool clay beneath the dusty topsoil. The contraption encircling his leg the outward manifestation of a deeper hurt. Pain in the marrow bone. The doctors would remove the screws, saw through the sweat-stained plaster, and the leg would appear shriveled and weak. In time, exercise would strengthen it. Only it would be a true leg no more. Robbed of its resiliency, aching in the cold, stiff in the morning. Disconnected from the time before the accident.

Disconnection. That's what this feeling is, George thought. Where were Cordelle and the optimistic farmers of his youth? What happened to his joyous role as a parent—ended first with a blue baby, and then when Joe became more of a silent servant than the enthusiastic partner he desired.

He had tied himself to the land because he understood it, and because it gave things back without complaint. Now, as George picked up a dirt clump of dirt, he realized the fields hadn't returned enough to fill the void inside him. Ruth and their pledge played shadow games with the truth.

George chucked the dirt clump down a row. It busted into powder.

"Nice throw."

George jumped as much as a sitting man can. Turning, he saw Frank behind him.

"God Almighty, Frank. You scared the living daylights out of me."

"Sorry," Frank said. He sidled up along side George. "I saw you sitting out here and figured you had fallen and might be needing my help."

"No, I'm just communing with my fields."

"Communing, huh." Frank took another step into the corn rows. This way, he shaded George's upturned face from the sun. Frank scanned the rows, as if lost in their lattice, too.

"Sometimes dirt's about the only thing that makes sense."

George squinted up at Frank's silhouette and nodded. "I was just thinking something like that before you come up on me."

"Oh, I'm a veteran of dirt. I've spent years riding tractors over it, asking question after question about this here arm. Guess what?" He leaned down so that George caught a faint wisp of last night's whiskey. "She don't answer."

George reflected on that nugget. Eventually, he nodded. Frank outstripped him by light years when it came to handicaps. George selected another dirt clump and rifled it down the row from his sitting position. It busted like the other.

"So what am I going to do Frank. I'm not much of a drinker."

"First, let's get you to your feet and back in that chair."

They got George reseated through the combined efforts of their six good limbs. With George spinning the wheels, and Frank leaning into the chair from behind, they managed to maneuver their way along the field road canopied by the box elders and ash. Sparrows chirped and flitted from tree to tree ahead of them. The two cripples reached the west end of the tree line and watched the sparrows fly to the roof of the machine shed. It, too, stood in a crippled state. The once scarlet wood siding had long ago faded into a dusty rose. Its mildewed shingles curled from decades of assault by the harsh Minnesota elements. The distinct smell of oil and grease wafted their way, overpowering the faint stench of chicken feathers.

George eyed the rusting Gleaner combine through the gapping door of the shed. He realized, now that his injury gave him time to reflect, that the whole darn place stood in disrepair. The farm was aging as fast and as poorly as George himself. Half of the outbuildings leaned like a beaten boxer. A good, heavy snow might collapse one.

"So drinking's not the answer, then?" George said, picking up where he had left off.

"Oh, it helps for a while," Frank said. He strained up a small rise past the back side of the steer shed. The young stock lined the fence, their eyes on the men, their ears cupped forward. Frank stopped dead center of the machine shed to catch his breath. "It gets me to sleep so I'm not plagued by dreams. Morning's are rough, though."

"I might have to quit farming now," George blurted out.

Frank still stood behind him, so George couldn't see if his epiphany caused any reaction.

"It'll be impossible once Joe leaves," he continued.

Frank rolled that over in his mind a few times. "Lots worse things could happen."

"What do you mean? "What could be worse?"

"I'm saying at least you have something to lose. See, that's been the curse of this arm. It kept me from ever getting the things I wanted. The things you have. A wife, a good kid, decent work. A place to call my own."

"So you don't think I've got a serious plight here?"

"No, you're wrapped up in the farm. It was your dad's, and now it's pretty much who you are. I can see that losing it would be a powerfully bitter pill."

One of the farm's calico cats appeared from around the north corner of the shed. A striped gopher hung from its mouth, wet and limp in death. The cat flinched when it saw the men. Then it leaped sideways into the tall grass to find an unobstructed path to its hidden young.

Frank, tired of standing, walked around the wheel chair and seated himself on the wooden tongue of a hay wagon that protruded from the shed's north door. He pulled a pack of Winstons from his shirt packet with his good hand, and shook one of the unfiltered cigarettes far enough out until he could grasp it with his lips. Returning the pack, he squeezed his left hand into a tight jean pocket in search of his lighter. He deftly lit the cigarette and set the lighter on its side on the wagon tongue.

"So just what are you saying? That you're more of a cripple than me?" George found himself growing upset. Frank had first disturbed his sit in the dirt, and hadn't eased his burden one bit since.

Frank ignored the question. He took another puff and then pointed to the parted grass where the cat had vanished.

"What I'm saying is you're like that calico. It's got a purpose. You've got the same purpose. A reason for living. Procreation. Passing something on so you'll be remembered. See, I can't find a purpose," Frank said, waving his dead arm animatedly. "No woman wants half a man." He pointed the cigarette at George. "You'll get better. And you've still got Ruth and Joe. They're what's important. Not the farm."

"But I've got to make a living." George grew madder by the minute. He leaned forward in the chair, his hands gripping the wheels tightly, wanting solutions. He couldn't just quit.

"Like that cat, I've got mouths to feed, too," George said hotly.

"Not saying you don't. But it don't have to be dairying. I bet Ruth and Joe wouldn't care what you did. They'd rather have you around more than always tucked alongside a cow."

George rotated the chair's left wheel and did an about-face so he looked back at the friendlier fields beyond the shed. He suddenly wanted to be left alone.

"Have you even seen him run?"

"Joe?"

"No, Jesse Owens. Of course, Joe."

"I see him running the roads," George answered. He remembered Joe running along side Bertha and biting her ear. He chuckled. "Saw him run down a cow, once."

"I'm talking about at a track meet."

"How am I supposed to get away to do that? It's because I'm working that he can even run."

"If he were my son, I'd try to be there every time. Wouldn't care if I were milking cows till midnight. My dad never saw me pitch. I wanted him to so that I could make him proud. But it never happened, and now it never will."

George half turned the chair back toward Frank. "You seem awfully chock-full of solutions for a man who hides in a bottle."

The cigarette a stub, Frank tossed it onto the dirt. Its final wisps of smoke stayed flat along the gravel. He reached for another. He remained silent until he exhaled the first puff of smoke from the second Winston.

"That's fair," he said at last. "I've been hiding a long time. Still would be if Ruth hadn't tracked me down at the VFW. On Mondays, with the hangovers, I wake up wondering how she ever convinced me. The funny thing is, she and Joe gave me a purpose. At least for a while I can help someone get something that the good Lord denied me. It's probably not healthy, long term, but right now, to be honest, I'm living through that son of yours. I'm going to be at the conference track meet, come hell or high water. I'm going to be affixin' some old dreams on Joe's shoulders."

He crushed the new cigarette out in the dirt at his feet as if this newfound purpose and Joe's upcoming race frowned on his smoking. "So I've got me some purpose. Just like that cat," he said, gesturing in the direction of the grass with his head.

Frank rose. "I've got to go straw the gutters. You want a push back to the house?"

"No," George said. "Thanks. I think I'll just sit awhile."

Night Running

It was a silly idea from the start, but he had run so far already, and not by coincidence in a northwesterly direction, that the thought stuck to his brain like a barnacle. He and Ruth finished milking about 8 p.m. He could have driven to Nancy's party—her second in a month, and been there in plenty of time to apologize to Annie for shoving her.

Joe hadn't talked to Annie in five days since the incidence. Every time he relived the shove in his mind and saw Annie hit the cement, his anger for Coach O'Reilly resurfaced. Joe blamed him for the affair, with Mark a close second. He wanted to show them all. Somehow improve his time so much over the next 17 days that he beat Mark in the conference mile and silenced Coach O'Reilly's one-point assessment of him forever. So he opted to go running in the dark even though he was exhausted. Both George and Ruth protested. Joe pointed out to them by lifting the curtains that the moon already climbed white and full in the east, promising a night of light. Plus, both parents knew Joe had earned the right to do anything he wanted with his yeoman efforts over the past couple of weeks.

Joe's route went west, lured by the salmon sunset. He reached Highway 17 quickly. He ran north facing traffic for another three-quarters of a mile, dipping onto the shoulder when a car or pickup approached, and slipping back onto the blacktop when they passed. Taking another left on County Road 9, he crossed the railroad tracks, the ones that daily brought the Burlington Northern train by which he measured his improvement. Here traffic subsided. Joe ran smoothly down the faint white stripes dividing the blacktop lanes. The telephone poles stood like totems against the gathering purple of night. His clip-clop snapped several farmyard dogs to attention, and their husky barks carried over the silent fields after him. Passing the slough between Spalding's and Anderson's farms, he heard croaking frogs in the dark ditch, and , then, the terrible screeching of raccoons fighting.

When he crested the hill near Anderson's apple orchard he decided to run to Nancy's. The fragrant apple blossoms reminded Joe of the smell of Annie's skin, and he vowed then and there to swallow his pride and apologize. Mark didn't matter, nor Coach O'Reilly. Winning didn't matter either. He just didn't want to be alone anymore. His whole life was defined by the isolation on the farm, devoid of even brothers and sisters, and he wanted no part of it anymore. He wanted Annie, someone who would listen to him and his many needs, and not turn away.

Nancy's home lay another four miles away. Running steady he could arrive before 9:30 p.m. He decided he wouldn't go inside Nancy's house, not dressed in sweaty shorts and shirt. No, he would ask Annie to come outside. He would pour his soul out to her. Surely she would forgive him. Things would be all right again.

Running downhill from the orchard, he glimpsed the distant lights of the Maple Crest development. It vanished out of sight whenever a hill or farm building came between Joe and its twinkling lights, but in about 20 minutes Joe drew close enough to the hamlet that he could discern individual houses. He once again faced more traffic. Some cars honked at him, the drivers startled when he appeared like a specter at the edge of their low beams. Soon he ran under streetlights, and cut across parking lots and lawns. Blue TV screens winked at him from first floor windows of the Tudor-styled homes. Joe didn't remember Nancy's house number, only that it was beyond Annie's. Her house, he knew well. He stopped in front of it, spied Harry and Donna watching "Gunsmoke" in the living room. No light shone in Annie's room.

He needn't have worried about a house number. At least 15 parked cars steered him to Nancy's place. Approaching, Joe slowed to catch his breath. He leaned against a maple sapling in Nancy's yard, trying to decide what to do next. Laughter wafted up over the house from the back yard. Joe heard the squeak of springs. Apparently, Nancy had acquiesced and let the guys use the trampoline again.

Despite the laughter, Joe hesitated. He feared being teased for coming to the party looking like a homeless person in his raggedy running clothes. Dave and Scott wouldn't care, which was worse. They might force him to stay and party when all he wanted to do was connect with Annie.

Actually, he feared finding Annie now that the possibility arose. She might refuse to talk to him, or make a scene. During his journey, he envisioned her embracing him and telling him in soft whispers that she forgave him. She understood the pressure he was under, and all was fine. Now, in the soft glow of the house lights, the fear of rejection poked at his resolve.

A shriek pierced the air. Loud laughter followed, and someone came running along the side of the house. Betty appeared, chased by Dave. They were almost upon Joe before Betty spotted him under the budding maple. Betty stopped, and Dave caught and squeezed her from behind, still unaware of why Betty halted, but glad for the chance to fondle.

"Dave, stop that," Betty said, slapping his encircling hands. "Joe, what on earth are you doing here? You scared the Bejesus out of me."

"Joe?" Dave peered out over Betty's shoulder, reluctant to fully release his grip.

"Hi, guys."

"Why are you dressed like that," Betty asked, eyeing Joe up and down. Then it dawned on her. "You ran all this way?" she asked.

"Yeah. I went for a run and then I remembered the party. Hope that's okay."

"Well little Joe, we'd love to let you join us but there is a dress code," Dave teased. He still hung on to Betty.

"Oh you be quiet, Joe's fine. Come on back with us. We've got sodas and some pizza left. And most of the gang is still here."

"Is Annie here?"

Betty and Dave exchanged confused glances. "Well no, Joe," Betty said. She called and said since you weren't coming, neither was she."

Betty freed herself at last from Dave and walked up to Joe. She knew about their fight and saw that Joe was upset. She gave him a consoling hug. "Her not coming, that must be a good sign. I mean, if she would stay home because she knew you wouldn't be coming. Why don't I call her now? If she knew you were here, she'd come."

"No, don't bother. It's pretty late. I'll run by her house on my way home."

"You're not going to stay for a while at all?" Betty asked. "We haven't seen you around much. We need to catch up."

"Next time. I've got to go. It's a long run home."

"Whoa, you're not running home in the dark, not with the storm coming. I'll give you a ride over to Annie's. Or all the way home, for that matter," Dave said, reaching into his Levis for his keys.

"It's suppose to rain? But it's clear," Joe said, turning to the west. A bank of incoming clouds blotted out the stars across the lower third of the western horizon.

"Don't you have electricity in that barn of yours? A radio?" Dave teased. "It's supposed to rain like the monsoons by midnight. High winds, lightning, the whole show."

Joe didn't want Dave to drive him to Annie's house. Annie wasn't home unless she was asleep. Either way, he wanted to find out on his own.

"Thanks, but if I head out now, I'll beat that storm. Or else I'll have Annie run me home."

"Suit yourself, and, hey, take care of yourself, too. We know what you've been going through with your dad hurt. We're here for you," Dave said.

"Yes, and let me know how I can help patch things up between you two," Betty added.

"Thanks, well, I better get going before the lightning strikes."

Joe waved goodbye and ran out into the darkness. He reached Annie's house in a few minutes. Her bedroom window remained black. He trotted up the sidewalk and rang the Jensen's doorbell. The light above the door blinked on, and Harry emerged, Scotch on ice in hand, through the opened door.

"Joe, what on earth? You out running?"

"Yes, sir, I am."

"At this hour?"

Joe didn't feel like defending his actions, especially since he didn't understand them himself.

"Is Annie home, Mr. Jensen? We had a fight and I need to apologize to her."

"Why, no, she's not." He opened the door further. "Come in, Joe."

"No, thanks. Do you know where she?"

Harry set his glass down on an unseen table behind him, and removed his bifocals. "Why, yes, she's over at Nancy's, at a party."

Joe nodded. "Oh, that's right. I've been working so much since my dad got hurt I forgot that the party was tonight."

"How is your dad?"

"He's home now. Has to stay off his leg, though."

"That was quick thinking on your part, Joe."

"Yeah, well, I just followed my gut." Joe fidgeted on the stoop.

"I'll hop you over to Nancy's if you want," Harry said.

"That's all right," Joe lied. "Now that I know where she is, I'll track her down. Thanks."

Nothing remained to be said, so Joe headed in the direction of Nancy's house. He waited for Harry to shut the door, then reversed his direction and started toward home. A dead panic fell over him. Annie had lied to both Nancy and her parents. To everyone. Where could she be? He ran blindly down the street, not knowing where he was headed. Eventually he emerged from the labyrinth of houses. He stopped alone under the arc of a street light. The moon still shone brightly to the southeast, turning the vacant fields across the road before him into gauzy shadows. Every thing was quiet around him, eerie and electrically charged. A sudden wind stirred the trees. Their branches dipped like demon wings around his head. Time seemed to stop. His neck hairs suddenly tingled to attention. His breath quickened. He closed his eyes and pulled his arms around himself in defense, all to no avail. Because he knew. He KNEW.

Joe bolted. He ran northeast, toward Troy. He ran to find Annie, hoping against hope that he was wrong. The first rumbling of thunder tumbled over him and, looking over his shoulder, he saw the fast-moving clouds gobbling up the stars. A bolt of lightning split the sky. The flash reminded Joe of another, happier night beneath the protective branches of an oak.

The storm beat him to the tree. First, the clouds snatched away the moon and his light. He relied on lightning flashes to guide his way. Then the storm's advance guard—random round droplets—pelted Joe and the highway. Minutes later, the rain rolled over him like a wet army. Joe was soaked in no time. He splashed through the sheen of water covering the paved road. After about five minutes, he reached the gravel road that led to the oak. He slowed his pace, knowing his world was about to change forever. He even stopped and turned momentarily to run away. His craziness pushed him forward.

The lightning struck more frequently now, and banged and cracked around him. It illuminated the leafy crown of the oak, the parked Impala convertible near its base.

In the midnight blue of a lightning flash, Joe saw the entwined bodies. The rivulets of rain running down the car window distorted Annie's face, but Joe caught her eye and saw the surprise and confusion. Then all went dark again, and the rolling thunder joined the roaring in his head.

Joe hurtled down the hill and into the meadow. The grasses tugged at his legs with every stride, but he ripped his way deeper into the lush wetness. Behind him, a car door slammed. Annie's voice came trailing after him, trying to undo what had been done.

Joe ran pell-mell into the night. He sought to distance himself from the truth revealed through glimmering glass, as if he could somehow keep ahead of it and be spared its agony. No escape came. The images of Annie and Mark clung to him like his wet clothes. His heart ached, and he couldn't discern whether it was from his hell-bent pace or if his heart had simply broken. He ran until he thought his lungs would burst. Several times he stumbled over pocket gopher mounds, falling into the dirt and coming up muddy. Tears and rain meshed. In another lightning flash, he saw the meadow sweep sharply uphill. He scaled it at a full clip until, cresting the top, he collapsed in exhaustion. Sobbing, he lay back into sweet clover, letting the rain pelt his face.

"Why? Why? Why?" he said aloud over and over again. His madness electrified his brain, shooting a hundred images at once into his consciousness. He felt about ready to climb out of his skin to find some relief. How could this happen? WHY?

The storms raged inside and out. Joe felt dizzy, so he sat up. Desperate, his mind raced in another direction—over the last week, trying to find what single act, what error could have caused such serious repercussions. He looked for a reason, and found twenty. All ended with the push, the stupid, damn push. He rocked back and forth. Still, none of the reasons were totally his fault. They were O'Reilly's doings. His dad's. If Annie had truly loved him, she would have understood. Would not have weakened. Worse yet, she chose Mark. Annie swore she hated his arrogance, his abuse. Yet she had been in his arms. The thought sickened him.

Joe sat for a long time. The front blew steadily eastward, the lightning and thunder trumpeting its advance. The initial bluster past, a steady, lighter rain followed. Joe's tears subsided, too. His mind played pinball with his emotions, bouncing between hurt and anger and self pity. Love was still too new to him, its betrayal foreign. He couldn't bring himself to blame Annie, so it hung like another storm over him. He cried out again into the black night,

"Why God? Why me? I've never hurt anybody. I've never done anything wrong. I've never had anything. Why did you take the one thing I want away from me?"

No response came. He sat alone, cursing a life that had brought him to this field in the rain.

At last Joe rose and searched for his bearings. He knew he was near the end of the meadow, close to Addison's farm, about four miles from home. He set his sights on the distance lightning, knowing that was east. In short order he came upon a gravel road. Awash with new puddles, it led him south. Soon Joe smelled Addison's hogs. No longer lost, he slogged along the muddy road, his legs tired beyond belief. He took his time, for no happiness awaited him.

Entering the house, his muddy condition and mad look startled George and Ruth.

"Where have you been?" Ruth asked, rising from the kitchen table and rubbing her hands together. "It's after 1 o'clock. We've been worried sick with this storm and so much lightning."

Pulling his drenched sweatshirt over his head, Joe mumbled through the wool. "I ran out too far tonight. I waited the storm out in one of Addison's sheds."

"Why didn't you call from there?" Ruth asked, still fretting.

Joe shrugged. "It didn't seem to matter."

"Didn't matter?" It was George, his voice agitated. He stood beside Ruth. Both looked exhausted from their vigil. "Do you know the sheriff is looking for you?" He pointed toward the door with one crutch to signify out there, in the harsh night.

"I said I took shelter," Joe said impudently.

"Joe, we've been just sick," Ruth interjected. "You could've been killed by lightning, running out in the open.

"Maybe that wouldn't have been such a bad thing."

"Don't sass your mother, or I'll . . ."

Joe shot George a cold, vacant stare. George's anger turned to fatherly fear, for the look belied something changed inside Joe. His Joe, who he had thought lost, then found. Joe's heroics the night of his accident were the only reason George stood alive across from his anguished son. In resignation, and to break the moment's awkwardness, he said with forced authority, "Go to your room. Go get warm. Ruth, call the sheriff and tell him Joe's home."

Joe sulked past them, up the creaking stairway steps and into his dark room. He closed his door without turning on the light. He slouched down at the foot of his bed until he sat looking out his single window. In the distance, the unseen lights of Troy glowed, polishing that corner of the night sky into a pewter gray. He felt numb and melancholy. The town reminded him of school and how uncomfortable he would feel when the news spread. Annie would avoid the subject, and him as well. Mark would share the evening's events with his cronies, though, and it would pass through the school like Asian flu. Joe suddenly hated Mark more than he hated anything else because he couldn't find it in his heart to hate Annie. Joe hated all the Marks—the boasters, the users. Those with the brashness he lacked. The power he seemed denied. They sat at the head of the table and lapped up gravy while people like him waited for the scraps.

What would he say to Annie? Would she call? Should he answer? He decided not to confront her, to let the thing between them end abruptly and silently, like finger and thumb extinguishing a candle flame. Trying to repair things would only lead to more self hate and, eventually, he knew in the core of his heart, hating Annie. He decided to spare her. No matter what she had done, she alone had made him feel, for a while, like he mattered.

Joe shivered through his wet underwear. He chuckled cynically. So this is what growing up is like, he thought. One minute willing to die for someone, the next fleeing the same person. Putting yourself down and standing up for yourself in the same breath. Learning the difference between trust and betrayal in the flash of a lightning bolt.

He shelved thoughts of Annie, and faced another issue. This was Mark's doing. His feigned friendliness had been a scam. Do I just let this ride, Joe thought, or bust his pretty face the minute he cracks a smile in my direction? No, that tactic resulted in expulsion for a day the first time. A repeat would finish his senior year. What senior year? He laughed inwardly at his own stupidity. Besides, Mark would pound the crap out of him.

So how to get revenge and regain self-respect, without ending up in a purple pool of blood in the school parking lot?

Suddenly the answer appeared as clear to him as the preceding hours' events remained muddled. His heart fluttered, and he rolled the idea over in his mind, as if coming at the concept from a different angle would test and prove its validity. He rose from the floor, stripped naked and stared once again toward Troy. The idea funneled through him like a fuse. "Could I do it?" he said out loud. Then he slipped dirty between the cool white sheets.

That's it, he thought. I'll beat Mark in the conference track meet.

His mind raced excitedly over the prospect. He pictured himself leaving Mark faltering behind him in a spray of biting cinders while Annie waited at the finish line to catch him in her loving arms as he collapsed, triumphant from his magnificent effort.

Joe snickered again. For sure Annie wouldn't be waiting. And he had never come close to defeating Mark. His best effort, when he boldly set the pace in their last race, was ultimately what drove Annie to Mark. That and the push. In that race Joe fizzled so badly after his fast start he actually finished further behind Mark than usual. And only 16 days remained until the championship. Doubts flooded in on him. Still, he clung to the possibility. Could he manage it, he wondered, as blessed sleep enfolded him.

EGGS

The previous night's storm sucked in a cold front behind it. The bells in St. Lawrence's steeple peeled in a clear blue sky as George, Ruth and Joe left the 10 o'clock Mass. Father MacDougall greeted them as they walked by, taking time to inquire about George's recovery. Other neighbors, still filled with the blood of Christ, gathered around George and Ruth. The wives insisted Joe's parents wait while their husbands dutifully fetched casseroles and desserts from the back seats of their cars. Before this neighborly manna could fill the Mitchell's Chevy, Joe crossed the street, and crawled into its back seat. Quickly, watching for parishioners, he stripped out of his Sunday clothes. The vinyl seat chilled him as he tugged on first his shorts and tank top, and then his sweat suit. In less than two minutes, Joe trotted west toward the high school.

He had spent most of his morning chore time trying to figure out how to defeat Mark. More sleep was a must, but it wouldn't be enough. With no apparent answers forthcoming, he quit looking internally. After bathing for church, he called Coach DeAngelo. His tone over the phone indicated a lack of coffee and little excitement, but finally, after much pleading, DeAngelo acquiesced.

Joe spied DeAngelo as he approached the school driveway. Huddled with his blue sweat shirt hood up to block the wind, DeAngelo leaned against one of the football field's light poles. His hands encircled a large thermos and, as Joe neared, he saw DeAngelo sipping coffee from its top. Upon seeing Joe, DeAngelo took a big gulp, shook out the cup's few remaining drops, and screwed it back onto the thermos. He set the thermos down reluctantly, knowing it carried the only heat of the cold morning.

"Morning, Coach," Joe said.

"Morning, Joe."

"Really glad you agreed to help me, on a Sunday and all."

"Well, you sounded pretty desperate over the phone," DeAngelo said, thrusting his hands into his pockets. "What's going on?"

Joe hesitated. "Like I said over the phone, I've been missing so much school, and I want to help us win the championship, so I need some coaching to help me improve my time."

"Why not go talk to Coach O'Reilly? He coaches you distance guys. I'm the dash man."

That was true. DeAngelo hailed from Chicago. He competed in the mile relay at DePaul University in his freshman and sophomore years. But speed didn't guarantee good grades. Flunking out, he entered a state college and eventually earned his teacher's certificate. He gratefully accepted the Troy school district's offer to teach algebra and American history. He coached track to help make ends meet, and remember his past glories.

Joe fidgeted before DeAngelo, etching a pattern in the track cinders with his spikes. "Cuz I can't stand O'Reilly's guts."

DeAngelo laughed loudly. "Well, I'm not fond of the man myself. He rides my ass constantly on how the relay teams are performing, or the sprinters. But I still go to the man. He is the Man, you know, and actually knows quite a bit about distance running. Come on, that's not the real reason why we're here, is it?"

"Okay, you want the truth?"

"The truth is always best."

"I was out running last night and came upon Perkins . . . with my girlfriend. I want to get back at him where it will hurt him the most. In the mile run at the conference finals."

"Oh, so that's it," DeAngelo whistled through his teeth. "Annie Jensen's the girl, right?"

"Yeah."

DeAngelo pieced together more of the puzzle. "And that scene between you, Mark and O'Reilly the other day explains why I'm here and not Ken. Well, I'm not too keen about spending my Sunday morning helping you get revenge."

"Just forget the reason, okay?" Joe said hotly. "I could give you a hundred other ones. I just want to win something for once in my life."

Stating the truth shook Joe, and he turned away, trying to check his emotions. He was weary from the night before, and not in control. He stared at the empty metal bleachers, and watched the debris of spring whip across the football field in the cold wind.

"Okay," DeAngelo said. Joe turned toward the young coach. "But here's how it's going to be. As mad as you are, get it out of your system fast. Anger will only keep you awake. Anger will distract you. I won't coach you if you come mad every day."

"Okay, okay," Joe said.

"And another thing. The only reason I'll do this is not to help you get revenge. Not to show O'Reilly was wrong about you. I'm doing this because I've been there—hell, we've all been there at one time. I know what it is to want something badly. Do this for yourself. Go into this with that frame of mind and, win or lose, you'll feel good about yourself when this is over. Agreed?" DeAngelo said, extending his hand.

"Agreed," Joe said, grasping it firmly and sealing the contract.

DeAngelo set to work immediately, as if he had known before he arrived what Joe sought. He instructed Joe to run an 880 at the pace he normally ran the mile.

"Run the first lap in lane 3, and the second in lane two. Don't cross over into the inside lane."

Joe stretched out on the infield. He ached terribly from the previous night's run. His legs felt as if injected with Novocain. He figured he covered almost 14 miles the previous night, about 10 of those running. Eventually the knots untied, the joints loosened. Joe shed his sweats and shivered in his shorts and tank top.

"Just two laps, about 80 percent of your regular 880 pace," DeAngelo said, looking at his stopwatch. "Starting . . . now," he said with the click of the timer.

Joe circled the field alone, thankful to be running as it warmed his body against the cold. He expected DeAngelo to holler out some advice as he completed the first of the laps and veered into lane two, but DeAngelo only studied his stride. After Joe passed, DeAngelo trotted to mid-field and continued to monitor Joe's progress. At the 700-yard mark, where the backstretch gave way to the far oval of the track, Joe strained into the northwest wind. DeAngelo waited for him at the finish line.

Joe eased up. He put his hands on his hips to catch his breath.

"Keep moving so you don't tighten up. You're going again in about five," DeAngelo said. Then he added, "Was that really about 80 percent?"

"Yeah. Why?"

"Not the fastest time. You have a long way to go to catch Perkins."

"I'm a bit tired from running last night. And I've been up since 5 this morning."

"Oh, that's right," DeAngelo acknowledged. "Those cows. Well, it really doesn't matter. Catch your breath and we'll go again. Stay off of the track." He walked away from Joe, and jotted notes onto a pad on a clipboard he pulled from beneath his sweat shirt. Joe tried to stay limber. His legs felt like pieces of cord wood, and the blisters he had bandaged on his toes painfully reformed inside his shoes. He donned his sweat shirt, and walked back and forth on the football green.

"Okay, you're up again, this time in lane one," DeAngelo barked. Joe trotted over to the starting line. "I want you to run a quarter, hard, as if you were given the baton with the lead in the last leg of a mile relay and Troy's championship depends on you keeping that lead. Do you know what I'm talking about?"

"Yeah," Joe said. "Puke your guts out fast."

"That's right. No mile or half mile run. Don't hold anything back. The 440 is basically a dash—only most people can't hold the sprint. You run the last 100 yards on dwindling power, depleted oxygen and pounding heart," DeAngelo, said, reliving his races of long ago, and forgetting that both he and Coach O'Reilly explained this fact at the start of every track season. The young coach positioned himself on the side of the track as Joe shed his sweats a second time. "Show me what you're made of, Joe. Starting . . . now!"

Joe burst down the track, arms and legs churning. He ran many quarters in practice, mostly for conditioning. He had even run a leg of the mile relay several weeks earlier. Unlike that relay race, however, today he couldn't motivate himself thinking about saving Annie from Mark's clutches. Now he didn't care if they both went over the cliff. So he simply went as hard as his leaden legs allowed. He headed down the backstretch under a full head of steam. He heard DeAngelo yell something from across the way, but the wind smothered it out.

By the end of the backstretch, DeAngelo's description of the 440 became fact. Joe leaned into the curve behind the goal posts, doubting he could even finish. His stride tightened. Mouth agape, he tried to draw in more and more oxygen, but no amount could replete his exhausted reserves. Ahead, DeAngelo gestured him forward with his right arm. Joe strained the last 40 yards, his arms pumping, his head light, until he passed DeAngelo.

"Good job, good job. That was a 63-second quarter after running a half." DeAngelo scribbled something new onto his pad. "Now tell me, what gave out first, your heart or your legs?"

"Wait a sec, I've got to catch my breath," Joe said. He bent over the track, feeling nauseous. He sweated despite the brisk breeze. His throat burned.

"Well you think about it while you cool down. When you have, pull on your sweats and do some stretching. Then come over here. And watch where you step."

DeAngelo walked up the track from the finish line. He pulled a black and yellow tape measure from his hip pocket, and busied himself measuring Joe's stride in each of the three lanes. He jotted down some figures and walked 50 yards in the other direction so he ended up 20 yards before the finish line. Again squatting, he took more measurements

Once Joe started to chill, he tugged on his sweats. He promised himself he would pamper his spent legs in a soaking bath in the afternoon.

DeAngelo returned to his first measurements, gesturing Joe to follow.

"Look here," he said, using the extended thin arm of the tape measure to point at the indentations from Joe's spikes. "We were lucky it rained so hard last night. We've got good imprints."

"What do they tell you?"

"Pretty much what I expected. Here, at the start of your first lap, I've got a stride of 65 inches." He moved the tape measure in an arc to another set of prints in lane two. "By the start of the second lap in the 880, your stride was 64 inches." He skooched over to lane one without rising. "When you ran the quarter, your starting stride was 64. Now let's go see how you were at the end of the half and the quarter."

DeAngelo rose, his knees cracking. They walked together to the second set of marked footprints.

"Boy, it's colder than a witch's tit out here," DeAngelo said, turning his back to the steady blow and walking backwards. "Doesn't spring ever come to this god-forsaken state?"

Joe smiled as he, too, rotated so his hooded sweat shirt took the brunt of the breeze. He watched DeAngelo play out more of the tape measure so he didn't have to bend.

"Now in lane two, you're tiring a bit at the end of a half. Your stride, 62 inches. That's to be expected, because as you tire your legs reach out less. It's too painful to fully extend your stride."

DeAngelo retracted the tape and did mental calculations in his head. "By the end of a typical mile, I bet your stride is only about 60 inches, if that. You can check that running on your own at home. Now," he said, moving left and straddling the inside lane, "let's check what your stride is when you're sprinting vs. running."

DeAngelo handed the end of the tape measure to Joe, who dutifully stretched it out as he stooped between his tracks.

"I've got 60 inches," DeAngelo said. "You can let go now."

Joe stood as the metal measure zipped back into its coil. "So what does it all mean?"

"Well, I was trying to determine a couple of things," DeAngelo said. "First, whether you're a distance man or a dash man. You see, your body type determines how you run. Think of a cottontail vs. a snow shoe hare. Or a cheetah vs. a lion. One runs on power, the other on smoothness and length of stride. It's all in the haunches and the legs, and your overall physical proportions. Now you, Joe, have powerful muscles. You're really a dash man, but you're too short."

"So you're saying I'm running the wrong race?"

"Basically."

"But I never won the quarter miles in practice. That's why O'Reilly moved me to the mile."

"How tall are you, Joe."

"Five-seven."

"You look shorter. Anyway, that's the other part of the equation. A person's running stride is about double his pant inseam. That keeps us in balance as we run. Your pants are about 30-30, correct?"

"That's right," Joe said, trying to drink up all this flow of information.

"So if you ran against someone identical in power and stride but five inches taller, you would have to take six or eight more steps to cover the same quarter mile at your height. That's a couple additional seconds at least."

DeAngelo raised his right arm, his hand tucked back into the sleeve to keep it warm, and swept around the track for emphasis. "Now Perkins is about 6', maybe 6'-1". Inseam's probably about 33-34 inches. That means his stride is almost 70 inches. Every step he takes he gains four inches on you. Easy. So it takes you about eight percent more steps to run the mile than it does Perkins."

Joe looked dejectedly at his imprints in the black cinders as the reality sunk in. He always knew he took more strides than his opponents because of his height. He just never did the math.

"Based on that equation, all things but stride being equal, Perkins should be beating you by about 12 seconds in each mile. Is that about right?"

At the numbers, Joe perked up. "No, it's been closer to 9 seconds. Maybe your math is wrong," he said hopefully.

DeAngelo smiled. "Hey, give me some credit. I majored in the subject."

"Then how do you explain the difference? You've measured my stride. Maybe Mark's not as lanky as you think," Joe said, still hopeful.

"No, there's probably a couple of other reasons."

"Like what?"

"You're a more determined runner than Perkins is. You're probably in better shape than he is because of your farm work. You've also got more heart, more muscle."

"What's the mathematical equation behind that?"

They were huddled close now, both vying for the light pole's protection. DeAngelo looked at Joe with affection.

"I've seen you run. That's why I made you run that quarter so fast after the half. Perkins would have found an excuse not to. He doesn't especially like pain. Besides, Perkins isn't a dash man. Remember the body build thing I explained. He's a glider. No, you're built more for speed. And you must have some ticker. Say, you have a ride home?" DeAngelo asked.

"No, I'll call my parents from the Standard station."

"How far out of town do you live?"

"About three miles, south on 17."

"Hell, I'll give you a ride home. Let's talk as we walk."

Joe hurried to DeAngelo's side, who strode with purpose toward his parked Ford Mustang.

"Getting back to your heart," DeAngelo resumed. "That's why I asked earlier which gave out first, your heart or your legs."

"I'm not sure," Joe said. "Probably my legs, since I ran about 10 miles last night."

DeAngelo stopped in his tracks. "10 miles? And you're out here running? Your body can't take that kind of abuse." Then he shook his head and continued up the southern bowl of the stadium.

"Anyway, we need to check. Tomorrow, when you wake up, take your pulse. It's usually the slowest at that time. Tell me what it is on Monday. Then the next time you run a mile, take your pulse as soon as you finish."

By then they had reached DeAngelo's car. The silver Mustang showed signs of patching and sanding where DeAngelo fought futilely against Minnesota road salt.

"It's open."

They sat in silence, thawing out, until DeAngelo had eased the Mustang through Troy's one stop light. There was no traffic. Most of the town's populace was in either the Catholic or Lutheran church. The others hunkered down in their homes against the raw day.

"Wonder what your heartbeat is," DeAngelo said, skipping from KDWB to WDGY on the radio. "MacArthur's Park" filled the front seat. "Jim Ryan's resting heartbeat is in the upper 30s. I bet yours is in the 40s somewhere with your lifestyle."

"Why is that important?"

"It's the converse of stride. If your heart is stronger, it beats fewer times. It takes longer to get to, say, 220 beats per minute where you're likely at when you end the mile. If your heart is 10% stronger than Perkins', it helps you take those extras steps you need because of a shorter stride. It keeps the flow of blood and oxygen to your head and body so you don't pass out or tighten up."

DeAngelo smiled sideways at Joe. "We're getting into the realm of biology now, so you'll just have to take my word for it."

They passed by the Standard station on the south edge of town. Roy Gerke was wheeling out bags of barbecue charcoal to replace bags of street salt. DeAngelo honked and Roy nodded his head and continued wheeling.

"You'd have to be crazy to barbecue in this weather," DeAngelo said blankly.

Joe wasn't paying attention. His mind swirled around "what ifs", thinking about inches and heart beats. "Coach, this all makes sense, but I don't see it helping. The way I see it, I can run harder and faster, but I'm doomed unless my legs grow in the next two weeks."

"That's one of the things we're going to do."

"How are we going to do that?"

"Put you on the rack," DeAngelo said. Then he chuckled. "Just kidding. Nothing quite so drastic."

"MacArthur's Park" ended and "My Girl" butted up against it. "I've got sunshine, on a cloudy day," DeAngelo broke out in falsetto song. He was finally awake, and actually excited about helping Joe. He rarely had to put his coaching acumen to the test, and Joe's raw talent and situation presented enough variables for him to strategize over.

"Sorry about that. I'm a Motown freak. Remember back there that your stride shortened the longer you ran? Well, we're not going to lengthen your stride so much as help you maintain the same stride you start with through the entire race. That way as Perkins' stride grows shorter, which it does, too, mind you, you'll make up some time."

"How do we do that?" Joe was like a sponge.

"There are exercises to strengthen your quads. We'll use some light ankle weights, too. I'll have both for you at practice tomorrow."

They glided down the highway to the purr of the Mustang's V-8, past fields silent on Sunday. DeAngelo soaked in the landscape, finding interest in the geometric patterns of the fields.

"It's the next left," Joe said as they neared his gravel road. DeAngelo turned on his blinker and waited for two vehicles coming toward them on the highway to pass.

"Two more things," he said, the cars whizzing by carrying farmers to the next Mass in Troy. "We've got to work on your arms—they're too active when you run—and on you getting some rest."

"I figured more sleep was part of it," Joe chimed in.

DeAngelo drove painfully slow to avoid the road's puddles and keep his Mustang clean. The north wind buffeted the car and bent the ditch grass flat.

"How much sleep a night do you get?"

"About seven hours. I'm up by five, working."

"What kind of work? Real physical?"

"Yeah, I'm forking silage, carrying pails, pushing carts, stuff like that."

"And you do that again after school, right? That's why you leave early from practice?" DeAngelo probed to learn Joe's routine.

"That's right."

DeAngelo shook his head in disbelief. "You must be exhausted all the time."

"I can sleep standing up. It's the farm on the right," Joe said, pointing.

"Well, you need more. In fact, you need to train hard one day and rest the next. That way the muscle cells you break down have time to be replaced by new ones. That's how your muscles get stronger." He turned slowly into the driveway toward the house, which was now surrounded by a sea of yellow dandelions. "I'll work out a regimen for you."

They circled around the cottonwood tree, the car splashing lightly through brown puddles, until the car faced the county road again. DeAngelo let the Mustang idle.

"Now here is one more secret weapon that will help you vanquish Perkins," DeAngelo said, throwing back his hood and leaning sideways in the seat. "You can't share it with anyone. Okay?"

"Okay," Joe said, willingly joining the conspiracy.

"Do you have lots of eggs?"

"Eggs? That's the secret weapon?" Joe looked perplexed.

"Yes, eggs." DeAngelo smiled. "You see, when you're in a dash, the race is all about power. You pump with your legs. Your arms move in unison with every step to keep you in balance. Your arms actually help pull you forward in a dash."

"So how do the eggs come into play?"

"When you're running distance, you don't want your arms to work so hard. Every time they swing they require your heart and lungs to work harder to deliver them blood and oxygen. You want that energy to go to your legs. And another thing. As you tire, you start to tense up. It happens first in your arms and then takes over your stride." DeAngelo made fists and pumped them as if running. "Think of all the energy that's going to your arms. For every stride with your legs, your arms pump equally. The folks in marathons, like Abebe in the '60 and '64 Olympics, run as if the upper halves of their bodies are sitting on a table. All the real effort is from the waist down. Think of yourself like a T. Rex with short, useless arms."

"Now I'm a dinosaur?"

DeAngelo laughed. He ran his fingers through his wavy black hair. "I know I've thrown a lot at you. So forget the theoretically stuff. All I want you to do is carry an egg in each hand the next time you run. When you start to tense up, you'll squeeze those eggs too hard and they'll break. They'll be a constant reminder not to tense up. When you can run a mile without cracking those eggs, we'll be in business. You think about that, and start picturing yourself running with the arms of a T. Rex. I'll have the rest sorted out for you by tomorrow."

Joe opened the passenger door and started to leave. He turned back. "I can't tell you how much I appreciate this, Coach."

"Tell me how much after you beat Perkins."

CHOICES

Annie's life turned into a living hell the minute she lost sight of Joe in the pouring rain. She yelled and screamed after him, then turned her hurt and anger at Mark. They argued terribly all the way home, the only respites coming when Annie bawled. Mark claimed it wasn't his fault Joe stumbled upon them. In his defense, he reminded Annie that only hours ago she had told him she was struggling with Joe. They parted with nothing resolved between them as Mark roared down her driveway and then sped away.

The squeal of tires alerted her parents. Donna was still sitting up due to the storm, but Harry came drowsily from the bedroom as Annie entered the living room, soaked from seeking out Joe in the rain. Donna and Harry were aghast at her appearance, and properly grilled her. Why are you soaked? *It was pouring when we ran for our cars at Nancy's.* Who brought you home? *That was Mark. He was at the party.* Did you see Joe? *Joe?* Yes, he came by. He was out running. Said he was going to Nancy's to find you. *No, he never showed up. Must have changed his mind. I'll call him in the morning.*

She slipped away unscathed by the Inquisition and carried her lies into her bedroom. Joe had come by. And what did he find? Betrayal. She flopped on the bed and cried some more.

Annie relived the previous few days, trying to find an explanation for the quandary she found herself in. The push started it all. Joe's anger. He spurned her, tossed her aside as if disgusted with her. The thought caused her heart to ache anew. In her own defense, she lashed back in equal anger. She avoided him in school, and coldly let Joe know by her silence that she would not tolerate abuse. Then a very non-abusive Mark appeared. He consoled Annie in her grief. He even defended Joe and said Joe was really lashing out at Coach O'Reilly when he shoved Annie.

An emotional wreck, Annie decided against Nancy's party. She didn't want to be seen without Joe and explain why she came alone. Then Mark called and asked if she planned on going to the party. When she said no and explained why, Mark asked if she wanted to go out to eat and talk about it. Because of their history, Mark suddenly became the only one she felt she could share her feelings with. She lied to her parents and said she was walking to Nancy's. Mark picked her up along the way. They drove to the edge of the city, and talked for several hours over burgers and cokes.

Mark never treated her better. Eventually, Annie took her turn at listening. Mark poured out his heart. He explained again how empty his life had become without Annie. He pushed all the right buttons, said all the right things. Mark fed off Annie's own expressed concerns that maybe Joe and her worlds were too disparate. He vowed he would change for her, and she knew from his tone and his open look that he truthfully meant he would try.

Mark's tenderness slowly folded back her resistance. She saw the Mark that had won her heart a year earlier. This time she wasn't another notch on his belt. Mark seemed to truly need her and was no longer ashamed to admit it. Toward the end of the meal, they laughed easily together. Annie felt unburdened, at ease.

When Mark pulled to the end of the familiar road, Annie spied the looming oak. She thought of Joe and the foxes, and guilt clawed at her conscience. Then she decided she needed to be loved, too. Half out of anger, half out of need, she clung again to the boy she had once loved.

Joe's appearance at the window tore away all her manufactured justifications. Through the lightning's blue light, she saw Joe's inner light extinguish in his eyes. She knew she had cleaved his heart in two in that one brief second. That's all the time she saw him, for by the time the next bolt lit the night and she stood outside the car, he had vanished. The one second loomed large enough. She could not shake free of it.

Annie eventually fell asleep on top of her covers. Anxiety-driven dreams streamed between Joe and Mark. There were rooms with locked doors that opened with her pounding fists. Then her friends were in her own house and she was unprepared to greet them. Despite the restless sleep, she awoke in a strange calm, accepting the truth that she loved both Joe and Mark to different degrees, and in far different ways. All during the Lutheran service with her parents, however, Annie knew she needed to make a choice. She prayed to God for guidance. She asked for a sign.

Later, while looking out the kitchen window, she saw a cottontail eating on the edge of their barberry bushes. It hopped ever so slowly and in such a tight circle, that its movements reminded Annie of a second hand ticking around a clock. Eventually the rabbit faced her. Even at 60 feet, she saw its jaws working overtime, its ears gyrating like signal corps flags. In time, the rabbit hopped away, and Annie rose to call Joe.

Ruth heard the Mustang, and was drawn to the kitchen window. She saw Joe and the teacher, Mr. DeAngelo, talking animatedly in the front seat. She returned to the stove, turning up the heat to finish the roast, lest Joe found her spying on him. Joe's behavior over the last 12 hours concerned Ruth greatly. It was unlike him to do something as irrational as his midnight run. The look of despair he wore to bed transformed into a steel mask of silence by dawn. Plus Annie had telephoned twice since they returned from church, both times requesting that Joe call her.

"How did it go?" Ruth asked as Joe entered the kitchen.

"Oh, fine. Coach DeAngelo's a good guy. He gave me some really good advice." Joe walked to the fridge as he talked. He grabbed the pitcher of milk, dehydrated from his runs.

"Dinner will be ready in about a half hour."

"Can I eat later? I really need to soak in the tub first," Joe said, pouring the milk into a plastic glass. He drank quickly awaiting permission, facing the cupboard.

"Joe, Annie's been calling. Did something happen between you last night?"

Joe stopped in mid-gulp. He focused on the cupboard, dirt smudged around its handles and its paint cracking. He was afraid to face his mother, afraid that tears would well visibly to the surface. Instead, he hid in the patterns of cracked paint.

"Annie and I are through," he finally said. "She's gone back to Mark Perkins."

"Oh, Joe," Ruth said, setting down her roasting fork. "I'm so sorry. What happened?"

"It's not important," Joe said. Then, despite his efforts, he began to cry. He leaned into the nearby doorframe and his body shook as the vision of Annie in the car once more cascaded over him. Ruth left the stove and rushed to his side. She held him, and Joe didn't resist.

"She was all that I've ever wanted," he sobbed.

Ruth let him cry it out. She stroked his head, something she hadn't done since Junior High. Her blond, happy angel had long ago grown up and distanced himself from her. Now she felt the hardness of his shoulder muscles, the faint smell of sweat from his run, and he was her child again.

"What can I do?"

"There's nothing you can do."

They stood together for a minute. Joe quieted until only the sizzle of the roast disrupted the silence. Ruth's mind searched for the right words. She felt responsible, certain that the events of the last few weeks led to this breakup.

"How about I go kick Perkins in the groin?"

Joe laughed onto Ruth's shoulder. She never said things like that.

"You can't do that."

"Why not? I would, you know."

"I know you would. But I don't know where he lives." Joe pulled away, sniffling and wiping both eyes with the palms of his hands.

"Well, let's invite him over. Or let's make another manure bomb."

Joe laughed softly again. "No, Mom, I'll be all right. I just need to get some sleep, and I'll be better. I promise."

"Okay, Joe. We can get through this."

Joe looked into Ruth's eyes. He saw the concern and love. "Thanks, Mom."

Ruth hugged him again. "Oh, Joe. Sometimes the world's a hard place. That's why you have parents."

While Joe soaked in the tub, George came in. Ruth heard him in the washroom first, swapping the wheelchair for his crutches. Soon he hopped through the washroom door into the kitchen and started toward the bathroom.

"You need to wash up here, George. Joe's in the tub," Ruth said, pointing to the kitchen sink.

"Is he all right?" George said, rotating on his right crutch.

"He and Annie broke up. I think that's where he was last night. He's pretty shook up about it."

George nodded, glad at last to have a reason for Joe's reckless escapade. He swung his way across the kitchen and washed his hands while Ruth dished the carved roast, carrots and potatoes onto two plates. They said grace together. After their amen's, Ruth asked where George had been.

"Just checking on the job you three are doing," he said, cutting a corner off the slab of beef.

"Did we pass?"

"Nothing but flying colors," he said, taking a bite. He chewed slowly, savoring the dark mellowness of the meat. There was much on his mind, and he didn't know where to begin. "I didn't think it possible, back in the hospital, when you told me. But you're getting us through this."

"It's more Joe and Frank than me."

"Now, don't discount yourself." He mashed a carrot into his roast potatoes and then said, "I'm real proud of you, doing the barn work and all, after swearing never to do so."

"It's because of the Pledge," Ruth said. She picked at her food.

"Ah, the Pledge," George said in acknowledgement. "The Pledge. What does Joe need to get through this thing with Annie?"

"He says sleep."

George chuckled, thinking back on his own previous week, and the decision made. "He's got that right. The only good thing about this busted leg is I'm sleeping late. Your mind gets unfogged. You see more clearly."

"And what are you seeing, George?" Ruth asked. She ignored her food completely now, her appetite ruined by Joe's condition.

"A whole lot," he said. And he had. Since Frank's sermon, George spent more time staring out over flat fields from his wheelchair. He thought of other farmers, like comedic Cordelle, who had transitioned out of dairying. In contrast, he reviewed his own life and found it wanting. He could count on two hands the number of time he had taken Joe fishing or to a Twins game. Vacations with Ruth or the three of them, on his thumbs.

"Like my life's passing me by," George said at last. "Like I chose farming and loved it, but now it's become too much."

George gently put down his knife and fork and reached for Ruth's hand. "Why have you put up with me? This struggle?"

"I married you. The farm came with."

"That's no answer, Ruth. Are you happy here, with the dairy?"

"George, what's gotten into you?"

George seemed about to explode. "Do you ever wish you were off this place?"

"Yes." She held firmly to George's proffered hand. "I've resigned myself to it after all these years. In truth, I like the place. The neighbors. My gardens. I like seeing the seasons change. It's lonely, though, George. And like you said, lately it's just been too much. And it will stay that way once Joe's gone."

George let go of Ruth's hand and returned to his food. "Remember the time I told you I almost drown?"

"Vaguely."

"I was about 10. It was Memorial Day and me and the Bettis boys decided to go swimming in some backwater on the river. The day was a scorcher, but the water was frigid. We swam anyway, buck-naked. I remember my pecker shrinking to about the size of a .22 shell.

"George."

"Anyway, we were having a blast, scooping up mud from the bottom and flinging it at each another. Caught Billie a good one right in the mouth. Then I stepped into a drop off. The current took me. I swallowed water and went all topsy-turvy. Didn't know which way was up. When I finally came to the surface, all I could see was this huge expanse of water. I started cramping to boot, from the cold. I was sure I was a goner. All that distance to shore. Panic took hold of me, worse than the cramps. I was just about ready to give up, let that water swallow me, when Billie yells, 'Turn around!' I rotate and I'm about 6 feet from the bank. I swam one stroke and I was on the bottom again."

George ended abruptly, leaving Ruth in the lurch.

"I don't understand."

"Since my leg, this farm's reminded me of that day in the river. I feel like no matter how much I struggle, it's got me beaten. I want to swim, mind you, but the river, the farm, it's become to big without Joe. But the near shore, it's still there. I just got to turn around."

"You're making no sense."

"I'm thinking about selling the herd."

His words, coming without hesitation, flabbergasted Ruth. She didn't know how to respond, things were so sudden.

"Joe's bound to leave, should leave. And this leg, well, we can't keep going."

"But George, you love the farm."

"Yes, I do. I surely do," George answered. He was calmer now, the explosion past, the devastation not as painful as he had expected. "But I have to be realistic. And take care of the other things I love. Like you and Joe."

Ruth felt on the verge of tears. She couldn't believe what she heard.

"If we sold the cows, I could still raise some steers, lots of them maybe. I'd like that."

George reached for his glass, and for a moment looked at its golden contents. "Selling the cows would free up a whole lot of acreage. Maybe we could start growing some sort of exotic cash crop. Like Jerusalem artichokes. I read about them in *The Farmer* magazine."

He took a sip of milk. "Or maybe start a nursery and strawberry business. The berries for cash now while the trees and shrubs grow. The city's coming this way, and all those suburban homes will want trees. And in the winter, I could find some job in town."

"Or I could work," Ruth added enthusiastically.

"Now Ruth, you don't have to worry about working. Your place is in the home."

"Then why am I spending countless hours in the barn?" Ruth countered. "Joe'll be gone. It will just be you and me. I could bookkeep for someone else if I'm not doing it for the farm."

George mulled this. Ruth was right, he decided. They would need the income.

"All right, we'll figure this out together. Convince Joe to stay and keep dairying until we've got a good plan. Get the crops harvested in the fall and sell them along with the cows. That'll get us the seed money for whatever we decide."

Ruth's mind spun. In two minutes, they had decided to change their life of nearly 20 years. Yet, it felt so right and natural and timely to Ruth that she wanted to dance.

"What about short term?" she asked, since decision-making suddenly came as easy as cracking an egg.

"You mean how do we let Joe enjoy the rest of the year and me with a busted leg?"

"Something like that. I think it's more important than ever that he finishes school and does well in track with this Annie crisis."

Just then, Ruth heard a truck enter the yard. She started to rise.

"You can keep eating, it's just Frank."

"Frank doesn't work on the weekend."

George smiled.

"George, what on earth is happening today?"

"Seems Frank feels the same way we do about Joe," George said, his smile broadening. "I'm a step ahead of you for once. Frank's agreed to work weekends until school ends."

"Oh, George."

"And I've talked to John Franksmeier. Now that John's crops are in, he says he'll help with milking and chores in the morning until haying time."

"He'll do it for nothing?" Ruth couldn't believe their sudden good fortune.

"Said he would. I promised him I'd give him a side of beef come fall, and the first shot at my best dairy cows when I sell. I feel better about it that way."

Ruth rose out of her chair and struggling to get onto his lap. With his bum leg, George's contorted effort to push back from the table caused them both to laugh. Ruth kissed George.

"Let me go tell Joe."

"No, let him go to sleep. We'll tell him later. Now, watch out for my dang leg."

Joe awoke to darkness, startled. Something was obviously wrong, as he had told Ruth to wake him at 4 p.m. for chores. He fumbled for the overhead light string and when the bare bulb lit the room, checked his clock. 10 p.m. He dressed quickly and ran down the stairs. Ruth, George and Frank sat in the living room, drinking beer.

"What's going on?" Joe asked, as all three smiled at him.

"We decided there was more than one way to kick Perkins in the groin," Ruth said.

"That's right," George added. He sat in his recliner, smiling. "The three of us, and John Franksmeier, have figured out a way to free you of some chores for the next couple of weeks. So your Highness can sleep in till the late hour of 6:30 a.m. starting tomorrow."

Joe sat down confused in the gold chair next to the TV console. "I don't understand. You mean I don't have to milk cows?"

"We'll still need your help at night, but Frank has agreed to work weekends, and John will help with milk mornings," George said, beaming.

"I don't know what to say."

"Say thank you. And promise us you'll win," George replied.

"Yeah, win," Frank chimed in, raising his bottle. "Winning would be real nice."

CONSEQUENCES

The next morning, Joe awoke to the sound of a wren warbling incessantly from an apple tree outside his window. A first. Something else was different. His room was aglow with sunlight and he was still in bed. He stayed there another 10 minutes, enjoying the luxury. He stretched under the warm covers, aware of the sheet's silky smoothness. It was if he were a prisoner released on account of good behavior. He couldn't get used to it. Most of all, he couldn't believe his luck. A key ingredient of his plan lay unexpectedly at his feet—rest.

Joe thought of the showdown race, and instantly Annie and Mark intruded upon his happiness. Part of him wanted to call Annie. The other half feared seeing her at school. What would he say? What would she say? His anxiety disrupted his lounging, so Joe channeled it into plotting his revenge against Mark. All the way to school, he tried to imagine how more rest would translate into seconds clipped off his mile time. Would intact eggs truly nibble away at Mark's winning margins?

As the bus rolled down the drive to the high school, Joe vowed to remain mum about Saturday's events. He avoided his locker, and went the length of the ground floor corridor to climb the steps to his first-hour class. Betty Carlson dashed his stealth plans the minute he reached the top of the stairwell. She deftly weaved her way through the morning tangle of students. She wore the face of a Nobel Peace Prize winner. Joe braced for the negotiations.

"Joe, I can't believe what I heard from Annie," Betty said, cornering him at the end of the row of green metal lockers. "You have to go talk to her. She's so sorry."

"There's nothing to talk about."

"Don't you want to know why she was with Mark? And how much she regrets it?"

"Not really."

Betty pressed on. "It was just something that happened. She was angry because you pushed her and didn't come to the party. She thought you didn't love her anymore."

"I don't."

"Yes you do. You've got to give her another chance."

Joe felt the anger well up inside him. "Why? If she cared about me so much, she would never have been in that car."

"You don't understand."

"No, I don't. And I probably never will, because I don't intend to talk to Annie ever again. You tell her that when you see her."

Joe pushed by Betty, who stood with mouth agape, as the first hour bell rang.

Joe took circuitous routes to English and History to avoid Annie, as he knew her class schedules and routine inside and out. Still, Annie's network of friends tracked him down. Each met the same angry Joe, heard the same terse message. With each peace-keeping mission, Joe's resolve hardened.

He couldn't skip classes, however, so eventually Joe saw Annie in Social Studies. She already sat in her desk on the far side of the room as he entered it at the last minute. She glanced over and held Joe's eyes for a moment before he looked away and feigned interest in Mr. Carter's continuing discourse on the election process.

Seeing Annie shook Joe to his core. His heart literally ached. He found it strange to learn that the expression "broken-hearted" was a physical reality. Part of him desired to reconcile. Maybe in time a broken heart can mend, he thought. But the fission in his heart still beat molten. Healing scar tissue remained months away.

As the school day ended and Joe headed down the stairs to the locker rooms for track practice, Annie intercepted him. Her eyes were red from crying, and for a moment he simply wanted to take her in his arms and forgive all transgressions.

"Not here," Joe said. "Let's go down to the gym."

The gym lay in semi-darkness, the only light bathing it spilled over the bleacher railing from the band and theater rooms above. In the quiet, they faced each other, their faces in soft shadows.

"Joe, I'm so sorry," Annie started.

Joe paced in a tight circle, ignoring her eyes.

"It's all a big mistake," she continued. "It's you I love."

Joe stopped and glared at her. "No you don't," he hissed.

"Let me explain . . ."

He cut her short. "There's nothing to explain. I thought you loved me. But you were with Mark, and I don't know why."

221

"You pushed me, remember? You told me to find someone else to take me to the prom. You've been so angry at the world. At me. It just got all confusing."

"So it's my fault. Well, I couldn't help it that my dad's accident kept me away. I just thought we had something strong enough to survive it."

Annie bowed her head. She fretted over how to proceed. "I can't explain now. You're too angry."

"You're damn right I'm angry," Joe shouted. He moved menacingly toward her until they stood a foot apart. Joe smelled the softness of her perfume, spied her moistening eyes. She looked like she hadn't slept since the storm.

This close, he weakened. This close, so close.

"Yes," I'm angry," he whispered. "You broke my heart."

Annie reached up with her hand. Joe moved to pull away, but her hand moved in unison. She cupped his right cheek gently. "Joe, I know what I have done. My heart aches, too," she said. "I know you won't believe this, but right now I hate myself more than you hate me."

Joe remained silent. The warmth of her hand was so soothing. But he could not forgive her.

"I have to go," he said. "Practice."

LESSONS TO LEARN

While Joe worked hard to avoid Annie, he didn't hide from Mark. He spied him at the end of the row of lockers. Mark must have sensed his stare, because he stopped unbuttoning his shirt and turned. A thin smile slit his face, and he nodded. The game was on. Joe nodded back. He turned to his own locker. Only then did he allow himself to smile. Mark didn't have a clue of his plan. Joe intended to keep it that way. There would be no conflict between them, no taunts before the race.

Joe went through his shortened practice. Mark and a healed Scott Hamre repeatedly led the distance runners in a series of quarter miles. Still fatigued from his Saturday marathon, and his Sunday morning races, Joe hung back in the middle of the pack. Coach O'Reilly noticed, and yelled from the infield, "You're not looking like that 1-point man today, Joe. Let's see some hustle."

Joe ignored him, his thoughts instead on the end of practice and his awaiting instructions. DeAngelo's had outlined his two-week schedule. They had jogged to the practice field together, with DeAngelo excitedly telling Joe that he had pored through coaching books and his own dog-eared notebooks from college. He even tracked down a couple of books about other famous distance men. The great Finn Paavo Nurmi, who perfected running by a stopwatch. "This one will help you understand how Mark runs," DeAngelo said. "By timing his quarter miles." And Glen Cunningham, who overcame fire-scarred legs and impossible odds to set the mile record. "To help you learn to run with pain," DeAngelo continued as he foisted the book onto Joe. DeAngelo beamed brightest over the book on Abebe, the marathon winner at Rome.

"The best distance runner ever. Period," DeAngelo said. "Read it to get inspired, but also to keep what you're doing in perspective. This is only a race. There will be a lot more important things in your life when it's over."

For Joe, at that moment, no life existed but the race. The race was everything. Validation of his worth, a means to sweet vengeance and, perchance, a way to cut the hate from his heart.

He began to browse through the training material minutes after Ruth picked him up in the Chevrolet. DeAngelo's instructions to get more rest prompted this change in routine. Ruth considered herself part of his training team now, so she left him alone as he focused on the typed notes. DeAngelo did his homework thoroughly. The regimen called for Joe to complete only four long runs over the two-week period before the conference finals. Between those treks, DeAngelo sequenced a series of quarter-mile exercises sprinkled with 100- and 200-yard dashes. Distance running concluded with a hard three-mile run the Friday before the conference meet. DeAngelo insisted on three complete days of rest before Joe's final mile.

The coach outlined exercises to strengthen Joe's quads and stretch his stride as well. DeAngelo also instructed Joe to use his chores to further build both his stamina and strength.

Joe dug deeper into the sack as Ruth turned off the highway toward their farm. At the bottom he found an envelope he had missed with his first cursory search. Inside he found a $20 bill with a note attached that simply said, "Egg money." Beneath that, he uncovered a letter. Unfolding the yellow paper, he read DeAngelo's hand-written note as the car bounced over the washer-board road.

> *Joe:*
>
> *Anyone who goes out for track is seeking something. Glory. Love. Something. Distance men especially are seekers. They run alone, living in their dreams. What else but a dream could pull them across so many tortuous miles in solitude?*
>
> *You, too, are seeking. Revenge for sure. Possibly redemption of some kind. I think you seek a way to accept yourself. You think winning the race will prove that you matter. Spend these next two weeks running knowing that you are already great. Winning or losing the race won't change that. Believe in yourself, now, and you've already won.*
>
> *John.*

"What does he say?" Ruth asked, as Joe folded the letter.
"Tips for winning, Mom."

Joe adopted his new routine that very day. He started with sleep, glorious sleep. With the help of his expanded support team, he slipped between his sheets every night by 8:30 p.m. and slept ten hours a night. He soaked up the needed rest as fast as raindrops on July dirt. He awoke every morning clear-headed and joyous because he believed by following DeAngelo's instructions he could beat Mark.

Twice that week he made the long runs home after practice. The first day he nestled six eggs carefully in Kleenex, along with a clean white dishtowel, inside his waist pack. He thought the half dozen would see him home, but he busted the first egg while straining up a slight incline early down the field road. The yellow yolk squirted all over the front of his shirt. He used some of the Kleenex to wipe his hand and forearm, and grabbed another egg from the pack. Joe traveled less than another quarter mile when the eggs in both hands burst simultaneously. This time, the sticky yolk struck his face, blinding one eye and covering his lips. The twin explosions struck his funny bone, too, and Joe laughed heartily. He tried to imagine what he looked like as he spit eggshell from his mouth and grabbed yet another tissue.

Minutes later, out of tissue and with two fresh eggs, he recommenced. His thoughts turned to Abebe, the great Ethiopian Olympic runner, and how DeAngelo said Abebe ran as if his upper body were detached from his churning legs. Joe tried to run that easily, to flow versus strain, to sense the smoothness of his running vs. closing down to the pain in his chest and legs. Still, he was not surprised when yolk, albumen and shell squeezed through his clenched right hand again. He plucked the remaining egg from his pack and stained the dishtowel yellow with yet another hand wiping.

Joe remained almost a mile from home when the last pair of eggs popped. He was thankful he had carried only the six, because the more tired he became, the more his arms and hands clenched up. At this rate, he would have to buy his own chickens. Still, the message of the yolks took hold. By clenching, he burned up energy as fast as he used up eggs. He sought a yoga-like peace to still his arms. Joe smiled again. DeAngelo was teaching him to run with his mind as well as his legs.

On the days Joe wasn't squishing eggs, he did his sprint work. He carefully measured out 100-, 220- and 440-yard lengths on the flattest section of the gravel road between the farm and highway. These distances he marked plainly with a can of red spray paint.

The sprints built his upper leg muscles. DeAngelo also provided a series of high knee jerks, plus striding and skipping exercises. The latter again sent Joe into hysterics. Some evenings found him skipping like a schoolboy down the gravel road. Occasionally a neighbor's truck passed by, the farmer frowning quizzically beneath his cap, lifting a finger in greeting from the steering wheel, and then shaking his head as he continued to watch Joe in his rearview mirror.

Once, Elaine Gathers, her white hair barely visible above the steering wheel of her Ford Fairlane, veered into the ditch when she took her eyes off the road to watch Joe hop like a kangaroo. "It's to strengthen my legs," Joe said matter-of-factly as he pushed her out. She drove away, shaking her snowy mane.

Despite this rigorous schedule, Joe didn't slack off during his evening chores. Every afternoon after school he climbed up the metal chute of the silo to fork down silage. Instead of settling into a steady rhythm, however, now he worked feverishly, as if the next fork would unearth a loved one. Joe reversed his hand grips on the fork so that he worked muscles on both sides of his body. He bent, scooped, turned and tossed. Bent, scooped, turned and tossed, so fast that when he finished, his breathing came as hard as at the end of any race.

Still he pushed himself to build his wind. Returning to the feed room floor, he filled the dented steel bushel basket with silage and hoisted it on his shoulder. He walked briskly beneath its weight to feed the young stock in the steer shed. Upon dumping the load into the trough, he now sprinted back to the feed room. In his tattered clothes, he looked like a petty criminal fleeing with a basket of treasures. He repeated this sprint between each of the seven bushel baskets of silage, and the five trips of ground feed.

By milking time Friday night of the first week, a strange serenity befell him. He became conscious of it while squatting against Nancy's side. He felt a shiver ripple underneath her black hide. Joe himself shook in response. It caught him by surprise. The feeling was not foreign. He felt it at every Sunday upon receiving communion. That's when he realized his healing had commenced. His anger was draining away. He missed Annie terribly, though he continued to rebuke her efforts of appeasement. The week of sleep and his deadeye focus on a faster mile run cleansed him.

There was more. Ruth. Joe watched her across the barn floor, washing cow udders caked in mud and manure. She had rescued him. Frank and George helped, too. But Ruth mainly plunged first into his icy despair. She broke her vow to never enter the place that she blamed for stealing her third child in order to save her first.

Joe held onto these affectionate thoughts as he pulled the milker off of the Holstein, and emptied its creamy contents into one of the pails. He moved to the next cow, the one just prepped by Ruth, and saddled the milker around her enormous gut. Ruth, in the meantime, removed the milker strap from Nancy and advanced it to the next designated cow. They met in the center of the floor as each finished their respective task. Joe reached out and hugged Ruth. He unashamedly put his head against her shoulder. Ruth, no longer startled by this affection, returned his hug.

"What's this for?" she cooed.

"For saving me," Joe said.

On Sunday after Mass, Joe had his parents drop him off on the southern outskirts of Troy. He changed first into his T-shirt, shorts and jogging shoes in the back seat. Ruth reached over the front seat and delicately handed him the waist pack laden with 10 neatly packed eggs. "Scrambled eggs for lunch again?" George chimed in. They all smiled, elated by the new familiarity among them.

Joe stretched out as his folk's Chevrolet rolled away down the road, kicking up swirls of chalky dust. He stood up and surveyed the fields in front of him. The arrival of May washed them in a spring palette. Greens of every hue. The clover fields dark and lush. The emerging corn stalks a translucent emerald. Rising oats like a carpet of minty sea grass. All undulated in the late morning breeze under an azure sky.

Along the field road, gold finches flirted among the stocks of last year's thistles. Fresh black mounds of dirt revealed the night excavations of pocket gophers. Overhead, a red-tailed hawk soared, looking for movements in the fields that revealed a striped gopher, or a hatching of garter snakes.

Among these many signs of spring, Joe noticed the redolent smells of the land. The aroma of blossoming lilacs, too, wafted from the homes on the town's edge. He could smell the long winter baking out of the trees and the soil; a warmth and dryness now seasoned all the earthly odors. They contributed to the inner peace that had befallen him over the preceding days and prompted him to hug his mother. That same serenity moved Joe to corner Frank on Saturday and effusively thank him for his help. Joe had been nonplused when Frank shook his head and said it was he who was thankful. "I'm doing this for me, too," he had said. "It'll be part of me in that race."

He thanked George last, just the night before. With the May warmth and the arrival of daylight savings time, George began rolling his wheelchair to different corners of the yard and sitting in deep contemplation in the evenings. Joe found him in the Saturday dusk overlooking Ruth's garden. It now lay fully planted, a large rectangle of dirt bordered by a windbreak of Scotch pine to the north, and a row of crabapple trees nearest the house.

George sat in the white caressing arm of a blossoming crab, his good spring jacket over his shoulders. Joe noticed a few white petals resting on George's extended injured leg as he drew near.

"Quite a setting, isn't it," George said, having heard Joe's approach.

Joe surveyed what George saw. May marked the best time on the farm. One witnessed the world reborn. No urban noises to interfere with the distinctive chirp of a courting robin. No neon to break the rosy horizon. At this time of year, at this time of day, they could sometimes hear John Randolph chasing his cows out of the barn almost two miles away, or the pigeons cooing from their roosts inside the distance silo.

"See the cottontail," George said, point to the garden's edge where the rabbit blended into the soil's color. The rabbit chewed contentedly on dandelions. "Ruth better not find out or it will be 20-gauge time." He chuckled. "What am I thinking? Of course she'll find out as soon as she sees the tops of her carrots chewed off."

Joe looked at the rabbit. He thought of the fox kill. It seemed so long ago now.

"I've been meaning to thank you for lining up John and letting me sleep in this past week."

"It's nothing. You've earned it."

Joe didn't know what to say. His dad and he rarely had meaningful conversations. Instead of talking, Joe reached out and put his hand on George's right shoulder.

"I wish I could have been doing it for you forever," George said. "It's just the farm, you know, it's so much work."

"I know."

"I wish we would have had some brothers and sisters for you."

The well-known silence between them returned as each drifted back over the past five years. So many countless hours spent working together. So little connection. They were of different worlds and different times. Yoked together by the farm, but destined to go separate ways.

"Whatcha thinking Dad?"

George shifted in his chair, his injured leg itching in its cast. He probed inside its darkness with a small branch broken from the apple tree.

"I was thinking of our two old draft horses, Maude and Queenie. How hard we worked them, and how willing they were to work. They were bred for it. Then one day we simply replaced them with a tractor. Forgot about all their years of service. Just like that. It's just the Farmall could do so much more. Oh, there he goes."

George pointed again in the direction of the rabbit with the branch, and Joe turned in time to see the white tail slip like a blossom beneath the pine branches.

"Something spooked her. Probably that fox over by Becker's. Anyway," George continued, "I was thinking I've had to use you the way my dad used those horses. Or me the tractors. I just couldn't get the work done without you."

Joe thought he saw where the conversation was headed.

"I'm not going to stick around much longer."

"I know. I blocked that truth for quite a while. But I've cottoned up to the idea."

"So what are you going to do?"

"Well, Ruth and I have been talking about selling the cows." He looked up at the blossoms above. A few honeybees crawled over them, excavating nectar. "Been thinking of starting a nursery or vegetable farm. Maybe berries. Something that's less work that keeps me close to the land but not sewn to it like dairying does."

Joe felt awash in guilt. He knew George's dream had always been to pass on the farm to him.

"I'm sorry, Dad."

George rotated in the chair. For the first time during their conversation, father and son faced each other.

"No need to be." Even in the gathering dark, Joe could see George's eyes moisten. "You've been the best son I could ever have hoped for."

For the second time in two nights, Joe found himself in the arms of a parent.

Now he faced the fields on a glorious Sunday morning, the Lord's wafer digesting in his gut, his parents nestled in his heart, and revenge pulsating in his mind. Joe set out smooth and strong, startling the finches, and was pleased when he passed the remnants of eggshells from his previous runs with today's first eggs intact. He traversed almost a mile before dealing with an oozing pair.

Well into his run, he spied the top of Becker's woods. Their place. The place of the fox. It tugged at him and threatened to ruin the run. More cracking eggs revealed the power Annie still commanded over him. The mess running down his hands and wrists reined his mind back in control. Joe covered another half mile. He noticed the wind in his face, and decided at the last minute to seek out the fox and her young. His search pulled him off the road and across a recently planted soybean field. He noticed the emerging green nubs in the pulverized powder at his feet. Since he was downwind, he held out hope. The foxes rewarded him. Two of the kits roiled in the grass at the edge of the burrow, the color of new rust. Then they heard him. Joe was close enough to see their ears cock in his direction. Then they bolted in unison for the hole.

The bitch fox came slinking quickly out of the pine to the edge of the mound. She eyed Joe and sniffed the air. Then she disappeared into the burrow as well.

Joe stopped and stood on the mound. The yips quieted and all was silent. Joe walked 10 feet away to where he and Annie had made love. He stood for several minutes, almost overwhelmed by the memories. Then he turned and climbed atop the fox mound. He unzipped the waist pack and emptied all of his eggs. They lay as white and cool as Annie's skin against the ocher ground. Joe knew he wouldn't need any of them to get home.

LANGLEY

One race remained before the conference finals. A triangular meet pitted Troy against rival Webster, and Gafton, a non-conference suburban school. For Mark, the race held particular significance because it featured Steve Langley. A lanky, pimple-faced kid with steely eyes and a steelier persona, Langley was Mark's chief competition. Coach O'Reilly referred to Langley as the "Mental Miler" for his renowned obsession with training. Langley commonly ran from Webster to Troy and back—a distance of 10 miles, stopping only for a Dairy Queen Dilly bar between jaunts. Langley sought every advantage. He shaved his head to remove extra weight, and ran without his glasses for the same reason. Both actions accentuated his pointed ears and nose. This gave him another edge, as he resembled Nostradamus, and literally psyched out opposing runners with his intense stare. He lived to run. His posted times from other meets approached Mark's, but this was the first competition between the two. All present knew theirs would be the race to watch.

Joe's interest in the race lay elsewhere. Nine days had transpired since he began DeAngelo's crash training course, and he felt stronger and more refreshed than before any previous race. He could not believe how the week of rest had scraped the accumulated weariness of the past months away. During his solo runs at home, he marked his slight but steady improvements against the punctual Burlington Northern. Joe knew, however, he could never push himself as hard as when adrenaline coursed through him in heated competition.

Joe experienced another new sensation. No butterflies. Before the race, he hung around Crazy Nolan, hoping Crazy might have an appropriate song or movie dialog to inspire him. Crazy didn't disappoint. By now, word of Joe and Annie's breakup had passed through the senior class like an intercepted love note. When Joe approached Crazy near the pole vault runway, Crazy voiced, without prompting, words from the Mamas and Papas song: "Oh Monday morning, it gave me no warning, of how it should be. Oh Monday morning, how could she leave, and not take me."

Joe squeezed Crazy's arm. He knew Crazy had selected the appropriate lyrics just for him. "You're crazy, Nolan," Joe said endearingly.

"And thus the name," Crazy said, bowing deeply.

The mile remained two events away when DeAngelo approached Joe.

"You ready?" DeAngelo wondered, too, whether his coaching would make a difference.

Joe nodded. "The extra sleep has really helped. I never realized how exhausted I was all the time."

"How many eggs are you down to?"

"On my three-milers? I'm down to three busted from 10 to begin with."

"That's good. That's good." DeAngelo seemed to be calculating something in his head. "Remember, you'll have to imagine those eggs today. A trick is to hold your thumb and middle finger together on each hand. That will help prevent clenching."

"Next event the 440. Runners to the starting line. Milers on tap." Both DeAngelo and Joe turned in the direction of the loudspeaker.

"Well, that's my cue," Joe said.

"One more thing," DeAngelo said. He looked Joe square in the eyes. "Are you having fun?"

Joe thought "fun" an odd choice of words. Fun? No. Was he more at peace? Enjoying his quest? That surely was true. "I'm happier, if that's what you're asking. But I'm bent on beating Mark."

"Well, good luck today, then," DeAngelo said, extending his hand. Joe shook it firmly, and trotted over to where the milers assembled.

DeAngelo watched him, and saw himself 15 years earlier. Anxious to prove himself. He remembered how years after his last collegiate 440, when he finished second in the NCAA Division III competition, he fell asleep nightly reliving that race. Each time he found some hidden reserve of energy in his daydream, and slipped past his nemesis at the finish line. Somehow he thought his life would have been different if he had won that final race, so he dreamed the dream a long time. Eventually all that sprinting, and later the marathons, wreaked havoc on his knees. The only time he ran now was rounding the bases in a summer softball league. Now he fell asleep not dreaming about winning that last race, but simply about being able to run without pain. That was his lesson. Abebe's lesson. Now Joe was his student. Don't just chase dreams. Enjoy the chase while it lasts.

The race lived up to its promise. Mark and Langley set the early pace, Langley leading. Joe found himself in the middle of the pack, and moved outside several other runners to avoid being boxed in. After the first quarter mile, the runners began to string out. Mark replaced Langley as the leader, but Langley kept close on his shoulder. Joe ran in fifth place, behind Gafton's best miler and a second Webster runner. He felt especially strong, and sensed the runners immediately in front of him were vulnerable. Just after the half-mile mark, he made his move. It surprised him how easily they disappeared behind his burst of speed. Now he ran down the backstretch, a good 20 yards behind the dueling leaders. It's time, he said to himself. It's time to see what I can do.

Almost imperceptively, Joe nibbled away at the gap between himself and the leaders. He concentrated on how lightly his thumbs and fingers touched, noticed how fluid his legs glided beneath him. Mark and Langley ran oblivious to him, caught up in their own struggle. The third lap ended with Mark still fighting off a persistent Langley. Joe had gained 10 yards on them in the last 330 yards. He grew tired, though, his energy ebbing. Still, he set little goals for himself down the final backstretch. Close the gap to only 5 yards by the 220 mark, then to three yards with 100 yards to go. He attained goal one and his confidence grew.

He noticed Mark pulling slightly away from Langley, and as Joe himself neared Langley, the Webster miler's shaved head bobbed red before him, flushed by his exertion.

Joe thought for a heady moment that he might actually take Langley. Maybe even Mark the way he felt. That prospect sparked a warning in Joe's revenge-ladened mind. Beating Langley would tip his hand. Alert Mark that it was he who posed the biggest threat at conferences. It would take away Joe's element of surprise. Joe eased up, feigning that his surge had spent all his energy. Langley pulled away steadily. Joe finished third, enabling the Troy milers to come away with six points.

While Joe leaned forward, hands on his knees, trying to catch his breath, Coach O'Reilly came up to him. He held his stopwatch in front of his chest.

"Nice race, Joe," he said. "I liked what I saw. You were right with the leaders till the end there. It's still your best time of the year by six seconds."

"Ran out of gas, though, Coach," Joe replied, breathing heavily and not for show. "I tried to catch them, but they're in another league."

"That's true, but you did well before you hit the wall. Do you think you can run that well or better next week at conferences?" Coach O'Reilly asked, his eyes hungry for the answer.

"Don't know, Coach. I think so. If I get enough rest."

"You see, even petering out, you ran a 4:40 mile, your best time. Perkins ran a 4:32. That's only 3 seconds shy of the conference record." Despite how close Mark had come to shattering the mark, Coach O'Reilly looked concerned. "The problem is, Langley finished at 4:35. If he hadn't gone out so fast, he might have beaten Mark. He had no oomph at the end, otherwise . . . ."

"Coach, I can't beat Langley," Joe replied, unsure what Coach O'Reilly sought.

"I know that, Joe. I was just thinking maybe if you finished fourth, you could get two points next week. That would help. In case Mark gets beat by Langley and only gets four points with a second place. That means you have to beat Andrews from Hermanville and Gieger from Elbow Lake. Gieger finished second to Mark while you ran the mile relay at Elbow Lake. They've both posted in the low 4:40s this year."

"I'll do my best, Coach."

"I'm sure you will, Joe," Coach O'Reilly said.

Joe could see clearly that Coach O'Reilly remained disturbed. He had mapped out Troy's margin for victory, and it came down to one point. That was the sole reason he sanctioned Joe's shortened practices, and allowed Joe to return to the team after the hiatus caused by his dad's injury. Joe was his 1-Point Man. Now Langley's shaved head and doggedness wedged doubt into Coach O'Reilly's calculations. Joe knew Coach O'Reilly would spend hours over the course of the next week trying to remove that doubt. He smiled a bit in self-satisfaction. Yes, Coach O'Reilly would specifically spend a good deal of time thinking about him, Joe Mitchell. He would treat Joe decently all week, because now Joe might have to become a 2-Point Man.

THE TRAIN

Dick Pearson ran the Burlington Northern Route 29 five days a weeks—six days in autumn when crops came pouring in like a golden flood from the surrounding counties. Route 29 was basically a ConAgra line. It connected a ConAgra's grain hub to its main terminal on the Minnesota River. Every day Pearson arrived at the hub. There, ConAgra employees maneuvered huge augured tubes above the slotted rail cars. On their command, corn, oats, wheat or soybeans swirled out of the tubes and into the empty cars, the wind catching the chaff and blowing it until it piled like golden fleece around the storage bins. The grain men worked quickly, rotating the tubes to tuck the grain into the far reaches of the rectangular cars. They wore face masks against the dust. Near the end of the fill, they stopped the augers and shoveled the various grains into the deepest recesses of the cars. Finally, the cars sated, hydraulics hoisted the augers away. Two men slid the car tops shut with a heavy clang of metal.

Pearson detested the clanging. It sometimes flashed him back to the Battle of the Bulge. He had been an infantry corporal, and the clanging reminded him of the magazines of U.S. artillery cannons slammed shut; or worst, of German 88s ripping apart the half-tracks and the Tiger tanks trying to stop the Nazi counterattack. A piece of one of those blasted Tigers landed near his foxhole, glowing red hot and sizzling in the snow. He grabbed it nonetheless, burning his fingers through his ragged gloves, and plopped it beneath him to keep his feet from freezing. It was just one memory of a hellish two days when the world went insane around him. Members of his division found him during their own counterattack, with frostbite toes, babbling incoherently, standing on steel.

After the war, because changing conditions panicked him, he decided on a railroad career. The precise schedules soothed him. Being locked onto the rails prevented him from going astray. His only stress consisted of coping with the clanging, and ensuring his load of railcars reached the river terminal by 1 p.m. That allowed the river crew time to empty the contents of the railcars into barges for a long lazy trip down first the Minnesota, and then the Mississippi River and on to Russia, India or China. By 3 p.m. he headed back with one last deadline. His engine, 30 empty cars and caboose had to be nestled inside the ConAgra terminal yard by 5 p.m.

Pearson became a stickler on time. He taunted the ConAgra dock workers if it looked like he might miss his 3 p.m. departure time. They laughed at him, told him to screw himself. They took to calling him Precision instead of Pearson. He resented the moniker at first. Then he wore the badge proudly. It meant he did his job well.

Pearson liked another part of railroading. The scenery. He purveyed a world most never saw. The deep corners of farmland only visited during plowing, planting and harvest. Flocks of famished migrating mallards, far from roads and hunters, feasting among cornhusks on March mornings as they returned to nesting grounds. He roared past drainage ditches alive with the drone of breeding frogs in early June, and crisscrossed by foraging muskrats in July. He saw wild roses wrapped pink and spindly around busted fence lines, thistles topped off in purple majesty in the late summer sun, and the hoar frost on rustling cornstalks in October. Even in the winter, when white drifts blanketed so much of his remote world, he found pleasure in the soft blue silent shadows of 4 o'clock snow.

Occasionally he had morning routes, and he liked the remote landscapes best in those early hours. The fields glistened with dew, and he was most apt to spy a Marsh hawk on the wing, or a whitetail deer browsing. Such sightings made his day. Once a killdeer foolishly made its nest in the gravel along side of the track. By Monday she sat on eggs. Every day for a week, with millions of tons of graffiti-strewn railcars roaring by her, she feigned a broken wing and fluttered along the ground to lure the train away from her nest. Mercifully, she disappeared the following week, whether out of better sense or a scrape with a predator, Pearson never knew.

In the afternoons, though, he favored the towns. His route took him through a series of rural hamlets until he traversed near the new suburbs seeking the bluffs and views of the river valley. Pearson didn't care for these pretentious manors. He enjoyed the backyards of the smaller houses the tracks skirted. He could tell a lot about people by those yards. That's where the business of living went on. Preschoolers scooted down slides, their young mothers nearby dragging on cigarettes in the mid-afternoon quiet. Farm wives in halter tops yanked weeds and shook the dirt from their roots with their practiced hands so the weeds were dead, good and dead, so they wouldn't have to pull them again. There were old couples holding hands in lawn chairs, their jackets zipped to their throats despite the June heat. In the next yard, another old man sat alone, bundled as tightly in solitude.

Pearson most enjoyed when school let out, and the children jerked their arms up and down, and he obliged by releasing a long moan from the engine's whistle.

Even without people, the backyards spoke to him. He paid attention to wash on the line to guess family size and the age of siblings. Over the years, he knew who made the baseball team or when a son or daughter graduated by their missing laundry. He kept an eye open for the Camaro jacked up alongside a blue house in Camden to learn when it might finally be repaired. He knew spring approached by watching wood piles disappear, or later, as the farm wives burned their lawns and the new green growth poked up through the black ash. In summer, he watched young boys in trampled backyards argue over foul balls in pickup baseball games.

He came to define his life by what he saw happening to others. That way he varied his life yet still controlled his own, always from a distance, always across the backyard fences.

Pearson's penchant for punctuality kept him safe, too. He never dallied. No slowing down to tell that young farm wife she looked awfully nice in that halter top. No stopping to ask what was wrong with that Camaro. No time to tell those boys that baseball was as beautiful and fair as the Declaration of Independence. He knew at every yard of his 228-mile daily roundtrip where he should be at 11:08 a.m. or at 3:49 in the afternoon.

That's why he became enthralled with a solitary runner starting in late March. Obviously, the boy was a distance runner for Troy, the closest town. Pearson first noticed him as a speck through the dirty right window of the engine on his daily return to Albert Lea. A week later, he noticed the runner again, this time slightly closer. Whether the runner improved or simply started his cross-country run earlier, Pearson couldn't know. He could only be sure of his time. He noted the spot and time where he saw the runner daily. 4:19 p.m. Every day, at 4:19, from the same part of his route, he looked for the runner. Sometimes he appeared. Sometimes he was absent. Regardless, the runner became another fixture in Pearson's journey, another person to build a life around.

Through the month of April, the runner edged ever nearer to Pearson's train, until by the end of the month, Pearson could discern blond hair, a steady gait. He scrounged through his basement one night and uncovered his Leica binoculars, and took to spying on this solitary soul. Through the lens he followed the runner's progress, watched him shed from sweatsuit to shorts, from leaping over pockets of gray snow, to pounding steadily down the field road. Pearson had forgotten that the field road existed since the previous fall, but with the spring he noted its path again up to and across the tracks, until they connected with the gravel road running parallel to the rails. From that he discerned the boy belonged to the dairy farm a short distance beyond. He coupled another layer to this new story.

Within the last several weeks, Pearson eagerly noted how close the runner came to his train at 4:19. He didn't even require the binoculars anymore, and, with the warmth of the ever-lengthening spring days, he began opening the engine's window and waving. The runner returned the wave, a quick acknowledgement with a right hand before it fell back into its rhythmic motion at his side.

Since the beginning of May, however, the runner's treks across the field decreased. At first Pearson feared the season might be over. Then, like a faithful dog, the runner returned. Now he ran with something white in his hands. Pearson peered back through the binoculars. Eggs.

Pearson marked down that he saw the runner on Tuesday and Friday the previous week, then on Wednesday this week. On Friday, May 14th, at precisely 3 p.m. as he left the Minnesota River with the sun gleaming off the tracks before him, he hoped he would again see his friend.

On Friday, May 14th, at 2:53 p.m., Troy's school bell rang. The students pushed their way to buses or waiting cars, anxious to get home. The prom activities kicked off with the juniors hosting the seniors' dinner at 7 p.m. Girls had a scant four hours to get ready. The boys were equally time pressed to wash their parents' cars and struggle with ties. The excitement was palpable, for the prom, not graduation, truly plunged them into an adult world. For many, this would be their first and only school dance. Many seniors lowered their standards to ensure an escort and secure the memory of what was suppose to be the romantic highlight of their years in high school. Chattering girls clustered hurriedly in groups, asking again what each was wearing, and where they would meet so they could sit together. The boys plotted their strategies for the weekend, their silence sexually charged.

One person did not join them. Joe spent almost an hour making up a Social Studies test. He had decided to try to graduate on time, and Mr. Carter stayed late while Joe proved he knew how the federal and state governments would tax him till he died. At 4 p.m., Joe left the school by the gym door dressed in his running gear. This was his last cross-country run before conferences. The last one.

Coach O'Reilly knew the date, too. He cursed the scheduling and pleaded with his team to sleep during the weekend days. The conference championships the following Tuesday carried more significance than a night of romance, he preached.

Whether anyone listened would reveal itself at conferences, but DeAngelo, remembering his own prom, assumed Perkins and every other trackster attending the Troy prom faced two long days and nights of eating, drinking and carousing. Some wouldn't sleep at all Saturday night. Nobody would miss the Sunday picnic excursions that might turn a spring romance into a summer of passion.

"Remember how tired you always were from getting up early all these years?" DeAngelo had asked Joe the day before. "Well, that's how most of the team will feel come Tuesday. It's your advantage. It's your time now."

My time, now, Joe thought. But time for what? A scant two months earlier he had set his hopes afloat, a fluttering kite in the March winds. He had sought a new perspective of himself, a loftier one. One not anchored by the daily drudgery of the farm. He joined the world when he put on spikes. Running helped shed his isolation like a snake shed its binding skin.

For him, he had dared much. Rejection in his pursuit of Annie, a rejection that had proved near fatal. The prospect of failing in every race he ran. The overwhelming likelihood that, in the end, this final race wouldn't matter.

Where had it all brought him? Joe asked himself as he began his final jog across the baseball diamond and up the hill to Main Street. What did he hope to accomplish? Win back Annie? Yes, that was it. Of course, that was all of it. Beating Mark was just the means, not the goal. Mark be damned, Joe thought, his agitation visible in the scowl on his face. He caught his reflection between the painted car prices on Brinkman's Buick's display window, through the same glass window that Frank Oster shattered with a bullet, left-handed fastball 11 years earlier.

Running gave Joe strength. He believed that by winning next Tuesday, whatever he lacked would materialize the second he broke the tape at race's end. And something new would exist. A fearless Joe. One free of doubt, invincible to ridicule, no longer a victim. What if he lost? He likely would. Then what? A fearful Joe? Destined to be buffeted forever by the demands or whims of those around him?

That was DeAngelo's repeated message, Joe realized as he crossed County Road 9. DeAngelo, despite all his encouragement, knew Joe's chances were remote at best. He wanted Joe to feel good about himself no matter what the race's outcome. He wanted Joe to like himself, for his effort and for who he was.

"Yes, it's my time," Joe shouted out loud to himself.

The day buoyed him along. The fields edged toward summer as tentatively as a new bride to her wedding bed, and the perfumed air left no doubt that May was courting June. The fields lay neat and still in their measured rows, new growth reaching skyward, rejoicing. Shapes at last distinguished the plants. The corn shouted hosanna with outstretched arms. The soybeans welcomed with their open green palms. They cheered Joe. He heard only his footsteps, felt only the cool roundness of the eggs in his hands.

He ran in this contented world until, in the distance, came the faint whistle of a train. His train. Joe pictured the engineer, commandeering the countless tons of steel across the terrain. The first time Joe ran this route, he had marked the train's position as he neared their farm. Over the last two months, he measured his improvement first by whether he even saw the train on his runs, then later by his ability to read the lettering on the sides of the railcars. CSX. Soo Line. Next came reading the flowing graffiti. Stop the War! C.H. + J.T.

Joe eventually caught the glint of binoculars. Then he discerned the gray of the engineer's cap, the blue of his shirt, until one day a stiff-gloved wave greeted him. In the past few weeks, except for the time he visited the fox den, Joe found himself a mere 100 yards from the train when it crossed the field road. Between the obligatory wave and the passing of 30 railcars, Joe's stride almost ran him into the train's caboose. Up close, the noise of the train was deafening. The empty cars roared and clanged as their couplings yawned and then collided back together again.

Now, Joe tried to estimate the location of his daily train. It still remained hidden from view. Again, he heard the train's whistle to the east. Probably crossing the viaduct just west of Franksburg right now, Joe thought.

Then, out of the blue, the idea struck him dead center. He would beat the train to the field road crossing. No settling for the caboose today. Mark could probably reach the gravel road beyond the tracks before the train arrived. If he believed he could best Mark in four days, he had to beat the train today. The train became Mark.

His legs and lungs protested, but Joe ignored their painful complaints. He shifted closer to sprint mode, the pace he reserved for the end of the mile. Sustaining it for the 500 yards that remained between him and the railroad tracks seemed impossible. Out of the corner of his eye, he saw the engine emerge from behind the windbreak of Bauer's farm, about a mile away. It came like a hungry python, its long twisting length revealing itself with steady certainty.

I can beat that train, Joe thought, pell-melling forward. I can beat Mark. I can redeem myself. I can win Annie back. I have to beat that train. I have to.

Pearson pulled the watch out of his overalls. Twenty years and I'm still engineering, he thought. He flicked the engraved gold lid to check the time. 4:18. On schedule, of course. Pearson began scanning the fields for his afternoon companion. Of late, he caught sight of the runner adjacent to a clump of pine. Searching that locale, he uncovered nothing but vacant fields. Disappointed, he thought again the season had ended. Then ahead of him, well down the crest of the slope from where Pearson expected, he spied the runner. At first the runner's location surprised him. Then it heartened him. He rarely saw the people he built stories around up close. As he gauged the angle between train and runner, and factored in the runner's pace, Pearson realized he would see his face today. Actually see his features. The thought pleased him. Even when the season ended, Pearson could conjure up the face to continue the runner's saga. He reached up and tugged a greeting from the train whistle.

The whistle blast warned Joe of the dwindling seconds he had before the train crossed his path. He bore down harder. One-hundred yards to go. The egg in his left hand turned to goo. The sleek locomotive loamed larger. For a second, Joe tried to correlate his speed to the train's to determine which would reach the field road crossing first. Another whistle blast blew any calculations out of his mind. All was gut feel now. Gut guess. He hoped he could cross the tracks first, and set his focus on that.

Pearson couldn't believe his good fortune. The runner's frantic pace would put him right below his window. That close, they could yell their greetings. He could add an audible texture to this life. In anticipation, he slid back the locomotive's window, and extended the right upper third of his body outside the careening engine. The wind pulled on his hat, but he snubbed it down tight. The two were so close now that Pearson broke into a grin and began to wave heartily.

Then, to his horror, he realized the boy wasn't slowing. He was on a hell-bent course destined to throw himself under the train's wheels. Pearson's left hand searched blindly for the whistle lever. Finding it, he pulled and held it down. There was not time to hit the train's air brakes. It was too late.

Joe surged forward, convinced he could make it. The engine began taking on height with its closeness. Joe noticed its bug-splattered front hood, the spray-painted bull's eye on the Burlington Northern mountain goat emblem. The engine's roar was deafening. Above it, the engineer waved desperately for him to stop. The whistle split his eardrums. But what about beating Mark? What about Annie? I have to beat it. Nothing else matters. Nothing else. Nothing.

Joe crossed the tracks, rolled into a ball and tumbled into the dirt. The ground shook as the cars behind him pounded past, and the train's vacuum threatened to suck him back. He hugged the ground. Looking west, Joe saw the engineer, now hanging out the left window, staring back at him, shaking his fist violently. Joe lay where he was, afraid that standing while the train cars roared by in their ear-splitting thump-thump, thump-thump he might still find his way beneath their deadly wheels. When at last the caboose rolled by, he rose. The engineer stilled stared. Joe went to brush himself off when he realized he still clutched an unbroken egg. He laughed jubilantly, and tossed the white orb at the receding caboose.

THE LETTER

On Saturday, while just about everyone he knew picked up black tuxedos and wrist corsages, or sat anxiously as the stylists swept their hair ever higher, Joe slept in until 9 a.m. He helped with the chores, and then sat on the tractor. The early corn stood nearly five inches high now, and marked the start of cultivating season. Joe drove the Farmall tractor and let attached curved cultivator blades uproot the carpet of sprouting weeds between the rows. As always, this mindless work freed him to dream. He plotted and ran his upcoming mile over and over in his head. He visualized his position in the race. Playing possum like in the most recent race against Mark and Langley. Letting them duel until, out of nowhere and on Mercury's winged feet, he swept by them to a surprise victory.

He stopped for lunch, and once again marveled at the mirth around the table. Frank joined them now. They obliged him with a luncheon beer, but it was obvious he no longer needed the alcohol to feel comfortable in the Mitchell household. He ate as family, and brought new stories of another life and farm to their plates.

After lunch, Joe strolled across the lawn toward the mailbox. Cut for the first time, the lawn lay like felt on a pool table. It was the height of spring, the harsh winter forgiven and forgotten by the day's kaleidoscope of greens, whites and blues. He reached the mailbox and pulled out the morning paper and a few sundry bills. Then he spied the small envelope. He knew the handwriting well. Joe looked toward the house, then walked part way back up the drive. He leaned against one of the apple trees, and tore the envelope open. On the light cream stationery, the blue ink of Annie's pen spoke to him.

My dearest Joe:

I keep trying to reach you, but you will not see me. So I am forced to write the words I wish to share face to face. I know I have hurt you. It no longer matters what the reason. All I can say is that I am sorry. All I know is I am still in love with you. There are things you don't know about me. There are things about you I don't understand. It is obvious we come from different worlds. But it doesn't matter. When I tear it all away, I see your heart, and it is true. I see your soul, and it is pure. And there is more. With you, alone, have I shared my heart, my soul. I am unafraid to do so only with you.

After seeing "The Graduate," I asked you how Ben and Elaine "knew," like you said, that they were destined. You said they just knew. I know now what you meant. There is something about you I cannot shake. I hope, in time, you will forgive me. Because I believe you are meant to be forever part of my life.

With all my love,
Annie

Joe reread the letter. He pictured Annie writing it, meaning it. He breathed deep, folded the precious words back into the envelope, and continued to the house.

RABBIT

Crazy Nolan stretched out, turning from pretzel to scarecrow in a series of contortions. Sensing Coach O'Reilly's presence, Nolan folded up protectively like a hermit crab.

"You seen Mitchell?" Coach O'Reilly asked, scanning the infield.

"No, but I'm sure he's warming up somewhere, Coach."

"I figured that," Coach O'Reilly said, annoyed. "What I don't know is where. So why don't you get up off your butt and go find him for me."

Crazy caught the menace in Coach O'Reilly's eyes and quickly hopped to his feet. He began jogging nowhere in particular when Coach O'Reilly hollered after him. "And Perkins, too. I need to talk to both of them."

At the far end of the football field, lying flat on the ground and near the goal post so that its skinny afternoon shadow shielded his eyes, Joe raised one leg, and then the other. He experienced the soft tingling pain of loosening muscles. Rolling onto his stomach, he smelled the sweet fresh-clipped grass. He did leg raisers and back arches, then pushups and knee-bends. Finished with his routine, he returned to his back. As he watched the puffs of clouds roll by, his thoughts, as they had since the letter, returned to Annie. When he entered the house that day, Ruth noticed something was wrong.

"Anything special in the mail?" she asked. She was wearing her glasses, poring over bills strewn across the end of the kitchen table.

"No," Joe lied.

Ruth noticed that Joe remained standing by the door after setting the rest of the mail on the freezer. She set her pencil down. "You can tell me, Joe," Ruth said. "Whatever it is, I'll understand."

She said it with maternal truth, yet Joe could not tell her. Sex created too wide a chasm. Joe feared telling would hurt Ruth, and he wanted to cause no more pain.

"Why did you and Annie break up?" Ruth softly pressed.

Joe shrugged with defeated shoulders. How could he tell? He didn't understand it himself. They had injured one another, and the wounds still bled.

Ruth removed her glasses and rose from the table. She didn't advance toward Joe, but stood with one hand on the table's veneer, as if it were the Bible and she sought divine knowledge.

"Love is not perfect, Joe," she said at last.

Joe remained anchored at the other end of the table. "Annie really hurt me, Mom."

"And you're still angry," Ruth surmised.

Yes, Joe said with a single, silent nod.

Ruth recalled her long ago anger over Kevin's death. She blamed George, rightly or wrongly. Keeping the loss inside was too painful. At the time, she thought it would kill her. So she directed her smoldering anger at George with no thought of his suffering. Through dinner silence and nighttime indifference. By offering minimum support to the farm and their marriage. George accepted this change as if Ruth's anger were but a stretch of drought. He weathered all she could deal out. Finally, because of Joe, because of a carved yellow rose, the anger ebbed, and through unclouded eyes, Ruth realized George still loved her, and how much she needed to be loved. They still possessed love. Maybe "not so much" anymore, but enough.

"If you still hold any love in your heart for Annie, do whatever you can to keep it alive."

Joe harkened back on Ruth's words many times. They lay next to him, now, on the May grass. In her own way, Annie had fallen in love with him. He truly believed that. Saturday's letter only reconfirmed it. There had been true intimacy, a level of feeling, touching, and baring souls, that was theirs alone. The pain that had shattered his heart came because love was so foreign to him. He had always pictured it pure and steadfast. He never fathomed that it came cloaked in human failings, or that it could be so fleeting. Love is not perfect, Ruth had said. As he watched the popcorn clouds above him collide, mesh and break apart again, these thoughts concluded like all the others over the past days. He could not deny it. Despite all that had passed, he loved Annie still.

"Hey Joe." It was Crazy, his usual smile revealing perfect teeth. "Coach wants you."

"What for?" He wanted this time alone to run through his strategy for the race one final time. "It's too early for the mile."

"Beats me," Crazy said, hunching his shoulders. "Wants Perkins, too. Better not dally. He's awful hyper, if you ask me."

Joe rolled to his feet and trotted toward Coach O'Reilly. Scanning the stands in stride, he saw his father and mother, and Frank, too. Ruth waved enthusiastically, and George saluted with a single crutch. Frank raised his good arm.

The stands overflowed. The conference championships, with its five competing schools, drew a rare crowd. With the baseball season concluded, most of the Troy team populated the bleachers, too. Joe looked for Annie, knowing she was among the hundreds of fans, but couldn't find her.

Mark stood by Coach O'Reilly as Joe approached. Neither had spoken since the storm.

"Good, you're both here," Coach O'Reilly said. He motioned to them with his clipboard. "Come with me."

Coach O'Reilly walked them away from the other milling runners. When they were 10 yards removed, he squatted down on his haunches. Mark and Joe followed suit. The coach paused and looked first at Mark, and then at Joe.

"Listen," he began quietly. "I want this championship more than I want a free night at Sally's Sauna. I'm tired of bringing up the rear of this conference, and playing second fiddle to baseball. For once I've got a chance to win a title," he continued, very agitated. "I've busted my butt—and yours—to get us this far, and I'm not going to let it slip away."

Coach O'Reilly shifted his weight so he could reach into his pocket. A half-finished roll of Tums emerged. He popped two white spheres into his mouth and crunched away.

"Thompson went and made it difficult. Damn African scratched on two of his jumps and only took third place," he said angrily, spitting a chalky gob into the grass. Neither miler said a word.

"The thing is, Joe, we need every point we can get from here on out to beat Webster. I've mapped things out a hundred times before this meet, and if Thompson finishes first, we're home free. Six points versus three. Hell, even second place by Thompson would have earned that boy four points. But I've got Thompson screwing up and who knows what else can go haywire."

Joe began to grow apprehensive. Coach O'Reilly was looking mainly at him.

"What does this mean to us, Coach?" Mark interrupted. "Want us to wax some pole vaults?"

"Quit joking, Perkins," Coach O'Reilly said testily. "This is serious." O'Reilly was a nervous wreck. He played with his watch, rotating the band around and around his wrist. He continued to froth with the Tums.

"Mark, you're good," Coach O'Reilly started in again. "You ran a 4:32 last week. Hell, you should break the conference record with the lack of wind we have today." Mark nodded and smiled confidently. "The thing is Langley stayed right with you in that last race. Now I'm betting you didn't get that rest I recommended with the prom and all, but I know Langley did. I don't know if it was Langley's prom, too, but he's too ugly to have a girlfriend. Even if he did, he wants to win too badly to have fooled around last weekend."

It was true. Spurned by Annie despite his honest offer, at the last minute Mark took Nancy Jones to the prom. Their evening ended without romance, but he still arrived home past 3 a.m., half-drunk, and picnicked all day Sunday.

Coach O'Reilly rose into a crouch, his haunches too old to support his weight so long.

"You beat Langley today and if we win the mile-relay like I expect, and bingo, we have 12 more points and we own the day. We don't even need Joe's point. But if Langley beats you, he gets the six points from the mile. Your second place brings in four points. Then I need Joe's point. In fact, I need Joe to place fourth and earn two points. The best we could hope for would be to match Langley's six points. Then we share the title, and that's like kissing DeAngelo. It doesn't leave a warm feeling in my gut. If Joe only gets one point and you lose, Mark, we kiss the title goodbye."

Joe piped in nervously. "I've been running lots better, Coach, and I got plenty of rest over the weekend. I'm good for fourth place. Maybe third."

"No way, Mitchell." He switched back to Joe's last name, a bad sign. "I know you've improved and I'm proud of you. I know you think that because a week ago you were humping Langley's skinny butt till 100 yards to go. But face it. You won't catch Langley today and Gieger's posted better times than you, too."

Coach O'Reilly tempered his tone. "Listen, Joe. I've let you run your own show on account of your farm and the accident and all. I did it because I thought you could help us win the championship. I still do."

"Well, then, what are you saying? You want me to switch to the half mile?"

"No, Joe, I want you to be our rabbit."

"Rabbit?"

"Yeah," Coach O'Reilly said, smiling now, the secret revealed. "The rabbit. The burner. The sacrifice. Go out too fast. Pull all the runners out after you. All the greyhounds."

Joe's faced whitened. His heart skipped a beat.

"You can't do that."

Coach O'Reilly bristled. "I can do anything I want. I'm the coach, remember? Anyway, it was you who gave me the idea."

"Me?"

"Yeah, in that race a couple of weeks ago. Remember the one where I tore into you two afterwards. You out to prove something by staying in front. Mark, like a fool, trying to keep up stride for stride. The fast pace almost cost him the race."

He scowled at Mark in memory, then put a fatherly hand on Joe's shoulder. "Look, this isn't the Olympics. Most of these milers run across cow pastures just like you. They don't know till the race is over if they've run faster or slower than the week before. Most haven't run this race more than 20 times in their lives, and most of them likely can't even spell STRATEGY."

None of this made any sense to Joe. All he knew was that Coach O'Reilly's plans threatened to ruin his own.

"So you want me to go out fast. For how long? I keep it up too long and I won't have anything left to finish."

"That's the point. Neither will anybody else. You go out as hard and fast as you can for as long as you can. Anyone who tries to keep pace will burn up, just like you. I'm betting Langley will take the bait, seeing as how you were on his butt last week until the end."

Coach O'Reilly seemed quite pleased with himself.

"Everyone will bite except Mark here. He's going to run his own race, marking his quarter times. He will do this because I will be calling out those times. When everybody else whose been chasing you is about ready to heave their guts out, Mark will sweep by them. First place. Six points. Best Langley and Webster can do is four points. The relay team wins. We nail the title."

"You think Langley will fall for it?" Mark asked, happily on board.

"For a while. I'm hoping for at least a quarter mile, or maybe almost the 880 mark. By then he'll be looking for you. When he sees you hanging back, the gig is up. By then, though, Langley should be history."

Coach O'Reilly looked back and forth between the milers. Joe visibly trembled. All his well-made plans! This can't be happening! Him the rabbit. He had no chance to win. No hope. Mark would ride home the winner at his expense. Mark, with his picture in the Troy yearbook, the Carver County Times. Mark, with another trophy on his parent's fireplace mantle. Mark, with another girl in his pocket. What has it all been for, he wondered? Why did people think they could just keep taking pieces of him?

"I won't do it," Joe blurted out.

Coach O'Reilly's face flushed instantly in anger. He hadn't expected any defiance.

"The hell you won't."

Joe spoke rapidly, pleading his case. "I can get you a third place. That's three points. A second and a third at worse from us. That's seven points. That's a safer bet. Seven's better than six. I know I can do it. I've been running extra at home . . . ."

Coach O'Reilly grabbed him by his left arm, shook him once and pressed his face inches from Joe's. His eyebrows pinched between his bulging eyes, and he licked his lips again.

"Listen son, nothing's going to take another 10 seconds off your time of last week. You don't want to be the rabbit, you take a hike and go jerk off somewhere. I've got plenty of bodies to burn. I've chewed enough Tums this past week to neutralize a battery, and I'm sick of it. I'll be damned if I let you ruin this meet for me. I give you a chance to help win the championship, to help the team—Christ, I let you skip practices from day one, and this is the thanks I get in return."

"Coach, please," was all Joe could muster.

"Hell, Mitchell, yes or no?"

Joe looked at Coach O'Reilly, then Mark. He felt trapped in the coach's web. What were his options?

"Yes," Joe said quietly. "I'll do it."

"Good," Coach O'Reilly said, relieved. "The plan has the best chance of working with you the rabbit." O'Reilly turned back to his plotting. "Here's what I want you to do. I'll station Probst, that worthless Thompson, and Hamre at the 110 breaks and have them yell out both your times. I'll handle the quarter marks. Joe, I want you to run that first lap around 65 seconds and the second the same or faster. The first lap will seem fast to some, but not out of line. They'll think you've just got title jitters. You burn them with that second fast quarter."

Joe listened in a fog, still stunned. A cheer went up behind him, ushering in the end of another event. He wanted to cry out. He looked in the direction of his parents. He looked for Annie.

"Now, Mark, you keep in the middle of the pack. Stay 20 yards behind. Even more, if necessary. Listen for your splits. Run to your splits, not to Joe's pace. Run your normal quarters. And if the other coaches catch on, so be it. We'll still have an advantage by the time they do. My bet is their runners will burn up like spit in a fire."

Coach O'Reilly left them. He hurried away to share his secret with a new set of conspirators—Hamre and the other timers. Mark's arm replaced O'Reilly's around Joe's shoulders. His face wore the same sincerity of the day he praised Joe's rescue efforts with George. It said I'm sorry for you Joe. It's not me. And it will get us the championship, and you'll be part of that. It said all that.

Joe was left to face his predicament alone. Around him, no one seemed aware of what had transpired. The mile relay runners, with gazelle-like bursts of speed, practiced baton exchanges a few yards away. A metallic clang signaled a missed pole vault, and the last heat of the 220-yard dash, a blur of colored uniforms, ended in a set of raised arms at the finish line. Joe remained oblivious to them all. The meet went on, while all his dreams tumbled down around him.

Joe's mind raced for a solution. Maybe if he told Coach O'Reilly what DeAngelo and he had accomplished on their own, he might change his mind. Or maybe he could start the race with a fast spurt, then settle into a normal pace. What could Coach O'Reilly do then? Plenty, Joe assumed. He did not think Coach O'Reilly above simply yanking him off the track in mid-race. Maybe it simply didn't matter, he thought, the plot now a poison numbing his senses.

His despair spun him back over the last two months. Suddenly the day that he and Annie first spied the fox loomed large in his mind. The day the fox barreled down the tracks, the rabbit seemingly resigned to its fate as it stayed confined between the rails instead of leaping to freedom.

Maybe that's all I am, Joe thought. A rabbit caught in the tunnel of my life. Locked in on all sides. Always the prey.

Through the chain link fence that separated spectators from the track, Annie watched Joe pace. She had witnessed the huddle between Joe, Mark and Coach O'Reilly, and knew from Joe's expression the outcome displeased him. That made her even more miserable. She found it unbearable when he was in pain. She wondered if Joe had read her letter or simply shred it unread out of spite. And so, her own broken heart ached as she watched him aimlessly finish his warm-ups. As he sprinted, with his speed billowing out his sweatsuit, she thought he looked like a blue angel.

"880 yard relay next. Runners to their lanes. Mile run to follow." The P.A. system above Annie's head barked her to attention. The commands sent runners scurrying. The relay men split in two, with half of them crossing the field to the 220-yard mark. The milers gathered between the track and the fence. Some sheds their sweats, while others huddled with their coaches for last minute strategy and encouragement.

Coach O'Reilly, concerned with every race, conferred with DeAngelo on the 880 relay. Joe assembled with the other milers. He drew lane five, front row, based on his previous best time during the regular season. He contemplated how fast he would need to sprint to gain the inside lane to put Coach O'Reilly's plan in motion.

"Joe," Annie hollered behind him.

Startled, Joe turned to see her.

"Joe, please come here. Hurry."

Joe hesitantly weaved his way through the other milers. At the fence he simply said, "Hello."

"Joe, did you read my letter?"

"Yes.

"And?"

"Can't talk now, Annie. I've got a race in a couple of minutes."

"Please Joe." She clutched the fence, and then bowed her forehead against its cool steel squares. Joe walked over. She raised her head, and Joe looked into the blue promise of her eyes.

"I just wanted to say I'm sorry. I wanted to say that you shouldn't spend time trying to figure out the 'why' of all this. It had nothing to do with you."

"That's the problem." He realized again he had not yet buried his anger. "Apparently, I wasn't enough for you," he volleyed, but it came out false and weak, with no belief behind it. He, too, leaned into the fence.

"That's not true and you know it, Joe." She lowered her voice to a whisper, conscious of so many runners staring at them. "I started out just liking you, thinking we could be friends, have a good time and go to the prom. And it would end as innocently as it started once school was over."

She took a deep breath. "But you kept getting in the way. You mixed me up. I don't quite know why. I've got to sort it out. That's what I tried to tell you in the letter. All I know is that I've hurt you very much. And that I'm so sorry. Because . . . I have never loved anybody the way I love you."

Joe stood silently before her. Annie extended her fingers through the fence. "I mean it, Joe."

Joe rocked gently back and forth. He wanted to believe her so badly.

"What about Mark?" he finally whispered.

"It's over with him. Joe, you're not listening. I want to be with you."

Joe raised his hand, hesitated, and then touched her smooth fingers. The touch was enough, as he knew it would be in reaching. It said forgiveness. He looked at her, and the smallest of smiles forced its way across his face.

"You mean I don't have to beat Mark in this race to win you back?"

"You never lost me. I lost you. You don't have to win this crazy race."

The smile—still tentative, still wobbly—suddenly grew stronger.

"Then I will," Joe said, turning.

"I love you, Joe Mitchell." Annie said it privately, between only them. Then she said it louder, feeling forgiven at last.

"I love you, Joe Mitchell."

Suddenly, Betty Carlson was at Annie's side. "She loves you Joe," Betty yelled. Annie looked at Betty, embarrassed. Then, the two friends laughed at each other and yelled in unison, "We love you, Joe Mitchell." Their chants sent Joe to his lane in the darkest shade of crimson.

"Runners to your mark," the timekeeper yelled moments later. He raised the small pistol skyward. The 15 milers tensed. They stretched across the track in three rows. Their team uniforms created a rainbow of colors. Their bare arms hung earthward from their loose tank-tops, their leg muscles bulged as they dug in for push off. All eyes faced forward.

Joe stood statuesque, in lane five, first row. Mark held lane one, his crop of black hair peeking above Langley's shaved head in lane two. Next to Joe in lane four, Elbow Lake's best miler, leaned forward. This was Gieger. Joe knew Swenson from Hermanville stood in lane three. He tuned out all the runners in the second two rows.

"Get set!"

All motion stopped, the runners as cocked and ready to spring as the hammer of the starter's pistol. From the bleachers, a few random shouts pierced the calm. Joe thought he heard his father. He shook his head, and focused on the parallel white stripes that lay before him, and those to their left that he had to cross quickly to perform his duty. Then he heard the girls again.

"We love you, Joe Mitchell!"

"Blam!"

As a unit, the runners sprinted forward. Joe sprinted fastest of all, cutting in a long diagonal line in front of the other runners. The cinder track crunched beneath his speeding feet. His initial surge was not unexpected. Outside lane runners commonly slid over. His move was still as disruptive as a car crossing lanes to make an exit ramp. It threw several milers from their stratagems immediately. Behind him, he heard jostling and stutter steps as others jockeyed for position.

After Joe secured the pole position, he didn't settle into a comfortable pace. Instead he accelerated. In a flash he opened up a three-yard lead, and, as if connected by elastic, the pack sprang forward to close the gap.

Joe rounded the first curve of the oval track, and propelled down the top of the backstretch. An audible roar of support rushed across the infield as the home-town crowd saw a Troy runner in front. The noise grew when his friends realized Joe held the lead. Joe immediately spied Hamre at the 220-yard mark, stopwatch in hand, waiting to help guide his pace. He felt the presence of all the runners behind him. Apparently they had swallowed the bait.

"31, 32," Joe heard as he streamed by Hamre. On pace. Very fast. Joe did not feel it. Adrenaline always carried him the first lap. And Annie's shout at the gun gave him a high that would leave a heroin addict envious. Both coursed warm through his veins—the words and the adrenaline—fusing into an elixir that lifted his spirits and guided his strides. Still, Joe was surprised when he heard Thompson almost whisper in his ear—so close did he stand near the lane—his 330 time. "45, 46, good pace, good pace."

Approaching the end of the first lap, Joe soaked up the growing crowd noise. The cheers were for him, the first place runner. No matter what happened after, no one could steal these moments. The Troy fans called his name. "Joe,

Joe, Joe." He almost started to cry. The chants gave him another injection of adrenaline. So he sped up. The cheers climbed louder.

Joe shot a look to the fence. Annie shouted excitedly, but the crowd drowned out her words. He scanned the infield next and found Coach O'Reilly nodding and smiling. Joe was being a very, very good rabbit.

"62, 63, 64" the timekeeper bellowed as Joe passed beneath the crowd's canopy of encouragement.

"That's too fast," the Webster distance coach said, looking in disbelief at his own stopwatch, pushing his way through assistant coaches and runners. Reaching the lanes, he waited for the last of the milers to pass, then stepped out onto the cinders to see the tail end of the pack. He asked no one in particular, "Who was that? Mitchell?" he answered himself. "What's he doing?" Frantically, he searched for his assistant, Finnegan, who, instead, just as nervous, found him first.

"Phil, that was Mitchell wasn't it? What's his best time?" the head coach demanded.

Finnegan looked bewildered, flipping hastily through his clipboard sheets. "Don't know. You had him down as a possible fifth, but nothing for Langley to worry about."

The Webster head coach, Burns, spun around again to follow the runners' progress. He leveled his gaze like two twin canons, squinting across the infield at the bunched pack rounding the first curve a second time.

"Where's Perkins? I don't see Perkins."

"There he is," Finnegan said, pointing over Burns' shoulder so the head coach could look down his long arm. "He's about seventh or eighth."

"The pace is too fast. Something's up," Burns said. "It's some kind of a trick."

Burns rotated and ran back to the finish line, looking for Coach O'Reilly. He almost ran into him face to face because Coach O'Reilly had also turned to follow the race. Coach O'Reilly stood, stop watch in hand, gleefully smiling as Joe maintained his lead after 600 yards.

"What's going on O'Reilly?" Burns growled.

"Going on? Why, I believe it's the mile run, Phil."

"You're using Mitchell as a burner, aren't you?"

Coach O'Reilly grinned from ear to ear. "We like to refer to him as a rabbit. It sounds so much nicer."

"But why? You'll lose his point."

"Maybe as head coach you should keep better track of ALL points," Coach O'Reilly continued gleefully.

Burns' face flushed, realizing at last the trap O'Reilly had just sprung. He went reeling toward the far bowl of the track, yelling as he went, "Langley, slow it down, slow it down! He's a decoy!"

Langley couldn't hear anything above the cheering because the runners were just beginning to enter the homestretch a second time. He didn't need Burns to tell him something was amiss, however. He deciphered the rabbit strategy himself after the first lap and a half when Perkins remained nowhere in sight, and the leader, Mitchell, churned in front of him like a mad man. With that awareness, Langley attempted to slow his pace. But the runners behind him didn't slow, and prodded him along. The trap had been sprung, and he was caught between its sharp steel teeth.

Ahead, Joe marveled at his pace. He could barely believe his splits, because as he heard each new one they seemed out of correlation with his energy level. His heart pounded, yes, but his legs reached out hungrily still. The sight of the rotund Webster coach galloping toward him down the homestretch signaled that O'Reilly's plan had worked.

"Steve, slow it down, he's trying to burn you up," Burns hollered through cupped hands as Langley sped by close on Joe's heels. "Perkins is lying in wait."

He was. Twenty yards back, among the milers who long ago lost hope, Mark glided as smooth as a thoroughbred. His eyes never left the leaders, especially Joe. Mark, too, had heard Annie's words, and although he owned the race, Mark now wished he had never agreed to Coach O'Reilly's strategy. He would pass Joe in the next lap knowing that Joe, his enemy, the car wrecker, the girl stealer, would receive partial credit for his victory. That tainted it. Joe had cost him everything he held most dear. Joe should pay the price. Mark didn't need a crutch. All he could think of as Hamre and Probst and Thompson controlled his race was that he should be in the lead. Conference championship, with one of the largest crowds of his life, and the cheers descended on Mitchell. Even his friends—Harrington and his basketball chums—heckled him. They, too, had been duped, and couldn't understand his lackadaisical performance. Mark grew impatient, and quickened his pace.

Ahead, Joe needed another infusion of something. The fix came from an unexpected source. Not from the screaming fans, but from John DeAngelo. He stood up the track, away from the main body of coaches and timers, his hands moving by his side, mimicking Joe's stride. As Joe approached, he saw that DeAngelo's hands held brilliant white eggs. He was reminding Joe to break his body in half. Sit your upper body on the table, the eggs said. Work below the table with your legs. Stop clenching your fists and wasting valuable energy with your arms.

It wasn't the telegraphed advice that helped him glide through the half-mile mark in 2:12. No, DeAngelo's presence meant one thing and one thing only. DeAngelo believed Joe could win. All his counseling about not running for revenge wasn't because he thought Joe would be devastated in losing. He simply wanted Joe to run for himself. To win for himself. To find joy in the running. In his opportunity.

Joe latched onto this realization like a drowning man grasping the cool, solid sides of a lifeboat. Every hundred yards required a new thought, some crystallization of hope to pull him along. Only that numbed the growing uneasiness in his chest and legs.

As Joe passed DeAngelo, and heard the coach chanting, "Abebe, Abebe", he thought of that barefoot Ethiopian conquering the cobblestones along the Apian Way in Rome. He tried to imagine the pain Abebe endured, remembered the determination on his face in the pictures. Joe recalled Abebe's quote in DeAngelo's book, when asked why he ran 26 miles barefoot to win the race: "I wanted the world to know that my country Ethiopia has always won with determination and heroism."

Joe, too, wanted to win with determination and heroism, not as some tainted trickster. The thought grew stealthily, and began to pluck at his resolve to obey. He was tired of obeying. He wanted the title for his teammates, too, but not this way. For two months he suffered the solitude of the fields. He sacrificed more than any of his teammates to arrive at this spot, 1,000 yards into the mile and a chance to place. Coach O'Reilly had stripped him of his right to earn his own points and help win the championship legitimately. Instead, only he had been asked to make the ultimate sacrifice. All because Coach O'Reilly carried a modicum of doubt on Mark's chances to beat Langley. This last insult cleaved his obedience in two. A renewed anger welled up inside him. He drank at its trough in deep gulps. Then, almost as quickly, the anger disappeared so fast that Joe peeked over his shoulder, to see if some weight, some piece of metal, banged and bounced in the lanes behind him.

Something foreign replaced this weight. Joe could not name it, but it spoke to him. It said, NO. No to Coach O'Reilly, to Mark, to anything and anyone who tried to use him. So Joe said "No" to his martyrdom. He heard himself say internally, "I am no longer the rabbit."

And just like that, his mind focused on how to win rather than concede the race to Mark. First came slowing his pace. He could not sustain it and hope to win. Even now, he knew his blistering pace had taken a toll. He slowed to the relief of the dogged milers strung out behind him. No one attempted to pass. They were as spent as Joe.

A lap and a half remained. Joe knew if he had a chance, it lay in the next 300 yards. DeAngelo said so much is made of the last quarter in the mile run. Who still has a kick. Who comes from behind. But it is the third lap that makes champions. By then, a body's senses flood the brain with urgent messages. Please stop, the legs scream. Can't you see we hurt? Then the lungs chime in. What are you doing? Can't you taste the blood in your mouth as our air sacs burst? The heart holds out, because it houses courage, but at last it, too, cries out for mercy. In the third lap you must push through these complainers, DeAngelo said. You must lash the flesh to continue, because this is the time that minds quit. The mind sees the remaining yards and conspires to convince the runner he can't possibly endure this much pain so much longer. It is the moment of truth. It is the devil tempting Jesus in the desert. The devil offers you the end of pain, the false fruits of quitting.

Joe kicked the devil in the ass and left him sprawling along with the sacrificial weight he had shed earlier. He rounded the far curve, 500 yards to go. If he could only continue to lead into the homestretch a third time, maybe the crowd would again buoy him forward.

This time, though, the roar started before he leveled out from the curve and propelled down the straightaway. He glanced over his right shoulder and saw Mark passing other milers. Mark seemed fresh compared to the haggard-looking wrecks he blew by.

Joe vowed not to look back again. Any unnecessary movement, like Mark's undisciplined passing in the outside lanes, cost a second. Any clenched fists over 100 yards cost another. Even with less than 500 yards left. It mattered. It mattered to Joe.

Coach O'Reilly loomed ahead, a jack-o-lantern grin lighting up his face. He had awaited this day through 11 years of coaching. He long ago lost excitement for teaching Industrial Arts. Nothing much in his life excited him. Coaching track started as a way to earn a few more bucks. So it had remained until this group of athletes. They made him proud. He recognized their potential early and correctly. And so he played with his spreadsheets nightly, much to the annoyance of his wife. Everything had always looked good on paper. Coach O'Reilly knew, deep down, that he had molded, cajoled and, at times, bullied this team into a winner. Made them accomplish more than they themselves believed they could. That was coaching. They would thank him for it. This race, unfolding as he watched Mark and Joe running neck and neck toward him, accented his effort. He counted points at night the way other insomniacs counted sheep. He stared now at six golden points emblazoned across Mark's chest.

"Good job, Joe!" he yelled jubilantly, as the runners passed. "You've done your job."

The only thing was, instead of letting Mark pass, Joe sped up and kept Mark in lane two.

"Let me pass," Mark spat out.

Joe said nothing. A word equaled a breath lost. He hugged the inside half of lane one, trying to shave off another few feet in this last circle of the track. Mark tried to sprint past him before they entered the top of the oval, but again Joe would not yield. They bumped shoulders, and for a second, it appeared all of Coach O'Reilly's dreams might crumble in a heap on the cinders.

Coach O'Reilly stared in disbelief as the two warriors sparred.

"What the hell is Mitchell doing?" he screamed at no one. Heads turned at his ranting. Coach O'Reilly watched in horror as Joe held the inside lane the entire sweeping curve. He cringed as Mark in lane two would not concede.

Showing unusual speed for a big man, Coach O'Reilly sprinted across the infield. He arrived at the 220-yard mark just before his two milers. He started to reach out to yank Joe right off the track, but someone jerked his arm down and then held him in a vise-like grip.

"Let him run, Ken, let him run," DeAngelo said. Coach O'Reilly strained against him, but DeAngelo was too strong.

"Besides. You've won. Look at them. One of them has won your precious title."

Confused, Coach O'Reilly looked at the dueling pair. Only Langley hung gamely in the race, but he trailed Joe and Mark by almost 10 yards with less than 200 yards to go. DeAngelo was right. One of them would win the race. But which one?

Joe ran on fumes. His world turned purple and muted, conscious of Mark and nothing more. His heart ached, his lungs burned, his legs felt dead. He knew his fists were clenched and he cursed his weakness, but even that thought vanished beneath the pounding of his heart. How he had held on so long, he didn't know. Could he hold on? He didn't know. The pain seared behind his eyes like an exploding sun. Everything was light and explosions, fear and hope.

Through this blinding pain, he suddenly saw Annie, illuminated by the lightning. He felt the wet grasses tug at his legs, pulling him down. He heard the young foxes whimpering softly below ground, as needy as Annie's whispers in his ears. He saw his mother humming by a lace curtain, felt his father's blood warm on his hands. He saw the engineer shake his fist in disbelief at a boy who would outrace a train. He saw a deformed fist raised in hope. He watched the pure oval of a white egg arc through the May sky and tattoo a caboose.

He ran not out of revenge. Not out of hurt or hate. He ran to win. This race, this test, that absolved him and made him whole.

And then it started. Or maybe it had commenced long before and his inner pain held it at bay. It rolled over the stadium. Even the opposing teams' fans picked up the chant until its thundering warmth enveloped him.

"We love you, Joe Mitchell. We love you, Joe Mitchell. We love you, Joe Mitchell."

Many happy years later, he said truthfully, he remembered clearly that the tape stretched taut across the finish line was powder blue.

The End

Breinigsville, PA USA
30 March 2011
258811BV00002B/17/P

9 781453 523025